12/18/08

May you never wa[lk]
your runway alone —
God Bless,
Rosemary Hamilton

MW01127364

Only When I'm High
The Runways Of A Southern Belle

by

Rosemary Hamilton

authorHOUSE®

AuthorHouse™
1663 Liberty Drive, Suite 200
Bloomington, IN 47403
www.authorhouse.com
Phone: 1-800-839-8640

First published by AuthorHouse   11/21/2008

ISBN: 978-1-4259-0146-2 (sc)

Printed in the United States of America
Bloomington, Indiana

This book is printed on acid-free paper.

Author's note:
Some of the people in my memoir have passed on; the rest will likely follow shortly after the book is published. The few chapters that cannot be completely substantiated by facts were written as such because as a Southern Belle, "you just know." Others were based on the opinions of countless psychiatric therapists because as a Southern Belle, "you just think they know." As for my affiliation with beauty pageants, insane asylums, Harlem, stand-up comedy, divorce, the airline industry, and anything else embarrassing to my family—it's all true.

Dedicated to
Dr. Merlyn Hurd
and
Dr. John Waid

And to Carol Waid. Thank you for those times you greeted me when I entered your husband's office for therapy—and for explaining what he was trying to say on my way out. Bless you, girlfriend, for showing me that friendship between two Southern Belles is about all the therapy either of them can handle.

Dear Pageant Committee,

Forgive me for being out of touch with you, but since my last letter I've been in rehab for my chronic Southern Belleness. According to the experts, I've been out of touch with myself.

Through the years I've rerouted my plane on numerous occasions and taken off from many different runways. Regretfully, not all those runways took me in the direction I intended to travel.

Nevertheless, I will attempt to answer your questions in much the same fashion as I represented the fine state of Arkansas on so many occasions—with the grace and decorum of a beauty queen and the humility of a Southern Belle—with one exception.

This time I've decided to tell The Truth.

After I was crowned Miss Congeniality at a mental hospital, I searched for something—I didn't know what—and then moved to Harlem and found it. I found myself in the hearts of my neighbors, and on the stage in the hearts of my audience, who gave me a license to be free—free of rules and expectations, stigmas and discrimination, runways and tiaras.

- *Free to be a cowboy riding a broom—or a housewife sweeping the floor with it.*
- *Free to grow real flowers in my rose garden. Free to put plastic ones on my door.*
- *Free to run with the wolves or dance with the strippers.*
- *Free to dance with the homeys or run with the honkeys.*

Free to be free, dear Pageant Committee, of you.

Today I'm no longer a comedian, nor do I live in Harlem. But make no mistake about it—I am still a Southern Belle. I am also free. I am a writer because I'm free enough to write about all the things I'm free enough to do. I wrote this book because God told me I should, with every challenge in every chapter of my life. I'm a flight attendant because if He was wrong, there's a flight leaving in five minutes.

And I can be on it.

Rosemary

From the runway of a Southern Belle to the runway of the southern beauty pageant, and on to the runway of a major airline—it was fairly predictable, my transition from one to another. But there was nothing predictable about those emergency landings in between.

As you travel through these chapters, if it seems you're going backward on one runway, forward to another, and skipping over the next—don't be too hard on yourself. You aren't confused; you're merely experiencing life as I have. You're simply searching for the right runway to avoid those rough landings—hoping to delay that final approach.

So, whether you choose to read this book as a linear biography or a series of vignettes, remember that time, in the mind, flows back and forth. Therefore, if you come upon a space between chapters, please feel free to add an episode from your own life. That is, if I haven't covered it already.

Contents

1. The gospel truth
  1. The tree 1
  2. The gospel truth (about the tree) 3
  3. The gospel truth (about my daddy) 8
  4. Nice little girls don't talk about dead people 13
  5. "S-h-h-h-h! Here comes Mr. Jones!" 16
  6. Charity begins onstage 18
  7. "Hold on to your hooters, girl. That baton's on fire!" 20
  8. Here she comes . . . *with her mother?* 26
  9. "If it's not one thing, it's her mother." 29
  10. Let me entertain you—whether I want to or not 44

II. Take off your tiara—you'll be here awhile
  11. P.S. If I fall off the runway, will they take back my crown? ..57
  12. The eyes of Texas 64
  13. Go to the back of the bus 68
  14. First Lady for the last time..74
  15. Turn on the light. I can't hear you.........................78
  16. Will the *real* action hero please stand? 82
  17. *"Do hush!!"* *86*
  18. For whom the Belle folds...90
  19. "There are things you can change—and others you go on
     vacation for. . . ." 95

III. The beginning of The Inn
  20. Nantucket, my ass! 101
  21. I never promised you. 103
  22. Somebody help me!
     I can't get out of this mess by myself! 124
  23. It would be my privilege. 127
  24. Fear of commitment...135
  25. Weller than well 147
  26. Southern Belle Disorder 150

27. "I was in circumstances that made the salary an object." 155

28. Still crazy after all these years 157

29. Somebody help the man! He can't get out of this mess by himself! 164

30. A promise kept 171

31. Free . . . at last! 176

32. . . . and she danced on roller skates forever 179

33. Maybe I'd rather have lobster...196

34. Maybe I'd rather have sex 199

IV. You can't pay your therapist with the scholarship fund

35. Self helped...205

V. Excuse me, am I on the right runway?

36. Could y'all please climb on my beverage cart while I push it out on the wing? 215

37. Tiaras in turbulence...223

38. Stand up and be funny 232

VI. Running out of runway

39. Troy and me in a 733 239

40. Don't touch that bag. She works for the company.............244

41. Cosmetically correct 246

42. The longest runway 249

VII. Men . . . (and other delays and cancellations)

43. I was picking up trash when I met him..............................265

44. I was taking out trash when I left him. 268

VIII. There was a Rose in Spanish Harlem

45. Sometimes you win. 273

46. There goes the neighborhood!...277

47. There are no pageant committees in Spanish Harlem (no first class, no coach)..280

48. With both feet on the ground, I was high.........................282

49. There goes the neighborhood—again! 284

IX. Only when I'm high
    50. The gospel truth about getting high.............................293
    51. The gospel truth about the Land of Oz.............................301
    52. The gospel truth about the gospel truth!.............................306

1. The gospel truth

1.
The tree

My first title was attached to my birth certificate. It came easy, without a runway, a judge, or a contest. But that's because I was born a Southern Belle—and sister, you don't compete to *be* one, you compete because you *are* one.

It had to do with my Family Tree, where it grew, and how its twisted roots embraced my world. My credentials were classic, in perfect order. Well, almost.

On Mama's side of The Tree was Granddaddy, whose political career took off when he was only eighteen—too young to vote and drink but old enough to be elected mayor and get hauled off to jail when he got "tipsy." It was during a dry spell that he was elected Arkansas' State Senator, which was years before his cousin was Governor and just after their cousin became Speaker of The House. When he married my grandmother, her daddy had already been Speaker of that same House while my mama, in their house, had little chance to speak at all.

But there was the other side to The Family Tree, and from those branches my daddy's people flew upside down, right side up, and inside out, in every wild and wacky way you can imagine—except for the politically correct way.

Daddy owned a liquor store and drank during business hours, but never went to jail. Just like Granddaddy, he embraced the people, shook their hands, slipped them money, hugged their babies, and then wrote it all off on his taxes. But Daddy never held any kind of *political* office, which automatically disqualified him as a "tipsy politician with a big heart and a keen eye for business," and reduced him to the ranks of the lowest and most unacceptable of all crooks and boozers.

So, while the branches on Mama's side held a long line of upstanding politicians, Daddy's side, who never voted for any of them, held a longer line of non-voters who—according to The Senator—spent their waking hours out on a limb, completely out of their tree, or simply barking up the wrong one.

Mama remained on her side of The Family Tree, always telling The Truth and living just exactly right, while Daddy only did so when it fit his purposes. But to me, his purposes seemed just exactly right most of the time. As his way of living continued to make more sense to me than hers, the confusion that followed would force me into various states of guilt and many offices of psychiatry.

Despite my suspicion that Mama also yearned to swing from Daddy's side, she clung steadfastly to her family's portion of The Tree while I, stuck in the schizophrenic split of its enormous trunk, managed to stay close by her side just the same. Unable to budge, I was trapped—dead center—in a house filled with mixed messages.

And set free by a life of fun and dysfunction, hairspray and lipstick, tiaras and tragedy—and this book.

2.
The gospel truth (about the tree)

"Number one on the runway!"

I didn't always strap my body to a jumpseat and prepare for takeoff when I heard those words. Oh no, I wasn't always a flight attendant.

There was a time when this tiara traveled in a different set of clouds, a time when this *Hey Miss* answered to *Miss Whatever's in Season*—Miss Peach, Cotton, Strawberry, Duck. I simply reigned where I was needed. It was a time when being number one on the runway required more of any God-fearing, decent southern woman than she should dare reveal, ever.

Just the same, brace yourself.

I'm about to reveal the myth of the Southern Belle—to cut through her grits and glamour, drama and insanity, and actually address the phenomena of Southern Belle Disorder. It's time to track this disease—and the women who spread it—all the way back to the roots (even though, in this case, they happen to be my own).

So buckle up.

We're going down runways where life is not always as it appears—where titles and labels rule and we make our choices because of the ones we wear.

I spent my youth on a merry-go-round, feeling insecure about one thing or another. My sister said it wasn't my fault, being stupid. She claimed I left my mama's womb with only half of my mind—then she, my brother and other sister came along and made off with all of theirs, plus the half of mine that got left behind. The impossibility of this goof-up, since two of them came *before* me, never really registered in my half-a-mind. Thus my journey down the runway of dysfunction commenced on that day and continued the rest of my life, with me accepting as Truth whatever I was told, and never making any stops along the way to check out the sources.

Having access to this information at an early age did give me a definite edge as it enabled me to respond to the often-asked question,

"Have you lost your mind?" in a fairly intelligent and forthright manner. I could honestly say I'd lost only half of it and knew exactly where that half was. In fact, when my brother chose a political path, his third made a very *public* appearance. When I saw the decisions coming from his office, I'll swear, I knew the man had abandoned his mind and taken on mine. (Lord knows, it doesn't take a whole mind to know when less than half of one has been at work.)

He first entered the political arena as an elected official in Arkansas—a Democrat to the core. Then he moved to a higher office— still in Arkansas, still a Democrat. When the administration changed, he stayed. To my way of thinking, he was now—correct me if I'm wrong—a Republican. But when a fellow Arkansan and Democrat took over the highest office of all, the administration changed again, as did my brother's job. So he wound up in Washington, D.C., where he was—correct me if I'm wrong again—*a Democrat!*

Are you paying attention here? The man served as both a Democrat and a Republican!

Of course, my brother was never one to make commitments *or* decisions hastily, if at all, and had never settled on either party—or, some said, any particular government for that matter—so all this switching back and forth worked out just fine for him. Obviously, his ambivalence was rooted in the troubled history of his Family Tree, dating back centuries to his ancestors on my mama's side.

They were monkeys.

That's right, monkeys. According to my granny on Daddy's side, Mama's people were half-monkey, half-human. And Granny told me the monkey tale every chance she got. Depending on her mood, the story line would change slightly with an unexpected twist from time to time, but the message was always the same, as was the image in my head. There they'd be—Mama's people on their side of The Tree, hanging from the branches like apes and monkeys. And there Granny's people would be—swinging on vines from the other side like Tarzan and Jane.

"It's the Gospel Truth," she would say. "Just like monkeys, your mama's people climbed up their side, intending to swing from branch to branch until they landed on the right one." Sigh. "But like humans, they clung to one branch for years until the bough broke, the cradle fell, and the ground below met them head-on, leaving every last one crazy as Betsy Bugs and fit to go into nothing but a mental ward or politics." With uncharacteristic concern for Mama's people, Granny would add, "Those poor little apes, every last great-great aunt and uncle, remained on the ground below The Tree, pondering and wondering and wondering and pondering themselves and each other nearly to death." She sighed again, louder than before.

"They wondered *which* branch to choose—*what* people would think—*where* they belonged—*if* they belonged—or *if* they belonged *anywhere.*" So according to Granny's story, my brother was a lot like those monkeys. The man simply could not choose a branch. But he was clever. A politician who could swing from the left to the right and back to the left again without attending anyone's party certainly had to be using his whole mind. Clearly, my portion wasn't involved at that point.

And my sisters? Girl, one of them has never used her *own* mind (much less the section of mine she was allotted), while the other one has jet-setted and yachted her share all over the planet! I mean, call me stupid, but how much brain power does it take to live well? Designer clothes, designer looks, Martha's Vineyard in the summer, Lincoln's bedroom in the winter, yadda, yadda. If you ask me, there are few things that require less thought than the stuff that comes out of Washington, but drinking champagne on the deck of a yacht is probably one of them.

(Crippling jealousy and unresolved sibling rivalry are possibly others.)

Although my choices have been limited—visualizations of doctorate degrees and presidential nominations were somewhat hazy—having half-a-mind was not a stumbling block to success on any runway I chose. I could date, be a beauty queen, marry a politician, and get through flight attendant training without a whole one. Besides, each time my grandmother threatened, "I have half-a-mind to put your butt on the Greyhound," I knew I wasn't alone.

Naturally, when your belief is that you've been short changed and the supporting evidence concurs, your landings will be as predictable as your transitions from one runway to another. Like a well-rehearsed talent routine, you'll perform the same dance on every runway of your life until each one becomes a boot camp for the next. I suppose it was a fairly natural progression that took me from:

1. The Runway of the Southern Belle to the
2. Runway of Dysfunction to the
3. Runway of the Beauty Pageant back to the
4. Runway of Dysfunction and on to the
6. Runway of a Major Airline.

I left out number five on purpose.

And sister, that wasn't easy. Not when most of my life people have said to me, "You know, you don't have to tell everything." And most of my life, I've answered—*"Excuse me?"* But not this time. Not in the second chapter of this book, for goodness' sake. Because that's what *Only When I'm High* is about—that number five runway, and my compulsion to drag you down each and every other runway of my life until I figure it out.

Two years. Number five lasted two years. Two horrendous years. And one of them was spent in such a god-forsaken hellhole that none of my runners-up could be found.

Anywhere.

It slips up on you. I'll swear it does. You think you know the rules and what to expect. But just when you believe Collard Green Queen is who you are, pure and simple, someone will observe that you are hyper, moody, disorganized, and a little depressed. From that day on, the opinions of others (which, I swear, follow discombobulated Southern Belles like pickup trucks) will take on a label and commence to accumulate in a big heap right alongside the titles. Trust me, each time I picked up a new label I fell off one runway, landed on another, and then crashed right back down onto the Runway of Dysfunction.

I exhibited symptoms of my first label as I blossomed into a slightly impulsive, extremely compulsive, and noticeably disturbed and neurotic young woman—behavior eventually misdiagnosed as ADD. That's because the erratic and frankly annoying behavior of the person with ADD (Attention Deficit Disorder) is identical to the person with SBD (Southern Belle Disorder) except that with a Southern Belle, the disorder is viewed as delightfully daffy, hopelessly helpless, pert and prissy, slightly seductive, and always and forever, just downright adorable.

It is understandable that I prefer the SBD over the other; titles, I have always believed, matter. And titles, of course, have no statute of limitations. That's why I am presently Arkansas' Junior Miss, and have been for going on three or four decades now, and will continue to be into the next decade, or until I figure out how to represent that state's typical teenage girl without bringing up world peace or bringing down the governor. Elevating my own title by stripping someone else of theirs is not now, nor has it ever been, my style.

Elevating my title by *marrying* someone with one—now *that* always *has* been my style. So I also hold the title of First Lady of a small town in Tennessee. I've held this one for thirty-something years, although some will argue that I forfeited all rights to it the year The Mayor began interviewing other candidates before passing my title on to the finalists.

Obviously, I've lived my life in search of the perfect title and correct label. Understandably, I've never found them. It is no wonder I now have a job with a stage, a captive audience, a title, and at least six emergency exits. But as I stand in the crew room of a major airline, where memos from the FAA form the backdrop for the annual "Appearance Fair," I know I've stayed at this one too long. Then I visit the booths of the image consultants, beauticians, and plastic surgeons who have assembled to conduct the fair—and it seems that we all have.

The goal is to improve my flight-attendant image, but after the fair, my image is that of a near-schizophrenic, totally confused, professionally embarrassed person. So help me out here. Am I competing for Miss Safety Professional or am I just flat too ugly to pass out pretzels?

I mean, really. Which runway am I on, anyway?

Although this one reeks of jet fuel, bad food, and the threat of the unknown, there is a strange sense of familiarity. I have landed in the galley of a 757-200 airplane yet, I'll swear, it's the same stage, same beauty pageant, same kitchen, same labels, same men, same curtain— different runway.

3.
The gospel truth (about my daddy)

I never thought much about how I got to be a Belle. I just knew that for the first part of my life it was the only runway in town. I knew how to get on and keep from falling off, and if I did fall off, I could do it so no one noticed—except for Mama. She always knew.

That's because Mama and I were walking down different runways, and Mama, or so it seemed, wasn't altogether happy with her own. If I did the *correct* thing, I didn't feel right. So I did the *opposite,* and *she* felt worse. If I looked *good* enough, then I wasn't *smart* enough, until someone said I was too *smart* for my own *good*, which meant I had to act stupid, which of course required me to be *really* smart, and that meant no matter which runway I chose, I failed. And failure—plain or dressed up and coiffed—was dreadfully incorrect.

But Granny, with no family history we could speak of, was not particularly concerned about correctness, political or otherwise. A stout, arthritic, and asthmatic woman, she had been scarcely able to "do for herself"—to clean house, cook, or lose weight—since "a whore made off with your Granddaddy" (who wasn't a senator or speaker of anyone's house, especially his own) thirty years before. Yet she could execute a near-aerobic routine in which she fell on one knee, clutched my quivering frame to steady herself, then wheezed *The Gospel Truth* into my ear. At grocery stores, movies, and funeral homes, she proclaimed it. Sometimes it was about relatives on Mama's side of the Family Tree.

"Gospel Truth, my dear, that one was born with a common streak."

But, mostly, it was about men on *either side* of *anybody's* Family Tree.

"Now, girl, do you see that fool over by the strawberries/in the choir/in the casket?" she would wheeze. "Child, he doesn't have sense enough to pee in a boot!"

Each time she proclaimed *The Gospel Truth*, the reality of my unusual birth resurfaced, and the significance of not possessing a whole mind was etched into the half of one I'd been given. I then renewed my vow to spend the remainder of my days avoiding the rain and snow and my grandmother—anything having to do with boots and not being smart enough to pee into one.

When I got to high school, Granny's prayer, "Oh! My Dear Lord and Precious Savior, save us all!" wasn't working. That's when church became my refuge—except when Brother Bob had a laying-on-of-hands spell. The devil, he claimed, overtook him. The devil, maybe. His wife, for sure. Every so often, tanked up on the communion wine, she'd think about that devil and attempt to beat it out of him. Nevertheless, I learned to forgive Brother Bob, cautiously turn the other cheek, and assist his wife in exorcising that devil with a gift of cheap wine every chance I got.

Brother Bob kept right on preaching against young ladies wearing shorts, playing cards, and jitter-bugging, especially when he had a microphone—and a tent. Yet before every beauty pageant he'd show up at the house with camera in hand, then spend hours photographing me in a swimsuit while stashing his principles so far back he'd forget he'd ever had any, or that he'd been in a tent the night before screaming about hell and all of us burning in it. But we all kept right on dancing and playing Old Maid, and Mama kept on believing Brother Bob was a disciple of The Lord who'd most likely been sent by the devil to come over and take pictures.

His wife continued to spend an inordinate amount of time at the church altar, setting up the wine. After the congregation left, she spent even more time putting away the leftovers as she enjoyed her own Happy Hour with the Lord. Mama declared that she was, just the same, a fine Christian woman working overtime for God. "You could eat off that woman's floor," is what Mama used to say about Brother Bob's wife. The rest of us suspected that after Happy Hour on communion Sundays, she probably did.

I clung to this emerging chapter of my life, a potpourri of the confusing values accumulated in my youth. However, I had finally traded in the earlier obsession with my mind for an obsession that didn't require one. I now embraced the inevitable, the insatiable, the tormenting:

Fixation on beauty

Again, someone had made off with my share.

It was partly this belief that precipitated my beauty pageant addiction and, ultimately, stripped my bones buck-naked and deposited the remains onto the runway of every beauty pageant from Little Rock, Arkansas, to Mobile, Alabama. Too bad there were no trophies for my real talent; as eating disorders go, mine was the best on the runway. As fixations go, this obsession with beauty was the one that hung on the longest and began the earliest. I was barely six at its onset.

Until then, I'd been content alternating the roles of Dale and Roy Rogers. But things took a turn when the lady next door converted her home into a beauty parlor and called herself a beauty operator. She was the first woman in town to abandon her family and follow a dream. Even though they were rumored to be trapped in her basement—cold, hungry, needing haircuts—the women in town didn't seem to care because they went to that house a lot. Some of them went every day.

The beauty parlor was filled with women in various stages of denial; its drawers were filled with magic potions that kept them coming back. On each wall hung Hairdo-of-the-Month pictures: beautiful, black-and-white or Technicolor women, all smiling. As the customers filed in, the beauty operator tied ugly plastic aprons around their necks as she asked what they wanted to look like. They pointed to a picture—it didn't matter which one. They all left looking exactly the same, which just happened to be almost identical to the beauty operator.

Looking back, I got the message: "Try to look like someone else and you'll look like everyone else." Sadly, my response was, "So, what's wrong with that?" It would pave many runways ahead.

To see the instruments on the countertop, there was a spinning chair I had to climb; but I had to see the beauty operator's tools; I had to know what this woman had done to the women on the wall to make them smile. Could I do it to myself at home with the kitchen gadgets? When I finally got a good look at the weapons on that counter, I shuddered. Scissors, hand mirrors, combs on long sticks, things that plugged in, bowls of bad smells. *What on God's green earth were the ladies smiling about?* It was a dentist's office up there! But my neighbor in the shiny pink jacket wasn't pulling teeth. She was making beauty.

I saw pictures of beautiful women on the wall, and me in the mirror, looking back at them with my rabbit teeth and skinny hair. At home I cried and clung to my brother who explained that trying to change things would most likely cause scabs on my scalp and a fear of

10

beauty parlors. But with each miserable permanent wave, one thing was abundantly clear: I liked bad permanents a lot better than I liked myself.

It was different around suppertime each night when Daddy's motorcycle pulled up in the front yard. That's when my world changed and my reign commenced. That's when I became Miss America. Or a cowboy. Or both, depending on the day. But no matter how many roles I took on, Daddy felt obliged to remind me that I was *really* myself. "You can be a cowboy or Miss America—anything or anyone you want to be—for make-believe, but the person you should always come home to is Rosemary," he would say.

It made no sense at all. But I sure couldn't turn to Mama for answers, not about that or anything else. Poor Mama never even understood Daddy or that he came home every night to see me, only. Mama never understood me, either. As Daddy pushed me forward, she pulled me backward until I wasn't playing cowboys and Indians anymore. I was in the middle of a tug-of-war—and Daddy's side was losing.

He never saw the pictures on the beauty parlor walls, so Daddy thought I was perfect. A perfect Miss America. A perfect cowboy. Smart, too. Of course, I knew I couldn't be Miss America and smart, not at the same time. But I tried to believe it was true, because if a cowboy hat could magically become a crown, anything was possible.

Daddy didn't know much about Southern Belle stuff, so I didn't have to remember the rules when I was with him. Mostly we just hung out at his liquor store and laughed with his friends—men of all sizes and colors, each with a different smell and hug—who came by just to watch me perform. When I told funny stories, that's when they laughed and liked me the most. They must've liked Daddy too, because they gave him money for the bottles on the shelves.

Most of my audience showed up about lunchtime and sat on big brown barrels until their wives came to pick them up, or until they got real happy and started smelling different, usually around suppertime. I always knew when they were ready to go because the barrels beneath them wiggled as they tried to stand and walk to the shelves with the bottles.

It was at my daddy's liquor store that I learned about life and how sometimes you have to stay put for awhile until you get happy. Or start smelling different. Or someone comes to pick you up. Whichever one comes first.

He was a fun-loving but kind and simple man, my daddy, with clear definitions, easy solutions, and rules that worked. Fat teeth and funny hair were acceptable while temper tantrums because of them were not. I learned that a girl can ride the range or walk the runway, and that there are things in this life you can change, and others you go on vacation for. But fit throwing is never, ever acceptable and many times only draws attention to bad hair and big teeth.

I lost my front teeth and my daddy all in the same week. With his unexpected death and my disfigurement came tales of angels in heaven, tooth fairies under my bed, and other bizarre phenomena. But at age six, with even half-a-brain, I knew The Truth: my teeth would never be back.

But my daddy was on vacation.

4.
Nice little girls don't talk about dead people

When my first grade teacher made me trade my broomstick horse for a bald-headed rubber doll (girls can't be cowboys), I got my first inkling that Daddy's rules had followed him straight from the gate of my corral up to the gates of heaven. It appeared he'd ridden off with the cowboys and a posse of women wearing dirty aprons (girls can be homemakers) had taken over the town.

One year later when Mama married a man with a movie theater, my fantasies took center stage (girls can have fantasies) and the women in dirty aprons were stampeded by a screen filled with skinny women in dancing shoes. It didn't take me long to join their troupe. But soon I discovered that the life of a movie star made no more sense than the life of a homemaker. Not one movie featured a daddy who started out as a good guy, then turned into a bad guy who skipped out on his own little cowgirl and her horse.

Funny thing about death when you're six—no one wants to talk about it. You try to remember what bad thing you did that made your daddy run away, or what bad thing he did so he got sent away, and was it just to his room or what? You wonder if he has food and a radio, and if it's forever, and if it is, how long is that? You wonder if the guys from the liquor store have all moved on and if the answers have moved on with them. But when those answers finally show up, you understand what everyone had been trying to tell you all along: nice little girls don't talk about dead people.

They perform.

I took my act from Daddy's liquor store to the beauty parlor next door and from there, straight to the grade school cafeteria. Then I brought down the house at sleepovers and almost got my mama banned from the church. It was simple. Anytime, anywhere, for anyone, all I had to do was stand up and be funny. With the turn of a phrase or a quick comeback, I could erase the pain. People hung around. No one died.

The answers had been there all along: comedy (1) takes away pain, and (2) brings love. Standing up and being funny was all I had to do. Trouble was, Southern Belles had to be careful about being funny—and with Daddy, being funny was something I'd never had to be careful about. Now I had to be careful about everything. Careful not to talk about him, his liquor store, and his friends. Careful, careful, careful. But being careful not to be myself became easier each day, as I lost touch with just exactly who that was.

Happiness seemed as illusive as the hairdo-of-the-month ladies on the beauty parlor wall next door. Daddy's rules ceased to work and I had no replacements of my own. But life kept showing up anyway like it didn't even care, until Mama found someone who told her *he* did. In place of mourning—nobody told me I could—my life would be filled with happy endings, movie stars, and the stage. Other people had to buy tickets for these fantasies, but I would get mine for free.

****

JONES THEATER
****

That's what the sign spelled out on top of the old building. All the big stars showed up there sooner or later, with their familiar faces posted on the billboards outside. They were either *Now Showing,* or *Previews of Coming Attractions.* But we all knew that the real attraction in my hometown was the gentleman who owned the town's only movie theater. He was my new daddy, and everyone called him Mr. Jones. He didn't look, talk, act or smell like my last daddy, so I too called him Mr. Jones.

He tried to tell the family that show business would not be easy—that selling tickets and food was hard work. We all agreed to pitch in. I was seven-years old at the time, and the hardest thing I could imagine was counting the stars—that big screen full of movie stars! But after the first few months, I saw that he was right. Whether I was chasing my friends from behind the food concession or learning to take up tickets, this *was* the hardest work I'd ever done. As the months passed it got harder, because in addition to my duties around the theater, I assumed the roles of almost every female movie star who came to Jones Theater. That was my real job. It took Mr. Jones a while to realize just how dedicated to my profession I'd become.

When I was eight, "pretending" was no longer fun. That's when I *became* Judy Garland, and I *remained* Judy Garland for quite some time.

Almost everybody who came to Jones Theater knew who I was, but sometimes when I was taking up the tickets, I'd sign autographs on the backs of their ticket stubs so there would be no doubt that I was Judy Garland—the woman who danced in the street and danced in the rain, and once even danced on roller skates! She kissed and she hugged and laughed and cried and sometimes she went to the Land of Oz. But she never ever went on vacation. People hung around. No one died.

Of course, every time I thought of Daddy I knew I could never be Judy Garland or anyone else because I was, and would always be, Roy Rogers and Dale Evans.

And I thought of Daddy every day.

5.
"S-h-h-h-h! Here comes Mr. Jones!"

A person who came to Jones Theater with fifty cents could live like a king. Admission was fifteen cents—popcorn and candy, a nickel. A hot dog was fifteen cents—twenty cents with chili. But the best thing you got for your money was the peace and quiet. Those who came in for other purposes were warned once or twice, then quietly escorted out. Sometimes I forgot. Once I threw my popcorn on Beth Burns and we both giggled out loud. The bag had no sooner hit the floor than we heard—

"S-h-h-h-h! Here comes Mr. Jones!"

I always sat next to the aisle, and when I heard those words I looked at the floor. That's so I could see the spot of light that got bigger and brighter as Mr. Jones approached. Maybe it was the light extending from his feet up the aisle that made him look like a giant, I don't know. But even though I knew that giant was trapped in a small man's body, when I saw him coming, I forgot. I hoped he would keep going, that it was the boys in front of me he was after. I wanted to tell him they had thrown Coke on the girls sitting beside me. But as I tried to make myself smaller in the seat, he stopped and shined the flashlight below my dangling feet.

I looked up and squinted, hoping that when I found his mouth the corners wouldn't be turned down. But sure as his forehead would be scrunched up and his jaws, jutted out—I knew they would be. I expected he'd be doing that thing where he pressed his lips together so tight words were afraid to come out. It was always the same. Whether the coloreds had slipped in the back door without paying or someone had talked out loud instead of whispering, that mouth and those jaws never knew the difference.

He leaned forward until his face was so close all I could see were the bristly hairs of eyebrows taking off in different directions, no doubt scrambling to escape that flashlight. When he whispered, "Settle down," I heard a faint laugh two rows up. It was Beth.

He tried to keep his theater as immaculate as his socks-and-handkerchief drawer at home. He got angry when people threw candy and gum on the floor. The black people who sat in the balcony sometimes threw their food on the white people downstairs, and Mr. Jones got real mad about that, too. So did the white people. A couple of the black women had worked for my mama. I'd even called one of them Mama Woman. But the day I saw Mama Woman walk up those steps and head toward that balcony, she turned into Colored Woman and she remained Colored Woman from that day on.

Mr. Jones liked children. There were steps to the water fountain they could climb. He liked fat people, too. They had double seats. I curled up in those seats on nights when Mama couldn't leave the concession stand to take me home. Teenage sweethearts sat together in the double seats and held hands. If they kissed, they knew exactly what to expect—

"S-h-h-h-h! Here comes Mr. Jones!"

Some children couldn't come to Jones Theater. Mama told me they had polio. Mr. Jones showed a movie about it and we all cried. Then we fought over who would pass around the cigar boxes for donations to help the children. There was some talk about one boy who always collected the money. People said he stole it from the box. If I had seen him, I would have told Mr. Jones. I told him everything.

Many years have passed since I sat in Jones Theater, and it's different now when I go to a movie. Oh, I still sit next to the aisle. But when the movie is really good and the folks around me get rowdy, I turn and look for that spot of light on the floor. Then I wait to hear those words and to see him coming. But I never do.

And they just keep talking.

6.
Charity begins onstage

. . . and the bus children and the beauty-pageant children, too—they all stood behind the big curtain, waiting for their names to be called. . . .

Belledom was about many things, but most of all, charity—charity and compassion. I think it was the "bus children" who taught me about compassion. I know it was my Aunt Allie B who taught me not to show it unless someone was looking.

They lived outside the city limits and were treated, you know, the way bus children should be treated. At the close of each school day they waited until the teachers shouted, "All you bus children better line up!" to leave their desks and walk out to the school buses. That was a long time after the rest of us, the "town children," had been picked up by our mamas. We sent food and money to the bus children and children of different races, too, so they could eat and go to school. This, of course, made us feel better about not letting the children of different races eat and go to school with us.

In third grade, the year of the big tornado, Principal Boutwell announced that a lot of the bus children had gotten sucked up and blown away while waiting for the bus, waiting for their names to be called. Tornados, he explained, mostly only happen to people who live in the country. (But since the bus children were in town when this one hit, I figured that tornados can find bus children no matter where they are.)

After the storm we gave even more money and clothes to the families of the bus children, and I talked about it for years. I talked at school and church—and in the coming years, at beauty pageants. Anywhere a public address system could be found, I openly, sincerely, and proudly professed my love for God and all his children, which, I believe, included the ones in my very own town. And the bus children as well.

I would discover that beauty pageant contestants were a lot like third graders, with everyone pushing and shoving to get onto the runway, all being judged fairly and equally—within their own categories, of course. Just like the town children and the bus children, the losers were separated from the winners, the swimsuits from the talent, the evening gowns from the sportswear, and the fat people from the face of the earth. I learned that folks need to stay behind the curtain unless their names are called—and some of them never are.

Years later I would greet passengers on an airplane and observe this sacred law of the beauty pageant runway (and third grade) being enforced on the runway of a commercial airline. I watched as the coach-class children were separated from the first-class children, waiting to be upgraded, standing behind the curtain, hoping their names would come next.

And still praying that the tornado—or worse—would not.

7.
"Hold on to your hooters, girl. That baton's on fire!"

Sometimes just a simple letter can set the stage.

Dear Parent:

    Thanks for submitting your child's application to the "Little Miss Perfect" pageant. In compliance with contest rules, please submit answers to the following:

        1. Is she potty trained?
        2. What is her talent?
                The Pageant Committee

Dear Pageant Committee:
        1. Yes she is.
        2. This IS her talent.
                Parent

The road to Belledom was lined with lessons, paved with fear. But I never stopped learning. The wrong note, a couple of pounds, a wobble or a zit could send me right back through the curtain, into another category, onto another stage, or out the back door to the car. "The world is a stage" was more than an expression for me now. It was my mantra.

The act that began in Daddy's liquor store had now survived slumber parties, state fairs, speedways, and duck callings, with more than one standing ovation. I had successfully laid the cowboys to rest and integrated the movie star, the comedian, and their mixed up inner-child. The stage was their home, my refuge.

THE FAIREST OF THE FAIR

The county fair queen stage was just a stone's throw from the midway and the sweaty, shirtless, riffraff carnies who worked each year to fill the children's fantasies—but more, Truth be known, the fantasies of the farmers' wives (and, behind the carnival tents, those of their daughters). Inside one tent was a bearded lady leading a parade of carnival freaks, all being observed by an audience much like the one ogling the fair queen contestants. But the scariest of all were the women of the church who went ballistic when their gingham-topped jars of jams and jellies went home blue-ribbonless.

Whatever the contest—beauty pageant, freak show, jelly-jar competition, or livestock show—they were all pretty much the same. Being the best at *whatever* you were competing for was what mattered. Winning was the goal.

Naturally, I had to focus on my own contest. If I'd gotten caught up in the hoopla on the midway—the rides, barking carnies, heifers, simulated piped-in organ music, and squealing pigs tromping through cow crap—I would have had to admit that they (the pigs and the crap) were more exciting than the fair queen contest or anything else at the entire county fair except for, of course, what went on behind those tents.

ARKANSAS' JUNIOR MISS

Dear Rosemary,
Ready for another pageant?
The Pageant Committee

Silly question. I was always ready. For me, life onstage was the only one that made sense. But when I received my entry form with the necessary qualifications for the Arkansas' Junior Miss competition, I feared this alien runway might leave me one tiara short of a title. I could hardly believe my eyes.

"A Junior Miss excels scholastically. She is poised and physically fit—the typical high school senior girl."

"Typical high school senior girl!" I shuddered, as I visualized the excruciating discomfort of pulling that one off. That was *not* what I wanted to be. Queen of the World, maybe, but *typical?* No way! I'd had the same reaction when asked to seek other thrones—Forest, Peach, Cotton, and Watermelon. I had reigned without ever revealing that I detested watermelon (and peaches).

Scholastic excellence and physical fitness would present a challenge. For the past year I had been too busy entering contests to excel or be fit. As for typical, I wasn't even sure what that was. But if this was what it took to win, I was sure I could figure it out. With less than three months to prepare, I studied, read every newspaper written in English, joined the cheerleading squad, and took over the vice-president's seat on the Student Council. Then I summoned my team.

Dr. Lusk, our family doctor and friend, had close acquaintance with my acne. He made house calls for it. "Don't be coming to me a week before one of those contest things and expect me to clear up that face," he used to say. "You need a month of these pills and shots. If you'd get off the chocolate, your measurements might be somewhere close to what you always write down on that entry form."

My Aunt Allie B was my seamstress. Her latest invention was an elastic gadget she had devised by cutting off and discarding the lower part of "just an old thing men wear in their swimsuits." The upper half had been sewn into many of my swimsuits and formal evening dresses in the past, flattening my stomach and making certain words impossible to say. But Mama said it was the same as telling a lie, and refused to let us affix it to the sportswear Allie B had made for the Junior Miss competition.

As chaperones went, Allie B was the best. She would go "wherever I'm needed," equipped with the South's first rat-tail comb. A few days before the pageant, she pulled up in her 1957 Ford truck, its back-end bulging with beauty secrets not even she could explain. Formal evening dresses were her specialty, so was recycling. So, when it was rumored that the rows of sequined ruffles on my Junior Miss gown once decorated the skirt of her daughter Billy Faye's double-wide, I wasn't surprised.

With a cigarette in one corner of her mouth, safety pins in the other, and chewing gum somewhere in between, she sewed each pearl and sequin on those formals—by hand, after midnight, when she was sick. I knew this because she told me so over and over again. Unlike Mama, Aunt Allie B was easy to read, an open book, especially when it came to beauty pageants. With her, you knew what you came for, what you'd have to do to leave with it, and how big the celebration would be once you got it. Everything she carried—from false-eyelash glue to swimsuit tape—was a weapon to be used in a war we had to win.

The week before the Junior Miss Pageant, Allie B had worked herself sick making dresses for the entire Arkansas' Southeastern Debutante Cotillion. "Lord knows, I have to be there for those girls," she said. "I just cannot depend on their mothers to get them dressed."

So that left Mama.

Uh-oh.

Mama. In the eye of a hurricane.
Mama. At a tent revival selling dildos and crack cocaine.
Mama. Having sex with the preacher in broad daylight.

These were only a few of the God-forsaken places my God-fearing Mama would probably have preferred to be than with me at a beauty pageant.

An accomplished pianist, she endured each talent competition graciously, praising the contestants for their efforts. While other mothers cursed the judges for their decisions, Mama was quick to praise the winner, whoever she was. And her mother. "Winning is not the most important thing in the world," she used to say. Someone like Mama had absolutely no place at beauty pageants.

Aunt Allie B never forgot anything. If she had been with me the night of the Arkansas' Junior Miss Pageant, we never would have left my sportswear in the car. Minutes before I was called onstage to model it, I realized it was missing. I shrieked and cried and was saved by a Jaycette who approached Cotton Plant's Junior Miss coming offstage. "Honey, you and this contestant are just about the same size. Now if she could just borrow your sportswear . . ."

Words cannot describe that girl's anger as she handed over her outfit. As I threw it on, smothering under her hot gaze, I heard the master of ceremonies call my name. I turned to thank her, promising she'd get my vote for Miss Congeniality, and tripped. Onstage.

She laughed.

And she continued to laugh throughout each competition. Finally, the MC called my name for the last time. I was one of the top five finalists. I could feel the piercing stare from the girl beside me. It was Cotton Plant's Junior Miss.

"How could you do something so stupid as leaving your clothes in the car?" she whispered.

That did it.

Stupid. She used the *stupid* word—an error in judgment that pretty much begged for the *bitch* word. But, like the *stupid* word, the *bitch* word was never used on the beauty pageant circuit. What *was* used was fifteen pounds of pancake makeup, a ton of hair spray, and a truckload of sequins, all of which successfully covered up anything remotely resembling stupidity. And that night, with Max Factor as my witness, I had it covered.

As for bitchiness, Cotton Plant's Junior Miss had that covered, too. In fact, she successfully turned it into a category of its own. It was the *Miss Most Obnoxious* competition, and she was winning.

"You really messed up," she snarled. The race was on.

"I always do," I replied, smiling, "just before I win."

She simultaneously sneered at me and smiled at the judges, a talent that far surpassed the flaming baton routine she'd just demonstrated. She stepped away and approached the microphone. It was question time. I didn't hear the question she was asked, but I believe she answered it by volunteering to live out the rest of her life as a missionary somewhere. I thought I'd gag.

It was my turn.

As the master of ceremonies read the question, I spotted Mama in the audience. She was visibly relieved because the question was one we had gone over so many times.

The question: "What would you do if you had a million dollars?"

The answer: "I would give it to the starving children."

But those words would not come. I'd had it with the bus children and the poor and starving children, too. Besides, Cotton Plant's Junior Miss had already done her version of that one—and if she was going to be a missionary, I sure didn't want to risk serving anywhere near her. My answer was as unexpected as the look on Mama's face when I gave it.

"In all sincerity, if I was presented with a million dollars at this very moment, I would share it equally among each and every one of the judges."

They must have needed the money. I won.

Even though this preceded my official diagnosis of Southern Belle Disorder, in retrospect, it was my first step toward the healing process— and, surprisingly, I hadn't broken my mama's rules to do it. Like her, I'd told The Truth; but like my father, I'd told The Truth only because it would get me what I came for.

Allie B and me

8.
Here she comes . . . *with her mother?*

Having done battle at least twenty times on the beauty pageant stage qualifies me more as an authority on this sport than, say, football. It has also familiarized me with the turf and the rules. And one of the unwritten rules is that there are three things beauty contestants leave in the car: their comfortable shoes, their cigarettes, and their mamas.

There are also rules about what they must *remove* from that car. So, when young ladies armed with rhinestone headgear and silicone chest pads take over prime time TV, that's good. The rules have been followed. But when someone slips in a new version—a production choreographed to promote mama and apple pie—you're looking at the *mother* of all violations! The same females who have fine-tuned the art of winning by proclaiming their affection for God, country, education, and each other, have now added another bold-faced lie to the mix.

Their mamas.

That's right. Their poor mamas are being dragged onto that infamous frontline known as *The Stage.* (Being dragged, well, maybe not. Not the mamas on my TV. They were right where they wanted to be.) So ladies and gentlemen, put down your remotes because *this* you've got to see to believe. I present:

THE MISS MOTHER-DAUGHTER USA PAGEANT!

Prime time. If I lie I die.

Mothers and daughters representing their respective states, posing side by side in swimsuits. That's what your average viewer saw. Unsportsmanlike conduct that defamed the pageant's creed, defeated its purpose and made a mockery of everything this business stood for. That's what I saw. It was, at best, incestuous. At worst—a freaking coming out for women who should have stayed in.

Two women crossing the goal line side-by-side. Sorority sisters, headed straight for that end-zone—stopping to dance around the goalpost like it was a friggin' maypole. The Super Bowl of the unthinkable is what it was. Nothing on TV quite as appalling—not since the year that Chinese girl from Honolulu got crowned Miss Teen USA. (National TV. If I lie I die.)

26

Whatever happened to the greatest of all American sports: young women bringing equipment to the field their mothers no longer, or possibly *never*, had and then exposing that fact beneath the bright lights of the pageant runway?! And Bert Parks? Where'd he go? You think he would've allowed a woman *his age* on *his stage*? I don't think so. The whole thing left me disappointed, saddened, confused.

Disappointed because these mamas had waited until now to claim their runways. Saddened because mine never did.

Confused because no one ever told them the rule about staying in the car.

> *Something you need to know about southern women and competition: the moment one of them is crowned, the real contest begins backstage—to determine the best loser. And when it comes to kissing and hugging, crying and congratulating, they are ALL winners! So, in the aftermath of defeat, the losers are still competing among themselves—to be crowned the best LOSER! And, really, there's nothing new about it. It goes back to the Civil War.*
>
> *As much as we like to win, southerners also love losing. As is evidenced in our re-enactments of that war—they celebrate it! In fact, when the high school band's version of The Star Spangled Banner prompted Bessie Moore's outburst, "It makes me wish we'd lost the war!" I reminded her of the war we actually lost, and all the times we've had to sit through its re-enactment.*
>
> *So, if the pageant losers from these southern United States had their way, they would return each year to re-enact the night they lost—over and over and over again.*
>
> *There are no real losers in the South is what I'm saying. Just so you know.*

RUNWAYS

I've been to a place . . .
where little girls and big girls
and women compete to see
who's the best winner and
who's the best loser and whose Mama
should've stayed in the car.

Where values are born and fairytales
die and the rules of the runway are.
Where young women vow to stop
world hunger. Such patriotic pride
(from those who haven't fed themselves
and would kill for a chicken. Fried).
And winners are given scholarships
that won't pay for therapy hours,
while losers are given floral bouquets
(you'd swear they were funeral flowers).

And the talent wasn't "life," and the
runways ran out, and they all
learned to hide the scar.
Because they had to be perfect.

You can't stay on the runway
. . . unless you are.

9.
"If it's not one thing, it's her mother."

Freud—most likely

I was a contestant climbing a never-ending, uphill runway with a mama who enjoyed the journey but had no intention of getting to the top. Just the same, I kept climbing—and I did it in my sister's one-size-too-small pointed-toed-high heel shoes and the upper portion of my brother's three-sizes-two-small (*Alterations by Allie B*) jock strap. I had family support, no denying that. With every step and every breath, I felt it.

Putting the excruciating pain aside, as I often had to, I was happy to have the smallest waistline on the runway. But while the upper half of a jock strap cinched it, my Aunt Allie B created it—a job she accepted with unbridled enthusiasm.

In her kitchen workshop, she ceremoniously commenced the procedure of removing that jock from the strap. With a cutting board and a sharp kitchen knife, she transformed the athletic supporter into a waist cincher and her favorite niece into a homemade version of Scarlet O'Hara.

Carefully, thoughtfully, with the precision of a brain surgeon, she sawed off the jock. As I watched that discarded remnant take off in the direction of the trash can, I heard the first sound of victory—the stabbing noise of the surgical instrument, as Allie B plunged it into the chopping block. Next, the *sign* of victory. From the same hand that performed the jock-ectomy, two fingers—seldom seen without a cigarette between them—formed a V. Then the climax—Allie B's signature laugh. Loud and raspy, with some bizarre overtones on this occasion, it could be heard from the boardwalk in Atlantic City to the headquarters for the National Organization for Women in Washington, D.C.

The burden of squeezing in my mid-section was now left to the remaining upper half of that athletic supporter, its seams taken in and reinforced by Allie B after some hard peddling on her old Singer sewing machine. Single-handedly, the woman was about to erase the evidence of every french fry and Hershey Bar I'd ever been exposed to. And ...

like so many of Allie B's creations, the device was multi-functional. It not only squeezed me in and pushed me up, it also removed the probability that something stupid might make its way from my lips to the judges' ears. I was speechless.

As the elastic torture chamber brought me to the brink of an unscheduled bulimic episode, my waistline approached the number Allie B had invented for the entry form. It was tiny, no doubt about that—especially in contrast with my enormous bust. Funniest thing. The instant that harness was placed around my waist, those two magical pageant digits—thirty-six—miraculously showed up above it. Encouraged by the mutated jock strap, my chest popped out like nothing I'd witnessed since Liz White washed her cheerleader sweater in hot water. On purpose, no doubt. If you knew her, you knew that.

But in spite of Allie B's efforts, the mixed messages continued. It seemed that while the *rehearsals* for victory were acceptable to Mama, the *victory* was not. Yet between pageants, she would footrace a tornado to get me to dance class and skip choir practice to take me to the dressmaker—then hide every last cupcake and cigarette in a place she claimed I had never shown interest in or been curious about. My mama was a mystery, alright.

To this day, I do not know what possessed her to choose that bookcase.

As for the bookcase she carried in her head, it has taken decades to understand the only book on its shelves—*The Rule Book for Getting into Heaven.* Each rule was more confusing, contradictory, and insane than the one before it. It was only after years of pageants, a collection of tiaras memorializing each one, and a collection of therapists analyzing each tiara that I finally figured out my mama and her book. I will never know the complete story, but in the collective opinion of the psychiatric crowd, the Cliff's Notes version was:

G U I L T

And sister woman, it showed up in every chapter of that book! There were chapters from *Mama's Book of Rules*, and *Mama's Own*

Mama's Rules, *The Tent Revival Rules*, and *The Rules of the Ladies of the Sunday School and Church*, as well as their own personal take on *The Rules of Jesus*.

I didn't have a snowball's chance in hell.

THE RULE BOOK FOR GETTING INTO HEAVEN

RULE I: THOU SHALT NOT CALL ATTENTION TO THYSELF

You read it right—no attention to T h y s e l f.

In Mama's manual, there were reasons for this rule which appeared to be closely related to sin, in one form or another. But, according to psychiatric manuals, the *real* reason for the rule was that calling attention to thyself just might lead to thy success. (As thy might suspect, just as failure was dreadfully incorrect for a Southern Belle, so was success.)

Like so many *Thou Shalt Not Do's* in this book, the actual rule obviously had little to do with what-it-claimed-to-have-to-do-with. No doubt, many were linked to that all-knowing, judgmental, buttenski of an intruder and destroyer of all things exciting and fun—heaven. And Mama wanted to get there more than she wanted a beauty pageant trophy or anything else. That's what her mission really was—getting to heaven—and by God, she was gonna get there come hell, high water, or the beauty pageant.

Problem was—while heaven had a track record for turning away women who flaunted what the good Lord gave them, beauty pageants were notorious for rewarding these same attributes. There were scholarships, trophies, contracts, money, and (my personal favorite) the wrath of every green-eyed monster over the age of three who ever put a tube of *Cherries in the Snow* to her lips.

In spite of Mama, I was one of those women. There have been labels for my kind since Jerusalem's first Jezebel exposed herself and her family in an open arena. Truth be known, the harlots who now peddle their wares on the legitimate stage of the beauty pageant are actually descendants of those biblical babes—and just like their ancestors, they know that exposing an inch of skin in another genre, or celebrating in the town square (Manhattan), will result in a public lynching and the immediate removal of *Oh! So much more* than clothes. In a public forum, they'll be stripped of crowns, banners, scholarships, self respect, and the unthinkable.

Their mamas.

There they'll be, those outcast beauty queens-turned-whores—those publicly branded strumpets, tarts, and trollops—thrown into the lions' pit, en masse, wearing little more than banners of scarlet letters forming the words of titles so shameful I am, to this day, prohibited from repeating them. (This would be partly due to my allegiance to The Pageant and my respect for The Church, but mostly because my closet is full of those banners.)

Just the same, I proudly exposed as much of myself as the contest rules allowed, entering the playing field as *Miss Whatever* and staying until I'd been crowned TOP something—*anything*. Top talent. Top swimsuit. Top evening gown. On top of the world. On top of the top. And I'll admit it right here, right now: I always vowed that if it ever became a category—and I believe it did—I would be on top of the judges as well.

Plain and simple, I had to have it all, and I wanted to be photographed doing it and ogled by the masses while getting it. Unfortunately, the opportunity often disintegrated before I could get a good hold on it when blindsided by Mama's "Runway of Public Approval."

And as far as I could see, that runway was never going to end.

Perhaps Mama's greatest challenge was dispelling the notion that we had come to those pageants with prior knowledge of a swimsuit competition much less, God forbid, an audience! I had likely been hogtied and forced into the tiny suit by Jaycettes, an organization of community do-gooders whose husbands, The Junior Chamber of Commerce, sponsored the pageant. Like over-zealous stage mothers, these backstage pageant wanna-be's had welded the suit onto my trembling body until my breasts were pushed so far over the edge you could practically hear their cries for more fabric. That's the only way it could have happened.

Well, let me tell you, smiling onstage was nearly impossible while being scrutinized offstage by females so hopping mad because they weren't as pretty as we were. And, too, they were married to Jaycees.

Truth be known I was probably an exhibitionist. But in case you haven't figured it out, so was Mama. Of course, she wouldn't have bought into that kind of talk, and announcing something publicly she couldn't even own up to privately was out of the question. In her mind, we were both wearing the banners of "pure in thought, word, and deed," and had come to that beauty pageant stage to spread those pure thoughts from one end of the runway to the other, which meant— *Oh! Patron Saint of the Beauty Pageant, forgive me for what I'm about to say*—

EVERYBODY *had to win!*

That's right; there could be no losers.

But Mama's purpose on this earth changed somewhat when she pulled out her second rule, which came close to contradicting her first.

RULE II. THOU SHALT NOT CALL ATTENTION TO THYSELF. TRUE. BUT THOU SHALT CALL ATTENTION TO THY NEIGHBOR AND THY NEIGHBOR'S DAUGHTER BY LOVING THEM BETTER THAN THOU SHALT LOVE THINE OWN DAUGHTER OR THYSELF—EVEN IF IT MEANS CALLING ATTENTION TO THYSELF IN THE PROCESS.*

Okay. Now, you may need to read this one twice. I did.

Accomplishing this rule required a ceremony that was every bit as confusing as trying to comprehend the rule itself. It started moments after my coronation when Mama appeared onstage to upstage my victory by turning things around. Minutes after I had bagged that title for which we had rehearsed and I had starved and we had rehearsed and

---

* Don't look for this one in the Bible. (Unlike Mama, Jesus was pretty big on calling attention to Himself. But kissing up? Not so much.)

I had starved some more, Mama tried to take back the glory—every last bit of it. *Oh, yes she did!*

Nobody else's mama did that. *Nobody's!*

With God as her witness and Miss Manners as her God, Mama headed straight for The Promised Land of the beauty pageant stage to earn her heavenly crown—by removing my earthly one. The minute she appeared, a new division was introduced that wiped out swimsuits, evening gowns, and all the rest. As the other mothers rushed from the front row to the stage to put down the winner (me) and console the losers (their daughters), which is—make a note of this—exactly as it should have been, Mama made a beeline from the back row to do the same thing! Once there, she began the arduous task of convincing the losers that they were winners which, naturally, convinced the winner that she was . . . well, you get the picture.

She praised every quivering voice and sour note; every pimpled face and bleached out head; every hoop-and-crinoline-filled evening gown; every sock-filled swimsuit top and fat-filled swimsuit bottom. There were hugs. Hugs and hugs and hugs. The losers got Mama's hugs and Jesus' hugs and hugs from people who, for one reason or another, couldn't be there: hugs from Emily Post, Martha Stewart, Mother Teresa, and the Pope. All hugs that should have been mine.

But get this. Only five minutes into the first competition, that same woman had delivered a message by courier to the unsuspecting makeup crew backstage.

And nobody else's mama did that, either. *Nobody's!*

Like a torpedo, that messenger shot down the aisle straight to the powers-that-be. With Mama's orders wrapped around a generous tip—which was, I like to think, the next Sunday's church offering—this dispatcher operated under a time constraint. His mission: to get that message to those in charge of the iridescent-blue eye shadow and jet-black eyeliner. Their mission: to put every last bit of it on my face before Cotton Plant's Junior Miss could put it on hers.

It was urgent, alright. In his hand, the man had one woman's immediate future and another's unfulfilled past, wrapped in church money, sealed with a prayer. But unlike a proper southern invitation on fine stationary engraved in gold, this was a beauty pageant invitation scrawled on the back of a pageant program, engraved in *blood*. It was short, but not sweet. It went off like a fire alarm:

GET MORE MAKEUP ON
CONTESTANT NUMBER FIVE!
**Put more socks in her bra,
more blush on her cheeks,
more red on her lips,
more black under her eyes,
more passion in her eyes...**

The message was not, of course, signed.

Oddly enough, it came from a woman who wore less makeup than anyone I knew—a woman with a love-hate affair with the beauty pageant that sure played havoc with the half of my mind and the whole of my body that loved the stage.

I had worked hard to create every genetically defiant curve in my swimsuit; to keep both glue-resistant butt cheeks above its elastic; to learn every tap and ballet dance step; to control every sprayed and ratted strand of over-processed, beauty-pageant-challenged-hair on my head. But I had help. Like two-contestants-in-one, Mama and I had been as loyal to our cause as a visiting evangelist was to his. We were all about saving people, alright. Saving ourselves!

But what really saved Mama was that she never, really, stopped honoring the most sacred of all rules. Deep in her heart and soul was branded the one you don't mess around with, not if you're born southern, and certainly not if you're a born a Belle.

RULE III: FAILURE, FOR A SOUTHERN BELLE, IS UNACCEPTABLE!!!

NOW we were getting somewhere. *That* rule was stamped on my birth certificate, for goodness' sake! *SUCCESS! WINNING! AT ANY COST!* That's what Southern Belles were all about. But failure? *Oh, I don't think so!* That I knew for sure, and no one could convince me otherwise.

One would think.

But Southern Belles were also wrong about being right. Then, too, simply going after what you came for would be way too pushy for any female south of the Mason-Dixon Line. So the next commandment appeared and wiped out the previous month's labors: the rehearsals, the jock strap, the chicken broth—everything I had worn, performed, and consumed to honor Rule III—*history!*

This one was right at the top of the list of *Thou Shalt Not Do's.*

It was big as the pain in my butt that spread to my heart and sent those mixed-up messages shooting through my psyche, each and every time *The Rule Book* opened to that page.

It was harder to ignore than the black yarn poodle on my pink felt skirt.

It was plain as the face on Cotton Plant's Junior Miss.

It was . . . well, you get the picture. As big and ugly as all the above, it was the impossible rule. It was Rule IV.

IV: THOU SHALT NOT WIN!

Now don't think for one minute that this is the grand finale because before I could take that one in, Mama turned to the rule that would jump off those pages and land in that small remaining space in my mind between total bewilderment and raging anger, next to clinical depression and just one step before the edge of the cliff. This one would be my one-way ticket to a stage where contestants were not just hysterical Southern Belles—they were certifiably insane! We're talking about people like those monkeys Granny told me about on Mama's side of The Tree who were so confused they could only go into "a mental ward or politics." (But hold on. Admittedly, I did go a little crazy, but I did *not* go into politics.)

This rule would take that two hundred dollar wardrobe from Sears, the scholarship to The College of the Ozarks, and that all-expense paid trip to The Memphis Zoo, and flush them all the way to New Orleans! And the fairytale ending I was expecting? Right down that same crapper. History. This was the rule that laid the foundation for many rocky runways to come and brought the whole mess to its final conclusion. It was Mama's rule.

RULE V: THOU SHALT NOT WIN. TRUE. (BUT THOU SHALT—JUST THE SAME—REHEARSE

TO WIN LIKE YOUR OWN MAMA'S LIFE DEPENDS ON IT!)

Well, sister woman, rehearsing to please my mama and figure out what routine she wanted me to perform on what day and why, is what I continued to do for most of my *not-so-natural* born life!

If Mama had been rehearsing to *lose*, she'd been rehearsing to *win* even more. Together, we had reviewed every scenario—every possible question, breath, and step toward victory. The night of the pageant Mama was in the ring with her eye on every ounce of makeup on every opponent's face and every pound of fat on every butt. Then, the only part heaven played in this match was that great big trophy in the sky! But no sooner had Mama donned her gloves than our opponents changed and I was forced to face my worst competitors: guilt and shame.

And what those guys did to my mama's face.

Yet in spite of her demons, the woman in the back row always mustered up the strength to come out fighting at least once during the pageant, and that took guts. It took guts for Mama to knock out her predators and send that messenger flying down the aisle to instruct the make-up crew. Of course, it took even more to cancel out the entire thing with her own trip down that aisle to do the right thing.

Years later, members of the psychiatric community would be fairly unanimous in their analysis of Mama, her bouts with victory, and life in general. Aside from using the Bible as a convenient excuse for avoiding success, there was her animosity toward her own mother for one thing or another and their rage about not having penises or ever being taught to drive anything with a stick shift, that sort of thing, which could all be traced back to those pesky sexual desires—some repressed, some not—that met the criteria for two or three of the Seven Deadly Sins. But with an impressive collection of good deeds, Mama could cancel out every last evil thought. Not that she'd had even one, not that she'd admit to.

The point is that in some religion somewhere, the title I had won was a sacrilege, and if not related to someone's faith, it was not in anybody's book of etiquette. It was not ladylike. It was not God-like. It was not southern-like. And the neighbors would talk.

It seems I never brought to the stage what Mama once did. According to my grandmother, she had been a brilliant student of classical piano in high school. In college, she taught that piano to play a boogie-woogie beat in a band long before women did that sort of thing. Most likely, it was only moments after those fond memories and love of the stage reared their vulgar heads that my Mama turned to the chapter in her book about women and their desires—located just before the one about the evils of sex. She would immediately cease any behavior indicating she was doing one, or had even thought about the other.

Maybe it was that church in Mama's head—with its members worshiping at an altar built from years of hypocrisy—that said "no" to most anything that might have allowed her to stand out in the congregation. Perhaps the church had brainwashed her into believing that people whose dreams were motivated by burning desires would find *themselves* burning in hell! Or maybe it was Daddy's early exit from her life.

When they met she was onstage, playing piano in that college band; he was a football star who was also onstage a great deal of the time, but in a "life of the party" kind of way. She was not even thirty when the life of her party died and left her with their four children. Now, this still-beautiful woman with such extraordinary talent seemed unable to care about her own life much of the time.

Maybe Daddy's motorcycle *had* pulled up at suppertime to see her, too, and now she missed him. Or maybe her behavior had less to do with Daddy than her own laws about not making waves or being different. Like not being different from the woman next door—or not causing some man in the family to lose an election—or not being reminded of lost dreams—or not burning in hell unless the woman next door was doing it too. Or not letting God off the hook for every bit of it.

Or not facing The Truth.

In retrospect, I believe that Mama's runway might not have had *everything* to with mine. Or God's. Or Daddy's. Or the woman's next door. Not even the runways of mothers with butt-ugly daughters. Not totally. Apparently Mama's was hidden beneath the dark cloud that can snuff out lights on the brightest of runways.

Mama was depressed.

But not 100 percent. When that remaining percent pierced the cloud and sent her messenger scrambling down the aisle, you knew *someone* meant business—and that someone wasn't asking to rule the town, the county, or the state. My mama wasn't asking for a seat in Congress and she didn't want to be governor. She wasn't asking to be a *man*, for goodness' sake.

All Mama wanted was to turn back a clock that had gone too fast for dreams to be realized or losses to be mourned. To bring back the days before children and husbands and books of rules, when she believed those dreams were within her reach. And Mama was as intent on getting to her dreams then, as she was now, on getting to heaven. In fact, she had once believed those dreams *were* about getting to heaven, right here on earth. Mama certainly hadn't needed a book of rules then. Like many Southern Belles, she knew exactly how to get where she wanted to be but got rerouted along the way.

Mama wanted just one more shot at that room full of strangers who hadn't been afraid to applaud, not even for a woman who played boogie-woogie piano in an all-male band in the year nineteen hundred and thirty-five. Just one more time, she wanted to own that stage and bring back all that preceded her performance on it: the rehearsals, the anticipation—the mirror. Mostly, she missed the mirror. Inside the frame she saw a face that reflected exactly what was going on inside her head, while so many faces outside seemed to be wearing masks. It was the one she was born with, and for her audiences, it appeared to be good enough.

An act of vanity to some—her obsession with that mirror—but I knew exactly what she saw in hers because it was the same thing I saw in mine. Beneath the layers of pageant paint was living proof of her uniqueness. Perfect or not, that face was hers, and in that moment nobody was trying to change it. In her world—*our world*—that was no small thing. So the night of her performance she checked the mirror one last time to be sure her face was still in it.

When she stepped onto the stage, there was more confirmation of her existence, but more importantly—her *right* to exist! From that gathering of strangers she heard applause. Reaffirming, loving, accepting, thunderous, deafening applause. And she would strut around the stage wearing next to nothing, then answer ridiculous questions about starving children and world peace—while feeling like a starving child with no peace of her own—just to hear that applause.

To find her own reality in the unreality of the fabricated world of the beauty pageant. That's what Mama wanted. Cheering, hand clapping, trophies; she wanted it all. She wanted applause she could hear. A crown she could touch. A banner she could see. *Something* she could pack up at the end of that pageant and take home to a place where nothing else made sense. Nothing else seemed real.

My mama just wanted to know that the face in her mirror was worthy of that applause—and there was only one way to find out: she had to win. That's all my mama ever wanted. That's all I ever wanted. And that's all my mama should have wanted for me if she'd been a Southern Belle worth her salt.

But apparently she wasn't. Because instead of hugs, I was being embraced by the embarrassment I had brought to her—and instead of applause, I heard the reverberation of shame as my victory rocked the foundation of the church and crushed the hopes and dreams of the poor woman next door for her daughter who lost. And I knew that not even the makeup requested by the woman in the back row would cover up that shame and make it go away.

Mama was simply defeated by her own set of rules. And I was defeated by Mama. Still, I had my dreams—one in particular.

Mama charged onto that stage like a bull in heat, mowing down every contestant and her mother until she reached me, the newly crowned State Fair Queen. And although the stage was permeated by cow crap and illuminated by a ferris wheel, she believed it was the Boardwalk in Atlantic City.

We hugged and kissed, as her jet-black mascara ran down her cheek and her pageant-red lipstick met mine. Then she grabbed the microphone, turned to the other contestants and their mothers and screamed, "Now, listen up, and listen up, good. My daughter and I have just won this pageant. We got exactly what we came for! You got that? My girl is the prettiest, smartest, and most talented one, and—eat your hearts out—she is built like a brick house!"

Mama headed offstage, then suddenly did an about-face and made a beeline for the still-smoking microphone. She picked it up, tapped it twice, and added,

"And that last part about the brick house? Well, take off your blinders. That goes for me, too!!"

In somebody's Book of Rules, perhaps Mama went too far. Of course, I didn't have a book, or any rules, so I held on to my dream. I clung to my secret, too. While Mama was earning her heavenly crown, and me, my earthly one, I always knew—even the night I shoved Rhode Island's Junior Miss from third to fifth place—that *God* was the only one who ever really gave a damn whether I won or not.

And the roses I took from the beauty pageant bouquets and pressed between the pages of Psalms and Proverbs? He cared about those, too.

Just one more thing about my mama. Make no mistake about it; she could have walked off any stage with a trophy for first place. In every category. Not a problem, not for Mama.

Swimsuit competition? In the bag. Especially if she could make good use of it by packing up her children during intermission and taking them to the pool across the street.

Mama could've attended that judges' luncheon; put together the menu and laid it out on a perfectly set table; starched and ironed everyone's outfits but her own; and shown them all a thing or two about The Ten Commandments and doing unto the other contestants better than she did unto herself.

Oh, Lord yes. She could've moved on to the evening gown competition and won that in her apron, then brought down the house with her special talent for keeping most of her dreams to herself and making the rest disappear.

But her beauty? Now THAT she couldn't hide. She had the kind not dependent on a drawer of tricks or well-thought-out wardrobe. She was the whole package, alright, with everything just as it should have been—from her thick, loosely curled auburn hair and flawless skin to her well-proportioned figure that refused to get fat. And did I say cheekbones? Oh, honey! Naturally high cheekbones, untouched by the sun-in-a-jar other mothers smeared where cheekbones should have been.

But if Mama had conformed—I'm just saying IF SHE HAD painted herself up—I'll swear, she could've passed for a movie star. Even unattended to, everyone said she looked like Loretta Young, a movie star of her era.

And Mama's platform? Well, she appeared to stand FOR more than she stood ON, if you get my drift. But God knows, she had time for promoting platforms with public appearances and such, what with being relieved of all the makeup chores and clothes-shopping marathons.

As for "saving the world," a prerequisite for anyone hoping to make top five, Mama went about that in a very private way which, bless her heart, was just one more peculiarity.

Still, Mama could've won any trophy, anytime, anywhere. Make no mistake about that. But, then, Mama wouldn't have had it for long because knowing her, she would have passed it on to someone who needed it more than she did.

But Mama was a winner just the same because in her class, there was no competition. Of course, Mama didn't know that, because somewhere along the way someone neglected to tell her. Some idiot forgot to give Mama her crown.

And that's all I'm saying to you about my mama, except that I—like the idiot before me—really should have said it to her.

MAMA

10.
Let me entertain you—whether I want to or not

Perhaps the hardest thing about living with a depressed parent is trying to solve the mystery. Dark clouds don't tell you much; mostly, they just hover. Maybe that's why I spent so little time talking to Mama and so much looking for clues, even though I knew if they ever showed up, every last one would point to me. In retrospect, I guess those unanswered questions aren't the hardest thing about living with a depressed parent. The answers the child comes up with on her own . . . that's the hardest part.

It was just like Daddy's disappearance, I figured. Mama's unhappiness was my fault. But no matter how many titles I brought home, or how sincerely I repented after I did, her sadness was still there, and Daddy wasn't. But Mr. Jones was. He was everywhere.

When I saw him in the audience, I'll swear, I almost switched my attention to the sadness on Mama's face. Anything would beat the pants off what he brought to that seat in the audience, and to me at home. Of course, he *had* taken on a wife in the beginning stages of a long battle with depression and four stepchildren whose father had died only one year earlier. Truth be known, that probably only proved the man wasn't thinking right.

After years of trial and error I did accept Mr. Jones, even appreciated, loved and respected him. But during those early years, there was a lot to learn for both of us—and Mr. Jones was quite a teacher. His first lesson was all about runways. He taught me that just like fathers and stepfathers, they are not all necessarily the same.

S-h-h-h-h! Here Comes Mr. Jones!

Daddy had been able to throw up a runway faster than Brother Bob could put up a revival tent. When there was an audience of two or more in that liquor store—steady enough to clap—I performed. But Mr. Jones was not Daddy. His creativity extended no further than the kitchen counter in his home, which became my home when he married Mama one year after Daddy's death. His contribution to my relationship with the stage would be all about that kitchen counter, a stage quite different from Daddy's. It would be the "Here she comes down the kitchen counter" runway—my own, personal runway from hell.

Daddy's departure, as well as whatever was going on with Mama, had taken its toll. In fact, I could have been the poster child for obsessive-compulsive jerks and twitches—habitual moves that were, even to me, annoying. My favorite one involved jumping as high as I could over a line in the sidewalk and then landing flatfooted on the other side. I repeated the routine until I got it right, especially the jumping part.

The higher the better.

With the completion of a successful jump, the magic I had created would be waiting for me just beyond that line in the sidewalk. It was a performance I kept to myself—or so I thought. But Mr. Jones was, apparently, watching. And he didn't like it. Or me. Not one bit. In retrospect I would imagine he'd heard his friends say, "She's just like her Daddy," at least a six-pack of beer and a fifth of whiskey too many times. It was most likely one of those occasions that prompted him to choreograph a talent routine that began with the public hanging of the town sweetheart and ended with the birth of the town idiot—the longest-running, most convincing show of all. Remarkably, Mr. Jones took me from being a star to a has-been in only one night.

Unlike his other theater—with movie stars, hopes and dreams—this one featured the sound of ice tapping against jelly glasses, and the smell of smoke encircling chips and dips. Short and narrow, slick in places, sticky in others—this runway was illuminated only by a lone yellow ceiling bulb; a few flickering cigarette lighters below; and an audience of onlookers who were pretty darned lit themselves. Lined with lipstick-rimmed glasses of whiskey and empty beer cans, there was a stove at one end of my runway, pigs-in-blankets in the middle, and a kitchen sink at the end. There were no trophies or tiaras. Victory on Mr. Jones' runway meant finding a way to escape it! My only hope was to be ignited by a spark from one of those cigarettes, leaving only the ashes of my compulsions and poor Mr. Jones with no performer. No show.

Most of my audience had formerly been the liquor store crowd, so I was quite familiar with them. But only minutes into my act, it was obvious from their expressions that my act was unfamiliar to them. In the midst of their partying, they were asked to direct their attention to the kitchen counter as Mr. Jones lifted me onto it. As master of ceremonies, he introduced me as a little girl who could blink her eyes over and over again, wrinkle her nose in between, and twitch and jerk 'til the cows came home. Without stopping. And she could jump. She could jump over anything, it didn't matter what it was, and she could jump high. And if she didn't jump high enough the first time, she did it—in even numbers—again and again.

"Do it!" Mr. Jones would shout, at least as many times as I twitched, "Show everyone how you jerk and twitch and blink. Show them how *stupid* you look! Show them how you jump! Do it. Go on, do it—over and over again. Do it without stopping!"

"Jump!" he screamed. "I ... said ... Jump! Jump over the glasses. Jump over the dip. Jump higher! Higher! Higher! HIGHER! JUMP HIGHER!

"D O IT!"

This performance required little rehearsal, but was one I would never forget. Unlike the titles I would eventually hold, stupid was not one I could pass on to a successor. Nor could I ever forget that jerks and twitches, excessive hand washing, and jumping over lines must be hidden right along with talking to grown-ups about dead people and asking, "What does 'He's at peace' mean?"

With each party, the fear of that kitchen counter runway resurfaced along with the compulsions, and I waited to be called upon for an encore. As things turned out, the encores would happen for the rest of my life. But never again on the kitchen counter.

A bewildered shrink would one day dive into his bottomless bag of psychiatric phenomena and come up with quite a diversified line-up of multiple personalities that should have stepped in following such trauma. At the very least, I was entitled to the kind of crippling fear that would keep your average person locked away in a subterranean vault for the rest of her life. But apparently my need to be on that stage was even greater than Mr. Jones' need to punish me on it. In fact, the man left me with far less fear of the beauty pageant stage than poor Mama's fear that Jesus was one of the judges.

Mr. Jones struggled with the difference in his Family Tree and Mama's. Even at seven years old I could see that. (Something to do with fertilizer, I always thought, and the way it takes to—downright favors—political roots.) Trouble was, everyone else could see it, too. Matter of fact, not since Daddy's people attempted to merge with Mama's had there been such a mess of mismatched roots—or a man as hell-bent as Mr. Jones on stepping out of our social order by exposing The Truth about his.

One twig at a time, it grew into the kind of Monster Truth that can uproot the best of families. It invaded our thoughts and watched every move we made. When we spent money, and when we didn't, there it was. It showed up at our family reunions and it *really* showed up at Mr. Jones' family reunions. Sometimes it arrived looking a lot like Archie Bunker and other times, Scrooge. It screwed up our wardrobes, messed with our music, and crept into our speech. Many times it sneaked up on us unexpectedly, but always — *always!* — it entered the room like a child who had not been invited to a birthday party—a little boy who'd been left out of the loop. And that little boy was mad as hell.

"I don't care if me or any of my people ever see or hear or go there. That's how I feel about that store," was Mr. Jones' unexpected, somewhat embarrassing—and, we all thought, downright low-class and exceptionally common—reaction the day I returned from a trip to Texas to see Mama's people. I had presented her with a fire-engine-red scarf in a Neiman Marcus bag, proof of my visit to Dallas' famous store.

"It's from Neiman Marcus. *It really is!*" I said to Mr. Jones just seconds before he megaphoned to the entire neighborhood how he felt about the scarf, Neiman Marcus, and every other "high-falootin" store outside the state of Arkansas. It wasn't the first time I'd seen him that angry. I saw that same expression the night I faced my audience and those pigs-in-blankets on his Runway from Hell.

"And Texas, too," he said, expanding the territory where one might encounter high falootin' stores and people. "Yeah, I don't care if my people ever see Texas, either."

His objection to the scarf had turned ugly and was opening the gates to rage I am sure Mr. Jones didn't know he had. "No, I sure enough don't care if me or any of my people ever go to Neiman Marcus or Texas or see a movie about it or even wear cowboy boots," he said, taking on the defensive tone of an illegal alien with limited knowledge of a strange new land. But Mr. Jones was not a man without a green card; he was a stepfather with second-class citizenship and no rights whatsoever.

But today was his. Mr. Jones had the stage and he wasn't about to step down until he'd had his say. "And that includes New York, Hollywood and Paris," he said, obviously pleased he had paid attention to the movies at his own theater—and sixth grade geography.

"Las Vegas. What about Las Vegas? Why don't I go there and bring you some naked women in bright red cowboy boots?" I fought back the urge to ask, but only because I didn't want Las Vegas added to the growing list of places Mr. Jones and his people would never see.

Like a soldier who'd strayed from his platoon, Mr. Jones marched single file across the living room to address the enemy. I knew his list of forbidden places was coming to an end as he called upon previous material to fill his remaining stage time. "Yes-sir-ee," he said slowly, like we hadn't just heard what was coming next, "I don't care if me or my people ever go to New York or Hollywood, either."

I was proud of Mr. Jones. I never thought of him as a man with opinions, only a man with secrets trapped inside some kind of monster rage he kept neatly tucked away in its cage. Most of the time, it worked. On the days Mr. Jones was in control, the monster was, too. But on those other days, Mr. Jones got quiet. Then he got mad.

I liked him quiet. Quiet moved in when control moved out. The less control he had, the cleaner the house got and the more perfectly everything in it got arranged. I especially enjoyed the way he lined up his fishing poles, bait and tackle, rifles, and frog gigging paraphernalia. Those weapons sure knew who was in charge. Every time they wiped out another unsuspecting creature, they knew.

From day one, Mr. Jones declared himself ruler of our roost as he took his place at the head of the table, got served first, and blessed the food he had hunted down and murdered. He paid our bills, operated his movie theater, and kept the car running. He gave a lot—I'll give him that—but not without passing out a few IOU's. Over the years, it seemed to me that Mama paid hers off many times over by selling bits and pieces of herself before finally handing over a pretty big chunk of her soul. When there was nothing left to sell, Mama closed up shop. Mama sold out.

The whole thing probably had something to do with Mr. Jones feeling out of place in our house. Actually, his world and mine were similar in that respect. We needed to find a place for everything around us because we couldn't find a place for ourselves. For me, acting on the obsessions mostly brought a sense of safety . . . well, not so much a sense of safety as a sense that *not* acting on them would bring on something unthinkable. I guess the biggest difference in Mr. Jones and me was that his compulsions were labeled "neat and organized," while mine had labels no one wanted to talk about.

It was after I returned from the trip to Texas that I began thinking about his former world and how he felt about the one he'd married into. I wondered about many things, like, if Mr. Jones and his people never wanted to go to Neiman Marcus, where *did* they want to go? Of course, nobody ever asked Mr. Jones how he or any of his people felt about Neiman Marcus or anything else which, I believe, was Mr. Jones' main problem.

Nobody ever asked.

Now we all suspected he had a past. We were *dysfunctional*—not *stupid!* Yet nobody was prepared for the shocking revelation that rolled down the wrong side of his tracks and slammed into our Tree. We simply didn't see it coming—not until Mr. Jones had totally flattened our family crest and made mincemeat of our Tree. Of course, we should have been prepared. I mean, we might have sent out mixed signals, what with being somewhat hypocritical and pretentious while being charitable, compassionate, and God-fearing at the same time. But we weren't *blind,* for gosh sake! On some level, we had to know it would happen. But as was often the case in matters that cast a shadow over the family, nobody would speak up.

Yet anybody could see that Mr. Jones was just *not like us*. No matter how long we lived under his roof; no matter how much he fed, clothed, and educated us or packed up the car and took us on vacation; no matter what the man did, he was just plain different. Not like us, not one bit. Not like us at all. He'd grown up in a different world, lived on the other side of the tracks, and traveled with a different crowd in a different vehicle.

That vehicle was big and it was yellow and Mr. Jones had once ridden home from school in it. Mr. Jones had ridden home . . .

on the bus.

Uh-huh. Mr. Jones had grown up on the outskirts of town in a house with people the spitting image of those children who got sucked up by the tornado—the ones who couldn't come to my house after school because Mama might have to drive them home and come face-to-face with something inside their houses more terrifying than the crap trapped inside *our own* tornado—the one that was shaking the shingles off our seemingly sound foundation. We sure didn't want to be confronted with God-knows-what in their houses or be forced to sit at their table and eat God-knows-what-else! Oh, yeah. Mr. Jones had been one of them, alright; he had definitely been one of them.

Pure and simple . . . somebody had to finally say it. It might as well be me. Mr. Jones had been . . .

a bus child.

Not to let him off easy, but that *would* explain his rage and dismiss most any way he chose to act it out, including an act of terrorism, the mass murder of his family, and the kitchen counter massacre of an unsuspecting stepchild. Then, too, much like Mama's Tree, Daddy's, and most everyone else's, Mr. Jones' Tree had suffered through far too many droughts. Well . . . on the night of the kitchen counter performance, *this* stupid stepchild remedied that.

As he swept me from the counter into the air, just moments before setting me down on the kitchen floor, I inadvertently demonstrated for my audience yet another of my disorders as my bladder—*without stopping even once!*—produced an unexpected stream of consciousness that drenched the runway, the pigs in the blankets, and the pig that put me on that counter in the first place.

You might say I gave Mr. Jones and his Tree a good watering—one that was long overdue.

In the years that followed, Mr. Jones developed quite a fondness for another runway—the beauty pageant. Well, not so much a fondness for *the pageant* as transporting me *to* and *from* it. In fact, preparation for the ride home topped any obsessive-compulsive act I could have ever performed on a kitchen counter!

Mr. Jones' relationship with the trunk of our 1959 Pontiac was as intimate as the one he had with his socks and handkerchief drawer at home and darn-near as impressive as his hunting-gear lineup in our basement. The packing and re-packing ceremony in that trunk was the highlight of Mr. Jones' pageant experience! In fact, the night of the Arkansas' District Forest Queen contest, the applause he received for squeezing in a three-foot blow-up of Smokey the Bear was uncomfortably close to what I got for winning the stupid thing.

As each piece of pageant finery assumed its assigned spot in that trunk, we observed, praised, and endured. But God forbid I should win because then the process was prolonged by the placement of—*Oh My dear Lord and Precious Savior, he hadn't planned on this!*—the roses, crown, and trophy. Inside the car, the hollowness of post-pageant gloom and doom generated an uneasy quiet that sucked up every morsel of triumph in its path before reaching the newly crowned *Queen of Whatever*.

It was a silence that felt like anything but the aftermath of victory—more like mourning the death of those poor murdered animals in Mr. Jones' pickup than celebrating the birth of a *queen* in his car! But the vacuum was eventually filled by that imaginary, though ever-present, Satan of the Beauty Pageant who joined me in the back seat and screamed words into my ear that would finally give a voice to this tomb of silence:

Well, you ungrateful little moron!! Why'd you have to go off and embarrass your mama and Mr. Jones? Are you stupid or what? God almighty, girl! YOU WON! You went off and WON! That was NOT what the rehearsals and trunk packing were all about! Let's just stop this car right now so you can think about what you have just done!

Think about the girls who didn't go home with a trophy!
Think about the losers!
Think about the starving children!
Think about the losers without a trophy who ARE starving children!
Think about Jesus!
Now, how do you feel? You selfish little hussy!

Or words to that effect.

For the rest of my life, would I be punishing people like Cotton Plant's Junior Miss because of Mama and Mr. Jones? I mean, just *think* about Cotton Plant's Junior Miss. Poor, poor Cotton Plant's Junior Miss.

DO IT! SHOW EVERYONE HOW YOU'RE THINKING ABOUT POOR COTTON PLANT'S JUNIOR MISS!!! DO IT OVER AND OVER AGAIN! DO IT, STUPID!!!!

Please.

The pressure hadn't come from her after all. The poor girl had gotten her falsies, swimsuit, and accordion glued shut for absolutely no good reason. The burden I drug across that stage had little to do with her, my acne, or those extra ten pounds—not even my obvious lack of talent. It was the woman in the back row who struggled with the demons that had taken over her own stage. It was those competitors—depression, guilt, and fear—that left my Mama as emotionally unavailable as her husband.

And it was her husband who earned his own trophy by packing a perfectly organized trunk for this Junior Miss so she could walk down the runway he had so perfectly taught her to fear.

II. Take off your tiara—you'll be here awhile

11.

P.S. If I fall off the runway, will they take back my crown?

My siblings left home and chose runways that would make anyone's mama proud. They had apparently escaped, ignored, or never experienced the turmoil that was my legacy. But knowing them as I do, I suspect they were simply smart enough to leave it behind.

For me, the next few years were mostly about bad choices. In the sixties, I made a bad choice to leave college shortly after I unpacked, and an equally bad one ending in divorce after that. There were more bad choices in the eighties, but a fairly decent facelift in the nineties. It was the seventies that made the other years look not so bad.

The act that began in Daddy's liquor store had now made a few stops along the way before accepting a limited engagement—my first marriage. During that two-year union, I gave several memorable performances, the most unforgettable being an impromptu impersonation of my mother-in-law that damn-near removed the roof and both our memberships from a country club out in Houston, Texas. But the most tragic of all performances was a few years ahead, and I'd been rehearsing for it all along.

It had become obvious that the weight of my crown was way too much for one Southern Belle to carry. Beneath its rhinestones were implanted not only my own feelings of unworthiness, but quite possibly those of my mother, her mother, and her mother before her. If there had been a Miss Ambivalence contest, we'd have all been winners.

Runways paved with opportunities and freedom were there—the opportunity for a woman to be a concert pianist, a cowboy, or a movie star. The freedom to be more than the politician's wife or daughter—to be the politician herself!

Eventually, Miss Peach, Miss Collard Green Queen, and Miss Everything Else would assume their proper places in my history and be remembered as little more than distant runners-up to the other opportunities those runways could have provided. But my father's list of endless possibilities had been replaced by only a cardboard crown, loosely held together by my hopes and dreams—securely held together with bits of pageant glitter and the glue of Mama's guilt.

It was clear by now that I'd done nothing for my mama. But I'd sure gotten stuck with that guilt.

Dear Rosemary,
    Congratulations! ROTC Queen at the University of Arkansas!
So, what's next—Miss Arkansas? Miss America?
Just as we predicted, you're flying high!
                       The Pageant Committee

My entrance and exit from The University of Arkansas were much closer together than I'd planned. My departure ended an old dream of representing the college in The Miss Arkansas Pageant. It could have been my year.

Some of my past competitors had gotten married; a couple simply disappeared—victims, most likely, of a sudden gust of wind. My main rival had been banned from pageants altogether after showing up drunk at a judges' luncheon and peeing about six feet short of the restroom (a definite point stealer, but grounds for disqualification? Hardly). But as I felt the opportunity for success closing in, I called upon the routine I'd rehearsed my entire life: I packed up my trophies and left.

It was shortly after my coronation as Honorary Cadet Colonel for the ROTC that I gave a final salute to the University of Arkansas and the troops. One last time, I turned to the squadron and asked, "What are the orders for the day?" and one last time, I asked them, "What the hell does 'What are the orders for the day?' mean?" Then I marched off the battlefield and kept marching through many battlefields for many years to come. In retrospect, my exit had nothing to do with the military, but everything to do with war—the war of the beauty pageant and the fear of winning that war.

But then I had to face my biggest fear—the marked similarities between me and the woman who had walked away from her stage much as I had marched away from mine.

Mama skipped out on her college band, forcing them to make *their* name without *hers,* or her piano. The gigs came, Mama went. But I couldn't think about that. Following in her footsteps would lead me straight to the heart of the Bible belt into an eternity of saintliness and a life filled with nothing but senseless good deeds and doing unto my fellow man forever and ever, amen. Well, I sure didn't want to see that happen. I mean, Jesus aside, who wants to do unto *any* man? Or worse—who wants to be like her mother?

But who doesn't, just the same, spend much of her life doing just that?

Coffee, tea . . .

Dear Pageant Committee,
I quit college. But I am flying.
I'll keep you posted when I land.
Rosemary

P.S. If I fall off the runway, will they take back my crown?

After jumping off the beauty pageant bandwagon and heading straight for college, one month later I boomeranged back home. Following several similar performances, I landed deep in the heart of Texas in the cockpit of a DC-3 airplane in the lap of a pilot. I was now traveling in old war planes with, mostly, old war pilots. I was, as airline folks said, a "stew."

Armed with hot-pink blusher, jet-black mascara, and sky-blue eyeliner that began somewhere around Wichita, extended from my eye to my ear and stopped just short of Topeka, I was, as airline folks also said, "regulation." I probably could've carried my cockpit keys and a small carry-on bag in my beehive-do, which today would never make it past airport security.

In those days it was rumored that we sat in pilots' laps and flew the planes. Since my abrupt separation from college was partly due to being blindsided by the "scholastic" clause in my scholarship (*Well, hello! Somebody should've warned me!*), this "sitting in pilots' laps" job sure sounded like something a girl with half-a-mind could, in time, learn to do. And I learned a lot.

Back then we had no legal recourse, so pilots had the freedom—with minimal skill—to sexually harass stewardesses. Then, my answer to the question, "Do you feel safe?" had more to do with layovers than landing gear, and *nothing* to do with weapons. In fact, one of my duties was to carefully, reverently, secure all artillery with blankets and hunting jackets, then shove them into the overhead bins.

As the rifle-toting hunters boarded the aircraft, a fusion of familiar smells with the sight of those guns brought back memories of a basement in Arkansas, with rifle racks lining the walls and ropes of catfish dancing from the ceiling. On Saturday nights a menagerie came alive in that room, with frogs' legs leaping over dead animal parts and duck feathers flying over muddy hunting gear—a final celebration before their presentation at the next day's dinner table.

Funny thing about the warm and fuzzy memories those weapons and animal smells conjured up and how happy Mr. Jones had been amid his trophies. Funny thing that this was probably the only place he could go in his very own house that felt like home.

The home of a bus child.

I had flown a year when President Kennedy got shot, I got married, and I got fired—three events that altered my beliefs about gun safety; the airline keeping a married stewardess on their payroll; and my staying married, forever, to a rich man. Then there was Aunt Allie B's fantasy about sewing up all the dresses for my wedding in Mama's backyard. That one got trashed, too. Thank you, Jesus.

It would have featured a "love in bloom" theme, an exact replica of my high school annual's full-page, color layout of the senior prom. Trouble was, there had been a passage of time since Allie B first had that vision. And while time, for her, was an unfinished canvas to be stroked with her broad brush of endless possibilities, for the rest of us—where Allie B was concerned—it was an invitation to disaster. By now, the white trellis could have grown into something resembling a giant McDonald's arch, covered in yellow plastic roses spilling randomly onto a nearby red plastic picnic table loaded with plates of Big Macs and side orders of fries. The remaining roses would have made their way onto the trains of the bridesmaids' dresses, the base of the wedding cake, the ushers' lapels, and the bodice of Allie B's dress, with the leftovers stashed away for her daughter's inevitable next wedding.

But the fantasy that really fell apart was the one about staying married forever to a rich man. The man sure wasn't forever. But he *was* rich. Down to his long-horned roots, the man was rich. But so was his mother, who was deep in the trembling heart of her son and, it would appear, most everything else in Texas.

I met him on a flight. Two weeks of dating followed by a three-week engagement culminated in a wedding celebration that lasted almost as long as the courtship. It was exactly what I'd dreamed about since those days at Jones Theater where I watched young women sing and dance their way into the arms of their perfect partners. Well, let me tell you, *my* perfect partner had definitely shown up, and he'd brought with him all that had been missing from my life.

The day of our wedding my dream played out on a screen big as Texas itself. The church was filled with roses, big yellow Texas roses, and music—big, loud wedding music. I started my long walk down the aisle when I got my cue from the organ. I don't know what everyone else heard, but the song that sent me floating down the runway—*Here She Comes, Miss America*—bore little resemblance to *The Wedding March.* I mean, really. Any Southern Belle knows that floating down a runway beats the heck out of marching—anywhere! (I could've done a lot for the guys in the ROTC, but not one of them had to do with marching.) Besides, *Here She Comes, Miss America* came with a guarantee that, barring any unforeseen scandal, I'd be holding on to my title for at least a year.

I continued gliding down that aisle to the beat of my own organ, ever mindful of the need to separate myself from the seven beautiful runners-up I'd chosen as bridesmaids (*What the crap was I thinking?*), giving them ample time to assemble in a big semi-circle at the altar. I walked slowly, waving ever so daintily to my audience while staying focused on the "you'd better be careful" portion of my Southern Belle Manual, which plainly states that a Belle must not cross the critical line between acknowledging an audience and appearing to be one of them. You know what I'm saying, maybe you don't. Well, not even *The Book of Rules* can put that one into words. (Sorry, you either know it or you don't.)

I was savoring every moment of my fantasy wedding right down to the aroma from those yellow rose buds in my bouquet. So, before that journey ended, I stopped just short of the altar and took time to smell the roses and look into the eyes of my perfect partner. Second row, stage left, there she was—the stage mother from heaven.* Then I took a few more steps and faced my soon-to-be husband—the man who'd brought her into my life.

I took my vows, even though the woman in the second pew had already taken them for me. She'd promised herself that like her son, I would honor and obey her forever. And that was okay, because she was the woman I had pictured in my mama's seat in the audience, cheering me straight to the runway of the Miss Arkansas stage.

In her, I saw a chance to hook up with a woman who wanted to win. She was Auntie Mame and the mother of Gypsy Rose Lee trapped in the same body—my Aunt Allie B with a pedigree—ruthless and determined, but more, come to think of it, like a Jaycette on speed. I tried to keep up, Lord knows I did, but next to her I was little more than an off-the-rack *Labels for Less* hanging on for dear life beside a *Christian Dior*.

She'd done it all. From her bloodline, southern royalty flowed freely, with dukes and duchesses, marquises and maharanis, oozing like sap from every root and shoot of her Family Tree. Like in *The Great Gatsby*, social gatherings were perfectly staged in her enormous antebellum home. The title she was vying for was never clear to anyone and certainly not to her, but the contest took place on a stage that covered the entire state of Texas.

She seemed intent on getting something before anyone else, but (except for her stash of alcohol) I don't believe she knew exactly where to look. Just the same, her desire was so strong for whatever it was she wanted, she would mow down and step over the dead and defeated from Houston to Fort Worth to get it—without looking back. No regrets, no stopping to make over the lifeless bodies of those she'd left behind, no apologies to God or ambivalence about victory or what she had to do to get it. None of that nonsense, none whatsoever. Her motives were open and honest, and there was nothing contradictory about them. She was the real thing: a perfectly turned-out, sure enough, gold plated,

---

*. . . the mother-in-law from hell.

ostentatious, controlling, pretentious, social-climbing bitch. And she was consistent. Not one day went by that she wasn't a bitch. Just the same, I took the heat for her; mostly, I took her hits.

Apparently, the stage mother my husband got dealt wasn't the one he wanted. In fact, he rebelled against that losing hand with every bottle of liquor available to him. I was an easy target. But I was so enamored with his mother that I ignored the bruises on my arms and face that appeared after almost every social affair. I saw no further than those elaborate parties and my wardrobe, selected and paid for by my perfect new mother.

She outfitted my house, too. With Neiman Marcus represented in every room, I felt like a queen—and I loved it. Her, too. I loved my husband's mother almost as much as Neiman Marcus. I couldn't understand why he didn't. "My God," I would say to him, "what do you *want* in a mother? What kind of mother do you want?"

Only when he got really drunk did I get an answer, "Your mother," he would say. "I wish I'd had *your mother.*" Come to find out, he did. He had a mother who was just as big a mystery as mine, and even harder to please.

Like Mama, I wasn't sure where this woman was headed, but knew I had some role in her journey—and that once again, getting there was all about the rules. I had to stay within the parameters of what another woman believed to be socially acceptable.

And that made perfect sense, of course, because everyone was watching.

12.
The eyes of Texas . . .

It was simple.

No one in her circle must ever know I'd been a stewardess, especially one who'd flown internationally. Everyone knew what these women did in airplane lavatories to earn their wings—even on short domestic flights, like from Houston to Amarillo—so the images of what must've taken place on a flight from Fort Worth to Paris, France, would open the most closed of all socialites' minds and dump them into the deepest of gutters on the wrong side of the tracks. I was extremely careful to adhere to the rules so that didn't happen.

But during those two years it became impossible to follow the rules while covering up bruises and keeping down panic attacks, as each seemed to have a lot to do with the other. Then, too, there was the social calendar. Seeing as how I'd taken on every role in *The Many Faces of Eve*, it was impossible to keep up with the parties and remember which face I was wearing. Alcohol didn't help.

I took up temporary residence in some of the finest Ladies' Rooms in Texas and became adept at warding off panic attacks and performing obsessive-compulsive rituals behind closed doors. I silently counted to ten as I washed my hands and, always, when I drank my bourbon and coke. Nobody knew the difference, except with the bourbon and Coke, on the nights I counted to ten too many times.

It was before anyone could count to ten that I pulled up stakes and left my mother-in-law, the country club, and my husband. The social whirl pretty much got the best of me while his mother, the alcohol, the social whirl, and my panic attacks *because* of his mother, the alcohol, and the social whirl, pretty much got the best of my husband. But I stayed long after I should have because come hell, high water, or my mother-in-law, I remembered those rules.

Rule II: Failure, for a Southern Belle, is unacceptable.

But after the annual Christmas shindig for the socially gifted, I realized that staying was no longer an option. So I choreographed my final farewell and pretty much made confetti of Rule I.

Rule 1: Thou Shalt Not Call Attention to Thyself.

Now that one was hard to pull off, what with a big bruise on the side of my face from the night before. Then too, there was the sauterne. I served it hot from a punch bowl the size of the Houston Astrodome and figured the more I drank of it, the less I'd have to serve. Made sense to me.

As luck would have it, after downing half a bowl of the hot wine I was unable to serve even myself, so I switched headquarters and positioned myself at the front door. With one hand clutching the coat rack and the other gripping a University of Texas mega-mug of sauterne, I began welcoming the women as they came in. "Welcome aboard, ladies," I said, greeting two at a time (okay, seeing double), "I am your stewardess."

From then on I made just one nose dive after another into that bowl.

"Please fasten your seat belts and observe the 'no smoking' sign," I sang, "and if there is anything I can do to make this party more bearable, please do not hesitate to call upon me." Since my routine had already destroyed life as I knew it, I decided to dive deeper. "Oh, and about the bruise under my eye," I said, stepping closer to my audience, "last night, damnedest thing, the stupid plane crashed!" I addressed my terror-stricken mother-in-law. "Your son is a *really* bad pilot, you know—when he drinks."

I thought my mama had a monopoly on the look coming at me from beneath my mother-in-law's flipped-up false eyelashes. Even her glittered and frosted lavender eyelids paled in comparison. It was *the look,* alright—the one that cut me off at the knees and then watched as I struggled to run for the hills. But it was too late for that.

I gave my audience time to sit and prepare their laps for the tiny plates with tiny hors d'oeuvres. Funniest thing, everything was miniature, even the cups for the sauterne (another justification, I thought, for drinking mine straight from the ladle).

With everyone seated, I took my assigned spot next to the punch bowl and addressed the group. After dispelling their petered-out old airline pilot fantasies (cockpit sex), I got on with the serious business of recruiting. "You women are missing out at the country club when there's a Mile High Club out there," I announced.

The desperate housewives were flying without a plane.

"And ladies," I said, as I carefully transferred them from the cockpit to the airplane lavatory, "Gospel Truth, joining this club has nothing to do with your husband's name or, in many cases, your husband. Period."

And that "period" also marked the end of this Yellow Rose's brief affair with the Houston social register and her reign as sauterne server for its members. In fact, she might as well have tied a yellow ribbon around an old oak tree—in the middle of the Texas Panhandle—and hung herself from it.

She was history.

Since my mother-in-law's weight phobia had kept mine teetering on the edge of anorexia, I took up modeling—local car and boat shows, a couple of TV commercials, that sort of thing—always careful to steer clear of assignments that might require the use of more than half-a-mind. There were also telethons—for every birth defect on the planet, except my own. Then there was a short stint as co-host for an afternoon teen dance party. That was okay; I could talk to teenagers.

But things took a surprising turn when the station manager put me in the co-host's seat on a noontime talk show. After the first airing, I realized I was smarter than I thought, as I actually had enough sense to quit before the next show. Then I realized I was smarter than anyone thought because I also had the good sense to date the station manager!

He gave me one more chance: an assignment that appeared to be as easy as flying an airplane from the lap of a pilot. In fact, it *was* a pilot . . . for an exercise show. My partner was a local wrestler known in the business as Mr. Clean. (I could not make that up.)

Dear Pageant Committee,
    I'm back in the ring, so to speak.
    I've quit the airlines, but I am doing a pilot,
    so to speak.
                        Rosemary

Our show would require minimal thinking and no talking, except for what Mr. Clean chose to think or say—which, Truth be known, was precisely what got the show cancelled even before the pilot aired. After that, jobs came and went, but with each one that required thought, I called on just enough to sabotage and knock down any chance of success before it got steady on its feet. After my work history began showing up in personnel offices throughout the city, it made perfect sense to head in the direction of home. Actually, I needed to talk to the family about Mr. Jones.

When it came to Texas and things of a high falootin' nature, the man had made a lot of sense, a helluva lot of sense.

13.
Go to the back of the bus

It was that dream again.

"Bus children! Bus children! Your buses are here!" the teacher shouted as I stood frozen on that playground and tried to remember whether or not I was one of them. I knew I'd been a cowboy the first day of school before the teacher jerked me off my broomstick horse, moved me to the other side of the playground, and forced me into unwed motherhood with nothing to show for it but a bald-headed piece of rubber wrapped in a pink blanket. But a bus child? I just wasn't sure whether I'd been turned into one of those or not.

As the children piled in, the doors closed and the bus slowly pulled away. Suddenly I realized that I was, indeed, a bus child—just one more thing my mama had failed to tell me. I stopped briefly to mull over the children now waving at me from the back window of the bus. What would a person have to do to be one? Did being a bus child have more to do with what you'd decided to be than what you'd been told to be?

I dropped my school books and ran toward the bus, knowing that once I joined those children, life as I'd known it would be over and I'd be looking at chickens, cows, and tornados (and myself, on the six o'clock news—running from something, most likely the tornados) for the rest of my life. Still, I chased that moving bus and frantically waved my arms as I pleaded with the driver. . . .

It was a recurrent dream that started when I was a child; I belonged on one of those buses. Just the same, every night just after my head touched the pillow, the bus took off without me.

"Stop! Stop!" I tried to be heard over the sound of the busted muffler. "I've decided! I've made up my mind! I know who I am!" But as I inhaled the last of its fumes, all I could see through the trail of smoke was a bus that was slowly disappearing. In that moment I knew I had missed my opportunity to be where I really belonged. The bus children were gone.

I headed back toward the playground, resigned to being a town child. But it was too late. The time to make a choice had passed. The town children had been picked up by their mamas. The town children were gone. Mama was gone. The buses were gone. Everyone was gone.

Everyone white, anyway.

I wasn't sure about the children who went to a different school and sat in a different place at Jones Theater. Mostly I knew them as children with skin so dark it could've escaped the scrutiny of Mr. Jones' flashlight—if he'd ever once walked up those steps to that balcony to check on them.

That dream taught me an important lesson about making choices: there were no free rides for children who couldn't make up their minds—only deserted playgrounds where they must spend an eternity trying to find a way to leave, and another one figuring out why they were afraid to leave after they found a way.

Of course, there was that playground on the other side of town where the children didn't have to make up their minds because the people on my side did it for them. But that playground was only for the children who got lost in the dark.

Everyone knew that.

After being away from home a few years, I had come back to a way of life that had changed very little. I was immediately aware that there were worse things than being a stewardess in Texas and one was being black in Arkansas.

Political connections had landed me a job at the state capitol in Little Rock. On the register of life's worst punishments, it ranked about one ladle below that punch bowl of hot wine out in Houston. Every day I rode the bus from that same crappy job to my same crappy apartment. I always sat pretty close to the front so I could get off first and I don't know why, because it meant getting to my crappy job or my crappy apartment just that much sooner.

Even though the blacks were now permitted to ride the bus with the whites—like illegal aliens crammed into the back of a pick up truck—they were imprisoned in their own section in the back of the bus. Some worked in those same government buildings, cleaning up the residual crap from the crappy jobs the white people had obtained most likely through political ties or sexual favors or because somebody's mama was a Chi Omega.

There were a few grown up bus children scattered throughout the bus and their function really hadn't changed that much. Now the grown up town children actually got to watch them get off in their slummy neighborhoods, which made their own neighborhoods and crappy jobs look a whole lot better. But on this particular day, I was more aware of the people who had made the long trip from Mr. Jones' balcony—to the back of the bus.

I hadn't been seated long when the bus stopped to pick up an elderly black woman. She stood beside the driver and scanned the seats, then braced herself with the pole above her head as the bus took off. She continued to search for a vacant seat; there were two. The one next to me was occupied by bags of government supplies I was transferring from my work office to my home office, something I did it on a regular basis. When she took her seat next to the white man across the aisle, heads turned. From the back of the bus, I heard a gasp. From the front, profanity. It was coming from the man she had just surprised.

Like a stuck pig, he flew from his seat to the aisle, staging his indignation for each member of the stunned white audience with front row seats. From clenched jaws came words that began as a whisper and grew louder and more threatening until they erupted into a full fledged attack. "You black bitch!" he exclaimed, as he stepped closer to the woman and repeated it again and again, like deafness was just one more down side of blackness. I wanted to disappear.

Suddenly I wasn't looking at that black woman anymore. I saw the little girl who had made herself small in her seat when Mr. Jones came after the white children with that flashlight. Then I saw the playground where she didn't fit in. I wondered if being a black woman on a bus with no place to sit was worse than being a white child on a playground with no place to hide. I remembered that sad little girl—and the running. Mostly, that's what I remembered. The running.

She ran and ran until she reached her house, hoping to find refuge from her teacher's obsession with gender and the stupid doll that was supposed to validate hers. Instead, she got rules for transforming herself into the proper young lady she had been running from her whole life.

I saw that confused little girl galloping away on her imaginary horse until she reached the house of her secret, colored friend. In her backyard she played cowboys and Indians and rolled in the mud until she and her friend were pretty close to the same color.

She wanted to scream so loud it could be heard at her house on the other side of town, "Look at me. I've changed! I've changed the color of my skin!"

She wanted to, but she didn't.

The man's cursing was getting louder and closer. He had targeted the seat next to mine for his next landing and was on his way. "That black bitch!" he mumbled, as he removed my bags from the seat while studying me as though sizing up a potential partner in crime.

I flew from my seat, waved my finger in his face, and shot back, "You white trash son-of-a-bitch!" As the aftershock of that outburst made its way through the bus, I trembled across the aisle and then steadied myself with the pole above the vacated seat. Looking down at the woman who had just been so abruptly abandoned, I cautiously asked, "Ma'am, do you mind if I join you?"

She smiled, "Oh, child, please do." I felt her sweaty hand squeezing my still-shaking fingers. She motioned with her head toward the man across the aisle. "Thank you, child, for not being like his kind," she whispered. "And God bless."

"Promise me you won't ever take a back seat to *anyone*—not unless you're sitting in the back seat of a limousine," I whispered back.

"You mean, when I'm sittin' 'all high and mighty?'" she grinned.

"Yeah," I answered, "I mean, when you're high—only when you're high."

As we approached her stop, she scooped up the bag of cleaning supplies she had lugged from her house to her job the week before. Now she was taking them home. "Government soap don't clean good," she said, tucking the bag under her arm, "so sometimes I bring my own."

I was caught off guard by her apologetic tone when describing how she transported supplies from *home* to *work*. It was the reverse of the uninhibited pride my co-workers and I exhibited when describing how we transported ours in the opposite direction. But then I remembered the difference in rules for her people and mine—specifically, the one about who goes to prison for stealing and who gets to stay home and keep doing it.

When she walked off the bus I was aware that the only thing between me and the man across the aisle was the bright-blue streak still looming from the cursing I had given him and the sound of the slap on my back I was giving myself for doing it. I slid over to her seat by the window and saw her standing tall and proud on the sidewalk—shouting and waving her fist in the air. Separated from her predator, she was free to put a voice to everything she'd been unable to say to his face.

I had felt a special bond with that woman. I wanted her to know that I, too, had an acquaintance with those people in this world who decide where we can and cannot sit. There was no doubt about it; I felt a kinship with the woman who had just been called a black bitch, and no wonder.

Damned if that black bitch and I weren't sisters.

A reasonably attractive young man, in a Clark Kent sort of way, moved to the unoccupied seat and introduced himself as a University of Arkansas law student. I envisioned him turning into Superman right before my eyes. I would continue to envision this—okay, hope and pray for it—over the next ten years.

"Wow! You've got some nerve," he said, as he studied me through the thick lens of oversized black-rimmed glasses. After a brief inspection of my chest, his eyes surveyed everything below and then traveled slowly up to my face. "You know, you'd make a good politician's wife," he said. "You've got guts." (Not exactly what he'd been checking me out for.) I tried to figure out what the hell he was talking about while he came up with his next line. "What you just did would sure get the black vote!" he said, enthusiastically. It was a statement I now recognize as the political BS he enjoyed hearing himself say, never mind that everyone else cringed. Of course, my actions that day were as hypocritical as his political platform, seeing as how I walked off that bus and resumed my place in a world of people who sit in the front and never look back.

In the weeks ahead, his interest in me overruled the disinterest of my building manager who persisted in withholding heat from my apartment unit. I accepted his invitations to go out, in retrospect, because I was freezing to death, but also because of the "You'd make a good wife" remark. Regrettably, I discovered too late that freezing to death would have been a better choice.

Jobs came and went as I searched for myself in each one, always hoping that whatever showed up in the workplace would solve the mystery of just exactly who I was. When that didn't happen, I turned to *Plan B* in *The Book of Rules* and hooked up with a man so I could become whoever he was, never once suspecting that this one didn't have a clue.

I celebrated his law school graduation by accepting a proposal of marriage and the three-part plan attached to it: move to his hometown in Tennessee, open a law practice, have children. I'd get to know him later, time permitting. I'd get to know myself . . . well, that wasn't in the plan.

It would be a big step, leaving Arkansas for the second time. Before, I'd traded Arkansas tornados for Texas dust storms and a carefree existence for the confines of Texas society. Now I'd be giving up my glorious year of post-divorce celibacy for another bout with mandatory sex. But, as always, my departure got easier as I vacillated between negative and positive feelings for myself. With the negative ones in the lead, it was not surprising when another family tradition took over as I—like many women before and after me—decided to go after success I didn't have to feel guilty about.

Because it belonged to someone else.

14.
First Lady for the last time

Dear Rosemary,
    We hear you have a new title. What would that be?
        The Pageant Committee

Dear Pageant Committee,
    First Lady.
            Rosemary

There was just one hitch to being First Lady, and it was The Mayor. I had to be married to him to be one.

He was quite different from my first husband, but a great deal like my first husband's mother—tenacious, ambitious, and smart. Tall and lanky with a bulging pot belly and thinning hair, he even looked like her.

Our roots had hardly gotten down good before he was elected mayor of his small Tennessee hometown. Eventually he would become a District Attorney with aspirations to be governor. But even though his titles changed from time to time, I chose to keep mine and have to this day, regardless of how many times it has been passed on to others. Actually, I held on to everything in those days, knowing how quickly things got taken away—never once suspecting one of them would be The Mayor. Unfortunately, I also held on to the title of "black sheep," which was, come to think of it, probably why I thought I had to hold on to The Mayor.

His law practice was thriving in a West Tennessee county known to be a hotbed of crime and corruption. Caught up in the wild and rowdy goings on, we were barely able to stay afloat in its sea of bad blood.

Outside our house, I'll swear, it was almost as bad.

But inside there were at least two good reasons for making that marriage work.

Our Family Tree
always blooms with joy,
because from every branch
there swings a little boy. . . .

Like our short courtship and hasty marriage, their father and I hadn't wasted any time producing two little stars. I willingly performed my duties each day for my audience of two who accepted me unconditionally—even on the days I believed my performance didn't measure up. I had finally landed a good job; I honestly thought I couldn't get fired.

Just one year apart, Travis and Sam loved all the things that little boys cherish—from the dead insects and frogs to swimsuits that never seemed to dry out. They were a lot like all the other little boys on the block . . . well, almost. Travis was deaf.

I always tucked them into bed with only a small nightlight shining up from the baseboard. It was on one of those nights after I'd gushed, "I love you," that Travis answered, "Turn on light. Can't hear you."

The doctors confirmed his deafness when he was two. I spent the next three years observing his progress behind one-way mirrors in special classes for the deaf. By the time he hit first grade he spoke well and was a champion lip reader. That was apparent the day he came home with the news,

"I've got a best friend and his name *looks* like Willie Stone."

Those were the days when my son thought grownups had no problems, so naturally growing up would mean growing out of deafness. But still, he had his concerns.

"Mama, when I'm 25 and don't need my hearing aids anymore, can I still keep my battery tester?"

I was working hard with Travis, but I had help. Jesus was back. Not the same Jesus I'd known before—not a full-blown Jesus, not even half. This was simply a "baby Jesus," and thanks to The Mayor and me, he almost didn't make it into our lives. We'd had a choice to make, and we screwed up, big time. Travis had wanted a baby Jesus for Christmas and we opted for a GI Joe instead. Well let me tell you, Joe was a pretty pathetic figure, propped up beneath the tree on that tragic Christmas morning.

"Jesus! Jesus! Where Jesus is?" Travis asked, as he pointed to his Tinker Toys, Easy Bake Oven, and GI Joe. Poor Joe. He waited with Travis for JC to make an appearance, but Jesus was a no show. We couldn't really blame Him; He hadn't been invited. Christmas morning had arrived and He hadn't gotten an invitation to His own birthday party, for gosh sake! I still can't explain it. Even though He was the present our child really wanted, The Mayor and I had made no attempt to get Him under that tree. Our credit cards had been maxed out on toys when we could've had a baby Jesus for next to nothing. There was almost always a surplus that time of year.

So now we had another strike against us, and a possible lightning strike at that. Not only were we failing at a marriage, we were sinners, with little more in our futures than the days preceding our impending trip to hell. This would surely go down as The Devil's Holiday—the Christmas that exposed The Mayor and me as little more than big lumps of coal, as useless as poor GI Joe absent his ammunition; standing beside that Easy Bake Oven; looking down at an unassembled train set; waiting for the coming of Jesus Christ. Of course, Joe was proud as punch to be standing in for Jesus, but in Travis' eyes, the action hero might as well have been Barbie on the Beach.

My search for Jesus began the day after Christmas. Unfortunately, I had to settle for a reduced-for-quick-sale, slightly damaged but still intact, wax-nativity scene, complete with a somewhat scarred-up plastic baby Jesus surrounded by a small flock of partially melted, seemingly disinterested barnyard animals. But Travis was thrilled. When I gave the manger-scene-on-plywood to him, he snatched the baby from His crib and tossed the supporting cast aside—sheep, cows, and wise men, the whole ball of wax. Then the tiny statue got stuffed into one of the pockets sewn onto the harness that housed his binaural hearing aids. Clearly, Jesus was a far sight more at home there than with that herd of crippled animals.

I knew their relationship was getting serious the night Travis stopped his prayer just short of "Amen" and asked, "Does Jesus wear hearing aids?" I saw this as a perfect opportunity to carry out my hearing and speech center assignment and let him know that *everyone* doesn't get to be deaf, not even Jesus.

"Travis," I said, as I moved closer and pointed to my lips, "*many, many* people are not deaf." I slowed down. "M a m a   i s   n o t   d e a f.   D a d d y   i s   n o t   d e a f.   S a m   i s   n o t   d e a f. And Jesus," I said, moving even closer, "Jesus is not deaf, either, Travis. Jesus can hear. Jesus does not wear hearing aids."

"No hearing aids?" he marveled.

"No hearing aids," I answered.

"Well," he frowned, "that be very very sad for Jesus. I've told him a lot of good stuff."

The next night I listened as Travis put in a request; this time he skipped the middle-man.

Dear God, this is Travis. Please make your Son ask Santa Claus for hearing aids so He can hear me when I tell him what to do. Amen.

15.
Turn on the light. I can't hear you.

With Travis I began seeing Jesus with the near-perfect vision of a deaf child—through lenses that filtered out old beliefs and ears oblivious to the voices of non-believers. His Jesus was not the judgmental jerk who stamped an R rating on beauty pageants and everything else of any substance. To Travis, He was a constant protector and friend, an action hero who put GI Joe and every other stud to shame.

The first time I saw them working together as a team, Travis was five. He sat on the edge of a hospital bed after having his hearing tested by an audiologist. A team of doctors poked and prodded his little body before taking him to another room for x-rays. There seemed to be no explanation for the sudden loss of what little residual hearing he had, or for the fact that it had somehow not registered in his brain—certainly not in his speech—that he had lost anything! The child was still functioning exactly as he had before his hearing flatlined on the audiogram, dropping from moderately severe to profoundly deaf.

I was relieved when his MRI was normal, but the doctors were baffled. He was still answering my questions. "He's lip reading; no wonder he's responding," one doctor said. Then he asked me to prove him right by posing questions to Travis.

I knelt on one knee, faced my son, and pointed to my lips. "Travis, do you want a cookie?" I asked.

"Yes," he answered.

The doctor believed I had proven his point. "Lip reading," he confirmed.

I covered my lips with my hand and continued, "Travis," I asked, "what *kind* of cookie do you want?"

He said nothing.

"See?" the doctor said.

"Do you want chocolate or plain?" I asked, still covering my mouth.

"Chocolate *and* plain," he answered. "I want both."

There was silence among the onlookers. Finally, one doctor conceded. "Well, there are things in medicine we cannot explain."

The audiologist stepped up. "I can explain it," he said. "I think it has something to do with that plastic Jesus he just removed from his vest pocket. He *was* awfully close to the hearing aid." The two doctors politely nodded and smiled.

Although they appeared to be giving their full attention to this audiologist's theory, I'm pretty sure Jesus never made it to one single page of Travis' chart.

The little apostle who was never supposed to speak began putting together sentences when he was four, but getting to that point took some doing.

For the past year he had spoken only single, some barely audible words, but had recently been on the brink of stringing them together. When he finally did, it happened in front of an audience—a group of experts in the field of deaf education. I stood with him in a mock-up kitchen on the classroom side of a one-way mirror as two professors and a doctor watched from the other side. Everything in that room was a tool for speech development and an opportunity for a deaf child to "listen."

I pointed to my lips and described our surroundings. The cabinets were made of brown wood; they were "up" and the doors were "open." When he slammed them shut, we listened. We touched the dishwasher and felt the vibration, then listened. We put objects "under," "on top of," and "beside" the kitchen table. Robotically, he repeated the words after me. But no matter what I said or did, the kid refused to say his new word—"high." And I needed him to do that. I *really* needed him to say that word. After all, we were putting on a show for a very important audience.

I guess that's how it happened—how I wound up on that tabletop, frantically shouting commands as I looked down at my child. "Say 'high,' Travis," I begged. "Look, Travis, Mama is high. I'm *high*."

No response.

I reminded myself that for every one hundred times a word is introduced to a deaf child, getting it back even once is a gift. Just the same, I was becoming very annoyed with my son's refusal to perform.

"Listen Travis, listen. Look at your mama's lips," I persisted. "Watch and listen," I said, as I became living proof that a mother could face personal challenges far worse than her child's deafness (*see chapter 12*). "Travis," I pleaded, with a look that screamed, *'Enough of this special education deaf gobbledygook. My credibility is at stake. Talk, you little shit!'*

Again and again I pointed to my lips. "Now listen to your Mama. Say it!" I begged, refusing to comply with the teacher whose expression screamed, "Give it a rest!" I continued to ignore the woman, knowing she believed this performance had something to do with the kid, when any fool could see it was all about me.

"Okay, Travis," I started out slowly. "Mama's not low. Mama's not down. Mama's not sideways. Mama's not under. Mama's not over. MAMA'S HIGH." I shrieked, "MAMA'S HIGH, DAMMIT!!! *Look at my lips!*"

He shut his eyes and cried out, "Stop it!" Then, tapping his finger beside his lips, he mimicked my plea, "Listen and look! Listen and Look! Stop it, Mama. Dammit! Listen and look!"

He had my attention. This wasn't just his first group of sentences; this was an honest-to-goodness paragraph punctuated with profanity! It wasn't about anything up or down, in or out, over or out. You couldn't see, touch, or smell it. It was plain and simple, pure old out-and-out— fed-up-with-your-mama—*DAMMIT-ALL rage!!*

About time.

I ended my part of our demonstration and watched as he removed his finger from beside his lips. Suddenly both his hands flew into the air as I realized there was more to come and, language break-through or not, frankly, I hoped there wasn't.

The kid had really crossed the line. This segment of the act had not been rehearsed, at least not by me. But he had obviously been preparing for this killer ending, the statement he'd been trying to make for God-knows-how-long.

"Listen, listen, listen, Mama!" he kept yelling, as he looked up at me. Again, he pointed to his lips. *"LISTEN!! LISTEN AND LOOK, MAMA. . . .*

DO HUSH!"

I stood mute on that table. My son was relating to the world with words he had chosen and emotions that were definitely his own.

His teacher clapped her hands and praised him over and over again as I began my long journey down from the tabletop. "I hope this breakthrough isn't something that happens only when he's so frustrated he can't take it anymore," she said to me, with the competitive tone of a teacher who'd just been upstaged by a parent. She wasn't through. "Or only when you're standing on a kitchen table!" she laughed, half-heartedly.

"Or only when I'm high!" I laughed back, whole-heartedly.

Just one more thing:

Although I was an agent to a winner and the best darned stage mother at the school for the deaf, in retrospect, I also bore a pretty close resemblance to some characters in my past: my ex-mother-in-law, determined to get her hands on that brass ring; my own mother, attempting to rekindle her brief affair with the stage; and of course, me—an aging beauty queen, putting the finishing touches on an old dream while driving herself and her son nuts in the process.

But you've probably figured that out.

16.
Will the *real* action hero please stand?

In the coming years our family moved at least once a year. Travis attended two schools for the deaf and numerous daycare centers, as I monitored his progress and made plans for the family according to his needs. I observed him through one-way mirrors and watched the other children mimic his speech. And that was okay, until the day he began mimicking their silence! When he stopped talking altogether, I jerked him out of a class—and I'm not proud of this—in the middle of a birthday party. Clearly, the only child who was teaching him anything was his younger brother.

Athletic and scholastic opponent, defender, best friend, worst enemy, language coach, and referee. That was Sam. He ran interference for his brother and used those same negotiating skills when his friends got into fights. The kid was a caretaker. He didn't know it, but that's what he was.

He had somehow escaped the fiercely competitive genes of his mother, father, and older brother, and would give up a victory when push came to shove. With his brother, push came to shove almost every day. Complete opposites, Travis had olive skin and dark hair while Sam was blonde with fair skin—a perfect canvas for the black and blue smudges Travis delivered, usually before an important occasion, like the annual studio picture. The one that became an important part of his history was taken when he was three and Travis was four.

Hanging on our living room wall was a poster-size reminder of the photography session. You couldn't miss that picture, no matter how hard you tried. In a fancy baroque frame with velvet mat, two little boys posed—sheepish grins, starched shirts, slicked-down hair, shined shoes. One brother was somewhat battered, but wore his scars like a purple heart, seemingly as proud of them as his hand-me-down suit. He had no idea that the picture would one day be documented proof of his participation in a war—one of many.

Sam sat in front of a blue, cloud-filled paper backdrop and smiled ear-to-ear, seemingly as oblivious to the kaleidoscope of colors forming around his eye as the perpetrator sitting beside him. The photographer had tried and failed to cover up the bruise with makeup. But Sam was smiling just the same. His eyes were still red from crying and he was wearing more makeup than his mama. But he was smiling. Like a Cheshire cat, he was smiling.

So what if he *had* just lost a fight to his older brother, he was just proud to be there. And you could be sure that if, in the middle of getting beat up, his brother had asked, "Do you hear Mama coming?" or "Do you want the fist on your face?" Sam would have let him know whether or not "Mama was coming," and then a speech therapy session would've ensued right there on the spot as he corrected his brother, "No! No! You said it wrong. It's—'Do-you-want-*my*-fist-in-*your-face?*'"

Five days a week, we rode two hours, round trip, to the hearing and speech center; then we sat for an hour and watched Travis behind a one-way observation mirror. After class, Sam critiqued his brother. The role of educator was one he seemed to enjoy so much I honestly believed that praising him for being good at it was enough. But by turning the spotlight away from himself and onto his student so readily, he often missed out on the real praise he deserved—for being the most selfless and caring little soul in the universe. Not that he would have responded to that praise if he'd gotten it. Sam was private—and the better at his job he got, the more private he became. I probably should've tried to find out why.

When we finally moved into the city to be closer to the hearing and speech center, the price of living went up, so I got a job. That's when Sam joined Travis as a "normal hearing stimulator" in his classes for the deaf. As always, I heard not one complaint. Not once did those dreaded words escape from his secret hiding place and explode out the top of his lungs—"*BUT MAMA, I'M NOT DEAF!*"

From the beginning, Sam had attended afternoon play schools with his brother and was often transferred, with little warning, from one to another. If Travis needed "free play," we went to the free-play school, sometimes for as little as a month. When I decided he needed a more structured environment, he got relocated. With each move, poor Sam got jerked off the see-saw—mid-air—and transported to the new school along with his brother.

It was inevitable he would join Travis in those morning classes for the deaf. It was also convenient. I could now drop both of them off at the same place on my way to work. I believed it was the perfect solution; who knew it would backfire. It never occurred to me that Sam would choose to follow the crowd. He just never seemed like the type. Oh, I always knew he *liked* the other children, but I never dreamed he'd want to actually *be like* them. So the day he decided to be deaf as the proverbial door, I wasn't prepared.

The teacher had been pleased to have him as a normal-hearing stimulator for the deaf class. In fact, she called him her "teacher's aide." But after a few days, it became obvious that his "deafness" was a vacation from "teaching" that was long overdue because he wasn't about to give it up. Unfortunately, since he'd turned stone deaf overnight and refused to lip read, talking him out of the whole thing was next to impossible. Thank God it finally occurred to Travis that for both their sakes, his brother needed to hear. He stepped in and wiped out the disability almost as fast as it had appeared.

After his hearing returned, Sam renewed his teaching certificate and got on with the job of coaching his deaf classmates. He was now, officially, an authority on deaf education. He reminded us of that daily as he continued ours. It could be an event as mundane as taking out the trash.

I'll never forget the morning I asked Travis to do it. Every inch of his brother—my little advocate for the deaf—took a stand as he pulled on my skirt and corrected me, "Mama, for goodness' sake, first tell Travis what trash *is* and then tell him to take it *out*."

Sam was good at his job and never refused a request, even the near-impossible ones—like the day I enrolled him with Travis in the be-all-end-all of structured daycare centers. Little did poor Sam know what would be expected of him.

There were two openings. Perfect. The only hitch was that the students had to be potty trained to attend, and Sam wasn't. Too bad.

Travis *had to go!* So Sam had to go, too—literally; Sam had to go potty. But Sam didn't know how. Well . . . the teacher didn't have to know that, and I don't believe she ever did. According to his brother, Sam followed his classmates into that bathroom line every day until he finally figured it out; then he gave instructions to the others. Even if his peers *thought* they knew how to pee, Sam showed them a better way and then provided words that appropriately or inappropriately described the act itself. That was Sam. That was definitely Sam. But that was also me. I hadn't even potty trained poor Sam, heaven forbid!

Of course, that fact occurred to me the day I cried as he tried a case before the State Supreme Court. I realized that if I hadn't potty trained him by then, it was probably too late.

> *Potty or no potty, Sam was holding a lot inside. But just as his brother refused to admit he was deaf, Sam wasn't about to let anyone know he was angry. It would not occur to me for years that these were two of the secrets they had been keeping.*
>
> *Travis was mainstreamed into a normal-hearing classroom in first grade, had a successful sports career in high school and college, and was principal of a residential normal-hearing high school for troubled youths. He speaks well, and often, and has never adopted sign language. Although he has held a few titles, including "coach of the year," he still refuses to accept anything remotely akin to "handicapped" (but admits to having parked in their spaces).*
>
> *In a book about labels and titles, it is surprising that I gave birth to a son who didn't know he was different. I tried to tell him, Lord knows I did. I guess he just wasn't listening.*
>
> *Sam almost pursued his dream to be a college professor but made an unexpected detour into law school. Shortly after he graduated, tragically and with no warning, someone told him he was a lawyer. Unlike his brother, he heard them.*
>
> *He did not, however, continue to follow the crowd, not into bathrooms or anywhere else. But he did continue to referee. Every weekend, he referees.*

17.
"Do hush!!"

"You, sir, are a liar. This woman's had her share of unanswered questions and conflicting messages," the psychiatrist told The Mayor. "We're staying here until we've addressed *your* issues."

I should've brought the sleeping bags.

The doctor walked across the room to shut the door, the second sign in the past two minutes that this was going to get very personal. He interrupted the trip back to his desk, stopping about two feet from The Mayor's chair. The meeting was definitely coming to order. "Let's talk about The Truth," he said.

After ten years and as many moves, The Mayor and I had continued to have problems which were mostly never addressed, so naturally they kept coming back, now with almost the same frequency as the checks we both wrote to make them go away. When he agreed to attend marriage counseling, I made an appointment for us with the psychiatrist in Memphis I had seen after my divorce.

"But I'm a mess," I reminded the doctor. I was unwilling to forfeit the spotlight for one minute, even if it meant taking a negative beam off the Mayor and shining it on myself. "Don't you remember?" I frowned. Perturbed that my inadequacies had slipped the man's mind, I began laying them out again, one at a time. Half-way through, he stopped me.

"Enough! This is not about you, woman!" Again he focused on The Mayor and The Truth. Well, *The Truth* turned out to be that unlike the IRS, I would let The Mayor off the hook. He would attend these sessions in absentia and I would do the talking for both of us which was, it occurred to me, probably what got us in this mess in the first place.

The psychiatrist's office was a three-hour drive from our home, so he suggested I spend a couple of weeks in the hospital across the street on a floor occupied by outpatients from out of town. "It's like a hotel," he told me. "You'll come and go as you please, and I'll drop in to see you every day enroute to the psych ward two floors up. We'll talk."

We talked, alright. But not near as much as the people back home.

The word that I had gone so mental I got myself locked up spread among them faster than Billy Joe Johnson's recurring rash or the Mayor's denial that he caused it. (Me getting locked up, not Billy Joe breaking out.)

Ours was a small community, populated with non-believers when it came to psychiatric voodoo and the doctors who practiced it. These were folks who believed that women's doctors were only for birthin' babies and psychiatrists were for those who had either birthed too many or hadn't been called upon to birth at all. "Attention is all them women is after, and they'll give upwards of seventy dollars an hour to get it," is what I once heard the preacher say, even though, word was his wife was one of them women.

There was, however, unspoken permission—bordering on pure adoration—for a woman who took off seeking help for her husband who did not believe in going to get it for himself. And even better, if the woman had taken to downing nerve pills and alcohol due to his business practices and philandering ways, she could expect the sympathy of all the womenfolk in town. More times than not, she would return home to a pantry stocked with strawberry preserves and pickle relish; refrigerator shelves loaded with cheese grits and deviled eggs; and a casserole of last week's leftovers trapped beneath a can of mushroom soup. And her house? You could eat off the floor.

But there was no tolerance for a woman who had gone mental due to her own screw-ups, bad judgment, and dysfunctional childhood. She would be turned away at the outskirts of town right alongside the beauty-queens-turned-whores, the muddy-skinned people of unknown race and origin, and the black people of obvious race and origin.

So as not to be deemed racists, the townsfolk would mix that last group in with a handful of hypocrites who ate supper before saying grace and had no paperwork confirming their baptisms. (Those lying sons-of-bitches might as well turn around at the county line. They would never step over it.)

His Honor's donations to our problems were mostly written off as the antics of a "good ol' boy," and were swept under the carpet with half the good ol' boy bullshit in town. That left only the "going mental due to her own screw-ups" category for me, which mostly involved that same carpet and a whole lot more sweeping. There were also whispered rumors of a scarlet letter, the early-morning greyhound, and a sack lunch. But not for this Belle. She'd be leaving in a Cadillac, tiara in tact, head held high. And rightfully so.

She wouldn't think of dishonoring the sacred rule: *Thou Shalt Not Be a Selfish Bitch and Think of Thyself and Thyself, Only.* She wouldn't dare leave town in search of a new life, then come back and flaunt it in the faces of people who still had their old ones. Good Lord, no. She'd fix *their* lives, too!

I vowed to find solutions to the problems in my house and the houses of everyone in town and swore on the Bible that no matter what or who came through my front door, I would travel the world to find out why I had left that door open. It wasn't such a big deal, not really.

I wouldn't be the first woman who'd left her home and family to figure out her life and everyone's in it; make her husband well; and fix everything—their marriage, weight, overspending, and, time permitting, a lovely picnic lunch—without him ever missing one day of work, a football game, or the fall campaign.

With the rules in place I started packing for this one-stop shopping spree, a short vacation that would take care of everything all at once— a long-overdue rest, I told myself, somewhat like the facelift of the seventies. Not a bad deal for a woman with two children, now ages six and seven. For the first week I did nothing but my nails.

ALL ABOUT ME . . .

The second week I did nothing but talk about myself and I was okay with that. But the doctor? Oh, *hell no!* He was dead set on butting in with positive affirmations from every self-help book ever written. With a happy face I was expected to greet myself each day with, "I am getting better and better," and "I deserve to be happy," crap like that. And hope. He was big on hope. So when those sessions became too full of it—hope and crap—I realized this amateur shrink had never worked with half-a-mind except, I would soon discover, his own.

I opened the floodgates and sent my resume rushing downstream. Yet, still blinded by his own cockeyed optimism, the man continued to ignore it. Finally I silenced his happy talk by acting out every illness I'd ever had—real or imaginary, mental or physical. When I got through, I figured no Broadway show tune on the planet could put a happy face on either of us. I was wrong.

With the virtual feast of dysfunction I had laid out, I couldn't understand why he was smiling. But soon it was clear I had opened a can of worms and he was in the precarious position of being attracted to it. The man was getting off on my pain! The sicker I convinced us both I was, the longer my sentence and the more goo-goo eyed he got.

Whatever his problem, I knew that the only way to fix a man was to let him fix me, which really shouldn't have been such a big deal. But it was.

Because this one didn't know how.

18.
For whom the Belle folds

"Help me! Somebody help me! I can't get out of this mess by myself!"

With those desperate cries for help etched in lipstick on their birth certificates, it is no wonder so many southern women came into this world by caesarean section.

Each day I woke up facing the inside of a deep, dark hole while the man with the shovel, go figure, was becoming as irresistible as the stars at Jones Theater. Like an old movie, my past was playing out, with me assuming the role of every helpless Hollywood starlet who'd ever driven herself helplessly insane and this doctor as my leading man—too macho and helpful to resist. But when that starlet got moved to the psych ward, the movie was over and the upcoming attraction featured a liberty bell as cracked as I had convinced both of us I was.

Though free to leave, I stuck around believing I could find the answers to questions neither of us had been able to answer, nor could either of us figure out why they ever got asked in the first place.

"Why didn't you want to leave your mama? Do you know what a symbiotic relationship is?"

"No. Do you?"

No answer.

"You have such potential."

"For what?"

Silence.

"When you leave here, you'll be 'weller than well.'"

"Good. But what exactly does 'weller than well' mean?"*

No answer.

"What about my husband? When are we going to start helping him?"

---

*Weller than well: getting well enough for three—the patient's therapist, the patient's husband, and if her insurance holds up, the patient herself.

90

And another no answer.

I added these to my list of unanswered questions as I tried to figure out why it kept getting longer. If the man was purposely recreating the confusion of my childhood so we could roll around in the pain, dissect, and fix it, it sure wasn't working. I felt more stupid than ever. He couldn't help me; I couldn't help him; I couldn't help me; and now—I couldn't help The Mayor.

My search for perfection became the perfect invitation for every compulsive act in my repertoire. I'd needed to be the perfect patient with the perfect therapist with the perfect answers, but instead, I was slipping into the bathroom, washing my hands to the count of ten, and jumping as high as I could over lines in the linoleum floor. It later occurred to me that slipping into the bathroom, or anywhere else, was a wasted detour; I was in a psychiatric ward, for goodness' sake! I was free to count out loud as I took every step and breathed every breath. I could jump flatfooted all over that ward, wash my hands in the water fountain—or pee in it! I didn't have to hide a thing. I could compulse 'til the cows came home because *hello!* I was not at the country club. I was in a looney ward! "Acting out" was what insurance companies paid these places for their policyholders to get to do!

Unfortunately, no matter how many rituals I called upon or where I performed them, nothing changed. I couldn't find the magic. But I *was* perfect, I'll give me that. I was a perfectly pathetic friggin' mess.

The hospital rumors were no surprise, certainly not to a Southern Belle trained in Advanced Helplessness and Seduction 101. *Nobody* stayed in a hospital psych ward this long! But as my focus shifted from my marriage to finding the meaning of "weller than well," the shrink extended my stay as he was, obviously, looking for it, too. Then, like things couldn't get more confusing, our roles were reversing. The man was crying out loud, whimpering, quivering lips, tears—the whole sissified scene.

"We don't *need* the answers to those questions. Maybe there are no answers anywhere," I tried to comfort him. Inconsolable, he was bound and determined that one of us would find them somewhere, even if it took a heavy dose of medication to do it.

Well, I sure didn't want to see him on medication, so I stuck around and searched for answers until it became as obvious as the absence of a diagnosis in my chart that I was looking at an obsessed, lonely man with a license to mess with the human (half-a-) mind. I waited until the end of a session and just flat out asked, "You love me, don't you?"

He welled up. "Yes, I do."

Well, shit.

It was all my fault. My history with men had made its way through the bolted doors of this psychiatric ward. Even though my calls for help could scarcely be heard over those of the certifiably insane—a startling reminder of how far this whole thing could actually go—the poor guy was hooked.

As six months turned into eleven, visits from my family grew farther apart. Phone calls from The Mayor stopped. Then a box of clothes arrived—some mine, some not. Those that were not, I tried to ignore. They belonged to another woman. Size two.

SOUTHERN COMFORT

The therapist either ignored the other woman or took advantage of the situation, I was never sure. I was comforted on chilly nights by the argyle socks he dropped off for me at the nurses' station. But it was a trade off. I could be sure that each night another pair showed up, the following morning my breakfast tray would not. Well, I told myself, those nurses may have kept my breakfast, but I had the doctor's socks. Sadly, I actually believed I had gotten the better deal.

My focus shifted briefly from my problems to what had made me so resistible to one man and irresistible to the other. But it really didn't matter; I wanted to go home to that other man, no matter how he felt—which meant getting "weller than well" as soon as possible. But the shrink could not give me a time frame. He just smiled and repeated, "weller than well," as I smiled right back and wondered what in the hallowed name of Elvis Presley's departed mother he was talking about.

"We don't need the answers to those questions!" I kept saying, hoping against hope the man would get a grip.

He ignored my pleas. "I can't give you your answers, and I'm too emotionally involved to be your doctor." He lowered his head. (I don't know why. The time for prayer had passed.) "I suppose that I, selfishly, needed you to stay. I believed I could take a near-perfect cake and put the icing on it. My need for you to stay a year was partially self-serving. I had feelings . . . too many. In fact . . ."

I interrupted. "But I don't N E E D the answers! Besides, if *you* don't have them, *who does?*"

"Do hush, Mama. Do hush!"

"There is a place, an upscale private treatment center," he said.

I cringed. (Not so much about the private treatment center as being in the room with a person who called it "upscale.")

"Although I've only seen pictures of the place, I am aware of its reputation. I've sent other patients there."

So I'm not your first screw-up. . . .

"I can no longer keep you here as my 'project'—to witness your transformation and see you 'weller than well.' When you arrived, I believed we could accomplish our goals, and for a time, I thought we were winning," he said. "Yes," he started slowly, like he was trying to work it out in his own mind, "I guess this is love. I certainly see you more than I see her . . . you know, my wife." He wiped his eyes. "Well, one thing's for sure, I wanted you to stay."

The man was hurting. I wanted to let him know that the shame he felt over unloading his professionalism and ruining my life would subside. All he had to do was flip through my chart and examine my past relationships to see that this whole thing would soon take a dramatic turn in his favor. It might take as long as thirty minutes, but the issue would ultimately be about what *I* had done to *him*.

On my last day, he appeared to have made peace with himself; still he struggled with nagging guilt and the need to confess. "I'm aware this extended stay may have had something to do with my own feelings,"

he said, hesitating briefly—too briefly. I'd heard enough. "In fact," he continued, "to coin your phrase, 'If The Truth be known . . .'"

Oh no, Don Juan. The Truth is NOT known for me now nor has it ever been! The only Truth I see is that you've kept me cooped up for a year on a stage disguised as a psychiatric ward while my big butt tap danced for your tiny ego as you applauded the same worn-out routine that helped put me here in the first place! I've got two little boys who could give a rip about tap dancing, but would sure like to see me waltz through their front door! I wasn't committed, but I've stayed because I thought The Mayor and I needed help. I took time out from my life to fix our lives and the lives of everyone in ours so another woman could move in and take over the one I left behind!!

The only Truth I know is that two little boys need their mother, but thanks to you I can't be anyone's wife or mother until I figure out what's wrong with me! Oh no, Romeo. I didn't walk into this place sick—at least I didn't know it if I was—but I'm walking out the door a basket case to be delivered to another shrink, and all I'm taking with me from this whole sick scene is five pair of socks! Look, dumb-ass, my boys don't care what happened to me when I was five, and until I met you, frankly neither did I; but now we've dug up so much crap I'll need wading boots to get through it all. And time. How much more of it do you reckon this is gonna take?

Oh, no-sir-ee, asshole. The Truth is definitely not known by me because THE TRUTH—look it up— SETS YOU FREE!

"Don't feel bad," I interrupted him. "You've done a lot for me. I don't remember the last time I held anything inside."

"Yes," he agreed. "You've been quite candid about your feelings."

"And don't you go worrying about my therapy," I consoled him. "*Of course* I plan to finish what we've started. You know I can't leave the contest until I win!"

Then I smiled at him—much as I would've smiled at a judge in Atlantic City, if I'd ever gotten that far.

19.
"There are things you can change— and others you go on vacation for. . . ."

What Daddy said just before he left on his.

I'm not totally stupid. I packed several suitcases, knowing it might take some time to uncover what in *my* childhood had caused me to make my husband lie, cheat, and write checks that bounced all over the county and then boomeranged back to our bank. And those phone calls from the IRS and K-Mart collections? I sure had to figure out why I fell apart like a crazy person every time those people cut off our credit and threatened to come get the house. Now on top of that, there was the psychiatrist. Obviously I had connived and hussied to strip him of his Hippocratic Oath, all his principles, and those five pair of socks.

Well, one thing was as sure as boll weevils on a cotton crop—I had a lot of work to do. A lot of work.

THE INTERVIEW

The administrator of a private treatment center, referred to by patients and staff as "The Inn," assured The Mayor and me that, through me, everything could be fixed. Beneath my obsessions and compulsions, we would find the problems in my marriage.

Untruth number one.

He also said that the Inn's interior was quaint; the setting, picturesque; and the staff, professional and caring.

Untruths number two, three, four, and five.

The only thing visible from his office window was a forest of trees surrounding the facility, so I took him at his word and agreed to be admitted, sight unseen. During this initial visit, I tried to assist him by dredging up all my shortcomings. They were right on the tip of my tongue and rolled off effortlessly like an alma mater from The School of Hard Knocks.

Obsessions, compulsions, and magical tricks. I didn't leave out a thing. Since childhood I'd taken my mind to a better place by simply counting in even numbers, clapping my hands, or jumping high into the air and landing on the other side of an object. Toys on sidewalks were

95

good. Cracks in sidewalks were perfect. Since he practically salivated over those, I decided to save the others for later. Of course, none of those compulsions were as bad as the one that made me talk when I should have been listening. It wasn't that I hadn't been warned.

"Listen, Mama. Listen. Dammit! DO HUSH!"

I continued. "But my marriage—which I once believed to be the main problem—is getting worse. God only knows what's happening at home. There aren't enough sidewalks anywhere to solve the problems in *that* relationship!" I laughed, thus beginning a series of one-liners that were funny to me, but to him—the early stages of psychosis.

He didn't want to address my marriage, or the other therapist who never addressed my marriage, or what I did to make him forget I was, in fact, married. He sure didn't want to discuss wrapping this thing up so I could return to my family. Nope, he didn't want to talk about the length of my stay. But he *did* want to talk about *the length of my insurance coverage.* My symptoms were all insurable—"grist for the mill," he said. I was definitely Inn material, and I could probably get in. I could be fixed. I only wish I'd thought to ask a question along the lines of, "And how long do you think something like that would take?"

But I didn't. Instead, I focused on the "getting in" part, and I think I know why. Telling a Southern Belle she *might* get in, any place, sets off a noise in her head like the ones coming from that party she wasn't invited to next door—or her best friend's new Jaguar pulling up to attend it. Suddenly, this illusive "retreat" took on the allure of pledging a sorority or belonging to the country club. I wasn't sure what would be waiting for me inside that building, but I desperately wanted to be a member, which, you can be sure, wasn't *near* as much as the administrator wanted me to join. According to him, there was no question I would fit right in, but still some concern about my *getting in.* "Well," he said, with *YOUR PROBLEMS,* if your policy will cover this, you'll certainly get your money's worth."

Following an unsuccessful stab at manly laughter came more references to money—from deductibles and co-payments to, "How much cash do you have on hand? Can you get a weekly allowance from your husband? How much? Is there a supplemental insurance policy? How much?" And on and on.

My past experience with people this hung up on taking my money was that I almost always hung up on them. But this man wasn't your run-of-the-mill bill collector, and this was no occasion for rudeness. I was about to be a guest in the man's home, for goodness' sake. Nevertheless, I had recently failed to ask the right questions, and I wasn't going to make that mistake again. So, many psychiatric labels and references to money later, I answered his questions by asking him another while giving him a label of his own. I was pretty sure I knew the answer, but I asked just the same.

"Jew?"*

> *Thus began my year-long, tumultuous relationship with this man and payback from him that far surpassed any dollar amount ever paid to any hospital, anywhere, by an insurance company.*

The next week I received a letter from The Inn. The insurance company had agreed to pay my room and board. Apparently these people and the administrator had the same sense of humor and, I would discover, were in agreement that he should get rid of mine.

So I was in. I was definitely going to The Inn.

"And how bad could that be?" I asked myself.

It was, after all, an Inn.

And I had, after all, loved Nantucket.

---

*It was just a joke—one of Granddaddy's favorites—but the first rule about those type jokes is that you don't tell them to the people the jokes are about.

III. The beginning of The Inn

20.
Nantucket, my ass!

Not even The Daughters of the American Revolution could save me now. . . .

An unusually enthusiastic (overpaid) housekeeper, a box containing a mystery woman's clothes, and a husband who appeared to be more supportive and concerned than ever. At least one of those clues would've been an eye-opening slap in the face for your average person. But I chose not to spend my short time at home figuring out clues. It made more sense to stick with the kind of denial The Mayor and I had always enjoyed, especially when making plans for the future—never mind that they almost never worked out.

This one seemed simple enough. I would return from The Inn knowing how to live with The Mayor and be a better mother. There would be many letters and visits, even more phone calls. It would be all about the therapy . . . almost like he was right there with me. When Travis called, The Mayor would pick up a second phone in the same room; he would face Travis and slowly repeat to him what I'd said; Travis would read his lips, and then answer me on his phone.*

The bases were covered.

Naturally, my husband would miss me terribly and another separation would be difficult for the children, but we agreed that the transformation of his wife and their mother would be worth it.

With our plans in place I said good-bye, knowing I was a woman on a mission to save a marriage, and time permitting, to find the meaning of "weller than well." Then, too, it would be a vacation. Of course, we never called it a vacation. We called it helping our marriage.

Well, I'm here to tell you I *helped* all right! I helped another woman move right *into my little white house and take over my title!*

No big deal.

---

*Soon the TTY teletypewriter for the deaf would eliminate the need for The Mayor altogether.

Now I'd never thought of myself as mental, not in any stark-raving-mad psychotic way. Depressed? Occasionally. An obsessive worrier? Sure enough. High strung? I'll say. A pitcher of conniption fits? My birthright. A pain in the ass? Regularly. Disorganized? As a drunk sailor. But crazy? I don't think so. At least, not before this particular vacation.

I guess the closest I ever came to what you might call an out-and-out nervous breakdown was the first day of that vacation when The Mayor drove me so far out of his voting precinct there wasn't a registered voter in sight. The brochure had depicted this retreat as a peaceful place, a refuge where I would stare at the trees and talk to a therapist—finally, I assumed, about my marriage. In retrospect, couples therapy would've probably cancelled the entire vacation. But it was too late now; this vacation had already started. And it would make my marriage look like a trip to Disneyworld.

On the positive side, there was that $136,000 a year—the cost for getting a room in this joint. Now that would surely pay for a boatload of "weller than well." On the negative side, the woman behind the counter at McDonald's—our final stop before The Inn—would be the last person I would see for quite some time whose outfit was color-coordinated and whose restroom had a mirror. As for those phone calls I'd be making to The Mayor and my boys . . . I'd have to ask for "the privilege" of using the phone.

And privileges, where I was headed, were about as scarce as The Truth.

21.
I never promised you. . . .

I beg your pardon. I certainly *WAS* promised a Rose Garden! But this was not it; this wasn't the place I'd packed for. Oh, sure, I'd done time in some pretty disgusting southern institutions. But that country club in Houston and the fall soirée in Nashville did at least pass out hard liquor at the door. I could think of nothing in my past I could call upon to prepare me for this place.

Not even the America's Junior Miss Pageant . . .

Just a little homework would have told me those private rooms in the brochure had padded walls—and the mint juleps at five? Poured from pill bottles. It was an honest-to-goodness, "she always was a little funny," "we told her to get saved," looney bin. It was the family gathering you didn't want to attend; the mental hospital movie you wanted to see but couldn't watch; the insane asylum your parents drove around the block to avoid; the black and white, low budget, nuthouse feature at the drive-in you climbed into the back seat and had sex to avoid. But today there was no block to drive around or back seat to have sex in—so this nut was about to take a front row seat.

Back seat, front seat, through the lens of psychosis or a glass of whiskey, this place was no Inn. There was no veranda with rocking chairs—just a bunch of lunatics who climbed into the fetal position and, rocking chair or no rocking chair, rocked just the same.

The Mayor and I pulled into the lush, 75-acre tract we'd driven past the day we met with the administrator. The entrance was marked by a black wrought-iron sign that omitted the word "hospital"; the shrubbery was shut in by a large iron gate. A curving, tree-lined driveway led to the main building, a four-story Gothic mansion set far back from the city. It felt like a small town frozen in the '50s. But when we entered the building, it was clear that the inside had frozen years before that.

I would learn that the place was an anachronism—a relic of psychiatry from thirty or forty years earlier, but with a price of admission from thirty or forty years in the future. Psychiatrists on the outside were appalled by its failure to use modern techniques. But on the inside, I was about to find the techniques used on me to be the oldest of all.

Danish modern furniture in the reception area did little to hide the musty shag carpeting beneath it. The room's resemblance to one of Aunt Allie B's garage sales should have been a dead give-away that we might be heading for the Dungeon of Doom, but I desperately wanted to believe the worst was over. So I believed.

Until we stepped into a vault-like, rickety elevator.

I was afraid it wouldn't safely reach my suite on the third floor, but when the door opened to a room swarming with crazies, I wished it hadn't. Before I had a chance to turn and run, I was visually assaulted by a parade of wardrobe no-no's. I escaped into the restroom and was damn-near leveled by the unmistakable essence of urine—the aftermath of what I would come to recognize as a daily battle fought by the soldiers of the ward, with their streams of ammunition aimed at the foxhole but landing on The Town Seat instead. I would discover that the only unsuccessful attack on the entire ward would be from buckets of ammonia fighting the smell of that urine.

The welcoming committee of lunatics was quickly rounded up and sent back to their black holes while the head nurse escorted me through the ward. This grand tour was normally conducted in the presence of the patient's family. The Mayor, however, was running as if he'd seen the IRS.

The visitor's lounge would become the room where patients acted out when visitors left. With the plastic-ware from their lunch trays, they attacked the demons in their paths, forking them unmercifully—chairs, plants, people, it didn't matter. But it was also ironically, the only room in this fort where sunlight had ignored the crisscrossed bars on the windows and summoned up the courage to come inside.

Inside, flourishing green plants lined the window ledges like a small garden—living proof that the sunlight hadn't been ignored. Of course, it was no rose garden—certainly not the one I'd been promised. But as God was my witness and tomorrow was another day, if I stayed long enough I knew I could make it one. Or at the very least, I could call it one.

THE ROSE GARDEN

SESSION I

You don't bring me socks anymore. . . .

Granddaddy said they would eventually take over the world and sure enough, now they were running hospitals and messing with people's minds. Well, he was wrong about one thing. These two looked nothing alike.

The administrator, a neatly groomed male version of Golda Meir, was a direct opposite from my therapist, a man whose strands of undomesticated grey hair appeared to be searching for their place in a coif that was less about grooming than how he'd slept the night before which was—one could only assume—alone.

I sat in his dust-covered office and observed a man with asymmetrical features accentuated, of course, by the hair. I wondered how his tiny head could sprout such a mane or house the huge shifty eyes that had, hopefully, never shifted in the direction of his big-and-tall antiquated attire, because if he had actually selected the red shirt with oversized collar and brown bowtie, I'd be taking advice from a man whose advice to himself about how to dress was insane.

"Well, thank goodness, a sane person," I said, as we began our first session. "Now . . . before we get started, let me just say this: I know you want to know all about what I think. I'm not exactly new at this. I mean . . . I've been down this road before. So, here's what I think. No, here's what I *know*. I *know* the administrator is an asshole. But I must say—and, good Lord, please don't take this the wrong way—I find you not only different from him but," I hesitated, for effect, "has anyone ever told you that you bear a strong resemblance to an old movie star? His name escapes me—but you know the one!"

I winked, attempting to rescue myself from the "old movie star" blunder. "But, of course, you probably aren't old enough to remember him," I continued, frantically trying to save myself. "I had hoped you wouldn't be—how can I say this—you know, nice looking. Has anyone ever said that to you before? I'm guessing, about a million times," I answered myself, and then repeated, "I mean, has anyone ever said you look like, you know, that movie star?"

"No, not that I recall," he responded. "Has anyone ever told you you're full of shit?"

Oops, wrong stage.

"Sure!" I shot back. "Isn't that why I'm here?"

"No," he snapped. "Frankly, I don't know why you're here. 'Full of shit' might have been a committable diagnosis where you came from. Here, it's like an unpleasant stench that people steer clear of. But don't worry; I'm not going anywhere. I get paid to sniff around."

So, there they were: answers to my questions. This shrink (1) had no sense of humor but thought he did; (2) had no intention of giving me his socks or anything else; and (3) wasn't going to try to save me—not even from the administrator. But at least, I consoled myself, this one probably *could* save me, you know, if he wanted to.

I tried to explain my relationship with the therapist who had referred me to The Rose Garden. "You don't have to," he assured me. "It's written between every other line in his notes. If the idiot ever had a medical license—do they give them out in Tennessee?—it should be taken away."

Do they give them out in Tennessee? Tell me he didn't just say that!

SESSION V

I accepted the loss of half of my mind. . . .

It seemed I had diagnosed myself right out of college, success, and life in general, into a couple of bad marriages. The previous therapist ("with credentials from the Harlequin School of Psychiatry") had encouraged the seductive performance I'd developed as a weapon against abandonment. His letters and calls to The Inn had been ignored.

"It was the easiest decision in my professional career," the therapist said. But his tone changed as he raised both eyebrows and shook his finger at me like I'd just soiled my training pants. "Please understand one thing," he scolded, "there's no place here for tea-party talk or that southern syrup you people pour on hard cold facts to sweeten them up."

"You mean The Truth—the *bitter* Truth?" I quipped.

"Right," he answered. "So don't try to get around it by asking how I'm doing, not today or any day. Don't even say, 'Isn't it a nice day, y'all!' This isn't about the day or the weather or me or how I'm doing or how you think I look. This isn't even about how *I* think *you* are doing or how I think *you* look. It's about how *you* think *you* look—on *the inside.* The only judge in this contest is *you!* As for that 'mindless' act . . . well, look around you. You've got some serious competition! And *they* aren't acting."

I felt one huge weight lifting from my shoulders as another came crushing down to replace it. As a Southern Belle with far too many charities already, it was a relief to be stripped of the most demanding one—the job of elevating and then nurturing the self-esteem of all men who entered my space. But at the same time, I was being denied access to my native tongue, so to speak, and I couldn't imagine how on God's green earth I was going to talk to this man without it.

"The tough part of believing you have half-a-mind—and I'm not saying you *don't*—is finding someone to fill up the rest," he said. "Regrettably, the people you've chosen so far think they're entitled to take over your *whole* mind, not just that other half! Then, too, most of them probably haven't been using their minds in their *own* lives, so what could they possibly offer you?" He laughed, and then added, "Present company excluded, of course."

"I guess I'm too stupid to hook up with smart people," I said.

"Could be," he nodded.

In my ongoing analysis of yet another shrink, I took note that this one's responses encompassed both concern and an obvious need to taunt. I wondered why he would risk further confusing a patient already reeling from a past punctuated by question marks. Of course, it was obvious the man didn't know me. Lord knows, I hadn't even been assigned a diagnosis . . . which might explain why he starred at me as though expecting my psyche to bust open and expose one.

"Let's find out what rewards have come with wearing the label, 'stupid.' As a child, do you have any recollection of *not* presenting yourself as helpless?" he probed.

"I'm thinking, I'm thinking," I said, like I was going along with his little joke, knowing full well this was no joke.

"You know," he said, like he had to spell it out for me, "a time *after* your father's death when you were rewarded for being a *big girl*—when you didn't have to be powerless to be validated?"

"Well," I nodded, "come to think of it, it was after Daddy's disappearance that I was blindsided with the disturbing difference between boys and girls."

"Your daddy didn't *disappear, HE DIED!*"

Jerk.

"Girls weren't supposed to play tough," I continued.

"They were expected to sit on their petticoats all flustered and helpless?"

"Petticoats? Good God, how old *are* you, man?"

"Strong. Girls couldn't be strong," he clarified.

"The playground was divided in half—girls' side and boys' side," I remembered. "I belonged on the side with the dolls and playhouse."

"Quite significant," he said. "Your father had just died when you were remanded to a *pretend* house that made no more sense than your *real* one. After that, you began believing *you* made no sense!"

"Yeah," I sighed. "But I don't think I did. That's probably why I was so hard to live with."

"Most pissed-off people are!" he said, sounding pissed off.

"Why was I so angry?"

"You believed no one else had noticed your father was gone. You felt alone, guilty—like you were doing something wrong. Maybe you had even caused your father's death and your mother's depression."

"Lord! Now I *really am* depressed," I joked. "But, I *was* the black sheep," I said, changing my tone. "I was a mess."

"How so?"

"Scatter-brained, showing off, making an F in second grade, always looking behind the liquor store for men who smelled like Daddy . . . *My Lord! Who makes an F in second grade?!*" I exclaimed. "Then there was that movie star phase. I went from worshiping them to believing I was one," I recalled. "But the cowboy stage was the worst. A *girl sheriff* was probably as unpopular in the late forties as a *girl band member* in the thirties."

"You mean your mother?" he asked, referring to our last session. "I know you don't want to address your similarities, but they're there—even though there is also a vast difference. It made for a very complex relationship."

"I've always tried to please her."

"Well, nothing personal, but that's a no-brainer," he teased. "Started way back, didn't it?"

"I think so."

"Think back."

I didn't have to think. My childhood was always accessible. It was my adulthood that was hiding out.

"I remember a hot afternoon—I must've been about seven—one of those times when getting a drink of something cold was just about all that seemed important. It was just before my life got complicated, and stayed that way for a long, long time. It seemed quite natural on that afternoon to handle trauma without drama. But Mama caught me doing it."

He was pleased with my recollection and I was happy to have his undivided attention. So I remembered more. "I'd been riding my bicycle in the driveway, but after falling onto the gravel, I took a break. I was standing in the kitchen drinking a Coke when Mama noticed the reddish blue scrape on my knee. She screeched, 'Oh, no! Good Lord, honey, you've hurt your knee!'"

"I looked down at my injury and remembered the fall, then got back to drinking my Coke and picking out the nuts from the chocolate chip cookies on the counter," I recalled. "I turned to Mama, 'I fell off my bike and hit the rocks,' I told her. She rushed toward me with such force I thought it was going to be about the nuts; but when she knelt down and zeroed in on my knee, I knew it was about my wound."

"Lord, child, it's bleeding! Your knee is bleeding!" she exclaimed. "How did it happen? Why didn't you call me? Did you cry?" Before I had a chance to tell her, she moaned, "Did you cry? You *cried*, didn't you?" she asked again, but this time in a way that told me there was only one acceptable answer to that question and I'd better deliver it.

I interrupted the story and turned to the therapist, "Like the rest of my blunders, this one was filling up that kitchen like a hot air balloon. But I wasn't about to watch it take off with my mama. So I tried to fix it. 'No, Mama, I didn't cry, but . . .' I thought Mama was going to cry. I'll swear I did. So I rushed to the good part. 'But, Mama . . .' I begged. *'But, Mama . . .'* I repeated, louder this time, still trying to exonerate myself. *'BUT MAMA!'* I had her attention. 'I GOT A VERY SAD LOOK ON MY FACE!'"

"Then what? What did your mama say when you told her you hadn't cried?" He leaned forward.

"Well," I said, "Mama smiled."

"Why did she smile?" He asked, puzzled. "You didn't *cry*. So why did your mama *smile?*"

"Because I got a *very sad look on my face*, and, where we came from, I'd done the next best thing."

He laughed. "What an actress! Woman, no wonder you're here! You could enter a doctor's office with an ingrown toenail and leave with one leg! You're very convincing."

He was right; he didn't know *how* right. I had a history.

Years ago I had stopped producing "sad faces" and started dealing in just plain fraud. Every time I got within fainting distance of a man with a prescription pad in his white coat pocket, I got turned on. If he talked down to his staff, I was in love.

It would begin innocently enough, with me sitting in this doctor's reception room, waiting to join his other victims—women whose names had come straight from the pages of his appointment book. In a treatment room down the hall, I would disrobe, strike a pose on an examining table, and anticipate the moment he would enter the room, whip out his instrument, and place it on my fibrillating heart. As sexually charged thoughts raced through my mind, a sickly voice began registering more complaints than there were body parts beneath my blue paper gown.

Oh, sure, I was just another of his fashion fatalities. I knew that. The gown I wore was identical to those passed out to the rest of his harem. It had obviously been cut from the same pattern (and made from the same material) as the filters the cheap bastard used in his coffee pot. Just like the doctor, I knew that gown had been around for quite some time and much like my obsession with him, it had no closure.

Today I knew I'd made progress. I wasn't experiencing any of those feelings with this psychiatrist. He'd obviously done an extensive study of the Southern Belle. He knew too much.

"What you've described isn't that unusual." He drew a long, exasperated breath. "Not in your neighborhood, anyway. There, you would fall under the *Drama Queen* category. It's all over the South. But you must understand," he said, raising his brow, "once those southern labels cross the Mason Dixon Line, they become *diagnoses*. So, for insurance purposes, I'll need to tag this one 'hysterical personality.' But get ready," he cautioned, "the administrator is determined to label it 'psychosis.' And, believe me, it will eventually become 'grist' for his infamous mill. Sooner or later almost everything winds up there."

"As for that 'Truth' you're seeking," he sighed, "you are ignoring it in this marriage just as you did in Houston, even when it socked you in the face—*literally*, socked you in the face! You just kept serving that hot wine for your mother-in-law, hoping you'd consumed enough of it to numb the Truth of that inevitable fist-in-the-face greeting you'd be getting at home!" Then he laughed, because that is, obviously, the kind of stuff Yankees laugh about. He assured me I would get nothing but The Truth from him.

"I'd prefer a fist," I mumbled.

He stood. "Your hour is up."

SESSION VII

"Let's talk about that recurrent dream you had as a child."

"Stranded at school, trying to stop the school bus, waiting for someone to pick me up?"

"Right. Did you ever get home?"

"In the dream? No."

"Tell me, how far was your house from the school?"

"Three blocks."

Dead silence. As dead as I would like to have been at that moment.

"Your confusion about where you belonged on that playground was actually the conflict about your rightful place in the world. The bus was your means of escape to that place. The bus children were like your father. They were different from the town children, much like he had been different from your family. When you tried to go home with them, the bus drove away. You were stranded. Of course, you could have walked home, but to someone who didn't want to go, those three blocks must have looked like a hike up Mt. Everest."

I normally sat on the man's couch with my legs intertwined into a twisted pretzel, not unlike I envisioned the brain he was attempting to untangle. I saw him as just one more in a long line of masters of my universe and myself as master of little more than the yoga position I assumed. It was becoming clear that any chance of claiming the exclusive rights to my mind were lost the day I signed it over to this hospital. But maybe not.

In the past, I had released my thoughts and waited for him to pick his favorites before analyzing them. But today, I don't know why, I chose to ignore him. I had felt safe in his presence but now, liberated at the thought of leaving him behind. I stretched out on his couch, starred at the ceiling, and gave a voice to the thoughts I was sending in the direction of no one in particular. As each one returned with surprising resolution, I wondered why I hadn't done this before. After all, it was *my* mind, wasn't it? Could I not send it wherever I pleased or, if I pleased, nowhere at all?

Had I been answering to this therapist like that judge and jury in my head, awaiting his verdict so I could abide by his decisions? If I stopped asking for opinions, would there even be a *case?* What would there be to deliberate *over?* How could I be *sentenced?* Or *abandoned?* Abandoned to *where?* If, let's say—just for instance—once upon a time, a woman ruled her own universe, isn't that where she'd be dropped off—*in her own universe?* And could she not turn her universe into whatever she pleased and invite into it whomever she pleased, or, if she pleased, no one at all? Could she not banish all evil from her land? (Or at least, God forbid, stop inviting it to move in with her?)

Perhaps if I had known more about governing my universe, things might have been different that blistering summer afternoon. Maybe I could have told Mr. Jones The Truth, even if it was mine, not his. But, then, my universe was only seven years old.

"Do you want to go or not?" he kept asking, as everyone piled into the car. *"Tell me right now, or we're leaving without you,"* he warned. *I froze.*

"Answer me! Do you want to go? Do you want ice cream? Or not? Yes or no?"

There was no doubt in my mind that in their minds, everyone in that car was 100% sure they wanted ice cream and 150% sure that they needed me to want it, too. Maybe I did, but what if I didn't? What if I was as different from them when it came to ice cream as I was about everything else? What if I told The Truth? What if I wanted to be alone? But what if I told The Truth and then got abandoned? Or . . . what if The Truth was weird—as weird and stupid as the eye-blinking and twitching? Would The Truth land my butt back on that kitchen counter? Oh, no! Not again! The clock was ticking and I had to come up with an answer. But what answer? Mine or everyone else's?

If I gave theirs and it wasn't mine, I'd be lying. If God heard me, then HE would abandon me! If I didn't lie, Mr. Jones would start that engine. But God wasn't going anywhere. Was He? He had to stick around and help me. Didn't He? Even Mr. Jones had once said, "She lies, God help her."

So as not to be exposed to God as a bold-faced liar, but mostly so that car wouldn't take off without me, I struggled to give an answer that would be acceptable to both God and Mr. Jones. "I don't think I want ice cream, but, then, I'm usually wrong about everything, so I probably really do. Want ice cream. Yes, I think I might want to go get some. Go get some ice cream. Yeah. I do. Maybe."

Wrong answer.

I rearranged it. "I think I thought I did."

Worse.

"But on second thought," I started again, "I can't say for sure. But I really do believe that I probably really did think that I thought I did."

And that was, unquestionably, the answer that put the key in the ignition.

Then, something akin to mob violence broke out as the occupants of that car turned on me. But I found the outpouring of laughter that followed to be much more annoying, as there was nothing funny about the look on Mr. Jones' face that told me to make up my mind—quick. Well, I couldn't. And Mr. Jones couldn't wait any longer. As I watched the door shut on that Plymouth Sedan, my mind began racing faster than Mr. Jones could rev up the motor.

My eyes shifted from the ceiling to the therapist, who seemed to have adjusted to the long stretch of silence. "My memories of childhood are mostly about feeling confused, trapped—wanting to be alone, yet afraid of being left behind; fighting against all odds to prove that my mind was working right; trying to find the right answers—not trusting them when I did; needing to please everyone else," I said. "Come to think of it, those are the memories I have of most of our sessions."

"Funny," he said, obviously disgusted. "And limiting. *Very* limiting. You've made your world small so it will fit into everyone else's . . . always living by their *right* answers."

"And what is *your* right answer," I asked, "you know, regarding my childhood?"

He leaned forward. "Do you really have to ask?"

"Apparently so."

He packed the tobacco into his pipe, sucked it into his lungs, then exhaled his answer.

"You really should have gone home with the bus children."

"So, how long before you *FINALLY* learned to drive a car?" he asked.

"Well . . . you know me. The engine was running but no one was at the wheel!"

"You got your license *when*?" he persisted.

"Not until I married The Mayor," I said. "Somebody gave it to me. City Hall, I think . . . *Happy*?"

Appearing neither happy nor sad he sat silently, as though suddenly overcome by unmitigated disgust.

"Yeah, it was the funniest thing," I said, sarcastically. "That Tennessee shrink and I got ours at the same place, same room, actually. He got his license to practice psychiatry and I got mine to drive a car. We suth'ners get our licenses for pert' near everything—driving, fishing, medicine, law, prostitution, whatever—at the same place. That way the tractor only has to make one stop."

He diverted his attention to the bookcase across the room as though expecting his next revelation to jump right off one of the shelves. "The day you took the passenger seat in other people's vehicles was the day you turned over your life to them."

"Never should've given up that broomstick horse," I mumbled.

"Ever think about which ones might have driven you straight to the front door of this nuthouse? What do you think your life would have been like if you'd been at the wheel?"

"My life? I'm sure I would've parked it caddywampus somewhere," I said.

"My guess is that you wouldn't have parked it here!" As before, he looked at me searchingly, as though expecting something insightful to leave my mouth. "But I can see how you believed this was the right destination," he continued. "You were programmed to stop here . . . like someone governed by a cult."

"Like a hippy?"

"A very frightened hippy. Always faithful to that 'Family Tree' you pay homage to—and those indisputable rules carved on its trunk."

"In blood."

"Afraid *not* to follow those beliefs, terrified to express your own . . ."

"Couldn't express them if I didn't know what they were . . ."

"There are names for . . ."

"Well, *of course* there are," I sang.

"'Brainwashing' is one," he said. "Then there's . . ."

"Paranoia!" I interrupted.

"Paranoia?"

"Sure. When you start believing all this "poor me" crap, you get paranoid as hell. At least, that's my opinion."

"'Mental institution' is yet another," he chimed in, reminding me that people with any opinions that weren't his opinions could find themselves and their opinions locked up and one-upped all in one fell swoop. "Case closed," he victoriously proclaimed.

But just like that mental hospital full of opinions and all those people who were out to get me, I figured this case would probably hang around forever.

I was right. The man had opened up one of those boxes belonging to Pandora Granny always talked about, and he sure wasn't ready to close it.

"You were a mystery to your mother—possibly not like anyone she knew. But you were like someone she had once known—your father; that's what everyone said. Problem was, those similarities—the things that endeared you to him—alienated you from her."

"So she was afraid I'd bring back good memories—or bad?"

"Probably both. No doubt, she loved him—and likely missed his adventurous nature. Wasn't he known to be a dare-devil—fun, a little wild, and fearless?"

"Nothing wrong with that."

"She wasn't sure. That was the conflict. But clearly, if you were like him, and he needed to be rearranged to 'fit in'—then so did you. Of course, he was a rebel who refused to change for *anyone*."

"Yet I was supposed to change for *everyone*."

"That's what you believed."

Again, I couldn't resist the opportunity to wallow in an old memory. I tried to make it through this one without feeling the pain.

"Why can't you be like your friends? Why can't you be like Judy Broach?" Mama wanted to know—like I could, magically, begin doing everything just right and suddenly, miraculously, my blouse would be tucked in and I'd be dressed like a proper young lady.

But then I jumped as high as I could and when I landed—voilà!— everything had changed. It was magic. "She's coloring inside the lines!" my teacher would say when she called my mama, "and she's playing little girls' games, on the little girls' side of the playground." Then, just after Mama hung up the phone it would ring again. It was the Sunday-school teacher.

"She knows her lesson perfectly," she would say. "Now she's teaching all the other children their lessons—Judy Broach, too."

Next I'd be talking about Jesus and crocheting perfect doilies for the old ladies down the street and I'd do it all while remembering to be real careful not to run into my room, shut the door, and laugh hysterically about the whole thing. But I couldn't stop myself because every time I thought of Daddy, I knew he was laughing, too.

"I figured I was stupid. Otherwise, what was all the reprogramming about? Too stupid to think for myself, too stupid to know how to act, and way, way, way too stupid to drive a car."

"Too stupid to drive yourself to a beauty pageant but smart enough to come home with a trophy! Now, figure that one out!"

"Alright, alright. I get it."

"You didn't measure up at home but went off and measured up somewhere else! In front of God and everybody, you had the audacity to *win* before you'd even gotten '*fixed!*' *The Loser WON!—as HERSELF!*"

"I almost always won," I said, as I repositioned myself a couple of times on the sofa—like shifting my body would somehow give credibility to the praise I was about to bestow on myself. "And it wasn't all about looks—*not mine!*" I volunteered, like that hadn't already crossed the man's mind. "Almost everybody on that stage looked better than I did. Lord knows, I wasn't a great dancer, either . . . *Man!* Those comedy acts sure diverted attention from a multitude of shortcomings! But I was a master at adding comedy—and even better at designing my wardrobe so *I* didn't look like the *joke!* I became an expert on every current event I understood and spoofed the ones I didn't. Whatever it took."

"Likely not as much as you thought . . ."

It occurred to me that my first pageant talent routine was simply a well-choreographed re-enactment of my life. I remembered that night like it was yesterday. Probably because it was. Yesterday and every other day of my life.

"I walked onstage and auditioned for an imaginary director. I began the first of several dances. Every step, perfect. Yet, after each one, he stood, turned, and headed straight for the door. 'Mr. Director,' I begged the invisible man, 'please sit down. I have other dances.' Frantically, I pulled another one from my repertoire. Each time he stood to leave, I changed the steps. I tap danced, toe danced, performed a jazzed-up ballet. But finally he walked away, and I realized there was no way to talk him into coming back. I shrugged my shoulders, plucked a black sequin from my dress, dampened it with the perspiration from my palm, and stuck it on a front tooth. *Wahlah!* A toothless smile! Like an inebriated rag doll, I cut loose into something similar to the 'buck and wing' dance I'd seen black performers do on TV. Truth be known, I'd never seen anyone do anything quite like this. Obviously, neither had the audience or the judges."

"But you were your own audience. . . ."

"I was, finally, performing for myself," I nodded.

"And how did you end the performance?"

"By winning."

"Why didn't I know that?" he smiled.

"After that night, there were no boundaries for me on the stage—no rules. If there were, I somehow got around them." I closed my eyes, hoping to experience another "high," as I reminisced. I wondered how my recollections of that time in my life could seem so vivid, yet unreal at the same time. I had rushed through them as though waking up from someone else's coma to borrowed treasures that had to be returned.

"*Lord, that person was ME! And I won! I deserved to win!*" I shrieked. "Did you know that I got . . . I got *THREE? I GOT THREE COLLEGE SCHOLARSHIPS! THREE!* Know how I got them?"

"For being *yourself*?"

"You got it."

"Creative, funny, and smart?"

"Sure was."

"But you didn't stay in college because you were . . ."

". . . Stupid."

He made an unsuccessful attempt at sucking tobacco into his lungs from an unlit pipe, then made that exact same attempt at humor. He chuckled. "I wouldn't be surprised if the main player in your dysfunctional childhood wasn't . . ." he began.

"Oh, Lord! Don't hold back," I chimed in, happy to take over. "Just say it . . . '*THE SOUTH!!!*' As long as *I'm* off the hook, you can blame it on whoever or whatever you damn well please. Pick one—The Confederate Flag, The Star of David, or The Grand Ole Opry—I don't care! *Just leave me out of it!*"

Obviously pleased that I knew about the Star, he flashed an unexpected smile that quickly vanished. "I don't know about that, but clearly, you got the fight knocked out of you early on," he said. "You walked into this office that first day like a sissy little girl, crying over a skinned knee."

Jerk.

"Caution: deaf child playing," was the sign I had wanted to plant in the front yard at home, but Travis' teacher warned me, "If you start now, you'll be putting up stop signs for him the rest of his life." I wondered if anyone was watching him now, listening for the cars. I knew Sam was doing his part, but was anyone doing anything for Sam?

My communication with their father had pretty much shut down at this point, so during the day I imagined what my boys were doing and at night, what we'd be doing if I were there.

Sam—soft, lovable Sam. I'd be squeezing him too hard at night as I tucked him in. The next morning I would sit by the window and watch Travis play basketball in the front yard, hoping the ball wouldn't roll into the street, dreading the sound of a car driving by, praying I wouldn't hear a horn.

I missed everything I'd taken for granted. I even missed the homework. I missed the dirty laundry. I almost missed those cars. It made no sense to walk past the empty pond on the hospital grounds when the one back home was filled with ducks, fish, and the mysterious squirmy earth-toned things that followed the boys home from time to time. I missed those creatures almost as much as the dirty laundry. I thought of Travis when I heard a word he might not know although, considering most of the words I was hearing, it was probably best that he didn't.

In therapy I was willing to meet head-on practically any aspect of my life, except anything having to do with my boys. Avoiding that subject seemed to be alright with the therapist who was dead set on talking about my mama. Mama, me, sex, and the South. He loved those subjects. Generally, they all showed up at the same time, sometimes in the same sentence. Well, at least my fears of having another shrink fall in love with me were unfounded. The man was having a serious affair with Freud, and on alternate days, with himself.

While he saw me as an unlikely candidate for hospitalization, the administrator viewed every well-insured patient as a long-term prospect. Like a big corporate ladder, the chain of command was set up with him at the top, looking down at those he had flattened on his way up. The therapist was groveling to keep his position on the lower half, as he held on to the small remaining piece of his dignity, which appeared to have slipped considerably and now teetered just a few steps above mine. I was on the bottom step, performing my duties as I always had—afraid to move up or down, always answering to those above me, never once asking how on this earth I had wound up on the bottom when I was the only one paying to be there.

The administrator's expectations of the patients were defined by people we never saw. Said to operate out of a room hidden away at the end of a long hallway on a floor beneath the ward, these mystery employees were shielded by vault-like doors, similar to those on the elevator, which, mysteriously, was not programmed to stop on that floor. As the story goes, this obscure, well-staffed department could first be identified by the strong smell of old money, then by a small sign on the door that read, simply, "Accounting."

That office's connection with my hospital stay would be apparent when each time my insurance was extended downstairs, the bar was raised upstairs. (Or lowered, depending on your point of view and which side of the bar [s] you were on.) Clearly, crazy paid better than sane and on my ward, crazy was king.

Ironically, I would find the *crazy* thing less disturbing than the *southern* thing. There wasn't one among them. My therapist swore I should be able to relate to *one* if I'd grown up with the *other*. Well, I don't think so. These people weren't just crazy. They were pale, malnourished, crazy damn foreigners, and worse. Some of them were Yankees! At first, I tried to make sense of it.

Was I the only southerner in this place or had the others been here so long you couldn't tell them from the Yankees and illegal aliens? Had no one else inadvertently wound up in a nut house while taking leave to simply fix a bad marriage and get a suntan? Had I signed up for that infomercial with those ragged, wide-eyed children? Or, God forbid, was I in a time warp, revisiting the America's Junior Miss stage as that chubby teenager, unable to give up—but more than willing to throw up—her cheeseburgers and fries, to become one of the emaciated finalists?

Like most organized cliques, divisions were drawn between members of the Society of the Insane. But it was difficult to know which group I should hang with, as there was a complete absence of any kind of social order; not one ounce of anything remotely suggestive of an upper and lower crust. Well, there was *one*—the most taboo of all crusts where I came from—the one surrounding every day-old lunchmeat sandwich in the cafeteria!

But my greatest challenge was ahead. In addition to your everyday mental hospital ambiance—cheap busted furniture, prison food, a dubious odor layered with Apple Blossom of the Asylum disinfectant, two psychiatrists with opposing views, and psychiatric aides, likely without green cards (dot heads and sheet heads in muumuus, all over the place)—I would be forced to face my "deep-seated prejudice." And here's the best part. I was supposed to face *THAT* while looking into the sleazy eyes of a bunch of fucked-up foreigners!!

Of course, I now know I'd been living with one all along. It was becoming increasingly clear that The Mayor was from Mars.

And sister woman, Mars was getting farther away every day.

Unless the girlfriend *was* a very small child, I couldn't understand why my last box of clothes from The Mayor had contained the dresses of a girl six, maybe seven years old. Unless . . . *Omilord! Surely not!* Had my boys' obsessions with that Easy Bake Oven transformed them into the little girls I never had? Or was this The Truth I'd been searching for? Had it come through the mail in a meticulously packaged brown cardboard box? Was there actually another woman, and had she brought along her little ruffled-up, frilly-frocked girl as part of the deal? Was her bad taste in men surpassed only by her kid's wardrobe?

The Mayor and an affair. It didn't compute. Of course, it was possible the man had finally been talked into having sex, bless his heart. Stranger things had happened. *"Remember?"* I asked myself. "Remember when you thought he'd never take time off work for the two of you to have a little vacation and then . . . *surprise!* The man packed up the car and drove hundreds of miles to a romantic little retreat too costly for two so he dropped you off and went home? *Remember?"*

But if there really *was* another woman, why had no one told me so I could send the bitch a note, just one perfectly crafted—no holds barred, from the depths of my soul—thank-you note? I mean, crazy or not, I was still a Southern Belle with social obligations. "She's gone so mental she can't even write a thank you note!" I could just hear it now.

For weeks I continued to search for answers. What was up with The Mayor? Was this a passive-aggressive message, mid-life crisis, temporary insanity, or all three? If so, "this too shall pass." It does pass, doesn't it? Besides, "what doesn't kill us makes us stronger," right? Then, too, "everything happens for a reason," that's what I've always said. . . .

Funniest thing about mental hospitals. You get answers. Like it or not, you do. But they don't come from the doctors. Oh, no. Not even from some treasure you discover after years of diving into your own half-empty glass. They come from the other patients. Whether you ask for those answers or not, your crazy neighbors will step up to the plate and give them to you. Here's why. The hopelessly insane are unencumbered by the endless justifications and rationales of people like us *NORMAL* folks.

US—with our sanity and ability to navigate our lives by navigating around them with: *"Maybe I misunderstood. . . ."* or, *"He probably meant . . ."* or, *"Not my wild imagination again!"* And every other imaginable excuse for anything too unimaginable to face.

THEM—with their insanity and ability to face anything, especially anything too unimaginable for the rest of us to face.

I wasn't surprised when my new family stopped the ruminations. The foreman stepped away from the group who had briefly abandoned their psychotic excursions to join him in deliberating five, maybe six seconds. There was no doubt they'd reached a verdict. I figured whatever came next could not possibly be as disturbing as what I'd come up with by myself. But I, of course, had been wrong before.

He spoke:

"Tell the Russian FBI to stop the shipment of mashed potatoes!"
he warned. "The factory sent the SOS through the watermelons!
So reroute those seeds to Vietnam. Now!" He paused as I, for one

*brief second, thought he might actually be putting some thought
into the next part of the verdict. Wrong again.*

*"The lying, mother-fucking, wetback, bastard Chinese sons-of-
bitches of Jesus and Buddha," he continued, as he raised his voice
another notch, "the Nazi Jew with a chicken shit Elvis Presley
car—that knocked-up Barbie doll in a turd house with a popsicle-
stick mother—that cheating fuck-head husband of yours doesn't
give a shit about your fat ass, so get yourself a divorce!"*

The man had just solved the mystery. It was like hearing, "You're
too ugly to be Miss Tennessee Walking Horse." Painful initially, but
at least you know it's time to get out of the race.

Before I could gracefully bow out, it was over. No one had called,
as promised, to work out the problems in my house; but just as the
therapist had predicted, someone had sure moved into it—problems and
all. As it became increasingly clear that no one was coming to return me
to my roots, I decided my roots would need to do some serious growing
right where they were.

Maybe this Rose Garden I hadn't been promised was the right
garden for me after all.

22.
Somebody help me!
I can't get out of this mess by myself!

I was beginning to believe that death and taxes would surely abandon me if I showed the slightest need for them. But each time Mama forwarded my mail, I knew there were those who would hang on forever, whether I showed the slightest need or not.

> *Dear Rosemary,*
> *We've lost touch.*
> *The Pageant Committee*

> *Dear Pageant Committee,*
> *So, they say, have I.*
> *Rosemary*

The black wrought-iron sign in front of the building had eliminated the word *hospital,* and so had the administrator. Even the patients and staff referred to it as "The Inn." I could understand how the crazies might have had hallucinations of grandeur, but the doctors and staff—*shame on them!*—knew better, and so did the insurance company. This was a full-blown mental hospital and I was as out of place as Mama at a beauty pageant. Clearly, I'd returned to high school, I didn't fit in, nobody liked me, and my clothes were all wrong.

Like they cared. Their minds were fixed on a game of pursuit in which eating utensils became weapons and I, their parole officer, both their parents, and on a good day, the devil herself. Running from them did fill up my days. But the fun and games would cease when the staff dutifully convinced me that integrating into the group would be easier than trying to leave it. Each day I felt myself taking one more step backward down the path to their Land of La-La. The seduction of madness had begun.

The letters from The Mayor stopped, the winter clothes never came, and those phone calls from the children—almost never. But the little boys who had once reminded me who I was each day now wrote letters to remind me that being a little "funny" was the part they missed the most.

> *Dear Mama,*
>   *Today we went to Doug Kennedy's birthday party and his mama forgot to wear a clown suit and act weird.*
>   *We miss you.*
>   *Travis and Sam*

I borrowed a coat from a patient who'd been at the Rose Garden for twenty-five years. Not surprisingly, her coat had been in and out of fashion about as many times as she'd been in and out of psychosis. Since this was one of the "out" years (for her coat), I figured I would finally join my housemates on fashion's worst-dressed list or would, at least, blend in.

Until now, taking on the fashion sense of those with no sense had not come easy. But with depression pulling at the sides of my mouth and a ripped coat lining pulling at the heels of my shoes, I figured I was in the beginning stages of that mental-patient look, with the mental-patient shuffle not far behind. Yet, after sponging down the coat, sewing up the ripped lining, and putting a scarf under the collar, my look was still that of a desperate housewife—an upper-middle-class woman hoping to be accepted into the country club, or at the very least, to stand out in the crowd. Well . . . there was little doubt that in *this* crowd, I did stand out and, like most of the country club crowd back home, this one was also crazy.

As the months passed, I learned to overlook the way my neighbors dressed and smelled, what with being lunatics and all. I, in turn, was forgiven for the inappropriateness of my—comparatively speaking—designer attire. Most of the time, we just sat around and stared, as some of us saved our imaginations and creativity for making wine out of apple cider, and others, for trying to break out. Any fleeting thoughts of saneness and singularity I had on my arrival vanished as I—*God, save me*—began fitting in, which—*God, thank you*—also meant I had definitely not returned to high school.

125

I remembered that first day when the head nurse said the plants lining the window ledges were grown by patients. The thought of watching those plants grow for a year would have been as unlikely as another year without my children. A year spent with a group of crazies in a mental hospital—*unthinkable!* I could not have imagined working at a hospital kiosk for one dollar an hour instead of—well, come to think of it, that *was* more than I was paid at home. But spending that dollar an hour for my own contribution to the garden on the window ledge? No way.

Today I was looking at that purchase—plants grown from seeds once covered with avocado, the main ingredient for my favorite, albeit forbidden, feast. How clever of me to send a psychiatric aide to buy that delicacy with my seed money! How brilliant I was to transform the avocados into my favorite treat! How many avocados I ate before prize-winning plants emerged from the seeds and joined the other plants! How thrilled I was when mine overtook the entire window ledge and then towered over all the rest! How understandable was my need to win—and that I can no longer tolerate an avocado.

How fortunate I was to have a roommate crazy enough to help.

The birth of that green delicacy took place in our closet, where the lights went on at 10 p.m. when the other ones went out. Requiring a surgeon's skill in its preparation, the peeling procedure began with the scalpel, my roommate's (formerly self destructive) fingernails, and was followed by the careful injection of salt and mayonnaise packets from the cafeteria. With the smooth end of a toothbrush, we blended the concoction before serving it up in the aired-out lid of a tennis shoe box. It was an operation quite different from our previous one, its success still evident in the scent that permeated every piece of clothing I owned. Changing those open jugs of apple cider to wine was a streak of genius, alright—one that brought me to my knees every time I opened the closet door. It had been as close to a godly miracle as anything I'd witnessed in this place. And the green substance in the lid of that shoebox?

As close to guacamole as any two mental hospital patients had ever gotten—in *any* place.

23.
It would be my privilege. . . .

. . . and the bus children and the beauty-pageant children and the mental-patient children, too. They all stood behind the big curtain, waiting for their names to be called. And some of them never were.

Although The Rose Garden shut out the world, for a lucky few there were "privileges" to visit it. Groveling to get them was, by all indications, a privilege in itself.

Like Christmas presents, they were awarded to certain patients by the ward's self-proclaimed king—an administrator who appeared to have been de-throned at some point during his reign or, a more likely possibility, had never sat on a throne outside the men's room. A one-man parole board, he dangled these tidbits of freedom in the faces of the inmates who sat in a big circle at weekly group meetings; then he read from a list of reasons why most of them hadn't earned the right to privileges or most anything else in life.

After each rejection was systematically labeled, "grist for the mill," the patients were sentenced: some back to bare (seclusion) rooms, others to the next group meeting, and a few to now-empty homes and former lives that would never be the same. Nevertheless, the residents waited for the verdict, because that verdict just might be freedom. And that's what they wanted.

They *longed* for freedom. They *prayed* for freedom. They sat in their rooms and *rehearsed the words* that would *beg* for freedom. They asked for the privilege to walk the grounds unrestricted—to break free from the group of patients herded by psychiatric aides to the cafeteria. They asked for the privilege to go to the bathroom unaccompanied, or to the kiosk, even off-grounds to dinner or a movie. Of course, leaving the grounds scared the bejezus out of even the truly insane, who were normally afraid of nothing but their own hallucinations. Just the same, almost everyone wanted freedom.

Yet almost everyone was scared half to death that they would get it.

Privileges for me would mean the freedom to bake chocolate chip cookies for my boys, but the whole process took some doing. Fortunately, the administrator hadn't heard about the late night guacamole-fest or the wine cellar in my closet, so after a few weeks of required groveling, he gave me the privilege of spending one night a week, escorted, in the kitchen. Escorted or not, privileges were hard to come by, so I was thrilled. Besides, this one would at least smell like home.

But after finally getting that privilege, it took another month of kiosk paychecks to buy the ingredients, plus two more weeks until the kitchen and the aides were available, and then another week to get permission to walk the one block, escorted, to the post office. Then there was the privilege to buy more ingredients for the cookies, since the eggs had gone bad and the milk had soured in the weeks of asking for privileges.

Weeks after the cookies had been mailed, I got the privilege to call my boys. Toward the end of the call, I nonchalantly asked, "Oh, and by the way . . . how were those chocolate chip cookies your mama sent you?"

The response was swift. "Cookies? What cookies, Mama?"

That day I awarded another privilege to myself—the privilege of putting together the necessary ingredients for blowing all working appendages from the body of whoever stopped the delivery of those cookies.

And that would be off-grounds and unescorted.

The privilege to see my family was awarded without a hassle, but I accepted it with trepidation. The month before, The Mayor had informed a hospital representative that a divorce was in the works. Shortly afterward I received papers confirming it—and secrets. On every page of the document, there were secrets. Now, in case I hadn't gotten the papers—and the secrets—that message was being delivered one more time. I was about to be dumped, in person.

I knew this might be our last time together as a family and I wasn't sure why. All I knew was that The Mayor wasn't going to provide any answers. I hadn't completely lost my mind, or my memory.

I was happy to see the children, sad because they had obviously been rehearsed on what to say. Fortunately, these instructions flew right past

Travis' hearing aids, since none of his lesson plans had ever involved *not repeating* what he saw on someone's lips! To him, secrets were exciting new "show and tell" material that brought inaudible praise from his teacher and old Halloween candy from the jar on her desk.

But no amount of coaxing could extract information from Sam, who had become skilled at keeping everything inside. I tried to bribe him, Lord knows I did. With my next door neighbor, crazy Steve, as a new kiosk employee with a history of stealing, I had the perfect accomplice/delivery boy. Candy bars by the box were the thing he liked delivering best. Delivering sentences in threes he liked even better.

"What do you want me to do?"
"What do you want me to do?"
"What do you want me to do?" Steve would ask.

"Steal from the kiosk."
"Steal from the kiosk."
"Steal from the kiosk," I would answer.

In less than forty-eight hours, Steve got to experience being hired and fired from the same job. But if you're into justice, it did prevail. I was punished in a recurrent nightmare in which I shared a cell with Steve. San Quentin didn't scare me. Sharing a cell with Steve did.

While Sam was a closed book, much of Travis' information fell into the "too much of it" pile, with unsolicited tales of a superwoman-in-residence.

"And Daddy's girlfriend is very very pretty and a really good cook and we can find stuff because she keeps the house good."

Still, there loomed the big question: *WHERE was this very very pretty really good cook keeping the good house?*

Travis could hardly wait to tell me. Our house had been sold. The First Lady-to-be was "in waiting" to marry The Mayor, but not to move into his new house. She was already there! Right along with the wicked, soon-to-be stepsister.

"And she got the good bedroom but we got sent to the cold, wet basement where we starved and freezed to death and nobody could ever hear us screaming."

With this unexpected shocker came the obvious question:

WHY had we never had a basement?

And how, pray tell, could our house have been sold without my signature *somewhere?* And wasn't this hospitalization a bit suspect—convenient, to say the least? Had I really been crazy enough to purchase a one-way ticket to this house of horrors, and so naive I honestly believed there would be a return ticket home?

And, above all, what in the name of Martha Stewart had happened to the cookies?

> *I never found out how the house got sold without my signature. I still don't know if my boys actually slept in the cold, wet basement, and I have no idea what happened to the cookies. If the First Lady-in-waiting gobbled them down as she had my home and family, I figured that just living with The Mayor was probably payback enough. Besides, I told myself, they were likely delivered to our old house that got turned into a state orphanage where a bunch of skinny waifs devoured them, never once suspecting they were made from sour milk and expired chocolate chips.*

The Mayor, the boys and I spent our weekend visit in a cottage reserved for visitors on the grounds of The Rose Garden. Travis was speaking well, and often, while Sam was dutifully passing on to him everything he had missed. As always, he added his own spin and then dissected each answer, fully aware that he'd get wrestled to the ground and beat half to death if he didn't.

Travis and I had the same intense relationship as always, but we had more in common than I had once thought—something I realized the day I read the head nurse's comment in my opened chart at the nurses' station: "The other patients will benefit from living on the ward with her. She's not psychotic." There was something very familiar about that moment. Today I was reminded once again what it was. It was Travis.

I remembered the years of driving him from one class to another, one town to another, searching for a place that would address his special needs. The day I thought I'd found that school, his teacher had made a pronouncement as disturbing as the head nurse's. Matter of fact, it was practically the same one: "The other deaf children will learn from Travis. He talks."

Travis would have made a lousy mental patient. At nine, he was true to himself and refused to be shoved into a convenient slot. The kid was a rule breaker, still is. Against the beliefs of some deaf communities, he decided early on to depend on spoken language and lip reading instead of signing. But no matter how much I had tried to support his choices, there always seemed to be someone standing by, waiting to slap on a label.

I had cheered him on the year he asked to join Sam's group of normal-hearing stimulators in their Christmas program. "But he belongs onstage with the deaf children," his teacher had said. I disagreed. He wasn't "just a deaf kid" any more than he was "just a normal hearing kid," or "just a town kid," or "just a bus kid." He was just a kid who wanted to be in a Christmas program with his brother.

I was glad I'd convinced his doctors to stop searching for him on the pages of their medical journals, that I hadn't taken the easy route. I thanked God he never wound up in the wrong file folder or got lost in a misplaced stack. I saw him now and knew I'd done the right thing. He had found his own niche these past two years. He had found his own stage.

It all made sense now. No wonder there were no classrooms for children like him. There *were* no children like him! Just the same, my search became an obsession that wasn't going to stop until I found the perfect school. I don't know why it wasn't clear, then, that I'd also been trying to make things right for my own first-grader within who still clung to the hope that somewhere there would be a better playground—and somehow, I'd be able to find it.

Why hadn't I been the kind of mother to myself that I'd been to him? Why had I slipped into a slot that seemed convenient for everyone but me? How easy it was in the classroom of the insane to get lulled into a state of apathy, to lose oneself in the routine of a life bound by a set of laws that were the same for every patient.

Once again, it appeared I had exchanged my beloved broomstick horse for a stupid rubber baby as I obediently followed the rules of another senseless game.

At least, that's what it felt like. It felt exactly like first grade.

Together, The Mayor and I told the boys about the divorce. Travis cried so long and hard I thought he would never stop. I remembered the "surprised" and "crying" face lessons at the speech and hearing center and how he'd chosen the crying face for show and tell that week, with encore performances for some time afterward. I recalled how proud of him I was for being able to fall apart on cue. Today was different.

Sam stared straight ahead, never shedding the slightest hint of a tear; yet he made sure his brother understood every word and was ready to fill in the blanks if he hadn't. But that's as far as he would go. He sure wasn't going to join him in those crying-out-loud spells. He'd have no part of that, none whatsoever. I wanted to cradle him in my arms until he felt it was safe to cry—to squeeze him so long and hard the tears would finally be set free. But Sam's emotions were as imprisoned as this hospital's inmates, held hostage by their own secrets—the kind that spiral until only barred windows and locked doors can contain them.

I released myself from the guilt I felt about Sam's secret-keeping by blaming it on his father's upbringing. Until I remembered my own.

Nice little girls don't talk about dead people. . . .

When I got the news of the up-and-coming stepmother, it had been a crushing blow, yet I was able to extract an ounce of satisfaction from my past by applying it to my present. It occurred to me that in addition to her title of *First Lady,* the new wife would be wearing the crown of *Second Mother,* placing her in that category of people viewed as little more than illegal aliens in foreign households. God bless America. God bless Mr. Jones.

Travis freely expressed not only what he was thinking, but what he assumed others were thinking, too. If there was a problem, he had a solution. The one he came up with the last day of our visit had appeared in a dream the night before. Once again this kid, who could bring up a rainbow at the end of an earthquake, was trying to make things right.

"It was a beauty contest," he said, addressing his father. "You were the judge. Then you looked at Mama and said, 'You're the winner, so I'm taking you home!'" He turned to me. "It's true, Mama. That's what happened in my dream."

No doubt about it, my son was a dreamer. His mama was no winner—and she sure wasn't going home.

For the past two days I hadn't allowed myself to think about my family's inevitable departure. But now my boys were stuffing their backpacks for the trip home. I still hadn't talked to them about this non-stop bus to nowhere I'd boarded, probably because I would then have to explain why I couldn't get off.

Travis had pretty much disintegrated into the puddle of tears that started just after he arrived. Even Sam was crying now. I was a mess. I don't know how their father got them to the car, but I hadn't even been able to walk them to the front door. I waited inside until I heard the revving sound of the motor and then inched my way toward the door and out onto the porch. They were gone.

I followed the tire tracks to the end of the dirt driveway and waited for the car to turn around and come back. I don't know why, but I believed it would. I could imagine how I must look to the mental hospital security guards, as I stood at first, then sat at the end of that driveway, waiting. I finally peeled myself off the pavement, got back on my feet, and walked the short distance to the cottage.

Inside, the only visible memory of our visit was Sam's terry cloth wristband on the bathroom floor, a ratty little reminder of him and his love of sports. I remembered the healthy competition that once existed between sports and baking cookies. The year he asked for an apron with footballs on it, I figured the kitchen was losing. When he traded in his oven mitt for a catcher's mitt, the verdict was in: he could no longer take the heat from the kitchen. Sports had won.

I collected my clothes as I surveyed the first house I'd been inside in almost a year. There were soft sheets, fluffy towels, and a little boy's wristband—no locked doors, psychiatric aides with keys, or wet commode seats. It was a real home. I'd forgotten how sleep felt without the intrusion of madness and misery. But although I had hated those haunting sounds on the ward, there were nights I would've given almost anything to throw in a few of my own.

Now I could. Without the threat of seclusion rooms and revoked privileges, I was free to vent. I could cry, moan and groan, throw skillets at the wall, scream at no one in particular, and shriek, *"WHY ME, GOD?"* It was a real home, alright. At least, from what I could remember, it was awfully close.

Sitting on the floor in the empty cottage, I tried to recall some facet of Sam's personality that would get him through this. But I was haunted by what he'd shared with me only months before my first hospitalization. For Sam, it was a rare heart-to-heart. For me, it sure wasn't offering much comfort now. I don't know what had prompted me to ask him, "What would make you feel really safe?" But he sure hadn't missed a beat in giving me his take on the subject. "Feeling safe," he had said matter of factly, "would be like I was in a big house with no windows and only one door and you were the only person with the key." He grabbed my hand and quickly let go as though suddenly aware of the answer he had released without proper editing. Like it was yesterday, I could see the smile that came with his closing statement,

"Yeah, that would make me feel real safe."

As I looked out the living room window at the hospital grounds, the moisture collecting inside my contact lenses blurred the image of the building that housed my ward. I strained to see through the tears to a slither of hope on the other side. But my former life had just walked out the door and my hope had left with it. There was nothing now but a fuzzy image of the gothic building across the grounds.

A couple of hours passed before I could bring that image into focus. When I did, the place I'd lived for the past ten months had changed. The sight of the barred windows was no longer followed by a series of cold chills up my back. The structure that once resembled a prison now looked like a safe haven. It was familiar, I deserved it, and no one was trying to take it away. I was going home.

Of course, the front door would be locked, just as it always was. I wasn't sure who had the key, but I knew it wasn't me.

24.
Fear of commitment

I'm not stupid. I understood that The Mayor needed a quick divorce so he could get on with the inauguration of the new First Lady. You know, the pomp and circumstance. Then there were those other circumstances. You know, minus the pomp.

He now had the task of explaining to his voters what had befallen the former First Lady, ex-Junior Miss, and member in good standing of The Garden Club. Would they ever believe that a woman who took leave simply to visit a rose garden had taken on the mind and body of a vegetable?

I could only imagine that, given the campaign promises these people had believed in the past, they could.

I was divorcing the newly elected Assistant District Attorney, which probably explained why the Tennessee lawyers I tried to retain went crawling off to their mamas like spineless little gummy worms. The one who eventually took my case broke in half and went slithering off in opposite directions while continuing to talk out of both sides of his mouth and practice law with one-half the morals of a common worm. Just the same, I felt absolutely no ill-will toward him or his profession, none whatsoever. Not my style.

The same insecurities documented on my insurance policy and two hospital charts were about to determine my divorce settlement. Convinced I had single-handedly destroyed my marriage, I asked no more from the union in its broken state than when I believed it was whole. My attorney asked for even less.

His answer to The Mayor's divorce complaint was written in legalize, but the message—"She doesn't deserve shit"—was unmistakable. The only place I could go for support was to my therapist. On the ward, the same objections I might have expressed in polite society were measured by a staff trained to watch for something resembling a ray of disease. The administrator? Worse. Now up to his ass in "grist," he threw this event into his overflowing mill where it got labeled, "just another symptom of insanity"—or at best, "just another screw-up." Well, I'll give him that one. I had certainly screwed up.

Despite my one-on-one classes with Steve, he stopped stealing from the kiosk, and like it couldn't get any worse, the wine jug in my closet was empty; my allowance from home was coming less frequently; the avocados were out-of-season; and that dollar an hour from my job was going for shampoo and deodorant. Life was sucking pretty bad now but I sure wasn't without support. The insurance company pitched in and offered more money for me to stay, and The Mayor—according to the administrator—a *forced* commitment if I tried to leave.

Commitment. A word once associated with long-term love and devotion now meant long-term hell—something a person with half-a-brain probably couldn't fight.

> *Dear Pageant Committee,*
> *Remember when y'all said the first-runner-up would take over in the event I couldn't fulfill my duties? Well, I need her NOW. And tell her to bring that flaming baton.*
> *She's gonna need it!*
> *Rosemary*

On the bright side I had, typically, over-packed.

On the dark side, I was about to be charged with insanity.

From what I could piece together, a sanity hearing would consist of hospital lawyers, the administrator, The Mayor, the ex-husband and his mother from Houston, my ex-boyfriends, and any other forms of low-life scum-sucking sons-of-bitches they could round up from my past, or in the gutter behind the hospital.

Although the therapist claimed I didn't meet the criteria for commitment, I feared that facing the aforementioned group could bring on every one of them. But in time I would discover that my fear of being committed by someone else was completely unfounded as I was more than willing to commit myself. The administrator was eager to help.

With an unexpected divorce on the horizon, he was now predicting my regression—a brief period of psychosis which I would live out in a "seclusion room" on a mattress surrounded by four walls and a locked door. It was a prison term that could last for years, five being the average at this place. As was my pattern, I spent the remainder of the year alternating between the fear of being confined to that room and the fear that my insurance would run out before I could get locked up. Go figure.

With so much at stake, I became obsessed with not appearing to be crazy while showing the proper respect and concern for those who needed me to be and, of course, for those who actually were. It wasn't an easy gig. But not to worry, I kept telling myself. I had signed myself in and could sign myself out. Of course, if this commitment thing happened, all bets were off. There'd be no place to run but into one of those cells. The hospital called them seclusion rooms; I called them hell.

I knew exactly what to expect. I saw them every day, faces of insanity peeking through the tiny windows on the doors. Inside, patients were deprived of the pills that had once kept them from the world of the insane and allowed them to remain with the extremely weird instead. In another hospital, those drugs would have been their "get out of jail free" card, but medication was viewed with distain in The Rose Garden, and discontinued on admission. Without it, the prisoners were sentenced to their dark kingdoms, with little more company than their own hallucinations and visits from the stampeding army of psychiatric aides.

One thing I knew without asking. I may have spent my life questioning where I belonged—which side of The Tree; which side of the playground; or which seat on the bus—but I sure knew which side of that seclusion room I was about to be facing. And let me tell you, I was determined to stay on the traffic side. If I was sick, I knew how much sicker I could get inside those four walls. I'd seen too much. A lot of people went in; I never saw anyone come out.

"Seems to me you'd feel right at home, hunkering down in your own private corner of that seclusion room," the therapist said, smartassedly, "a safe distance from those pesky Jews and bus children, not to mention the occasional black balcony kid!"

"I can't tell you anything."

"It appears to be part of his strategy, this fear tactic," he continued, as we dissected the motives of the administrator. "It steps up the process of getting the patient into regression and on to recovery. The hospital supports the man and so do I, in some cases," he continued. "Patients are forced to face their demons head-on by removing medication and distractions. Daily visits from their therapists are just about their only diversions. It's all about. . ."

"*. . .Money!*" I exclaimed. "For every patient thrown into one of those rooms, this privately owned hospital adds another wing onto the owner's house on the hill—that mansion overlooking this hell hole! The more patients locked up, the longer someone has to pay for them, and the fewer staff members needed to take care of them! *Perfect!!* 'Out of sight, out of mind!' Right? Or, is it 'out of *mind,* out of *sight?*'"

"If I really believed that, I'd lock you up right now and throw away the key!" he laughed.

"Seriously, doesn't that therapeutic journey to hell and back sometimes take ten—twenty years, or longer?" I asked.

"Sometimes," he nodded. "But you do understand the concept, don't you?"

Well, now, lemme see . . . how does it go? I'm in the real world but I'm not facing the demons in it so I regress and regress until they show up and I confront them so we can all wallow around for years on a urine-soaked mattress in an otherwise barren room with peeling walls and no windows— and if everything goes as planned I return to the real world, coincidentally, about the time someone stops paying my bill, but by then I've been away so long the real world looks bigger and badder than when I left it; so help me out here. Why was it that I left it in the first place?

"Of course I do," I nodded. "I understand perfectly."

"But there's no way you could be committed or locked away in a room—not without those demons. Nobody gets in without those guys," he said, trying to comfort me. "Look, I'm not sure what's up with you and the warden. Have you done or said something to the poor man? Has that one-track train of yours derailed from its narrow south-bound railway? Come on now, what was it that set him off? Was it one of those cute little put-downs that aren't really put-downs because your granddaddy kept a list of them pressed between the pages of his Bible?" He laughed. "You really got to him, didn't you?"

"Not that I recall."
"Not one word, huh?"
"Maybe one."
"When?"
"When he labeled me."
"As what?"
"A mental patient."
"And?"
"And he wouldn't stop talking about money."
"*Money?*"
"Yeah. How much it would take to fix me."
"And you said *what* to him."
"I just sort of asked him the same thing."
"What same thing?"
"You know, could *his* label be fixed?"
"What label?"
"It was just a joke."
"What label?"
"Jew."
No answer.
"You're one, too, aren't you?"
"I'm one what?"
"You're a Jew, too."
Still no answer.
Because he was.

I grinned. "No wonder you won't stand up to the man. You people sure stick together, don't you?" He didn't answer me directly, but more in what you might call a passive aggressive way.

"Your demons—and I mean no disrespect for *YOUR* roots—aren't behind a locked door. They are those competitors on that southern runway, racing to get to the crown at the end." He paused. "And why are you so angry with the administrator for trying to 'fix' you? Like *that* has never happened before! As for your fear of being thrown into a seclusion room—when *haven't* you been incarcerated? Guilt, discrimination, fear of success . . . *they've* kept you imprisoned most of your life! As for that abandonment phobia . . . well, you can blame your father for that one. Even those beauty pageant audiences were viewed as potential deserters." He stood. (Not a wise move, I thought, so soon after bringing up the abandonment thing.) "As for that 'magical thinking' farce," he sighed, "how many lines will you have to jump over to make the world see things your way?"

Are you catching on here? Every time I say the "J" word, one of them goes off on me!

He sauntered back and forth from the table to his desk, determined to dredge up as much crap about me as he could. I had to respect that; it was his job. I thought of how much he looked like the mental patients in the halls of the ward—pacing tirelessly, getting nowhere.

"After awhile, those obsessive thoughts can sure zap the strength from a person," he said. I marveled at how a man could be an authority on another's thoughts when he gave so little to his own. He sat and reached for his pipe, a move I had come to recognize as the precursor to sudden insight, invariably followed by a pensive pose. "Probably no more exhausting than the magical thinking. . . ." he added, orchestrating the brainstorm with his pipe. The man was in his element, obviously impressed with his own mind but more, it always appeared, with that pose.

Then, too, maybe he was just tired of pacing.

I cut in quickly, hoping to head off his next revelation. "This is probably not a good time to tell you how very much you remind me of a preacher back home who works out of the back of his truck."

"Probably not," he said, as he gave me the kind of look you'd expect from a Yankee psychiatrist who'd just been compared to a southern street preacher.

As he chomped down on the pipe I wondered how a man who believed himself to be so wise could be smoking an unlit pipe. Then, like he'd just discovered a sidewalk sample sale outside a retail store, he looked at me through eyes that had almost doubled in size.

"Oh, those choices we've been taught to make!" he exclaimed. "It starts early. For you—*very* early. That's probably why you lost your mind—well, not *lost your mind*, exactly, but more like lost the ability to *use your mind*. Can you imagine how different the world would be if more people had been given permission to think for themselves, then given *themselves* permission to make their own choices? They would likely be climbing off the tired backs of those donkeys and elephants, eager to form their own parties. . . . "

He rambled on, asking questions and answering them—for I don't know how long. I was drifting in and out. "Your granddaddy would roll over, wouldn't he?" I heard him ask. I attempted to respond with a knowing look, you know, like I, basically, gave a shit. "Well, I can assure you," he said, "I would've liked you a hell of a lot better if you'd remained that tomboy who beat her own drum!"

And that's what this is all about, isn't it? BEATING YOUR DAMN DRUM! Pleasing YOU! Sorry, I've pleased my quota of shrinks who need to have their drums beat! I pleased the last one all the way into an insane asylum!

"Your 'runways' were built from rocks of stigma, and that pedestal you created stood on those same rocks. If I were you right about now, I'd be taking off my tiara and chiseling away!" he said, annoyed. "Just look at your son! He seems to be hearing the *whole* band, not just a select few. What if you had slapped a label on him as you have on everyone else?"

Oh, good Lord, man. The kid's deaf, not Jewish.

"I'm convinced you've never really confronted your own myopia."

Like I needed another disorder nobody's ever heard of . . .

"Well, I'm sure you won't experience any discrimination when you leave here. There are millions of ex-mental patients out there who wouldn't *think* of judging you."

"Bastard."

"Of course, that will limit you somewhat—you know, to just one group. Not that you haven't always been, you know, limited."

"Bastard Jew."

"Go on, tell me how you really feel," he smirked.

"Okay," I said, "since you asked, here's a good one: 'You people wouldn't pay a dime to see a pissant pull a freight train.'"

"Already heard it," he said with a chuckle, most likely a lingering response to one of his own, earlier knee-slapping come-backs. "Listen," he perked up, "I've got one, too." He made a pathetic attempt at a southern brogue.

"Girl, yer the spitting image of yer mama!"

"*Spittin'* image," I snapped.

"Rich, poor, bus, town, black, white, first and last runner ups, Jews, protestants, Democrats and Republicans," he said, laying out a list of society's fortunate haves and unfortunate have-nots that fell quite short of being complete, if you know what I mean. "No wonder you stay so frustrated. How can you possibly decide who to eliminate? So many choices . . ."

If I had one now, I wouldn't be sitting here with your smart ass.

Dear Rosemary,
How is your family?
The Pageant Committee

Dear Pageant Committee,
Crazy as ever.
Rosemary

I was now a member of the most dysfunctional family on the planet. Inside the gates of our home—we liked to call it The Inn—my life was mostly about survival, that and loneliness. I was afraid my depression would consume the small slice of sanity I had somehow preserved—a fear that was being supported by the administrator who saw me as little more than a sumptuous feast for the panel of commitment cannibals at that sanity hearing.

I became fixated on the seclusion rooms—black desolate holes, much like the one in a recurrent dream I'd had after Daddy's death. Every night I had waited for a heroic rescue, but that never happened because my hero was gone. Granny told me the dreams weren't real and Granny was right about most things. But she was sure wrong about those dreams. The Mayor had vanished. Allie B was sick. Granny was dead. And Steve's newfound independence had reduced him to little more than a disobedient slave, greeting each new assignment with, "Fuck this shit." "Fuck this shit." "Fuck this shit."

I was afraid to stay, terrified to leave. It was just a matter of time until I'd be certified as a blithering idiot with nothing to save me but a fast-dwindling insurance policy. Maybe I was paranoid. But it certainly seemed to me that, given my ongoing affair with tragedy and continuing decline, I could be declared—by a board of the hospital's most impartial psychiatrists—nuts. Besides, if I wasn't crazy now, I had to have been a certifiable fruit loop the day I signed myself into this place.

Sometimes I visualized Aunt Allie B driving right up to the gates in her pickup, it's bed (in the shape of a glass slipper) filled with magic wands. A makeover on the seclusion rooms would be performed in preparation for a picture spread in the society section of the local paper back home. Allie B had always made me laugh with her ability to transform most anything into whatever she needed it to be. But this wasn't funny. Like a reality TV show gone bad, the place was extreme-makeover proof. This most likely explained why my small audience of close friends back home had tuned out this place and switched the channel to the town's big event—*the wedding of the Mayor!* Not that I blamed them.

Clearly, there was no one in my present to save me from the impending future—certainly not my therapist. Just as he *really* knew I was sane, I *really* knew he was a yellow-bellied wimp. And what did he know about me, anyway? A proponent of anything sexual, the thing that made a person certifiable in his mind was a blatant disinterest in it.

But maybe I *really was sick.* I hadn't told him the whole story about first grade. I can't believe I'm about to tell you now.

It wasn't my fault the teacher made me sweep the playhouse floor with my horse's tail. Damn that woman! HE WAS A HORSE, for goodness' sake! He was supposed to take a little girl into the wild blue yonder to find her daddy's secret hideout. Was I the only person who knew that? Apparently so.

The more I swept the more dirt I stirred up and the more dirt I stirred up the more I swept and the more I swept the angrier I got. In the sacred name of Gene Autry, The Sons of the Pioneers and Roy and Dale Evans— what was this teacher's problem?

Now what? Would I join the crowd and start sweeping poor Daddy under the rug like a pile of dirt? Would I be standing in one place forever and ever, amen—a buckaroo in an organdy apron with no more to hold onto in this life than a broom handle? Would I sweep and sweep until I came to the end of the dirt and discovered I'd swept my way into hell where I would spend an eternity for being a queer cowboy grinding a poor horse's butt into the dirt—or worse. For wasting my entire life standing in one place sweeping?

Not if I could help it.

My shirt, age 5.

"Girls can't be cowboys," the teacher said that first day of school. As she ordered Trigger and me to the girls' side of the playground, I wondered what happened to Daddy's words: "You can be anything you want to be." Then I remembered; they died with him.

As I swished Trigger's backside across the playhouse floor, I decided if I couldn't revive Daddy, I could sure bring back his words—and I did. The harder I swept, the louder his voice got, until his message was clear as the sky that formed the roof of that playhouse.

"You can be an Indian," he was saying.

"You can be an Indian warrior," he was getting very specific.

He didn't have to. The pow-wow was over, and this warrior had work to do.

While my assigned doll was napping by the tree trunk (growing from the center of the living room floor), I grabbed it by the hair and ran for the (swing set) hills. I used Frances Stone's jump rope to tie my prisoner's stiff little rubber body to the broom (stake), which I jammed into the muddy ground—all in preparation for the great burning.

"Quick! Get those matches while I take this white woman's clothes off and give them to my squaw," I screamed to the boys on the other side of the playground. I hoped the boy with the matches had heard me. He'd shown them to me earlier in the cafeteria. "Hurry!" I screamed again. "I've got her tied up! Get me those matches!"

The teacher arrived about two seconds after the matches and was so mad I was pretty sure she believed the white woman about to be burned at the stake was her.

Yeah, come to think of it, maybe I was crazy.

But maybe not. Lady Justice stepped in to remind me that from day one, I could simply have packed my bags and walked out the door. Of course, I always knew that. But just as this place fostered dependence, there was also regression. Each day I was more convinced that the thread I was hanging on to was connected to only half a brain. As luck would have it, just enough to be brainwashed. I found the broken end of a patient's plastic spoon easier to take than being told by the administrator I had brought the attack on myself. Probably by flaunting something. Most likely, my sanity.

"How could the outside world be more 'unsafe' than *this?*" the therapist asked, as he stepped up his campaign to get me out of The Rose Garden and into outpatient therapy. "Obviously, your depression is related to your fear of *leaving*. Don't you see a pattern here?"

"A problem with leaving?" I quipped. "No. Other than mamas, bad marriages, and mental hospitals . . . it's never happened before."

"Well, "he said firmly, "if you don't see the problem here, you never will! *This* place is enough to depress anyone—anyone sane. I get that way every time I walk onto the floor of that concentration camp you call home. Of course, living in the South would . . ."

"Uh-huh," I stopped him, "and we'd be pretty torn up too, knowing a Yankee was dragging his carpet bag through our cotton fields—slithering along like a snake on a boll weevil's back."

(Now, you and I know that statement made absolutely no sense—and the reason *I* know is because *he* laughed.)

I continued wallowing in what I perceived as escalating mental illness—battling dark thoughts and taking time out only for regularly scheduled rounds of self-analysis. Anything preceded by the word "self"* would do. As I became more attached to that word, I felt myself slowly, unattractively, going crazy. Not psychotic crazy, but the kind that comes with depression and makes you wish *were* crazy—crazy enough to escape the depression.

I tried to diffuse the administrator's seclusion room threats with humor. "Maybe I belong somewhere between crazy and sane, you know, like in a room with a bunch of shrinks or my in-laws, something like that." I mustered up a smile. "Isn't there a second choice?"

He didn't answer; he didn't have to. I was quite familiar with the way things worked: everything was black or white, town or country, cowboys or Indians. If you didn't choose one or the other, you'd find yourself alone on a playground with nothing to keep you company but the charred, blackened remains of that pale-faced white woman you'd stuffed into your lunch pail to take back to the tribe.

If I'd learned nothing else in life, I'd sure learned that.

---

*i.e., self-help, self-awareness, self-gratification, self-respect, self-destruction, self-effacing, self-love, and so-self-ish-I-can't-get-my-mind-off-my-sorry-assed-self-long-enough-to-think-of-anyone-but-myself.

25.
Weller than well

The day I got the last seclusion room warning, the administrator declared me well and told me to leave. I didn't know if it was positive thinking or an act of God, but apparently what I had come to find had shown up. It was magic—as magic as my actual departure. How else could I explain it when my insurance and I ran out at exactly the same time?

Recap:

I was asked to leave just after The Mayor left me which was just after my best friend hooked him up with her new best friend who left her house and job and most likely her own husband and/or someone else's (who could keep up?), moved into my house, brought her kid and took both of mine—along with my title, various articles of clothing, and several sacks of unopened Avon.

Shortly thereafter the administrator came up with a diagnosis for me. It was "Fear of Abandonment."

If I lie I die.

The news of my upcoming departure sent my depression back to its pre-mental hospital state of just your common ordinary run-of-the-mill, pissed-off rage, as it made a beeline for the administrator and a chain of people all the way back to the mother-in-law in Houston and that bitch who taught first grade. It had taken many grueling sessions but now my anger was coming faster than this shrink could get it down on my chart.

Clearly, I had tapped into my volcano-within and stirred up eruptions that had been bubbling beneath Lord-knows-how-many pancake masks for Lord-knows-how-many runways. I was ridding my space of predators, but if one slipped in, he'd get a dose of unmitigated wrath like the one served up with that hot Houston sauterne, only from a deeper bowl. The therapist couldn't have been more thrilled with my progress if it had been his own (and, as I was about to discover, it was).

My plan was laid out. At a privileges meeting I would be awarded the privilege of a shopping spree, unescorted, for a jump rope, matches, and broom. The administrator would mysteriously disappear. Suddenly his ashes would blow onto the grounds of The Rose Garden and form two humongous monuments—one, in the shape of a Blue Cross; the other, a Blue Shield. In his absence, I would conduct the next privileges meeting beneath a big tree beside the monuments where everyone would be denied the privilege of attending the memorial of his death but awarded the privilege of celebrating it at the after-party. Years of kiosk paychecks would go toward the purchase of beer, tacos, and anti-psychotic prescription drugs which the attendees would consume as they watched their un-milled grist pile up beside the monuments.

In the psychiatric kingdom revenge is huge—certainly more amenable to therapy than depression. I had arrived.

"Is this what the administrator meant by 'a danger to myself and others?'" I asked the therapist. He sauntered toward the door, which was normally his signal to me that our hour was up. But today he stopped mid-way and stood beside the couch where I was sitting.

"I don't know what he meant," he laughed, "but these homicidal ideations are what I view as a giant step for you."

As I stood to leave, he placed his hand on my head and gently eased me back down onto the sofa. "Wait a minute," he chuckled. "You can't leave until I pronounce you *weller than well.*" He paused a moment, then added, "And I can't leave until I pronounce me the same thing."

There you go. I'd expressed the therapist's own desire to snuff out the administrator! His anger had come up for air after years of being suppressed by his unconscious need for a paycheck.

The man was making progress, I'll swear he was.

THE CONFRONTATION

I never imagined God would show up in a place like this, and certainly not with the missing spine of my therapist! But there it was—an honest-to-God backbone on this follower of Freud. His once-yellow streak had suddenly turned a macho shade of redneck red as he clenched his jaws, stepped up to the plate, and called a meeting with the administrator and me.

"Your fixation with putting her in a seclusion room—now *that's* insane!" he said to the bewildered leader of my ward. "There's not a psychotic thought in her head. Not now. Not next week. Not ever! And you *knew* that!" His face was on fire. "She should've turned around and walked right out of here the day she arrived!" He hesitated, I assumed, to search for words that would take it all back. Instead, he'd worked out a killer ending. "Outpatient therapy is where she belonged—and frankly," he sighed, "that would've been just fine with me."

This Yankee shrink had just done a near-perfect impersonation of a rifle-toting redneck protecting his chicken-eating mad dog from being locked up or blown out the back of a pick-up truck. In my attempt to help the man, I had taught him that expressing anger was a good thing, and he was sure giving it a trial run—as a southerner, for some strange reason, but he was doing it, just the same. Obviously, I'd neglected to tell him to stay within his (Yankee) comfort zone. I'd also forgotten to teach him about humor.

"Why'd you do that?" I asked him, as I watched the administrator walk away like a sissy little girl. His jaw dropped. "Dammit," I threw up my hands. "You should've asked me first!"

"ASKED YOU? ASKED YOU WHAT?" He was losing it.

"Well, maybe—just maybe—I wanted to be a lunatic!" I said, basking in the success of what I was pulling off. I stepped closer and raised my voice. "In this place, joining a group of people who don't know where the hell they are was beginning to sound pretty good to me!"

If he hadn't been concerned about what Freud would think, I'll swear, the man would've taken his own life right there on the spot.

26.
Southern Belle Disorder

"The irony of this whole thing is that you are probably less imprisoned here than you have been most of your life! Of course, it's easy to see why you signed yourself into this place; you've been masquerading as a mental patient for quite some time now. I'm sure the paperwork was easy to fill out! But if you weren't *committed*, we need to address what got you *admitted*. It wasn't psychosis," the therapist said, shaking his head. "If only it were that simple," he mumbled. "'Southern Belle Disorder' is a perfect name for the culprit."

SOUTHERN BELLE DISORDER! If you honestly believe I'm the most prejudiced person in this room, I have some old beauty-pageant memorabilia in a farmhouse on swamp land next to a cotton field crawling with Mississippi boll weevils to sell you.

In this our last session, he laid it all out. *This* misinformed woman hadn't started out as a half-brained child after all. "Issues? Yes," he said. "OCD . . . yes, again. A learning disability? Probably. But stupidity? No! In fact," he grinned, "it took a pretty good brain to talk your way into two mental hospitals."

I guess the part about not being half-brained should've been good news, but it wasn't. I mean, call me stupid, but this new label sounded like it would be harder to cure than the congenital, half-a-brain thing I'd struggled with up until now.

Southern Belle Disorder (SBD)* was a condition he blamed on most everything not found in his medical books, which seemed to include most of my problems as well as our regional and religious differences—with emphasis on all the times I'd offended him by calling attention to them. The only cure was to dismantle and reconstruct the Southern Belle within.

Today the renovation was all about sex.

As always, we examined my upbringing—like how I wore swimsuits onstage and then carried Bibles at home to be forgiven for it. And exhibitionism. Mine was constantly lurking, but not solely for me; it

*A made-up disorder that began as a joke—until this shrink started believing it was real.

150

was also for my mother. My mother, who had a need to hide so many of her assets, had an even bigger need to have them recognized.

And get this. According to him, the lemon meringue pies that showed up at practically every church social and Bible study—the same meringue women slaved over for days—had actually been ejaculated. Since he obviously enjoyed that kind of talk, I went along with it, although, for the most part, I had not one clue what he was talking about, as no men in my family would ever do that sort of thing and were not allowed in the kitchen anyway. Besides, it was the women who were obsessed with piling on the meringue.

The higher the better.

Eventually I came to understand that EVERYTHING in the universe, good or bad, stems from the expression or repression of sex—and that holding it back actually lies at the bottom of hysterical neuroses. Now that got my attention!

I hadn't been sure what a hysterical neurosis was, but knew there was a lot of the other kind I wanted to shake, so, when I got out of this place I would solve the whole mess. Okay, stay with me here.

According to this theory, all I had to do to stop the compulsions was replace them with sex. But I had a better idea. I would transfer those annoying urges to the bedroom! By integrating the jerking, jumping, eye blinking, wiggling, and fidgeting into the sex act itself, I would be expressing (sex) with the very things I needed to repress (the neuroses). Perfect! I'd be performing the act that would free me FROM the compulsions WITH the compulsions! Are you catching on? Can't you visualize it? Well, I sure could. I could even imagine clapping my hands during the act and washing them afterward. But finding someone to do it in even numbers?

Now that would turn out to be a problem.

"Oh yes," he said, "Southern Belle Disorder is harder to fight than any mental disorder I've encountered. I'm taking on everyone who ever told you how to think—every teacher, minister, southern politician, relative, beauty pageant judge, and town gossip. You need to understand that this disorder escorted you right up to the locked doors and barred windows of this nuthouse," he said, "and by taking on the label of 'mental patient,' you have once again assisted others in determining who you are. Naturally, you're being treated accordingly."

Oops! Did I miss something here? Just exactly who is passing out labels? When a Yankee tells a woman she has "Southern Belle Disorder," what do you think that is—chopped liver?

I shook my head in agreement before asking him, "And how long did it take you to get your label . . . I mean, title? You know, 'psychiatrist?'"

I didn't expect an answer. Good thing.

"And one more thing," I snapped. "You surely don't believe that SBD, as you describe it, is limited to the South—or to women!"

No response. His label for me was, obviously, "absent."

He kept on. "You will not find the answers you are searching for until you're free of everyone else's expectations and opinions of you—mine included—and are introduced to yourself, a person, I predict, you will regret not having met sooner."

"But, then, that's just my opinion."

The Fantasy of the Cold Wet Sheet Pack

Okay, so maybe I hadn't gotten to know myself all that well in this place, but I was sure becoming acquainted with sex—specifically, the sexual fantasy.

It started with room service.

Thank God, instead of ordering what my neighbors were getting in this hotel, I had the good sense to opt for the *fantasy* of what they were getting, instead. I didn't need to set the scene; the choreography had already been worked out, big as life, right there on the ward. I had stood in the wings and listened to the process until I had it down.

It was all about cold wet sheet packs (CWSPs) which, given their abundance in this hotel, turned out to be the most logical choice on the menu. Mind you, I never got a real one, but that was probably best. Reality, as I was discovering, is not always about happy endings while fantasies, as I already knew, are.

Commonly used in mental hospitals before the advent of Thorazine, CWSPs were an archaic, drug-free method of restraint. The sheets were kept in ice-filled coolers which, like most everything else in the place, frequently doubled as urinals for the insane. But, seeing as how this was going to be my very own fantasy, I took the liberty of eliminating that part from it.

The movie I produced and directed in my mind was the one thing in The Rose Garden I could orchestrate. In fact, the only medication this place dispensed turned out to be the right drug and the perfect dosage for me.

THE REALITY: The psychiatric aides delivered and administered the cold wet sheet packs to agitated patients and, really, they were no big deal. Not in an asylum. About three to four times a day alarms would go off, followed by the sound of stampeding young men—virile, muscular, drop-dead gorgeous-if-you'd-been-confined-as-long-as-I-had-or-married-to-The-Mayor—psychiatric aides. They stormed the hall, then entered the room of the screaming lunatic who was stripped to his or her underwear, placed in a hospital gown, wrapped like a mummy from neck to ankle in icy white sheets, and then strapped to a bed for several hours. The process was supposed to induce shivering, followed by womb-like warmth, and, ultimately, exhaustion.

Precisely the same thing I felt during the fantasy.

THE FANTASY: The whole ceremony was nothing more than a perverted outlet for the sexual desires of the horney male hospital staff—just another trumped up excuse for S-E-X. My fantasy sometimes starred "the insane women of the asylum," others, "the homicidal babes from the cell block," and others, "the subservient nuns of the convent," and my personal favorite, "just your average, everyday, horny housewives." All four featured helpless, tormented, trapped-against-their-will females—and, of course, every last one of them was me.

The movie played out on the blank screen of my sexually challenged-but-eager-to-learn-mind each time I heard the mental patients'/inmates'/Sisters'/housewives' screams, followed by flailing and wailing, moaning and groaning, and begging for mercy, as their straight jackets/prison uniforms/habits/aprons were ripped from their quivering (perfect) bodies in preparation for the inevitable mummy wrap. At least, through the peeling walls in my room, that's how it sounded to my naked ear.

Forced Sex. Sex as it should be—out-of-my-control sex, with no way I could *EVER* be held responsible. Think about it. A brigade of hungry male animals, taking advantage of this poor, defenseless, deranged, politically and socially misguided woman, with such liberal leanings, her fantasies were ex-rated. This would be perfectly acceptable, clinical sex—unabridged, guilt-free, unprovoked, down and dirty, completely sober (yet-southern) hospital sex. And the whole thing would be staged by the staff and paid for by none other than ... *are you ready for this one? THE INSURANCE COMPANY!!!*

Oh, sister, pay those premiums!

At the administrator's staff meeting, it was decided that never should a cold wet sheet pack touch my body because it was as obvious as an erection that the procedure, for me, had a sexual connotation with orgasmic overtones and absolutely NO aspects whatsoever of the archaic, cruel, and unusual punishment for which it was intended. Sex was obviously not his thing while for the therapist, it was not only his thing—it was his treatment plan.

Once again, I appeared to be standing in the shade of that ever-present Family Tree; trapped inside the schizoid split down the middle; answering to two opposing sides, as opposite as any two sides could be. Outside a person's immediate family, that is.

27.
"I was in circumstances that made the salary an object."

— Mark Twain

Even though my departure was imminent, the strict house rules at The Rose Garden remained the same. In fact, *leaving* had now climbed to number two on the charts of hell (with actually *living* there still on top). As long as there was the possibility of squeezing one last dime from a patient, the hospital kept a tight rein. Ironically, the whole thing was now working in my favor; I had no place to go.

Since the pricey hospital-owned rental property across the street was the target for my next move, The Rose Garden was happy to let me stay on the ward until I found a job to pay the rent. My own plan was somewhat similar to theirs, but with a slight twist in the clause concerning rental arrangements. I *was* looking for a job to pay the rent, true, but it didn't involve the place across the street.

I interviewed with three government agencies. Each told me to expect a call in the next few days. I gave them the ward's payphone number, then waited for it to ring and prayed to God I would be close by when it did. Like my earnings from the kiosk, I guarded that phone. For twenty-four hours, I lived beside it, took my meals there, read there, dressed there, slept there. I did everything but, big mistake, go to the bathroom there. Nothing could possibly go wrong.

Except for a couple of trips to the bathroom, I stood beside that phone and challenged anyone, no matter how insane and combative, to pick it up. But upon my return from one of those necessary trips, I rounded the corner and saw the receiver slowly, tragically, approaching crazy Steve's ear. Next came the all-too-familiar voice of insanity speaking into that phone. I went numb. In decibels that could burst an eardrum, he was answering, "Yes, Rosemary's in," as I lunged for the phone and grabbed it from his hand—but not before he added, "her room fucking dogs."

Since the pay phone number had been left with three prospective employers, I wasn't sure which one had called. But I was pretty sure that fucking dogs was not in any of their position descriptions.

In an unusual streak of luck, I didn't have to confront the problem, as there was nothing but a dial tone when the phone, finally, reached my ear.

My feelings were mixed. The young man who had answered the phone, my friend Steve, had been in and out of La-La-Land, mostly in, for ten years. Until today he had repeated every sentence three times and that sentence had predictably been, "What do you want me to do?" "What do you want me to do?" "What do you want me to do?" although recently his repertoire had been downgraded to, "Fuck this shit." "Fuck this shit." "Fuck this shit."

I had anticipated the day this twenty-five-year-old man would move beyond those short sentences delivered in triplicate. Today he had. His new vocabulary had been taken for a trial run as he stepped outside his comfort zone. I only wished he hadn't chosen this particular day to step out of his and tromp all over mine.

I cherished my friendship with Steve. Unlike other relationships, this one was uncomplicated and terribly consistent. In the beginning, it centered on a cookie and a psychiatric aide: Steve pointed to the kitchen; I found a psychiatric aide to unlock the door; the aide gave me the cookie; and I presented it to Steve. As he got better, Steve learned to reciprocate by picking up cookies and anything else I needed from the kiosk. I intended to continue his classes with lessons about paying for these things but decided that with no other marketable skills, stealing might be his only ticket to survival in the outside world. Besides, I couldn't bear the thought of poor Steve hanging around a cash register squawking, "What does this cost?" "What does this cost?" "What does this cost?"

I did the right thing.

About those prospective employers: they were all from the National Institute of Mental Health and—Gospel Truth—I eventually came clean about the past two years and got hired. Of course, it was the federal government and I did have a year of on-the-job training at a similar institution.

28.
Still crazy after all these years

"Say it! Say it! *Dammit, Rosemary*, tell the woman. Tell the woman. Tell the woman you are mentally ill!"

The social worker was completely out of control.

She had accompanied me to the social security office because, understandably, the job offers were not rolling in from the National Institute of Mental Health, nor was money—from any source. The hospital was still operating under the misconception that I was going to pay rent at their half-way-house across the street or, as I like to label this particular fantasy, "It'll be a cold day in hell."

I had now been discarded and replaced by The Mayor, cut off by the insurance company, and written off by the people downstairs. Soon I'd be standing in line for a block of government cheese beside the poor souls who slipped in the back door at Jones Theater and ate popcorn off the floor.

I sat in this government office and begged for money like I was groveling for the administrator's approval. In fact, it was exactly the same. "I am mentally ill. I have been mentally ill for two years, and I will remain that way as long as you need me to be," I pleaded, as I dutifully presented my case for that hospital-owned housing. "I need to live across the street from a mental hospital, you know, just in case I suddenly turn on myself or someone else. But with my allowance, insurance, and husband running out on me—Lord knows, I can't afford to be crazy."

I was one sip of Ginger Ale away from hurling on the document I had just sworn to when the social worker jumped in. "And she can barely take care of herself and certainly not her children so she needs support at this time and she will eventually be okay alone but in large groups we just don't know and she can't type but she can answer the phones and she is broke."

Well, I'll give her one thing. I *was* broke, but I beg her pardon. I sure as hell could type.

Thank you, Lord.

I was awarded a sum of money nowhere near what I had given these people over the years, but far more than I currently had. By my calculations I could now afford an apartment, and I had a few options: six months of rent with three roommates, or four months of rent with two. Or two months of rent with one. Or one month of rent with none. Or one year of Jack Daniels and a seclusion room.

The day I received the severance check, I traveled to that small corner in my half-a-brain where life made sense and everything always came out in my favor. There I remained until I understood how blessed I was to be awarded such a small amount of money, because the big bucks were reserved for the *truly* insane who had to give their money to mental hospitals anyway.

> *And another thing about that check. Historically, Southern Belles have had a tendency toward exaggeration, and I also have that tendency—so let me preface the following information by telling you that this is The Gospel Truth: Two days after I finished this book, I received a letter from the social security disability folks stating they had inadvertently overpaid me $250 thirty years ago. A statement for that amount was attached. I could not make this up.*
>
> *Had I known this a few decades earlier, I'll swear, I would gladly have given up my apartment for the seclusion room and a case of Jack Daniels. Just so you know.*

On my last day, I met with the therapist. He assured me he hadn't fallen in love with me during my stay and in his wildest dreams, could not imagine how the other therapist could have.

I laughed, but only because he needed me to.

"First I want you to know that I had considered writing a book about this experience." I said.

"So, what's stopping you?"

"Not wanting to sound paranoid is what stops me. Everything I write about my life and psychiatric therapy makes me sound really *paranoid*. Everyone seems to be trying to incapacitate me in some way—this place included. No, this place especially. So . . . where did all these predators find the time and energy to ruin my life? What made them put their lives on hold to mess around with mine? Sorry. It makes no sense. No sense at all."

He nodded knowingly. "Look, if we had placed all the blame where it probably belonged—on you—therapy would have gone on forever! It's simply more time and cost effective to hold others accountable: family, hospital, ex-husbands, the new First Lady, mothers-in-law . . ."

Oh my Lord, I think he's serious!

He reached into a drawer and retrieved a small package wrapped in brown paper, held together with a shoelace bow. Inside was a pair of socks with a couple of holes in the toes and at least four other threadbare reminders that I was not their first. I looked across the room at the previous owner and tried to come up with a Freudian connection.

"They're the ones I wear with my running shoes," he smiled. "I should have given them to you the day you arrived! Of course, *that* woman would never have considered a pair of socks with holes in the toes, or leaving a place—not even a marriage—not even a mental hospital—where she didn't belong." He gazed out the window facing the road, then turned to me. "Just the same, on some level I hoped you would turn and run from this place before it sucked you in." His smile caught both of us by surprise. "But I'm glad you didn't. We've done some good work. You've come a long way."

"Not really," I said, as I prepared to turn a moment of slight discomfort into many moments of excruciating stupidity. I jokingly revisited our first meeting. "Has anyone ever told you how attractive you are?" I hummed.

Undaunted, he continued. "Despite a few setbacks, like the performance I just witnessed, I believe you've begun the laborious process of dismantling the Southern Belle within. But have patience," he grinned, "the reconstruction process will probably go on for the rest of your life."

So here was this psychotherapist/wanna-be comedian, who had been my only ally in this madhouse—this Albert Einstein/Woody Allen on a bad day look-alike Yankee—who had found such joy in tapping into all things sacred, sexual, and southern. And here was this southerner, who had wanted so to connect with anything or anyone disconnected from this hell hole of a concentration camp. But through the process, had this southerner developed a fondness for the man? Or was he simply all she had left? And, how did he really feel about her? Was she as irresistible as she thought she was? Only one way to find out.

One more time. Enter: her seductress-within—kittenish purr, sexy pose, the whole package. Next: the weapon handed down by her father—sharp wit, with an edge guaranteed to cut through the pipe smoke and Freudian funk surrounding the throne of any shrink. Add: the repeated screwing of herself, an act of masochism likely more painful to watch than to perform.

"Now . . . you've often asked me why I signed up for this vacation," I said slowly, southernly, half-seriously, half-not. "Well," I teased, "let me ask you: 'what is a nice guy like you doing in a place like this?'" My left eyebrow went up as my corresponding shoulder moved forward, indicating a genuine interest in his answer—maybe more. I had his attention. "I mean, you have been such a joy, so delightful to talk to. I really hate to leave. I wonder why?" I asked, playfully. To which he, who had obviously graduated from a different charm school, replied,

"Because you are so fucking crazy."

For the second time with this therapist I had the good sense to cancel any further seduction and/or humor; for the third time, I knew there wasn't a snowball's chance in hell that he had fallen in love with me; for the first time, I was absolutely positive I had left my seductress-within back at that other hospital.

I looked at the clock. My hour was up but he seemed to be ignoring it. I wondered how much longer we would dance around my departure. "Before you leave, tell me . . . *why now?* " he asked. "Why didn't you leave sooner?"

"You know," I sighed, "you may be a psychiatric scholar, but you are sure clueless on the subject of The Southern Belle—this one, for sure. So let me give you a snap course. It's like this: a Belle doesn't leave *anyplace*—even an *abusive place*—without making 'nice' on her way out. And it doesn't matter if she's leaving one predator or one hundred, she sticks around as long as it takes to absorb each morsel of pain, then searches every last nook and cranny for pain she might have missed, knowing if she racks up enough of it—like frequent flier miles—she'll earn a free trip to The Land of Hope which, typically, means seeing the whole mess to its bitter end even if, in the end, it means seeing *herself* to her *own* bitter end. From a crowd of 100 men or women she selects the one with the most pain to give who likes her least, then devotes her time and energy to the process of turning things around. In The Rose Garden the obvious choice was the administrator—the only judge in this contest whose vote seemed to count."

"So naturally you focused on winning him over."

"Sure did. And, predictably, it got me exactly what that sort of thinking has gotten every woman in the universe since the reign of Adam and Eve."

"What's that?" he asked.

"The SOB got worse," I said. "You all do."

A perfect parting remark, I thought. I reached for my purse, but he kept talking. "There's something I need to know about you. . . or, actually, about southern women," he said.

"Sure, ask me. Ask me anything."

"Well, no offense, but it's your language. I was under the impression that a bona-fide Southern Belle doesn't swear."

"She swears only when referring to Yankee men," I laughed.

"Get serious . . ."

"Okay," I complied, "this *impression* you were under—was this the same one that compelled you to attach my entire existence to that 'Southern Belle' label? Have I ever blamed *your* every move on *your* label, you know . . . 'son-of-a-bitch?'"

"Yankee Jew SOB," he corrected me.

"And was this the *impression* you were under when you grouped all southern women together like a bouquet of wilting gardenias, defenseless against the elements, hovering beneath the dark shade of a phallic parasol, with our petals turning a shade browner every time they got poked by its oversized handle?"

"Until they turned all the way black?" he asked quickly, as though determined to jump in and reclaim his role as Freud the Fabulous.

"Could be."

He shook his head, "Talk about your sexual fantasies! That one had you abandoning your own race! My word, woman! *Black sex?*"

"*BLACK SEX?* Where did that come from?" I shrieked, louder than I meant to. "Lord, man! Don't we all do it pretty much the same way? In some circles, you'd be labeled a racist SOB!"

"A Yankee racist Jew SOB!" he said, almost proudly.

He quickly switched back to the 'cussing' question as it seemed to have something to with another of his fantasies. It also relieved him of having to confront being a racist SOB. Then, too, it delayed my departure—again.

"So, do the rest of you southern gals swear—or are you going to blame your language on us 'damn Yankees,' or the insane, or both?" He laughed.

"Is there a difference?"

He almost grinned. Another perfect time to leave, I thought, as I started toward the door. He got there first.

Awkwardly, he shook my hand and said a quick good-bye.

I was out the door and on my way to the elevator when I heard my name. I turned and saw him standing just outside his office door. "Frankly, I'm disappointed," he said. "I thought you Southern Belles were, as *y'all* say, 'ladylike'—you know, demure, classy, sophisticated. . . ." Before I had a chance to answer he asked, "Or is that—now, how do you so delicately put it?—'*bullshit?*'"

As the elevator door closed in front of me, I realized the man hadn't come as far as I'd thought. By now, he should have known to stay away from Miss Scarlett's Web.

But, alas, he was caught. When that psychiatric phenomenon known as The Disorder of The Southern Belle crossed the Mason-Dixon Line and penetrated his protective armor—girlfriend, he was toast. The Yankee shrink who had finally convinced this southern woman that she deserved to be free, was, today, refusing to let her go. With each replay of *Gone with the Mental Patient,* his own issues blocked her exit.

Was the man a sissy little girl, crying over a skinned knee, or simply paralyzed by his own fear of abandonment? Or . . . Ohmilord! Was it possible this carpetbagger had enjoyed Tara more than he meant to? Had he actually given a damn?

It looked that way.

Well, fiddle-dee-dee. I couldn't concern myself with that now. My time was up; my job, finished. After all, I *had* taught the man to express anger and, in a round-about-way, affection. My only regret was that he knew nothing about letting go. Poor baby. He had not one clue about how to say good-bye.

Not to a Southern Belle.

29.
Somebody help the man!
He can't get out of this mess by himself!

I was still questioning this extended vacation as I sat in the chair facing the administrator's desk. My feet—that had seemed to dangle from this same chair at our initial meeting—were now touching the floor. I was a big girl, for the moment.

At this our final meeting, I continued my attempts to ease the nervous tension between us, but bungled it worse than ever. Today I made a joke about leaving The Rose Garden with his diagnosis, "fear of abandonment," after being dumped by my husband, thrown out of the hospital, and deserted by the insurance company. "How's that for irony?" I asked. Like always I laughed, and like always, he analyzed what I said that he didn't laugh about. This time it was all about my laugh, itself.

Play it again, Sam.

"Have you ever paid attention to your laugh?" he asked. "Have you listened to it—*really listened to it?*"

No chance to answer. He answered for me.

"It's so—well—*forced,*" he continued. "Your laugh isn't real."

Seizing the opportunity to throw it in one more time, he said, "It's grist for the mill. Your laugh is definitely grist for the mill."

Uh-huh. And your mouth is definitely getting on my last nerve. Thank God you're a damn Yankee talking fifty miles a minute because if your venom came oozin' out like it's supposed to—slow and easy like molasses rolling off a snail's back heading straight for an open wound—I couldn't sit here like a lady and take this shit.

Like a starving man with only minutes to devour a large turkey, he chowed down. "And, too," he frowned, as I envisioned the ticking clock, "in your next relationship—if there is one—I hope you won't make the same mistakes that ended your marriage."

(The only thing that kept me from laughing out loud at that statement was knowing how much the bastard hated my laugh.)

"And another thing," he said, "I really don't know what it is about you—I think it's your offbeat sense of humor, maybe that's a regional thing—but people sure get the wrong idea. . . ." He leaned forward. "Again, I'm telling you for your own good—be careful."

Trouble was, Southern Belles had to be careful about being funny. Careful, careful, careful . . .

"As they say," he persisted, 'just because you think you're paranoid doesn't mean you're not being watched.'"

"You got that right," I concurred. "For as long as I can remember, I've been watched."

It seemed that each time this man and I got together, I went kicking and screaming all the way back to the confusion of my childhood. Today memories of those years raced through my mind with such force I was sure the expression on my face would give me away.

I have to be careful. I don't know why. I have to be someone else. I don't know who. I have to hide, and I don't know where. I have to watch out for those people and I don't know who they are but if I find them, I'll be afraid. Then just like always, I won't know why. Maybe it's because they might think I've been thinking thoughts like those I've been told to be careful about, even though I have never learned what those thoughts would have been if I had actually been thinking them. But I'm only six years old—too young to understand grown-ups and why they think like they do or what they expect little girls to think or what they think about little girls who look for their fathers, play with the coloreds, laugh too loud, and dance in liquor stores for applause and popsicles and such.

"Yes, I've always wanted to say something to you about your laugh," he repeated. "As I said, 'it's so forced.'"

Once again he validated what I already knew; I needed to change.

As a child, that message had sometimes been straight out, other times not. It was those other times I wanted to trade places with the boy who sat across from me in first grade. Oh, sure, his skin was a canvas for the red stripes and occasional open wounds you saw the moment he walked into the classroom—but that boy *knew*. Every time his mama said, "Cut me a switch," he knew she was getting ready to scream about what needed fixing. And when he bawled, she'd say, "I'll give you something to cry about," and then he knew he'd need to fix the bawling, too.

Me, I never got whippings. Sight unseen I had to hunt down the bad parts of myself I wasn't sure about. The others were labeled, "She's just like her daddy," and I knew exactly where they were. They were tucked away in that place where I kept Daddy alive. Taking pieces of myself from there was like chipping away at the parts of him I still had access to—like his big, loud, laugh. It was like no one else's except, I always thought, my own.

So now I was facing the man who could sweep me back to the pain of my childhood and then return me to a near-identical present. But today the woman who had so willingly reinvented herself for him this past year had changed her colors for the last time. The chameleon was dead. After he dumped my laugh into that bottomless pile of "grists for his mill," *that was it!* My laugh was all I had left. There was nothing more to attack.

Oh, but of course there was! This was The Rose Garden. There was always something else to attack.

"And another thing," he continued, "everything you say sounds so *rehearsed*. Everything that leaves your mouth is so measured, so *PLANNED*."

Now that's just great! With no rehearsal, I'm expected to walk onto your stage au naturale' without, most likely, makeup. I must be impromptu—but not funny; needy—while asking for nothing; crazy—but just crazy enough to keep the checks coming in; and sane—but just sane enough to snap out of being crazy when the checks stop. Well, I don't think so. Not this Southern Belle. I've performed on your stage for the last time!

Well, hallelujah! It was over. The bastard had finally reached the bottom of his barrel and damn-near drained mine. He'd taken my identity, my family, all of my insurance, and a good portion of the tiny bit of self-confidence I'd had on my arrival, and now he wanted me to walk out the door with the same insecurities that had plagued me my entire life. *And my laugh!* Now he wanted to take my laugh! Oh, I don't think so. *This was it!* Cinderella was leaving this ball. The party was over, and not one mental hospital minute too soon!

Okay, not completely over.

I heard a familiar voice, mine unfortunately, questioning the ethics of an obsolete, run-down private hospital that charged its residents the equivalent of a new home and kidney. That same voice denounced the inhumane treatment of people locked away for years in seclusion rooms. In an effort to finish me off, it accused the staff of not doing their jobs. Then there were detailed, albeit *unrehearsed and spontaneous,* instructions as to where their leader should stick his mill and all the grist in it.

To accurately convey those instructions, I tapped into the cesspools of my crazy housemates' minds and retrieved the appropriate words. After I settled on a few old favorites—motherfucker, fuckhead, and fucking fuckhead—I worked them into my instructions, then thanked the Lord for the mental patients who taught them to me and the insurance company that funded my one-year, hands-on training.

I approached the door, lingering just long enough to misuse *and* mispronounce "mozeltoff!" and to kick myself a couple of times for doing it. Suddenly I envisioned the administrator's office as a seclusion room and him as a prisoner, surrounded by the undesirables whose names had reverberated through seclusion room doors—*whores! Mexicans! Redneck sons-of-bitches and lawyers!*

As the door shut behind me, I wondered if his mill could hold just one more grist.

Oh, but of course it could! This was The Rose Garden. There was always room for just one more grist—just one more grist for the mill!

I threw open the door. "And just one more thing. In the dictionary, 'grist' is defined as 'a potential source of advantage or profit to somebody.'" I laughed. "Well, my grist has sure lined a few pockets around here, don'cha think?" Without giving him a chance to answer, not that he would have, I proceeded. "But you know, I think you were right—after all, you're *ALWAYS* right. As predicted, I *have* gone stark raving mad! Listen! I'm hearing the voices of those angry gods, right here in this room, shouting through the grist. Do you hear them?" I asked, more loudly than I probably should have. Suddenly I realized the time for turning back was passing—and that was okay. I chose to go forward.

"Listen, listen closely," I commanded, as he backed up a couple of steps, then stood motionless, obviously befuddled. "The voices are telling me the balance of power has shifted! Looks like you'll have to find another inmate to intimidate and humiliate—and did I say 'depersonalize?'" I took a step toward him. "*S u w a n n e e!* Just look at yourself . . . drowning in your own grist! Well, look at it this way. I've sure loaded up the ol' mill with it today! And, best of all . . . not one thing I've said was P L A N N E D!"

Do hush, Mama!

When he stepped back, I assumed he was edging toward the phone to summon that on-call army of psychiatric aides with their tubs of icy sheets. I didn't stick around to find out. I made a dash toward the door but was stopped by another familiar presence. It was the witch I portrayed for the boys every Halloween. I stood powerless as her voice took over mine.

"Have you ever paid attention to your laugh?" she cackled. She wouldn't let me stop. I circled him as though guarding my brew. "I mean, have you ever *really* listened to it?" I screeched. "Of course you haven't," I answered myself, "because you've never laughed one day of your miserable life!" Then I laughed. I laughed out loud. And then I laughed out loud even louder. And then some more. I laughed and laughed and laughed. It was inappropriate, drunker 'n Cooter Brown, raucous, high-pitched, screaming-out-loud and obnoxious as Aunt Allie B-cutting-off-jock-straps—laughing. Hooten' n' hollerin' lunatics-in-seclusion rooms—laughing.

Suddenly I remembered the *one* laugh I had enjoyed such a long time ago. So, following the bad laughs of everyone I had ever known, I gave the man a big dose of that laugh Southern Belles have to be careful about. It was the one I had locked away in the seclusion room of my youth—my wonderfully spontaneous, unstoppable laugh. It was the laugh of my daddy and every bus and balcony kid who'd ever been shut out of my childhood!

But, like any laugh that comes over you suddenly—unplanned, unforced, unrehearsed, and real—I forgot to stop and listen, *really listen,* to it.

I had just walked away from my third marriage without signing the papers that would set me free. But I was always free, wasn't I? Of course, my third husband *was* The Rose Garden, and you don't ever really divorce a mental hospital.

On sheer faith I had pledged to honor and obey, for better or worse, in sickness and health, with the understanding that if my marriage to this place actually caused the sickness, I would claim it as my own and see it through, regardless of the consequences. Expecting no more from this union than others, I enjoyed only the bogus sense of safety I got from merely being in it, with no clue I had signed up for another cruise on a sinking ship–with an over-zealous tour guide.

It was a contract. People like me have conditions they agree to in most all their relationships, and it doesn't matter whether those relationships are with people or mental hospitals. A contract is a contract. But it hadn't taken me long in this asylum to realize how much the one I agreed to as a child looked like the one I had signed to take on mental illness! Unfortunately, breaching either of them had turned out to be trickier than I thought.

As the seasons passed in The Rose Garden, my platform had looked more and more like the magical stage of the beauty pageant. My performance would have to be perfect. Whether it should be "perfectly crazy" for the administrator or "perfectly Freudian" for the therapist, I was never quite sure. "Perfectly perfect" for God I was sure about. I may have been stupid but, Lord knows, I knew from the get-go that He wouldn't want to get involved.

The Rose Garden supported my belief that the world was too big for me and, though the therapist had a different opinion, it was no surprise that the voice of doom was the loudest. It was the one I had answered to throughout a very troubled childhood.

In the administrator's world, I was headed toward a small room still occupied by the lingering hallucinations and unanswered cries for help of its former residents. In the world of my psychiatrist, I was headed north, east or west. Any place that wasn't south. In the world of the psychiatrist at the first hospital, I was headed for . . . Oh, I don't know, I had a couple of theories. "Weller than well" was certainly one, while The Holiday Inn across the street from the hospital ran a close second.

Whatever the expectation or idea of perfection, I knew how to rehearse for it and I did. For two years I had followed the rules in two hospitals—rules I never understood, yet knew very well. My life was all about pleasing other people—measuring up to their idea of who I should be. There was an unspoken promise that when I got it right, I would move on to somebody's definition of perfection, found only in that perfect world of perfect women. But just exactly what that world was, who those women were, and what I had to do to sign up, has remained a mystery ever since.

Small and familiar, my universe had extended no further than the wrought-iron gates barely visible from my window; yet I asked God every night to keep reminding me I belonged in the real world, on the other side. Unfortunately The Rose Garden, with the house rules of a cult, shut it out. My only hope was to admit I was lost and then relinquish the reins to my partner, an all too familiar union, with one person promising the other a better life—for a price. But this partner had nothing left to give, and all she had left to lose was her mind.

Fortunately, she had lost her insurance, instead.

30.
A promise kept . . .

"There were no free rides for children who couldn't make up their minds—only deserted playgrounds where they must spend an eternity trying to find a way to leave, and another one figuring out why they were afraid to leave after they found a way."

I passed the lounge and those plant-lined windowsills on my way to the elevator. It was visitors' day and the room had been cleared of crazy patients and urine smells long enough for the head nurse to conduct a tour for a potential new patient's family. As always, there was special emphasis on the plants—but today, even more on the patient whose plants were the biggest of all.

She interrupted the tour to say farewell to her "star patient," the one who had come the farthest, the one with the exciting "future." I, in turn, said farewell to the head nurse, the potential new patient, his family, and my plants. Then I joined the nurse in praising the other patients for growing theirs, while concurring that the biggest and tallest were, indeed, mine. But it was my parting remark, "As for me, folks, I tower over no one, never did, never will, and—in spite of the $136,000 it set me back—I sure as hell haven't grown . . . ." that ended my tour of The Rose Garden, and, I like to think, the potential patient's tour of duty as well.

It occurred to me I was leaving on Halloween Day, yet these ghosts and goblins were sporting the same ghoulish masks they'd worn all year. I had been their best friend, an incarcerated Mother Teresa with kitchen privileges—bearing love, guacamole, and apple-cider-turned-to-wine. I had been queen of the mental ward, the mother to its children—and a lot like the woman who had been a mother to me.

Caring for the sick while feeling guilty that I was well, I had wanted to leave them much earlier but was afraid to take my place on the outside where I belonged. Yet I knew that I could put every psychiatric aide, doctor, and administrator in the place on the outside world's stage and, in the mental health category, very few would make the finals. But I knew my place. I was, after all, my mother.

But I was also me. So I had mastered the art of walking this runway—doing as I was told and being told what I already knew: I was different from the normal folks—my family, The Junior League and The Women's Bible Group. Now, like I needed another group, The Insane. I had been the most compliant, helpful contestant, befriending, protecting, counseling and entertaining the other patients. I was firmly planted in this rose garden, alright. It had become my runway—just another stage for a perfect Southern Belle. And, best of all, there was no competition for my title—not one chance in hell of losing it. I made sure of that; it's all I had.

I was *Miss Rose Garden,* a title I had won over and over again in a pageant for which I probably never qualified. But it had made sense at the time, possibly because life outside those gates appeared to be over, while the ones on the inside were in need of a serious makeover. I was needed.

I was leaving an audience who had forgotten how to laugh, turning my back on depression I couldn't cure. But no matter how long I stayed, I couldn't change it. I was abandoning this family I had tried to be a part of but wasn't, and I couldn't change that, either. I saw my mother in their faces and felt the escalation of her sadness with each step I took away from them. I remembered the day I left for college and wondered if this family's pain would have eased as her's did—when I returned home one month later.

My goodbyes said through the tiny windows on the locked doors of their rooms reminded me it was time to call upon the escape mechanism in my brain that functioned very much like theirs—the one that enabled me to survive the present moment by finding something reassuring about it. Think about it, I said to myself, these prisoners would no longer be expected to attend the warden's group meetings—to ask for the privilege to visit the outside world and be denied—or to be part of that privileged group who would be granted the privilege of leaving but were afraid to go.

Or those who were forced to leave but had no place to go.

Best of all, they would not have to face that god-awful Danish modern furniture.

Today it was business as usual for the staff and patients. At one end of the hall, a piercing alarm system brought the devils and demons from the darkest recesses of their masters' minds to assist in the daily warfare against the brigade of psychiatric aides armed with cold wet sheets. On the opposite end, a patient was threatening to cut off everyone's penises with the empty plastic Jell-O container from lunch—just another of those mental hospital moments when, penis-or-no-penis, a woman had to wonder if she was about to lose hers. But on this, my last day, the whole thing seemed like little more than a small family dispute.

Why hadn't I left when the therapist first questioned this hospitalization? Why had I chosen to stay until it all became commonplace? A year too late, that decision made me mad as hell; still my guilt, with its pigheaded resolve, was pushing its way through the rage. My neighbors were taking full advantage.

As I approached the elevator, they acted out their displeasure. Angry voices passed through the bars and windows and followed me out the front door of the building and onto the grounds. Just the same, I was about to breach that old contract and I was ready—even though, clearly, the remaining residents of The Rose Garden were not.

As I walked toward the taxicab, their cries—begging me to turn around, to unlock the door behind me—were muffled by the silent ones of my mother. I stepped up my pace, determined to leave home.

Their screams and my guilt ended the moment I opened the taxicab door and realized the paper-scented pine tree hanging from its rearview mirror had nothing to do with masking the smell of urine. I was free. The driver started the cab, then turned to me, "Will you be alone?" he asked.

"It's looking that way," I answered.

"Were you visiting someone or do you work there?" he wanted to know.

"I was visiting. Family, you know," I said.

"The whole family?" he laughed.

As we drove away I turned, and from the back window of the cab, there was no Rose Garden. At that moment I realized I had gotten away without looking back even once, until now.

"Well, they're not really *family*," I replied. Just distant kin. You know, from pretty much the same Family Tree as most of us . . ."

He cut in. "It's none of my business, lady, but if it was me or my people or anyone in my 'Family Tree,' as you say, we'd just go to one of them psychiatrists—like, in an office somewhere."

"That's what you call 'outpatient therapy,'" I said, "and you're right. A person would have to be crazy not to think of that."

I wondered if I was taking anything away from this experience other than the satisfaction of having survived it. I certainly hadn't followed the treatment plan by going mad and then making the slow climb back to sanity, nor was I fully convinced that had I gone there, I would have bought a ticket for the return trip back up. I sure hadn't made the transformation into a perfect wife and mother, or a perfect anything else. But as things turned out, there would have been no one at home to witness it if I had.

I had clung to the belief that after this two-year hiatus I would return to my husband and children a whole person. Instead, I had graduated magna cum laude from a school that kept me isolated from the real world, one that convinced me I didn't belong in it. From the first day, my objections had been discarded as symptoms of a disease—the irrational crazy talk of a mental patient. At the end of this journey, I had no clue that I had rights, especially the right to be a mother again. I accepted this, although the letters from my boys said something else.

> *Dear Mama,*
> *We miss you. Today we jumped off the big diving board.*
> *Tomorrow someone's gonna learn us to swim. Come home.*
> *Your sons,*
> *Travis and Sam*

Second only to the day I stepped off The Rose Garden's rickety elevator onto one of its wards, my biggest regret was the day I stepped back onto that elevator one year later, but left the mother of my children behind. Today, I'm not sure I know the woman who agreed to share their custody, but I do know it never got shared.

As paradoxes go, the hospital's label for me, *fear of abandonment,* was my favorite. As for their promise that I would leave the place without that fear, they were right.

The day I walked out the door and felt no fear of abandonment whatsoever, I knew that this was one promise The Rose Garden had kept.

31.
Free . . . at last!

The Kennedy Center and a physician from Alexandria weren't the only highlights of my first real outing without the crazies; there was also my dress. It was small and black and in the sitting-down position, the neckline and ruffled hem met right around the crotch area. Too late to be useful, I realized it was a style that could not have gone out because it had never been in. I'd been away longer than I remembered, it would seem. Like I cared. I was free! Finally I was doing normal things. Soon I'd have those usual irritations: a run in my hose, being overdrawn at the bank. No more of the other kind: being thrown out a window or mistaken for a commode.

The King and I had never been better. The Kennedy Center had never been better. *I* had, however, been better. I stood with my date in the lobby during intermission and nervously drank red wine from a plactic glass. I was in the United States of America, yet I seemed to be sinking in foreign soil.

Cigarette smoke filled the air and though I'd never smoked a day in my life, I welcomed it into my lungs like a long-lost friend. Seemingly intertwined with mental illness, smoking had been a favorite pastime in The Rose Garden and I had become addicted to receiving my share second hand. Much like the illness itself, I had taken in far less than everyone else, yet I felt like a part of the group. But not *this* group. Everything was different here, even the smoke. Was there an actual scent to sanity, I wondered, or was it the absence of those other scents that left this room so empty? Maybe it had nothing at all to do with smell. Could I simply be bored out of my mind because no one here appeared to be out of theirs?

I waited for someone to do something unthinkable. A blood-curdling, hair-raising, earsplitting confession to the assassination of JFK would be a nice change of pace. Or sex. Was no one going to take this opportunity to declare Jackie a worthless fucking nymphomaniac whore . . . the Queen of Porno and First Lady of Satan? Couldn't someone stop making small talk long enough to step forward and piss on the Presidential Seal? I looked around for one—just one—uninvited guest to crash the party. But there wasn't a Hitler or four-headed devil in the place, not even one.

I had forgotten about the calm, quiet predictability of sane folks in these settings—the correctness of their every word and move. Obviously, I hadn't been exposed to sanity in a long time and therefore knew nothing about the current methods of bringing it out in a person. I knew a lot about cold wet sheet packs, but very little about tranquilizers—even less about how much alcohol it took to wash them down. But I could sure spot wellness when I saw it, and tonight it surrounded me.

I was adapting somewhat and had even managed to drown my recent past in the red wine—until we took our seats for the second act and I heard the commotion behind me. "*S-H-H-H-H!*" "*S-H-H-H-H!*" someone kept repeating. It was getting louder. I smiled as I thought of Mr. Jones lumbering down the aisle with that flashlight. Then I heard an all too familiar voice. It was coming from the back of the room.

"Rosemary, when did you get out?"
"Rosemary, when did you get out?"
"Rosemary, when did you get out?"

"Rosemary, what do you want me to do?"
"Rosemary, what do you want me to do?"
"Rosemary, what do you want me to do?"

I knew only one man who repeated everything three times. And I'd never known another one who asked, "What do you want me to do?" Not even once. But it couldn't be Steve. Not Steve from the Rose Garden. Not Steve, my errand boy! It could *NOT* be him.

But I hope it is. No, I don't! Do I?

What if it is—and he's naked? Sometimes he wore clothes, didn't he? Like, on visitors' day. He always wore a necktie for company. Oh, no, not *just* the necktie! *IT CAN'T BE THE NECKTIE AND NOTHING ELSE!* Not the Elvis Presley blinking-guitar, sequined hound-dog necktie! It's not Sunday. Is it? "Get a grip," I told myself. Tonight I was a guest at The Kennedy Center—mingling with my people, the *normal* people.

The boring people . . .

The familiar parrot squawk got louder as it traveled from the back of the room down the aisles past the minks and moutons, through the audience, then into the orchestra pit and onto the stage with Yul Brenner himself.

"A friend?" my date laughed—the kind of nervous laugh that you just know will be his last one of the evening, maybe ever. I turned.

It was Steve, dressed. Waving his arms while calling my name, he was planning a journey down the aisle but was restrained by the psychiatric aide whose hand took possession of his coat tail. Another reason, I noted, to be thankful he was dressed. As I saw the group from The Rose Garden behind him, it all came together. Field trips.

I had forgotten about those field trips.

"Yes, he is my friend," I answered. "He's been a friend for quite some time now."

I wanted to say it three times but was able to resist the compulsion which was, it occurred to me, just about the only difference between Steve and me.

32.
...and she danced on roller skates forever

I was the woman on that movie screen. She danced in the street and danced in the rain, and once she even danced on roller skates! People hung around. No one died.

Fear of abandonment.

Wearing that label while being kicked out of The Rose Garden was, I thought, the greatest irony I would ever experience. But that changed the day I accepted a job with a psychiatrist from the National Institute of Mental Health—an expert in the study of The Stockholm Syndrome, the phenomena of hostages becoming sympathetic to their captors.

"Given your previous residence," he joked, "I'm pretty sure you're overqualified for a job involving the study of people who convince themselves their situations aren't really unbearable."

"Sounds like a bad marriage," I smiled.

"Or being locked up for two years," he shot back.

"So you're saying I was . . . a hostage?" I asked, cautiously.

"No joke!" he replied.

When I got hired as the man's administrative assistant, there was a joke, alright. But it was on the government.

Right off, I turned down an invitation to lead a consciousness-raising group—a human chain of people who had experienced the mental health system first hand. I wasn't about to be an advocate for the mentally ill. I hadn't turned back when I left them, and I wasn't about to start now. Besides, most people suspected that these ex-mental patient activists were simply exhibiting symptoms of their own illnesses, and I, who have exhibited mine on every page of this book, *knew* they were. Then, too, I had way too many questions of my own to answer anyone else's.

Obviously, being a federal worker *did* play havoc with my sense of self and complete psychiatric recovery. After all, I was now just another inmate in a system with no parole board, diagnoses, or individual labels

179

for its workers. We were all exactly the same. Truth be known, it was this affiliation with and comparison to the *truly* insane that brought about a monumental moment in my life—that epiphany in which I discovered my own sane, creative, and resilient mind, and that Daddy was right. I'd had a whole mind all along.

Given my recent schooling, I was unequipped to handle such a revelation, so it took some time to react. But when I did, I was Judy Garland dancing on roller skates forever, headed straight for The Land of Oz. I was an advocate for everything liberating, fun, forbidden, and free—a woman freed from her captors who was finally in charge of the records she played. I was a disc jockey.

But I was *not* an advocate for the mentally ill.

A PERFECT PARTY

I took my act from Daddy's liquor store to the beauty parlor next door. . . .

By simply giving a name to the performance I'd begun as a child, at night I became "A Perfect Party by Rosemary," and I took it to

Washington, D.C., Georgetown, Northern Virginia, and as far into Maryland as my van would travel. I hit Air Force, Naval and Marine bases, discotheques, singles' clubs, country clubs, hospitals, political gatherings, weddings, and bar mitzvahs.

I packed a fancy sound system and music from every era into an aging red van. Padlocked and insured to the max, its piercing alarm system was a mere whisper compared to the words that danced in big yellow letters on the outside. "A Perfect Party by Rosemary" was an invitation that screamed to every perverted murdering crook and hijacking rapist in the vicinity, "Come on in, take the disco equipment, and Rosemary's as well."

After unloading and setting up my equipment, I disguised myself as a mobile disc jockey and started the music. But as the night progressed, my fifty-foot microphone cord took me out among the troops and onto the dance floor where I became a comedian. The rest was easy. Handling hecklers I had picked up at The Rose Garden. Saying and doing most anything to please my audience and get compensated for it, I got from beauty pageants. Doing that exact same thing in a government office, I got from my social worker.

"SAY IT! SAY IT, WOMAN! For the love of God, are you crazy or what? If you want that damn disability check, tell these people! Tell them you are mentally ill!"

I became a deaf comic, oblivious to the cries of insanity: "Shut up! Get off the dance floor! Bring on the Bee-Gees! We want *Saturday Night Fever!*"

Somewhat prematurely, I gave birth to the first of my stand-up routines at a Marine base in Virginia. It was the night I was shocked and awed by the most hideous and demeaning display of decorations I'd seen since the year my Aunt Allie B held the family reunion in her daughter's double-wide.

I approached the stage at this non-commissioned officers' club where I had spun records for eight of the twelve months I had been out of the hospital. Now, on my first night back following a one-month hiatus, I was surrounded by a makeover gone wrong. The walls and ceiling of the stage, formerly a nondescript shade of foxhole brown, were now a definite 42nd Street and Broadway twenty-five-cent peep-show red. The whole scene left me with an upset stomach and a deep longing for the original.

My sound system and disco lights were bouncing off a backdrop of gold-flecked mirrored squares of linoleum and had multiplied at least 50,000 times as they looked back at themselves in utter awe. Plastered in between were about a million red, very plastic roses, their only apparent purpose being to fill up the spaces, with no regard for the social or esthetic ramifications. There was more plastic on that stage than I'd seen since the "Love in Bloom" theme that went way too far the night of my senior prom. On that occasion I had witnessed the meltdown of an entire graduating class as they became a puking pile of pimple-faced drunks, an event I always attributed to the plastic roses and their exposure to them.

I was making every effort not to repeat that event as I stood on this Monument to White Trash that surrounded me. I had turned my eyes toward heaven for assistance when there appeared a sign. Taped to the rafter above my head was a cardboard poster the size of a Volkswagen! And it was framed with—*would they never run out!*—the leftover plastic roses. Big black letters, at least three times the size of the gold-flecked mirror squares, made the message on that poster almost impossible to ignore although, God knows, I tried.

WELCOME HOME ROSE! WE MISSED YOU!
Your family

It was huge. I stood speechless but my mind was running full speed.

My family? MY FAMILY! They cannot be SERIOUS! What makes these men think I'd like this tacky mess? What must they be thinking of me to put that trash in my background? Don't they know about my background? What would my family think? My sister travels by private airplane and yacht, for gosh sake, and my brother does something in Washington so important even he hasn't been let in on it. There are five lawyers in my family, and I divorced a man who honestly believed he would be the next governor! Jesus, don't they know I have a certain standard to uphold? Have they never been exposed to CLASS? And what the fuck have I said to make them think I don't have any? What did I do, say, think, wear, imply? How could they think I would want fake anything? What WERE they thinking?

Just a disco beat away, my answer came from the dance floor. "Well, you haven't said one word about your new stage, Hamilton." This was one agitated Marine. "We knew you'd hate it. We knew it wouldn't be good enough, not for your stage. Not for the throne of a southern snob—excuse me, 'southern royalty.'"

That did it. It was time to take the microphone out among the troops. I lowered the music and followed the smells of pickled boiled eggs and bad cologne to the gathering of Marines on the dance floor. They were now awaiting an answer. The one they got was brief and to the point.

"It looks like a whore house."

It worked. They started again with the "southern royalty" routine, only this time everyone joined in. I walked back to the stage and grabbed one of the roses taped to the mirrored squares, then tucked it into what I hoped had become cleavage after the hard yank I'd given my disco dress when I turned away. I adjusted the volume of Barry White, then decided to cut him off and devote all my attention to getting theirs. With a walk more sensual than anything Judy Garland could've pulled off, I headed for the dance floor.

"Fell-o-o-o-w-s," I drawled, as I gave my blouse one more yank, this time coming quite close to exposing the cellulite on my thighs. "I said it looked like a whore house. Did I say I felt *out of place?*"

From that ice breaker came my first comedy routine, fifteen minutes that began with more references to that stage—"Come on, guys, just tell me where you keep the grenades"—and ended with the kind of self-deprecating humor one would expect from a comedian whose last gig at the local mental hospital had lasted a year. There was laughter, I think, but it was hard to hear because of the applause, and hard to enjoy because of the guilt—or was it the *absence* of guilt that was bothering me?

Until tonight, I had tried to be their somewhat mysterious but always proper DJ/sister/girlfriend—there to help them fight their battles, sometimes with words, others with a disco beat and a strobe light. But tonight, had my role changed? Had I taken that short journey from debutante to whore?

Was I the girl in high school who had a baby out of wedlock or the cheerleader who got knocked up by the football team because she had "asked for it?" Was I deliberately disregarding the rules in Mama's Manual for a brief flirtation with inappropriate behavior? Had I been jerked up by the devil and thrown into the wrong side of town where everyone's parents smoked, drank, and had sex with the door open? Was I low-life, common, indecent white trash with no redeeming qualities, not fit to go to any well-brought-up person's house after school? Or worse. Had I been this way all along? Was I one of *those* girls—the ones my granny warned me about? Had I been walking around all these years with a common streak?

Probably so.

I should have been in deep shame, having lost the respect of this entire Marine base with word now reaching the men at sea, their mothers, aunts, and sisters. But something had changed. I seemed to have lost the capacity to care.

Oh, sure, I had been aware of the word—R- E- S- P- E- C- T—since my first bedtime story from *The Book of Rules*, and I'd heard it at least five times that night from the left turntable and somewhat warped but no less determined voice of Aretha Franklin. But my whole life I never got a grip on exactly what it meant.

Tonight, feeling as safe and loved as I had in a very long time took center stage over everything else. It was as though I had taken this entire troop of soldiers back in time to a place where there was no judgment or shame. No bars on windows. No home and children on the other side. Just a quaint little liquor store deep in the heart of a small town in Arkansas where everyone stayed in one place until they got happy.

I was proud to be a part of this family. They were loyal, true, honest, and dedicated. They were, after all, Marines. Still, being a member of this family reminded me that I'd been part of another one less than a year ago. I remembered the social worker's prediction.

She will eventually be okay alone, but in large groups, we just don't know. . . .

Who did I think I was—pretending to fit in with normal people? And what in the consecrated name of Gladys Presley made me think *these* people were normal?

The process of dismantling the myth of the Southern Belle had been in full swing that night, from the moment I stepped down off the stage and connected with the troops below. I had entered their worlds this past year in a very personal way, bringing music, comedy and caterers to their weddings, anniversaries, and engagement celebrations. I'd been to backyard barbeques and a military funeral; turned a dishonorable discharge into a gala event; laughed at their heckling; cried in their beer; and played for the annual Marine Corps Birthday Ball.

Through it all I tried to represent what I believed to be their fantasy woman—a Tennessee version of the Japanese lotus blossom. I was a symbol of Truth, perfection, and immortality—blooming fresh and clean in contrast with the muddy pool of water surrounding me. Or, another possibility: a blooming idiot, as artificial as those plastic roses I'd just snubbed—only minutes away from being found out and stomped into the ground by muddy, Marine combat boots. Well, it was time to come clean—time for a pow-wow with my adopted family. But first it was time to take another swig of bourbon.

I wondered if I could tell The Truth to an audience, to *anyone*, and keep them in their seats at the same time. I didn't have time to think about that. I didn't even have time for more bourbon—or maybe I did. I wasn't sure how much time it took to tell The Truth. But hold on. Wasn't it onstage that I first revealed The Truth about myself—*to myself?* Wasn't it there that I forced an audience to look at the Belle beneath that ton of makeup? Wasn't that the talent routine I had labeled, "comedy" when, in fact, it was just The Truth delivered with a clever punch line? Wasn't that what won me points?

It was.

But tonight was different. I was a woman with only a microphone in her hand facing an audience with drinks in theirs—mugs of happiness, on tap, that were about to be chased with a mega dose of Truth. I wasn't even sure they could take it. Oh, sure they could. They were Marines.

I surveyed the room for a place to land—something high.

I guess that's how it happened—how I wound up on that tabletop, frantically shouting commands as I looked down at my child. "Say 'high,' Travis," I begged. "Look, Travis, Mama is high. I'm high."

And I found it.

From a seat on the bar stool, I delivered a zinger or two while scoping out my stage, the bar. With obvious difficulty, I commenced my trip. Suddenly I felt the strong hands around my waist of a soldier attempting to lift me onto the bar. I stopped him briefly to honor a flashback that had somehow survived the rising sea of bourbon in my brain—a rerun of that battlefield from my past—another man, a kitchen counter. "No, thanks, I don't need any help," I said, remembering that horrific page from my childhood. I unlocked his grip from my waist and heisted myself onto the bar. As I pushed aside the glasses of booze and overflowing ashtrays, the audience observed my attempts to steady myself.

"If we can get her on her feet, betcha' another round she'll strip," a newcomer exclaimed loudly. When one of the regulars gave him the slim-to-none odds of that happening, he liquored himself up and retreated back into his fantasies, likely searching for a better one. He hung his head, raising it only to throw back shots of the cheap government-issued whiskey. Soon his agitation accelerated into a drunken rage which he introduced to every soldier at the bar, until one of them introduced him to a clenched fist.

Poor schmuck. Like his homecoming from Vietnam hadn't been a big enough joke, now some idiot had hired a stripper too drunk to even undress herself.

I wasn't particularly happy about having my job description so clearly defined by the other soldier. For one glorious moment I had been mistaken for that stripper in the first soldier's fantasy. And... okay, I loved it. I had come a couple of hooks, a pair of support hose, and a barrel of whiskey from baring all—as though I didn't have a frigid bone in my body.

In an aborted attempt to rev up another fantasy by striking a sexy pose, I struck just about everything else. First I scooted into a bowl of peanuts, then turned over a drink and dumped an ashtray into the lap of a bewildered Japanese woman. "Look, Geisha," I slurred, ". . . mind if I call you PEARL? Thank you. Now . . . it's not that I *HARBOR* any resentment, *PEARL*, but I won't apologize until your people say they're sorry for dropping that . . ."

Hush, Mama!

This time I did.

My audience was visibly relieved when my squirming body came to a complete stop as I twisted it into the once-popular calendar girl pose, nonchalantly supporting myself with one hand behind my back as I dangled my legs off the bar. It occurred to me that I had inadvertently staged a scene from one of those old black-and-white war movies: the smoke filled club, the soldiers, the Asian girl, the cheap beer.

I wasn't sure about my role now. Was I the local call girl or the unattainable, yet provocative and mysterious, leading lady? Maybe I was the feisty little side-kick girl who never landed the man but always landed on the dance floor. If so, I'd need to jump off that bar, grab a soldier, and break into an impressive jitterbug. Singing would be better. I had never wanted to sing like I did at that moment, but I wanted to smoke even more. What I *really* wanted was a 1940's hair-do and shoulder pads, big ones. Of course, no matter what part I assumed, I would always play second fiddle to that titillating mistress behind the bar with those enormous twenty-five-cent-beer-on-tap JUGS!

Time to confess. "So, you want to know where I was the last two years, huh?" I teased, as the soldiers' expressions told me they thought I had lost my mind which, it occurred to me, fit right in with what I was about to say. "Well, I can assure you," I smiled, "that the institution I came from isn't so different from the one you're in right now."

The material from that one unfortunate detour in my life was the nightmare a comedian's dreams are made of. Using my own incarceration as something my audience could relate to . . . well, take it from me, comedy doesn't get any better than that! But it can sure get worse.

This would've been a perfect stopping point, but Jack Daniels had other plans. "Now, let's talk about war," I slurred. "I've had close

acquaintance with those politicians who decide which ones we fight."
The troops were, understandably, puzzled. I'm not saying I hadn't just
made a profound statement; I had. But for me, profundity and making
sense do not necessarily go hand-in-hand, never have. All I could really
count on now was that I had struck a fabulous pose and would look as
good going under as anyone ever had.

"And another thing, guys," I said, as I wondered how I could still be
sober enough to change the subject, "yes, I have served my country (*who
asked?*). I've gone through basic training in a society that taught me to
attack anything that looked or acted different from me and my platoon.
But you guys know something about that kind of war, don't you?"

They nodded, but were obviously more confused than ever, especially
after what came next. "Sure you do. There's not a 'funny' guy among
you, not one who'll admit it." Silence from everyone, especially the
'funny' ones. I continued. "I thought about it just last night, cleaning
out my closet. You know what they say, 'If you've got anything that's
been in the closet for over a year, get rid of it' . . . so I kicked out my
son—sent him to the Marines."

Jesus if love me, take me out right now.

"Bigotry! Discrimination! They force us to make choices. Lord
knows, I've struggled my whole life over the Wars of the Runways—and
the ones I've been *expected* to choose." Another perfect stopping point.
But I couldn't. "Now I am wondering why I was recruited at birth to
make those choices and fight those wars in the first place!"

Like an alcoholic manic-depressive tripping out on ADD, I switched
subjects. "Now . . . let's talk about 'feeding the hungry.' When it comes
from the platform of a First Lady or an anorexic movie star, could it
be more about feeding their own images than the starving children?"
Painfully aware that the platoon was drifting away, I knew my next
move would need to involve free drinks or nudity and that either choice
would likely dull their senses even more. "Or feeding the refugees in
Vietnam," I said. "Yeah, like Vietnam." I had their attention. "You
know, like a celebrity trekking through the rice fields of Vietnam,
passing out food to the hungry, with Jesus by her side and a camera
crew to make sure someone besides Jesus was watching."

I wasn't concerned that the United States Marine Corps didn't seem
to know what I was talking about and likely didn't care where I'd been,

how I felt about Jesus or anything else, or who I *really* was. It didn't even faze me later when they conducted an intervention outside the Ladies Room and advised me to "just stick to being funny." Actually, nothing really mattered now, maybe because I'd consumed as much Jack Daniels as Daddy probably sold in one day—or perhaps because I still believed an Academy Award would be forthcoming for my speech about not performing good deeds for awards.

About the time it seemed that nothing was going to stop me, running out of material (almost) did. But even as a soldier grabbed one of my hands to help me down from the bar, my other one was tightening its grip on the microphone. From a seated position on the bar stool, I carried on. "Of course . . . I'm still separated from you people by a thing called 'taste,'" I reminded them. "I still hate those damn plastic roses!"

After that evening of true confessions, I never again felt the urge to share another one with my family of Marines. After all, you know what they say about families. If they don't ask, you don't tell.

For the next year that Marine base became a place to explore the fascinating world of stand-up comedy until I found my voice. I would discover that the closer I came to that voice, the farther I got from the Disorder of the Southern Belle and the less I saw of her, the more in touch with myself I became. My family of Marines was supportive, non-threatening, non-judgmental, and available. But just like any other family, they were also, make no mistake about it, hecklers.

Following a successful gig at the Marine Corps Ball and local newspaper publicity, the jobs came. I landed high atop the Washington "Hill," spinning records for an institution that would rival any I'd ever heard of, including the one I had recently been released from.

In the Caucus Room of the Senate Office Building, I set up my sound system and played for two of the wildest parties on the planet—Democratic and Republican—as my 700 watts per channel got swallowed up by a colossal space with no apparent purpose or ceiling, insulated only by the bloated egos and floor-to-ceiling BS of drunken politicians. Bombarded by all-too-recent memories of being confined in a large building with the certifiably weird and insane, that night I lost the will to live, vote, and perform.

After a few months of spending days with the federal government and nights with politicians, I saw that life on the outside was where the real mental patients hung out. So when the Director of Activities for The Rose Garden asked me to entertain at their Saturday night dance, I accepted. But as the date grew closer, I wondered why I had booked this particular group. Was I crazy?

Apparently not. The night of the gig, my fears subsided as I grabbed the microphone, signaled my assistant to lower the music, and barreled out onto that dance floor. My routine was about the hospital and its workers—the administrator, social workers, and psychiatric aides. Then it shifted to the art of making wine out of apple cider and guacamole from avocados, all from a make-shift kitchen in the closet.

. . . as close to guacamole as any two mental hospital patients had ever gotten.

And disco lights. It was about disco lights.

"I know you people!" I shouted over the music. "You were seeing these lights *before* I turned them on!" (So, they couldn't tell the difference between disco lights and their own hallucinations. Big deal. Neither could the politicians.)

A year ago I'd been a member of this exclusive club. Overnight I was blackballed when my insurance expired and I was declared well. Tonight I was no longer a member, but was getting paid to entertain its members instead!*

Funniest thing, I had taken on two jobs, partly to put this nightmare behind me. I was a government employee by day and a disco queen at night. *A Perfect Party* had brought back an old friend, the stage. Equipped to extinguish the worst of memories, this party came with blasting music, disco lights, and alcohol. Yet nothing was ever loud enough, bright enough, or strong enough to erase memories that remained as real as everything this place had taken away.

*Even a blind woman with half-a-mind had to see a truckload of irony coming down this pike!

But the people on my dance floor tonight were no longer reminders of the horror movie I walked into that first day; they weren't just a bunch of crazy people trapped in an antiquated system. These were the people who had helped me *survive* that system. I'd found sanity in their insanity, Truth and openness from their "here-today, gone-tomorrow" minds I'd had to share with their demons. I'd waited patiently for them, anticipating the moment they would leave their worlds and enter mine. They jumped in quickly and left the same way, seizing each moment, aware that their time would be brief and each second had to count—no time for soft selling or editing; no running their opinions past friends and family, a committee of their peers, or their individually assigned shrinks. Best of all, unencumbered by the remote possibility they might be insane, there was no need to beat themselves up trying to fix it.

No matter how fleeting their time in my world, what my friends had brought to it was like nothing I'd experienced outside these gates. Socially, politically, and every other kind of "incorrect," they had delivered the kind of raw Truth respectable folks try to keep hidden from themselves and their loved ones. Their art, music, and poetry were as unfiltered as their language, as real as their pain. And you could be sure that most of them knew more about heartache and being desperate for love than those who screamed about it—in piercing but perfectly planned beats per minute—on the turntables in front of me.

But tonight my best friends were not here to entertain and enlighten me, nor were they representatives of the world of the weird. Tonight they were here as the honored guests at a perfect party—*my* Perfect Party.

As close to A Perfect Party as any ex-mental patient had ever gotten.

During a break I was approached by a young man whose outdated suit and tie took nothing away from his obvious confidence and movie-star good looks. As I shuffled through my record collection for his request, it hit me. This was a clean-shaven, scrubbed-up, seemingly sane version of my old friend Steve.

Sure, I know her. She's in her room. . . .

The inmate who had just asked for "Jailhouse Rock" was a former prisoner of psychosis who had somehow escaped. As I removed the record from my collection, I felt his hand on my shoulder. I turned.

"Hello, Rosemary," he said.

The greeting was followed by a very slow presentation to me of a napkin with a cookie on top. Oh, yes. This was the real thing. No doubt about it, this was Steve.

"I think I owe you a few of these," he smiled.

"About ten jillion," I nodded.

Our relationship centered on a cookie and a psychiatric aide. . . .

It was a miracle. Steve had escaped from the dark kingdom, alright. He'd served a ten-year sentence in The Rose Garden and, judging from the progress he made during my stay, I had estimated he would be sentenced to at least that many more. I had said good-bye to him through the window of a seclusion room door. (Steve had regressed—something to do with stealing, of all things.) He had shown up just a few months later, still crazy, at The Kennedy Center. It was obvious the miracle had not kicked in at that time. Now he was being released in two months. As we talked about his departure he knew exactly what I was thinking and he answered before I could figure out how to ask.

"Sanity was all I could come up with to get me out of this place," he laughed.

"Running out of insurance works, too," I added.

"Yeah, and a family who stops paying the hotel bill for a seclusion room and puts out the big bucks for medication instead—now that really fucking unlocks the door!" He laughed. "Ironic, huh? They put me in this place. Now they're getting me out!"

"Your parents?"

"No, drugs."

I caught a small glimpse of the old Steve as his expression changed. He leaned forward and whispered into my ear a secret which I fully expected to involve his fantasy about my past relationships with dogs.

She's in her room. . . .

Instead I was relieved to hear, "Well, it was actually more than medication that set me free. It was medication . . ."

"And Jesus?"

"No. It was medication—and a couple of cookies, as needed." He smiled.

It was a joyous reunion, though somewhat bitter-sweet. Steve was on his way out of The Rose Garden, yet I had serious concerns that he might one day be facing incarceration behind another set of bars. Hopefully, just as he had forgotten how to be insane, he had also forgotten how to steal.

I cued up the music again, feeling much better about The Rose Garden now. Someone had actually gotten well there. And it only took ten years.

Son of a gun.

It's a Return Engagement by Rosemary was the sign posted on the outside of the building. My assistant and I were heaving disco equipment into the van when we noticed it. "Looks like you've played here before!" he said, pointing to the sign. "No," I answered. "It's probably just somebody's idea of a mental hospital joke."

But since I was now an aspiring comic and free to make my own rules, it seemed appropriate to have the last laugh. For my performance and music, I adopted the pay scale of those who had hired me. In other words, I hit them up for $70 per hour, exactly what their psychiatrist had charged me, with one big difference.

I was worth it.

And so was Steve.

Now *that* was funny!

33.
Maybe I'd rather have lobster

It was no surprise that Mama's obituary was mostly about who her father was and his father before him and her—for the most part—successful children. There was little room for anything about who she was or had hoped to be, but I'm not sure anyone really knew. The closest I came was the night she took a stand at a steakhouse in Memphis, Tennessee.

Mr. Jones always sat at the head of the dining room table, while Mama almost never sat at all, except on her special night when we ate at Mr. Jones' favorite steakhouse. The only cloth napkin in our house was always carefully placed on his plate. Each time Mama folded it, I wondered if he would find fault in the way it was done. Actually, the only thing I truly enjoyed about the steakhouse outing was the exact moment he picked up that paper napkin and stared at it as though this time, surely, it would be cloth.

Mama always answered the waiter's same old question with the same old voice—sadly, softly, reciting the same old answer. "Steak, medium, a baked potato with butter, no sour cream, and a salad with bleu cheese dressing . . . when you have time."

But on this night she had been unresponsive, likely struggling with what I now recognize as the chronic depression she lived with. Impatiently, Mr. Jones turned to her, "The usual steak and baked potato?" he asked.

I almost replied for her, "Well yes, pig. What other choice does she have? It's all they serve in this rat hole!" I'm glad I didn't.

No one expected Mama's answer, but I'll never forget it. Her expression changed and she sat erect. With a voice that was neither sad nor soft, she looked directly at my stepfather and replied, "Maybe I'd rather have lobster."

I heard those words as I'd heard her music in the past, spoken by a piano demanding that its request for lobster be heard. Her words to that waiter *were* the music that ran through her veins and echoed throughout the house when she thought she was alone. They were not the words of her husband as he chose his favorite restaurant for her, nor had they come from her mother's sheet music or the church's hymnal.

They weren't the songs her children had requested or the sounds of a truck pulling into the driveway at twelve noon, her signal to position that cloth napkin at the head of the table.

Mama took charge of her keyboard like a high-ranking officer, with total confidence the troops would do as they were told. She never asked those keys to play anything that hadn't taken a trial run on the ground level of her soul. Her private concerts were played softly or loudly, depending on her mood, with her bottom side taking on the role of conductor for the whole thing, as it started midway on the bench and made its way to both sides several times before she struck the last note. I always hoped she would take her dusty banjo ukulele from the attic and play that, too. But I was more than happy with what I got.

She was closer to seventy than sixty when her piano was silenced. Her "favorite music" was played at her funeral while those who had selected it witnessed Mama, one last time, beating everyone else's drum. Like the dress she wore, the casket she slept in, the preacher's sermon, and the good-byes from family and friends—the music was impressive. But it would have worked just as well for the minister's wife, the beauty operator next door, or the woman who sold Avon on Saturdays. It was a tradition that would have been enjoyed more by me had I, like Mama, not been there to enjoy it. Nevertheless, it looked good and it sounded right, and it was for sure, proper.

I, on the other hand, was not. I longed to hear the music Mama had played in those private concerts—to watch her bounce from one end of that old piano bench to the other, and to see the look on her face when she got caught. I missed the day she left that bench, hiked up her skirt, and danced "The Charleston," as I stood and welcomed the imaginary preacher behind her. "Oh, Brother Bob!" I shrieked, "How long have you been standing there?" But I really longed for that one nanosecond when Mama seemed to be disappointed that he wasn't.

I missed her old dresses and the guilt and shame I felt when she wore them to shop for my new ones. *Dammit! I was sitting on that church pew big as life at my mama's funeral, longing for the guilt!* But more than anything, I missed hearing the notes that had unleashed her spirit and given her permission to take on life right then and there, on her own terms. I needed to see her that way one more time, if only through her music. But that music would not have been suitable for the occasion.

So I watched and listened as Mama's final farewell was presented to others appropriately and properly, much as the life she had lived in the same way.

At the cemetery, a woman removed the artificial red roses that had been placed among the mounds of real ones that covered Mama's grave. They were inappropriate, she said, for Mama. They were not even real.

Not real, it occurred to me, might be one way to describe much of the life of the Southern Belle we put to rest on that day.

34.
Maybe I'd rather have sex

I guess that's how it happened—how I wound up on that tabletop, frantically shouting commands as I looked down at my child. "Say 'high,' Travis," I begged. . . .

Along with her depression, Mama left me with an abnormal craving for lobster and a lot of questions about sex. I hadn't conquered the depression, nor could I afford the lobster, but I was well on my way to figuring out the sex.

I had taken up with a self-proclaimed master of the canvas—a life-drawing instructor whose nude models sometimes outnumbered the students in his studio. Women lined up to take their clothes off in his classes; much to the amazement of his pumped-up ego, I wasn't one of them.

"A perfect opportunity to study and draw the naked body," was the justification for taking his class on a field trip to a strip club. It made perfect sense to me, but in those days, I could rationalize almost anything—even this man's need to publicly humiliate me from time to time. On this night he went too far.

It began in his classroom as I sat with his students, waiting for a model to show up. There was, as usual, an abundance of local talent eager to take her place. I cringed as a student asked him why I didn't stand in. His answer was delayed because he waited until we got to the strip club to give it.

The dancers—on tabletops, the stage, and the bar—had just begun to disrobe when he looked in my direction and shouted his answer over the sultry music. "She can't even remove that beauty queen exterior. We'll never know what—if anything—is underneath!" He laughed robustly. "But not to worry, class," he reassured them, "you are not at risk. It's a southern thing."

Could be. But if he'd done his research, he'd have known what southern girls do when they don't want to be held responsible for what they're about to do. After this one finished off her sixth glass of Wild Turkey, he was moving dangerously close to finding out. This Southern Belle was fixin' to dismantle.

I found the manager of the club sooner than I'd hoped. I hadn't quite mustered up the courage to ask for an audition when I bumped into him in the hallway just outside the restroom. It was unavoidable. What his three-hundred-plus pounds were not taking up of that hall, his cigar smoke and male chauvinism were. As we exchanged pleasantries, I became more concerned than ever about what was about to take place on that tabletop in the other room.

"Well, babe, your butt better be good," was almost as scary as the thought of the sight of it—as untrained as it was unfirm—on that table. I convinced the man I was a pro (finalist, Miss Mallard talent competition, 1961), but with every word that left my mouth, it was apparent that whatever I did for his customers would never equal the performance he was getting at that moment. He led me to a room filled with almost non-existent costumes, open jars of makeup, cigarette smoke, umpteen bottles of liquor, and strippers who were not giving any of it time to go to waste. After they welcomed me like a long-lost sorority sister, I was taken on a shopping spree. Every costume I tried on was critiqued until we arrived at the perfect pink chiffon, feathered nightie. It was the most glorious moment of my life.

But it was just that, a moment. What had begun as my best idea and sexiest getup ever, now brought on an avalanche of remorse reminiscent of the morning after every bad idea I'd ever had—times one hundred. As I made eye contact with myself in the mirror, I knew I had once again eliminated the sobering-up part from my fantasy. I looked like, I'll swear, a pink, shivering, Thanksgiving bird, just a wobble away from a good plucking. And this turkey (you just thought it couldn't get any worse) was about two drinks away from doing the chicken.

I tried to back out. Lord knows, I tried. And Lord also knows, I hope, that I proceeded only because I had no choice.

It was those women backstage—those Jaycettes.

But when I suggested to the club manager that we alter the plan and hold the audition in the dark corner next to my date's table, the man's reaction was immediate, and loud. It was also my fantasy, big as life! This brute with the butt of a cigar attached to the corner of his mouth, was giving me no choice as he warned, "You get your butt on one of them tables like the others, or you get it out of my club. You aren't no different from the rest of 'em, girl. All or nothin.'"

No choice whatsoever. Against my will. Forced again.

Whatever I did after this point would be completely out of my control—just one orgasm short of a cold wet sheet pack. It wasn't my fault that I was about to have the most memorable evening of my life.

> *Dear Rosemary,*
>> *Where are you?*
>> *We're wondering if you ever pursued that dance career.*
>> *The Pageant Committee*

The next step in the dismantling of the Southern Belle was also the demise of the dignity of all God-fearing, decent women everywhere. It was cheap and degrading and would surely damn us all to hell. It had to be all of that and more because this girlfriend was loving it, whatever it was. Oh, sure, I had removed my clothes on the legitimate stage of the beauty pageant, but never, ever, for another audience.

As I danced on my boyfriend's table, his response—though I'll never forget it—was the least significant of the trophies I would take home that night. I was getting "thumbs up" from the women onstage, and victory signs from the others as they adorned the tabletops surrounding mine. It was the first time I could ever remember being onstage with women and truly enjoying it. Later, in the dressing room, I awarded each of us the title of Miss Congeniality and proclaimed us all winners of the talent competition.

Until that night, I did not know that a group victory was even possible.

But I did know the repercussions would be staggering. It would be the end of everything: my membership to The Association for the Preservation of Tennessee Antiquities, the fund-raising meetings for The Symphony Ball, and—just cut off my arms and legs—*The Symphony Ball itself!* No more luncheons with the Ladies of the Men of The Bar Association . . . and The Pageant Committee? History. It would be the end of pageant committees everywhere. And could you blame them? Imagine, women onstage, half-naked, bonding, with not a college scholarship in sight—and each in her own right, a winner. It was a mortal sin, make no mistake about it, especially the bonding part.

I tap danced, I disco danced, I did the chicken. It's all I knew. But I never followed my original plan to take off my work clothes, not one dyed-to-match bead or feather. In retrospect, it was a massive error in judgment, no doubt brought on by the sobering shock of my reflection in the full-length mirrors surrounding my work space.

It was surprising that my thoughts were of my mother, and they weren't cabboosed with guilt. There was no pondering over what the neighbors would think; no striving to be a finalist while fearing it at the same time; no administrator to tack years onto my sentence; no flashbacks of the preacher, the tent revivals, or that kitchen counter. Oh, no. It was all about a woman's funeral.

This was the way a woman should be remembered! *This* was what the preacher should include in her farewell tribute. *This* is how she should be laid to rest.

For God's sake! *The woman danced!*

I was pretty sure Mama was thinking the same thing as she looked down at me. I had taken just one more step toward our liberation. We weren't *sitting* at the head of the table, we were *STANDING* on it! In a room filled with admirers, my mama and I were, finally, having lobster, cloth napkins—the works!

She was proud. My mama was so, so proud. And this time she was in a safe place, safe enough to admit it.

Although I never went back to that or any other strip club, I could have because it seems that my co-workers put in a good word and I did get the job. But my performance accomplished far more than a job ever could. That night I put together more pieces of my life.

And in my garter was enough money to hire someone to put together the rest.

IV. You can't pay your therapist with the scholarship fund

"My dysfunction was no different from most in that it was 100 percent someone else's fault, and had its beginnings in the twisted roots of my Family Tree. Unfortunately, years of psychiatric therapy have failed to reveal the identity of that person. So, I have wasted the majority of my life and most of my money getting back at each and every member of my family, knowing that from time to time, I am surely reaching the right one. . . ."

35.
Self helped

(Just give me a minute to find some people to help me find myself.)

After I left The Rose Garden, I often found the "real world" to be less real than the one I'd left behind. In fact, it was easy to see how this one could drive a perfectly sane person into that other one.

After a few years of therapy, I discovered several alternative routes to self discovery. But as I began my journey I found that of all my grandmother's words of wisdom, "Be careful what you ask for" was headed straight to the top of the list. I was about to combine eastern mysticism with western occultism and southern gullibullism. As they say in the business, I was about to be enlightened and altered.

As they say back home, I was about to be ripped off.

BIOFEEDBACK AND HOW TO STOP IT

It took years of biofeedback, books, groups, seminars, workshops, and a couple of hippie retreats to get over the therapy—but not nearly as long as it took to get over the biofeedback, books, groups, seminars, and hippie retreats *because* of the therapy. With each shrink, group and seminar, there had been a different opinion about who I was, and a new plan for what to do about it. But nothing to explain or justify serving time in The Rose Garden.

The years advanced as did almost every stage of every disorder I believed I had contracted along the way. I was forever in search of or trying to survive a label, diagnosis, or dysfunction—consistently living out the last one I had acquired. My favorite one demanded that I live my life out of control, oblivious to repercussions, and without regret. As you may well imagine, perfecting this one afforded me unlimited freedom in living my life, composing this book, and screwing up a good portion of both. But not to worry. You can be sure the behavior has been covered with a label, the label slapped with a diagnosis, and me—you guessed it—not responsible for any of it.

Understandably, there are days when my inability to remember exactly who I am—an obvious symptom of the disorders—forces me to carry a list:

- ADD — (Attention Deficit Disorder) Disorganized, inattentive, and compulsive with a convenient inability to remember any of it.

- OCD — (Obsessive-Compulsive Disorder) (a) Worrying over and over and over about how disorganized, inattentive, and forgetful you are (see ADD, above) and (b) subsequently performing compulsive acts that have nothing to do with anything, then (c) worrying over and over again about why you're still so disorganized, inattentive and forgetful.

- MHC — (Mental Health Coverage) This is not a disorder but is important to those of us who have been labeled with one. It has to do with the patient's obligation to act out the label that is being paid for. (Check your file. It's right there between diagnosis and follow-up appointments.)

- PRDD — (Post-Realization Depressive Disorder) Crippling depression that shows up at the conclusion of therapy when patients figure out who they *really* are and then start being themselves. Tragically, most of them overdo it. This disorder is rare as few people ever finish therapy.

- OPOMD — (Overcoming Peace of Mind Disorder) A common reason for beginning therapy.

- SBD — (Southern Belle Disorder) A fun-filled combination of all the above.

Well, if I've learned one thing, it's this: you cannot have that many disorders without doing something to respond to them. But as you might expect, my addiction to the solutions became just one more disorder—and each disorder became an invitation to read another book or join another group or seminar where I developed new disorders, each of which was validated with another label. (Don't even try . . . just keep reading.)

THE BOOKS

God grant me the serenity to accept the
self-help books that work,
the courage to reject the ones that don't,
and the wisdom to know the difference
before I get to the cashier.

THE DRUGS

In these years I also came to understand drug therapy and how it enables one to continue the same old dysfunctional patterns, but without the self-loathing and guilt. In fact, absent the painful consequences, I found I could up my dosage and get around to stuff I'd had on the back burner for years!

Just the same, in my quest for The Truth it was impossible to avoid those who congregated for the purpose of destroying, en masse, any morsel of self-respect somehow overlooked by a person's family and/or psychiatrist. Just a bunch of people sharing, in a group—you know, so if one person misses something abnormal about another's mental and/or physical makeup, there are others eager to point it out.

THE GROUPS

I have come to believe that the only thing more damaging to a woman than beauty pageants, bad marriages, and living with lunatics, is a psychiatric label. Given my dependence on them—and growing collection—it shouldn't have surprised anyone when I headed straight for their manufacturer: group therapy.

At the first session, it was apparent that my new labels might be a whole lot worse than the Fear of Abandonment, ADD, OCD, and SBD I had collected so far. From day one I had felt a familiar uneasiness. By the third session I knew what it was. Better toilet facilities and a long table filled with snacks was the only difference in this place and the looney bins of my past.

At this, a typical session, I took notes:

Susan's chief complaint was that she'd been dumped by a man. The group leader determined that Susan was from a dysfunctional family and suggested other groups: Survivors of Incest, Tough Love, Victims of Abuse, and Adult Children of Alcoholics. When Susan explained that no one in her family drank or molested, the doctor concluded that her father was a dry drunk. He didn't drink (or molest), but acted like he did.

Poor Susan. She got so busy group-hopping, she finally lost sight of the problem that brought her to the group in the first place. The solution, as I saw it, was obvious.

Hello, my name is Susan. I've been rejected by a man. I'm depressed.
Hello, Susan. Fill out a change-of-address card on this jerk. Have his mail sent to a government agency in Washington. Shop 'til you drop. Eat your way into oblivion. Depression may be just the excuse you need for having a real good time.

Gloria ate like a pig. She dieted for awhile and then binged on fattening foods. That was before group therapy.

Hello, my name is Gloria. I now eat health food and I do herbs and minerals. This regimen has changed my life. I now know that I binged on greasy, fat-laden food because I was compulsive. Compulsion is a pathological relationship to a mood-altering thing that has life-altering consequences. I had the need to repeat.
Hello, Gloria. Repeat this: grease'll clog me up and make me think funny, but talking about it will make me sound even funnier. Lay off the fries for a week, hon. Then you can start again. But don't tell anyone in your group.

There is help out there when we want it and also, when we don't. I encountered this last week at lunch with friends.

Mary admitted to being in two of the aforementioned therapies. She shared books, workbooks and tapes with us. We all confessed to behavior characteristic of the profiles in the books and tapes. Mary informed us that we, too, were from dysfunctional families. All six of us, especially Judy. No doubt about it, Judy was the victim of alcoholism.

Judy recalled that the only person who drank too much in her family was her grandfather, and he quit years before she was born.

"He was wonderful," she said, reminiscing. "Being with him was such a joy. There was never a dull moment."

Mary understood totally.

"Yep. You are a typical adult grandchild of an alcoholic. You people are addicted to excitement, living on the cutting edge."

Judy turned to me, upset. "Grandpa was the best part of my childhood. I thought I was so happy then."

"Well, you weren't," Mary assured her.

Hello, my name is Judy. I thought I had a happy childhood.
Hello Judy. If you were wrong about this, you were probably wrong about many other things. Get help.

For my children, I guess it's too late. They are the Adult Children of a Procrastinator, the Survivors of Divorce, and witnesses to the highs and lows of a chronic dieter with a distorted body image. Any way you look at it, they're the victims of something I tried to do right, but screwed up.

I'm a simple person. I want to go back to the days when the solutions were obvious and free, back to the days when my Granny had only one label for me and it was, simply, "Scarlett."

Hello, my name is Scarlett. There's nothing left to live for.
Hello, Scarlett. Of course there is. There's tomorrow.
And tomorrow is another day.

THE CULTS

Cults bear such a strong resemblance to group therapy and mental hospitals, it's hard to believe they aren't covered by insurance. Most people head straight from one to the other as each is known to attract the lost, the needy, the weird, the self-absorbed, and the lonely. For reasons I chalk up to just another unsolved mystery, I always fit right in.

With this particular group, I found another "family" with the inside scoop on *The Truth*. I also found a man with money. The new family was a cult and the man with money, their leader. We called ourselves *The Children of the Eternal Flame*. Now for most normal-thinking folks, that name would conjure up a right accurate image of what was coming down. I, however, was not one who was thinking normally. I was one who had the hots for their leader—the most reverent spiritual guide.

Our safe space was a weekend retreat at a chicken farm on the outskirts of Baltimore. In the morning, two groups were formed. The women baked bread in the kitchen while the men communed with most anything that couldn't commune back; nature was a favorite. That afternoon, the men attended a class on the art of therapeutic touch followed by another class on the legal pitfalls of performing it incorrectly. At the end of the day, both groups met and formed a deep spiritual bond as they discovered commonalities in their dysfunctions and inabilities to fit in with normal people.

They made a big deal about experiencing the here and now—"living in the present moment" and "blooming where you are planted," stuff like that. But after only one weekend, it was clear that I was enjoying my present moments with these idiots least of any present moments I'd found myself presently in.

After a month I found that being in complete and total harmony with the Universe and spelling Love with a capital L just did not sit well with my essential nature and human condition. I could no longer watch my space fill up with stuff about who I was *not*. If I was *not* my body and I was *not* my mind and my spirit was *theirs* and their head honcho guru guy was *God*, then what the *Hell* with a capital *H* was left for me to be—and wasn't that the whole point of this charade, anyway—to find *Myself*? I mean, really, if *Man,* with a capital *M*, can create his own reality, would that not apply to women, with a capitol *W*, too? And if so, then what on earth was *this* woman doing in the Universe of the Children of the Eternal Flame which was obviously ignited by *Men?*

Well, I was fed up with their New Age and Perfect Universe, and I missed screwing up in my old one. I longed for my spirit. I was sick to death of theirs. And I was *really* sick of living in *their* present moments. But oddly enough, it was their philosophy that inspired my new one:

> *Life is a cow pasture.*
> *We can step forward or we*
> *can step backward,*
> *but we must never*
> *step in it. . . .*

I not only ditched the "present moments" of the cult world, but briefly discontinued the practice of jumping high and landing, flatfooted, in the middle of my own. In a nutshell, I mastered the art of being *who I was not* both in the past and in the future while using *the present moment* to just *think* about it! As for "blooming where I was planted?" Come on, now. You know that one has never worked.

Not even for those with cow shit on the bottom of their shoes.

V. Excuse me, am I on the right runway?

"Most of my life, I've flown by the seat of my pants, trusted a man on automatic pilot, and prayed that a stranger in some faraway tower would navigate me safely to the ground. I have, basically, traveled blindly into the wild blue yonder. . . ."

36.

Could y'all please climb on my beverage cart while I push it out on the wing?

. . . and the bus children, and the beauty-pageant children, and the coach-class children, too. They all stood behind the big curtain, waiting for their names to be called. . . .

1. Abuse.
2. Lies.
3. Mental hospitals.
4. A year as a federal employee.
5. A *Southern Book of Rules* that made no sense.
6. Years of never getting a straight answer from anyone.
7. Exposure to a cult.

Yep! I was prepared to work for an airline, alright. But even though I had every qualification to head straight for management, I accepted the job of flight attendant and fought them instead.

I started at the top.

My Airline
President and CEO
Somewhere in the USA

Dear Mr. President and CEO:
 On a recent flight we discussed what I consider to be the airline's deteriorating passenger service. You asked for my input in writing, so I'm taking you up on it.
 What it comes down to is this: I cannot take it anymore! We greet these passengers with that dreadful two-bag-carry-on-of-a-particular-size-and-shape-rule, then hit them with the hang-ups-in-the-closet-no-more-than-three-inches-wide-rule, which I cannot even begin to understand, while the potheads, terrorists, and escaped convicts who carry these bags go completely unnoticed! Then, just to make sure the bad guys turn violent and the innocent ones burn their frequent flier miles, the flight-attendants-from-hell who enforce these rules continue, throughout the flight, to assert

their authority in an effort to prove to themselves that they actually have any.

Thank God for cell phones so our passengers can call their analysts. Too bad our rules prohibit the use of cell phones!

I remain as confused as ever,
Rosemary Hamilton
Flight attendant

THE RULES

I'm not sure when it began—my aversion to being handed someone else's agenda carved in stone, or, in this case, an Emergency Manual carved in airline-speak. But most likely it started during those early days of Belledom, followed me to beauty pageants, and then peaked at The Rose Garden. But this I do know. *NEVER* had I witnessed rules being enforced with such vigilance, nor had they made less sense than the day I became a flight attendant. What made even *less* sense was to turn to an organization that made *no* sense.

THE UNION RULES

Like Christmas presents, the privileges were awarded to certain patients—and having to grovel to get them was, by all indications, a privilege in itself. . . .

I had no sooner secured the position that would protect my *future* than I found I needed protection *from my position.* So I turned to the Flight Attendant Union and sure enough . . . been there. It was just another "group," begging for privileges and being denied. But this time they were all about benefits and working conditions—insurance, salary, cabin safety, that sort of thing. Almost made a woman miss the good ol' days when all she had to beg for was the privilege to walk, unescorted, to the restroom.

Naturally there are days I wonder . . . *which runway am I on, anyway?*

> *Dear Rosemary,*
> > *Where are you?*
> > > *The Pageant Committee*

> *Dear Pageant Committee,*
> > *You tell me.*
> > > *Rosemary*

Okay, this is what I know:

- I know I'm not on the beauty pageant runway. Here, emergency procedures are about *saving* people—not *eliminating* them.
- I'm definitely not in a nuthouse. The crazy people in this place aren't downgraded to seclusion rooms; they're upgraded to first class.
- I'm certainly not under the rule of just one crazy administrator. I'm answering to the entire Federal Aviation Administration!

My current title combines two of my previous ones: I possess the arrogance of the Southern Belle (my granddaddy was The Senator and yours wasn't) and the confidence of the beauty contestant (I won and you didn't). That's because I am a flight attendant. I look good, my nails are red, my hair is big. I can greet you, chew gum, and toss your carry-on oxygen onto the jetway all in the same breath. I can tell you when to sit down and when to stand up, and, if you ring the call bell, I can tell you nothing at all. I am on this runway because I am a safety professional. I was on the others because I was young and cute and a little confused. But there are days, I'll swear, when being here is just like being there. It's like someone sneaked in an unwritten position description for flight attendants with fine print from the sixties.

Aunt Allie B and me:

Her: "Honey, tell the judges about the year you were a lifeguard and wore that little bikini?"

Me: "You mean the year I saved the woman from the sharks?"

Her: "Forget that part. No one cares."

Flight attendant supervisor and me:

Her: "Your uniform's a mess! What happened?'
Me: "It's blood. I saved a life."
Her: "No one cares. Did you finish the meal service?"

THE TRAINING RULES

Each year the memo announcing flight attendant training arrives with rules about studying and dressing—*how* to study for training, *what* to study for training, *what* to wear *when* you're studying for training, *what* to *bring* to training, and *how* to dress when you *finally get* to training: casual clothes, not too casual; comfortable shoes, not too comfortable; big hair, not too big. Yadda, yadda. Then the follow-up rules arrive about *how to dress* on the plane *enroute* to training.

It's no wonder I am confused when I arrive at training and find that my instructor obviously didn't read the memos because she hasn't followed the rules of the airline, Homeland Security, the FAA, and least of all, any fashion magazine on the planet.

"Don't you watch the news?" I want to ask the woman in middle-eastern hijab—long dress, veil-draped head, you know the look—but, seeing as how we're not supposed to take notice of how she's dressed or where she might be from or her method of worship or what rules she follows or what she thinks of ours, I keep my questions to myself. Still, I wonder: where was I when we merged with Islam Airways? And how politically correct was *that?*

I rack my brain to figure out how someone on the government's "no fly" list could be an instructor! No need to panic, I tell myself. She's *teaching, not flying!* But a Muslim female instructing a class of post-911, pissed-off flight attendants on the art of *self-defense?* Give me a break! Well, I'm thinking, good thing for her the airline never sets aside more than five minutes to teach its flight attendants to defend themselves. And, too, the torment this woman probably endured back home will make her a shoe-in for the segment on passenger service.

Of course, I'm not supposed to share these thoughts because then I'd be accused of "profiling." And Lord knows, if I wanted to do that I would include our baggage handlers and caterers.

THE EMERGENCY RULES

Sometimes when I'm sitting on my jumpseat in coach class and the fasten seat belt sign is on, I'll see a child turning red and gasping for breath. Inevitably I'll say to myself, "To hell with that seat belt sign rule, I'm gonna get up and give that kid a bottle of water and some oxygen." But then I recall the *You cannot serve the whole bottle or can of anything in coach class* rule and realize the kid might ask for a whole bottle and I'd have to say no and besides there's that other rule we say during the safety demo, *Be sure to secure your* own *mask first before assisting your child,* and of course that's not possible because this isn't my child and, too, I don't even *need* oxygen and most likely there's a rule about not using the passengers' supply even if I did, so I remain seated (with my seatbelt securely fastened) and turn my *Flight Attendant Manual* to the section on *Irregular Situations* but find the rules to still be *regular*. I conclude that in this business a rule's a rule—even when that rule precludes the rare sudden onset of a flight attendant's own good judgment and just plain common sense. Take, for instance, mine:

- Babies in FAA approved infant seats. *Hello! We have overhead bins!*
- Intoxicated passengers with hand grenades and rifles. *Not necessarily terrorists. Just stop serving them liquor.**
- Federal air marshals. *Start serving them liquor. (Anything to make them do their jobs.)*

THE HALF-ASS RULES
(Denial—not just an airline in Egypt!)

My whole life—yes, there were rules. No, they were not always clearly defined. That's why today, when a part of the puzzle is missing, it's no big deal. I just proceed with the information I've been given.

A perfect example? Those wretched carry-on explosives.

Although we aren't encouraged to talk about *who* might've brought *it* onboard or *how* that person might look, we are instructed on *where* to move one if it is discovered after takeoff. Since we don't know *how* the thing got on the aircraft in the first place, we just assume it

_____

(*But if you hear "NRA," throw their sorry asses off the plane. They're Republicans!)

219

happened on the "hair gel, hairspray, and mouthwash" day down at the security checkpoint and the "hi-jackers and explosives" day was the week before.

Yeah, we tell ourselves, that's probably how it happened.

THE RULES ABOUT THE RULES

A rule is a rule is a rule and God forbid you should break the one about making up your own! Take the one about who gets to use the first-class closet and lavatory—or the one about knowing *what class you actually are!* You don't *even* want to know what happens to the uppity coach-class sons-of-bitches who open that curtain and slip into first class—for *anything!* Their ratty coats, cheap-ass luggage, and Billy-Beer bladders better damn well stay behind that curtain. It's a rule.

Burning aircraft? Same thing. Rules.

Fortunately, like a well-scripted pre-nuptial agreement, there is *always a way* out of a crippled aircraft. There is only *one federally mandated way,* but there is a way. It starts with the seat assignment rule.

Let's say, just for fun, that the left engine is on fire and your seat is on that side of the aircraft. Too bad. You'd better get right with the Lord the minute you hear the flight attendants shouting their commands— "Jump! Jump! Leave your belongings, come this way"—because you are in the section that jumped out the *left* side of the 737-mock-up aircraft in flight attendant training last week. (It was, in fact, a test question.) That being said, "come his way" just might lead you straight into a jet-fueled inferno. I'm just saying, you know, it's a possibility.

"Leave your belongings?" No different. It means exactly that, and you damn well better LEAVE YOUR BELONGINGS when you're told to! Otherwise, you'll be sent right back into that burning aircraft with those belongings you were repeatedly told to leave there!

Here's another one. Remember how you begged to sit in that exit row? *You just had to delay take-off to get that window seat with more leg room! You made a scene!* Never thought you'd be taking that seat with you! Never dreamed the nice lady sitting beside you would relinquish her seat to a man-eating shark! So now, bless your heart, you're begging for the seat you were originally assigned. Well, d o n 't e v e n   t h i n k   a b o u t switching back now. Too late. The rule is:

you go first. But here's the good news. After you hit that water, you'll never have to ask for leg room again.

Then, too, you're likely escaping the screeching sound of flight attendants blowing those other commands out the end of emergency megaphones as they delight in scaring the bejezus out of every passenger who ever asked for a second cup of coffee or tried to go to the lavatory under ten thousand feet. You can't imagine how long they've waited for this glorious moment.

"Jump! Jump! Leg, body, leg!" the sky goddesses will command as the passengers attempt to get their large asses through that tiny window exit, because they know that when a flight attendant says jump, they damn sure better jump, never mind what's below! Oh, sure, we'd all like to believe that grabbing our seat cushions, jumping into the Atlantic Ocean, and floating around like human canapés, is a good rule to follow. Yet, to our welcoming committee of sharks, I'm sure *their* rule—grab an hors d'oeuvre, crack open its tail, remove the claws, and chow down—makes just as much sense.

But don't forget the up side to the whole thing, you know, the leg room.

THE MENTAL HEALTH RULES

Having spent the past few centuries in therapy or recovering from it—with a nice collection of labels at this point—I have found there are always those who are licensed and adequately compensated to pass them out, but not as many willing to accept and appreciate them. That being said, let's take a look at a commercial airline as it relates to psychiatric labels and mental health, specifically, mine.

First, in case you've been traveling by bus, you know that flight attendants are, as a rule, hostile, conniving, and cruel. These, however, are job requirements. I, who am not only terrified of the female flight attendants, but also without the skills and confidence to pull off those requirements, have become quite adept at another means of survival. It is one I have found to be just self-effacing enough to either keep these sky goddesses at bay, or to make me their new best friend.

"Please forgive me, hon. I have terminal ADD with OCD overtones," is what I recall saying to this particular flight attendant minutes before we took off for Paris, and would regret all the way to hell and back and into the next decade.

A few days later I got *THE CALL* from a man who claimed to represent just about everyone. He headed up the airline's Professional Code of Conduct Committee, which included the flight attendant union, the caterers, mechanics, ramp people, management, and baggage handlers. At least that's the way it sounded to me. It would the first time in airline history these groups had come together and agreed on anything. But now they were all in concurrence that if I had somehow made it through security and actually boarded one of their airplanes with ADD, OCD—or any other form of severe mental illness conveniently labeled "disorder"—I should not talk about it. Ever.

Well how much sense does that make? Excuse me, but I thought the mental health coverage was what we were all here for, anyway. I mean, how many lucid exchanges with an airline pilot has anyone ever had?

"Forgetfulness could be a safety issue, you know," the airline representative repeated three, maybe five, maybe seven times, but not in *even* numbers, as I clearly recall. After what seemed like an eternity in flight-attendant training hell, he wrapped it up by apologizing for having to make the call, but was obviously so friggin' proud of his pathetic self he could not wait to finish me off and check his files for another flight attendant with a diagnosis.

"Rosemary, we're just concerned with safety as it relates to ADD and forgetfulness," he repeated, like he was rehearsing for his next victim.

"I understand, Jim," I said.

"My name is Bob," he answered.

37.
Tiaras in turbulence

There are those who are afraid to fly. Me, I'm afraid not to. I guess it's all about safety and what the word *safe* means to each of us. For me, it kicks in just after the airplane climbs out of ten thousand feet and I give passengers permission to turn on their electronic devices. That's when I unfasten my seatbelt and give myself permission to turn on as well. Much like landing on the other side of a sidewalk line, the magic takes over.   In an airplane, that magic is my captive audience. And that captive audience is my safety.

That's why I love my job and am, frankly, enraged by books written by flight attendants who don't. That being said, it was not my intention for this one to include a section about flight attendants and their rage toward the passengers who pay their salaries, any more than I planned to write about my rage toward flight attendants and everyone on the planet's rage toward the airlines for hiring these people who not only enrage the customers but also each other! But the entire industry is so compatible with my ongoing theme of mental illness, it would've been a shame to leave out those who have played such a big part in perpetuating mine.

First, let's get very clear about one thing.

PASSENGERS HAVE EARNED THE RIGHT TO BE ANGRY!

Prior to being humiliated by flight attendants, our flying public has been molested by security officers, maligned by agents, and exposed to eating establishments with "Wok," "Taco," "Crab," "Krispy," "Chili," and, my personal favorite, "Black Muslim" (it's a bakery,* folks—if I lie I die) somewhere in their titles. So, even before flight attendants finish them off, these people have already racked up a good bit of abuse. Top this off with the deep-vein thrombosis they develop after being denied bathroom privileges and water for five hours while strapped to a seat beneath a blanket shared with the drunk in the next seat who is battling a runny nose and loose tray table, neither of which has been washed since the last outbreak of Scarlet Fever, and I believe that passengers should be allowed to express their rage with the weapon of

*Oakland Airport. Don't take off without the banana pudding.

their choosing, especially the sharp ones they sneak through the security checkpoint while the TSA* employees check out 95 year-old nuns in wheelchairs and one-year old lap children who as a rule don't even look like Arabs and if they did, they'd be rushed right through.

Most of the time when these security officers are summoned to the aircraft to remove an unruly character—drunk or on drugs—they're either confronting off-duty airline personnel or a federal air marshal who is simply trying to blend in, which is totally impossible since they all dress alike and show their badges ten times *before* they board the aircraft and again *when* they board the aircraft just prior to taking the same seat they've occupied on every flight since someone came up with the "heightened state of security" that makes us all feel so safe.

I say, the TSA should train their employees to go after the people they're supposed to, do the job they were hired to do, and stop acting like they don't know who those people are or what the hell that job is. *Duh!*

Once again, it might appear that I have digressed when I haven't, not really. You see, these frequent deviations from my story also bring home the unintended yet secondary theme of the book: "all about me, how clever I am, and how my ADD so often takes me completely away from my story." Bear with me. We'll be on the ground before you know it.

Airline Story #1

Repeatedly, I had asked a passenger to turn off his headsets as we descended below 10,000 feet. He obviously heard me but ignored my request. On my third attempt, he removed the headsets and shoved them into my chest. Hard. He snarled, "They're not on, lady, but if you think you're so smart, why don't you tell everyone what you hear?"

I apologized and told him he could put them back on if they were, in fact, turned off. No big deal. But again, he returned them to me

---

*TSA: Transportation Security Administration or Texas Society of Anesthesiologists. Take your pick. One is asleep while the other induces it.

with the same force and attitude, "No, lady, you say they're on—so tell everyone what you hear!"

I asked him again to stop shoving the headsets into my chest as I, typically, allowed him to continue doing it just the same. Finally, I leaned in close and politely spelled it out. "Sir, when you interfere with me while I am performing crew duties, it is a federal offense. But let's say, just for instance, I slap the shit out of you for interfering. Now that would just be a simple little misdemeanor."

A fight. It was exactly what the man wanted. After another brief go-round, I eagerly complied with his wishes and placed his headsets on my ears, pausing only to catch the attention of my audience, which had grown considerably in size since the show began. The curtain came up. I was ready.

"Okay, sir," I said, as I adjusted the headsets, "I'll tell everyone *what I hear.*"

I squinted as I pretended to listen, then removed the headsets as quickly as they had been shoved into my chest. "Was that your wife I heard, Sir? Does she leave messages like this often?"

Silence.

The look on his face was almost as startling as the tattoos that began beneath his ears and stopped just short of his elbows, an unfinished portrait no doubt commemorating the exact moment he had offended and/or injured the tattoo artist.

"Wait, let me rewind this," I said, as I took two steps back and prepared to turn my voice into a human megaphone.

"Okay, folks," I shouted, "this is what I'm hearing: 'Honey, you wear my nightgown and high heels one more time and you can keep your tattooed ass in Houston!'"

(Shortly after this incident I was summoned into an office and advised that I should have called airport security. I disagreed. My way of handling incidents of this nature was a lot more fun and really good practice for the hecklers I would encounter at New York comedy clubs— and, of course, the New York heckler I would move in with.)

Airline Story #2

Turbulence takes on many forms.

Ever notice before a flight takes off how you see ten, maybe fifteen flight attendants—and in the air you can only find one or two? This is because, more times than not, flight attendants have an intense need to kill each other. Sometimes with the beverage cart, others with intimidation and terrorization, and quite often, with the airline food. In other words, they basically just perform those god-awful passenger service skills on each other.

But this all ceases when circumstances require that they bond.

Kim and I strap ourselves in the jumpseat, preparing for an emergency landing. She loses it. Obviously convinced it's all over, this beautiful black, stone-faced woman has now decided to shift gears. With a seat belt as the woman's only defense against extreme turbulence and my only defense against an unsolicited lap dance, she traps my leg between both of hers and squeezes as her hands grab mine. Next she expresses her unconditional love for me and all older women, mostly white ones, and, basically, sucks up.

We land safely. Afterward, at a meeting with the crew, the captain perspires, frowns and fidgets as though oblivious to the news that we had not crashed and burned. He addresses the crew: "This was very serious—*very* serious," he says, authoritatively. "So, I'd like for each of you to tell me exactly what you learned."

One-by-one, the flight attendants rattle off the emergency procedures that were employed and blame each other for the ones that weren't. About now I am praying this pilot won't address me as I did not participate one bit, having no idea where to even begin to look for emergency equipment and just the thought of it scares the crap out of me. I can't even find my Ritalin.

He turns to me. "Rosemary, what did you learn?"

I had to tell him.

"Kim's a bisexual."

Airline Story #3

It is not unusual for passengers to board the aircraft and leave their manners in the gate area or for their brains to wind up at a security check point after being sucked up by the metal detector. And it is even less unusual for professional ball teams to board without either one and then to make that fact known to the younger female flight attendants. On this particular flight, they made it known to me.

I had made several unsuccessful attempts to reach the forward galley by way of an aisle that separated at least ten rows of neatly jelled, well turned-out testosterone. Each time I started out, my trip was cancelled as the athletes passed a girlie magazine across the aisle to their teammates. This woman in the altogether—staple in her navel, NBA drool most everywhere else—continued to occupy my workspace as she got passed up and down the rows and across the aisles. I saw a lull in the action and seized the opportunity to start back down the aisle toward the galley. But once again I found myself trapped by the magazine, mid-aisle—cornered by the woman sprawled out on its dog-eared pages.

Obviously pleased with himself, the jock in charge of entertainment raised the magazine into the air. Then, assuming I'd lost my eyesight and hearing along with everything else, he stood and held the magazine level with my face. Like I'd somehow missed a breast, a leg, or a thigh, he pointed them out, one at a time.

"So, wha'cha think about her, stewardess?" he exclaimed, raising his eyebrows.

To which this stewardess answered, raising her eyebrows right back, "Makes you wish you were straight, doesn't it?"

Airline Story #4

On my forty-ninth birthday I hailed a cab outside my Manhattan apartment. It screeched up to the curb and I followed my luggage into the back seat.

"Airport, please," I sang. It was a familiar tune sung in a cutsie voice I hadn't called upon since high school. I volunteered, "I'm headed for my high school reunion—wearing the same size jeans I wore back then! I *really* am!"

When we stopped at a red light, the driver turned to me, winked, and said, "Lady, from two blocks away—*wow!*—you looked really young!"

My dream was trashed. I wanted to die.

He proceeded to amend his remark a bit, as New Yorkers often do when their venom has somehow missed a vein. "I mean, lady, from *two blocks away*, you looked like a ten!"

At the airport I paid my fare, collected my luggage, and shut the cab door.

"No tip?" the driver asked.

I passed a quarter through his open window.

"From *two blocks away* it looks like a ten!" I said.

Airline Story #5

I was working a trip as the lead flight attendant with a crew of three other female flight attendants. For three days, a very senior captain had invited each of us to be a part of an audience obviously assembled only to witness his crude performance. On the fourth day, he asked to borrow my key to the cockpit. I inadvertently produced my apartment key, which he took. Realizing my error, I asked him to return it, explaining that I had given it to him by mistake.

"Oh, I'm keeping this," he smiled. "Tell me, what are we going to do when I come to your apartment?"

I motioned for him to come closer and whispered, "Well, for starters, I have a little suit I'd like you to wear."

"*Suit?*" he asked, with a sudden burst of energy. He stepped back. "Okay, now, what crazy stuff are you into?" His tense expression might well have come from the strain of trying to remember what to do next, given the fact he'd probably gotten nothing up but the wheels of an airplane since 1975. When he leaned forward, panting sounds accompanied hot breaths that traveled up my neck and deposited the unmistakable aftermath of bad airline food into my nose. A likely explanation for the man's intimacy issues, I said to myself, since convincing a woman to stand within twenty feet of anything on his body would zap the strength from even the most virile.

He whispered, "What kind of suit are we talking about?"

"It's called a sexual harassment suit," I answered. "Think it'll fit?"

Airline Story #6

A commuting company pilot was boarding behind a disgruntled passenger who had stopped traffic with his demands. "Oh, yes, you *will* put my luggage in the closet," he snarled. "And don't give me that airline crap about it being full."

The pilot stepped forward and whispered, "Ma'am, do you think my piano will fit in your closet?"

"No," I whispered back, "but I'll just bet your organ would fit in my coin purse."

Airline Story #7

My legs are my best remaining attributes. At least, that's what I tell myself. And that's also what I told the seamstress when she altered my uniform skirt.

As I waited in the L.A. terminal for my flight, a west coast-based flight attendant approached me. "Look," she said, "it's like, you don't know me but, I'm just saying this to help you. I mean, you know, don't get upset but I think you need to know that I have a friend who got put on a month's suspension for wearing her skirt too short. And it wasn't nearly as short as yours."

"You mean, like my Granny used to say, 'Law, girl, pull that down—I kin see plumb to the Promised Land!'" I said, Lord knows why.

"What?" she said nervously, as she backed up two steps.

I comforted her. "Oh, girlfriend, of course I know where you're coming from, and I'm not the least bit upset. Lord knows, we have to stick together! Look," I said, "I just got off a three month suspension myself."

"For what?" she asked.

"For slapping a flight attendant who said my skirt was too short."

Airline Story #8

It is next to impossible—and Lord knows I've tried—to write a book about stereotypes and labels without addressing that sometimes misunderstood segment of humanity: the airline pilot. So if, in the process of exposing these men, I destroy a myth or wreck a fantasy or two, well, as the airline pilots say . . . well, I don't really know what they say, but I do know that it is almost never clever.

Anyway, I would like to say that this is not a pretty picture. But, honestly, most of the time it is. There are days I open the cockpit door and would swear I'm opening the pages of *GQ*. But don't get me wrong. I don't care what these men *look* like, I really don't. What I *do* care about is layovers that are, well, fun. So, what I want to know is, *when's it all gonna start?*

As for sexual harassment and sex, itself, I have honestly experienced more of both on the number six local from Grand Central to Union Square!

It would appear that, for the most part, these are fine, upstanding, dedicated professionals who simply do their jobs and go home to their families.

They make me sick.

Airline story #9

The captain announced that he was unable to get the landing gear down. Shortly afterward he called the flight attendants and gave the all-clear. The gear was down and we would land in ten minutes. He asked me to tell the passengers. I made an announcement that was obviously ignored by the still-terrified-white-knuckled group, so I began my long journey to the back of the aircraft and my jumpseat.

All too aware this might be the performance of my life, I was determined to convince these passengers that we were out of danger. As I walked past their rows, I personally assured each of them that we would be landing safely. It wasn't working.

Half-way down the aisle, we hit a gargantuan air pocket. I used the force as an opportunity to land on the lap of a perfectly gorgeous man who was occupying an aisle seat. "Sir, I think we're going to be O.K.," I said, loudly, "but just in case we're not, I'm really lonely." He stood up, releasing me from his lap.

"Ma'am, he responded, even more loudly, "I can tell that you're really lonely and I hate to ruin your last moments. But I'm really GAY!"

The last Airline Story #10

There are times when, like it or not, I have had to share my stage with others. Sometimes those people are celebrities; other times they, somewhat like me, just think they are. But the late, great David Brinkley was for real. Since the first night he brought the world into my living room, we were friends. So on this occasion, I expressed my appreciation for all those visits by calling upon the power flight attendants innately believe they have.

"Mr. Brinkley," I approached his aisle seat. "We're landing. You *don't* have to return your seatback and tray table to their full, upright, and locked positions. You *may* keep your trash, talk on your phone, open up your luggage and use unapproved electronic devices . . . wanna smoke?"

He unfastened his seatbelt and stood. David Brinkley was about to have the last word, not a quality I find attractive in a man, especially just after I've had mine.

"Thank you," he smiled, still standing. "I've waited my entire life for this moment."

His performance was followed by laughter and light applause from the other passengers. I didn't like it one bit.

Sometimes I wonder why I have to win. Then I remember the 1959 Miss Mallard competition when I didn't and suddenly understand why, thirty-something years later, I have the need to prove that I could have.

I tossed him a pillow and the last word.

"Sit down, David. And goodnight."

38.
Stand up and be funny

*"The answers were clear: comedy (1) takes away pain, and (2) brings love.
Standing up and being funny was all I had to do."*
Six-year old me

It was inevitable I would one day take my act below 30,000 feet, but I never expected such a rapid descent the night of my first gig.

Twenty minutes—two ten-minute sets. That's what the comedy club owner asked for the night I performed. No music. No U.S. Marines. No little girl in her daddy's liquor store. No familiar airplane full of passengers. Just strangers in a small smoke-filled room and me—standing up, being funny.

The comedian who preceded me was black. In case we hadn't noticed, he was black. He was black, black, black, and his routine was all about—what else?—the color of his skin. It was sure enuf black. Well, I'll give the black man one thing—he had an unfair advantage over those of us who were not. And sister woman, he took it.

Just about the time he impressed me with his comedic range, he threatened to move into my neighborhood. *Oh, sure!* Like this white woman would pack up her Pradas in her Louis Vuitton and leave her cushy life! *I don't think so!*

But she *was* about to visit her old one.

The comedian hadn't been on that stage five minutes before he dug up my childhood and dumped it into my lily white lap. The next twenty minutes were like watching an old movie as my mind traveled back in time. On my screen, I saw the alley beside Jones Theater and me, standing beside a very young version of the comedian. I couldn't have been more uncomfortable had the young man in my movie summoned the entire balcony of his peers to join us.

We stood beside the COLOREDS' sign on the door of the makeshift bathroom attached to the side of the theater. I felt his hand squeezing mine which, in those days, would have gotten him possibly killed. Just the same, in my mind, that's what he did. After all, I had a dream. . . .

I returned to the present long enough to see him grab the microphone from its stand. I heard the roar of laughter as I was being pulled back into that alley. Hand in hand, we walked across the street from Jones Theater to the town's only other place of recreation. It was Betty Jo's Place, the old streetcar-turned diner, with jukebox, pool table, and soda fountain.

Betty Jo's was everyone's favorite hangout, everyone white, anyway. But Betty Jo was not without compassion. Betty spared this young man and his friends the embarrassment of another COLOREDS' sign on the bathroom door inside as the one on the outside, WHITES ONLY, meant he couldn't go to the bathroom at all.

The dream fast forwarded to another frame. It was all about a summer day in Little Rock, a bus ride, and the man who intended to sit in the seat next to mine, until I changed his plans with an unexpected critique of him—"You white trash son (and his mother) of a bitch!"

In retrospect, I'm pretty sure some of those words were also meant for Betty Jo.

The man *was* funny. So funny I could look into my immediate future and see a white woman on a black man's stage, drowning in a pool of sweat. It wasn't fair. Who gave *him* permission to call upon his past to further his present? I mean, give us a break, bro! Haven't you people done enough?

The black people threw food on the white people below. . . .

As he wrapped it up, I realized the redneck routine I had planned just wasn't going to cut it. For starters, a woman from Queens had done it earlier. It always made me uncomfortable, anyway, as it came just a little too easy. Certainly easier than to a woman from Queens. Besides, it had been done ad nauseam and there was nothing particularly funny about it when it was.

But being black? Now that had always been *hilarious!!*

Well, I certainly couldn't pass as a black woman, and I damn sure wasn't going to base my act on being an aging white one. Or, the more popular combination—a horney, aging, fat, white, redneck woman.

That also came a little too easy.

The red light was flashing the comedian off the stage when I had a light bulb moment: the perfect routine. It was irreverent, in bad taste, and slightly mean-spirited. All I had to do was throw in a few choice expletives and I'd have an acceptable set. I approached the stage. The comedian whispered, "Break a leg," as he passed me the microphone, with no clue that (even before he could pick up his popcorn and take his seat in the balcony) it would explode. His routine had made me angry; it made me mean; it made me preach; and it made me all those things because it made me, mostly, guilty.

"The recipe never changes," I sighed. "You take your black comic. You add your white audience. You sprinkle on your blue humor. And, *whamo!* You got your chitlin' pizza! Honey Chile, it's enough to make this honkey grab a cotton sack and beg, 'Lawsy mercy me, just this one time, let's get *off color.*'"

I had just made history as the first comedian to base her entire routine on putting down the comedian who preceded her. "I mean, folks," I said, as I tried to get a grip on a microphone now dripping with a bead of sweat representing each audience member, "for a man who could have served up a ten-course banquet on fine china, I got chitlins on a paper plate! Now that's a little hard to swallow."

People hung around. No one died. . . .

The captain had definitely illuminated the applause sign, and the approval meter was registering in the standing ovation range, minus one. The comedian had taken a table toward the back of the room, and he wasn't laughing. Well, boo hoo. My response simply fit the crime. Who dredged up the whole ugly mess in the first place? All I did was (1) rip his act apart, (2) reduce him to second-class citizen status and (3) segregate him from the rest of the audience so I could (4) watch him sit in the back of the room and take it. Not exactly an unfamiliar gig for the man. He should've felt right at home.

And I should've stayed there.

Maybe it was that black power thing, I didn't know. But some kind of spell sure took over my second set. No one could have bombed that bad without intervention of one kind or another. Well . . . according to my shrink, something intervened, alright—and it wasn't black power. It was the kind of guilt and confusion that either make a woman suicidal or turn her into a first-rate comedian. The more the audience laughed, the more anxiety I felt, but nowhere near as much anxiety as they were feeling because of mine. I was determined to screw up, and I did.

Those unresolved racial issues weren't the main offenders. Unfortunately, as was often the case with me and guilt, the kind that *should* hang around usually didn't. Sabotaging myself, now that was something altogether different. That was so well rehearsed and performed with such skill that at first it appeared to be part of my act. Of course, it was actually part of my life, but so was art, and tonight my art was most definitely copying my life.

The faces of the audience twisted into huge question marks but their bodies found the answer: they would heckle me. But they would not just heckle me. They would do what comedy club audiences love to do. It's *body language heckling*, and it works like this: the folks closest to the stage simply turn their heads and their bodies *away* from you while their evil inner spirits turn *on* you. It's as though they know some dark, personal secret from your past.

She's in her room fucking dogs. . . .

I felt guilty, alright. But not about the comedian—or the dogs. It was my performance. I had done what I came to do; I'd brought down the house—and I was terrified. Of course, it wasn't my first run-in with laughter, and it sure wasn't the first time I'd been afraid of the stage. During that second set, all the old tapes in my collection began serving concurrent sentences in my half-a-mind:

"Success! Winning! That's what Southern Belles are all about!"
"But Southern Belles have to be careful about being funny—careful, careful, careful . . . ."
"Go on, do it! Show everyone how stupid you are!"
"Have you ever listened—r e a l l y listened—to your own laugh?"

I had heard that when it comes to the death of a comedian, audiences don't usually hang around for the funeral. But this group wasn't going anywhere! A woman was about to be thrown to the lions and they could hardly wait to witness it. From the sight of punch lines scribbled on her hands in black ink, being carried away by an avalanche of perspiration, to the deafening sound of those ill-chosen words falling flat on every ear in the room.

235

The jerks knew I was dying before the ink hit the floor.

It wasn't like I hadn't been warned. Just before my first set, one of Rodney Dangerfield's writers had stopped me as I passed his table enroute to the guillotine. "Do you do drugs?" he asked.

"No," I frowned.

"Too bad," he sighed.

About three minutes into that second set, I agreed.

As I crawled off the stage, Dangerfield's writer stood, "Next time, I'll write you some good stuff, babe," he said, like the smartass he was. I assured him all the way to my car that I was perfectly capable of getting no respect on my own.

Driving away from the club I remembered Daddy's advice, "If you can't change things, go on vacation and if you can't go on vacation, go fishing." I fished for a very long time until finally things became clear. No matter how proficient I'd become at baiting my own hook, I could never catch enough—not to make up for or understand the little girl who believed she belonged in a Rose Garden or the woman who stayed there too long.

Again, what I probably needed was more therapy, but this time I decided to trash that idea for the sure thing. It was time to recapture my youth—to bring out of hiding the young woman who once braved so many beauty pageant runways.

And if I couldn't find her I would, for sure, turn to drugs.

VI. Running out of runway

39.
Troy and me in a 733 . . .

The celebration of my fiftieth birthday took me back to the year my children rounded up a houseful of relatives—on my ex-husband's side—to reminisce about the "good old days." I approached that event with the same blind optimism that saw me through acne at fifteen, near-insanity at thirty, and divorce at thirty two. But facing this birthday stripped from my memory every cute and comforting cliché.

"This too shall pass" offered no solace as I watched mini-skirted flight attendants running rampant through the airport terminal, each still going through some phase of the divorce/acne/mental illness thing. "Beauty is only skin deep" didn't work, either. Not since the day I realized I'd heard it only from ugly women.

So, the whole freaking universe was, still, a beauty pageant stage. And on this particular one, I was losing. This time, it was all about the luggage.

WINNER: Pilots put your luggage in the overhead bin; pilots take your luggage from the overhead bin; pilots call the hotel van; pilots tip the driver; and pilots take you for dinner and drinks.

FIRST RUNNER UP: Pilots put your luggage in the overhead bin.

NOT EVEN A FINALIST: It's your luggage, bitch. Deal with it. Stuff it with mini-bottles; hitchhike to the hotel; eat in your room; tape back your jowls; bleach your hair blonde; beat yourself up.

Rock bottom, I'd hit it. I was a fifty-year-old flight attendant with a supervisor named "Missy," for gosh sake. My personal baggage was extending into the aisle and had far exceeded the size and shape to put beneath the seat in front of me. The skycaps had all gone home.

But it was the day before my birthday. And I had to fly.

(Above or below 30,000 feet, I have found that avoiding the aging process is not nearly as difficult as avoiding those who remind us we are

doing it. On this, the day of my birthday, I would find that the late Troy Donahue was not one of those people—and certainly not someone I wanted to avoid. Our brief friendship will forever be a reminder that our fantasies really can come true, on our fiftieth birthday, or any birthday. That is, if we aren't afraid to fly.)

It was the second day of my four-day trip. I was unsure which time zone or what city I had waked up in, but was absolutely certain of how old I was and that it was my birthday. With the popular notion that my whole life would shape up after thirty minutes on the treadmill, I headed straight for the hotel workout room.

The flight attendant who greeted me was working out for what was, obviously, not *her* first time in two years. When she stepped off the treadmill I was eye-level with the words, "Party Naked with Me." That her t-shirt could carry all those words was astounding. That she had the forethought to advertise the exact way she chose to party—unbelievable!

There she was, my worst nightmare—a beautiful young blonde flight attendant ready to party on what was, most likely, not even her birthday. And there I was—an older but wiser flight attendant, ready to party on my birthday, but with no t-shirt to tell me how.

There are those who claim that these young women have all been replaced by unenthusiastic, aging old fossils. Well, not without enthusiasm, I would like to say that these people lie through their teeth. I *am* an aging old fossil and I haven't replaced anyone. The young ones are still out there. They're *everywhere*.

Some days the average age of the front and backend crew appears to slightly exceed puberty. When I look at these young women—I call them Barbie dolls—I have no recollection of ever being young, without gray roots, an angioplasty in my right coronary artery, or arthritis in my left knee.

On the fourth and final day of our trip, as we prepared to take off from LaGuardia to Baltimore, the twenty-three-year-old lead flight attendant instructed me to give the passenger count to the captain.

As I turned to leave the cockpit, the first officer asked what the cabin looked like. I was thinking it looked like *The Jerry Springer Show* as I gave him the standard, "Luggage is stowed, passengers are seated, and flight attendants are ready to go."

As I walked back through the cabin I heard the flight attendant call bell and I approached the ringer. My first mistake.

"Ma'am, are you in charge here?" the gentleman bellowed.

"No, sir, I'm just the oldest. Can I help you?"

I knelt beside him so that when he waved his finger for emphasis it would be precisely in my face. He demanded, "I want to know why those girls up front wouldn't hang this bag in the closet. And don't tell me again that it was full."

I attempted to resolve this man's dilemma without repeating that the closet was full, as I noticed his suitcase extending into the aisle, a computer in his lap, a cell phone attached to his ear, a suit bag beside him, and what appeared to be last year's poinsettias emerging from the overhead bin.

He shrieked, "I'll never forget this, lady. I'll never forget you!"

"Yes, you will, sir," I assured him. "It's my birthday. The kids forgot me. My family forgot me. Trust me. You'll forget me, too. Be patient with yourself, it'll happen."

I had just checked the rest of the cabin and was preparing to strap myself to my jumpseat for take-off when I heard two rings. I picked up the phone—it was the cockpit. There would be a slight delay to wait for passengers from another flight. I started back up the aisle, hopeful that the man who would never forget me, had. But I was met mid-aisle by the lead Barbie who was working first class. It was immediately clear to me that something was terribly wrong.

The poor girl! First the broken fingernail in Orlando. Then someone—we suspect the agent in Chicago—borrowed her chocolate chip cookies from the galley. Now what? Her hair spray? Her *Seventeen?* She pulled me aside and whispered, "There's an old movie star in first class. He's old, but it's like, you know, he's pretty tough looking. I'll bet you know him. You gotta' come look. I mean, he's pretty old, but . . ."

I marveled at her limited vocabulary as I tried to count the times "old" had slipped from her young lips. When I grabbed the passenger manifest, I expected to see, maybe, Mae West or George Burns.

241

But the name that leapt from that page almost sent me out the emergency exit and over the left wing. I don't know what came first—the chills, the memories, the music, or the sudden spurt of energy that had me reaching in my pocket for my lipstick, tucking in my blouse and my stomach and pushing the Barbie aside as I made my way to the front of this 737-300 airplane. And I did it all in perfect time to the music.

"There's a Summer Place. A place where w-ee-eee can go . . ."

TROY DONAHUE! It was really him. *Oh Troy! Oh Troy! Where have you been? I've missed you so!*

I approached him—this movie star. This man I idolized, this man whose blond hair still tousled. Whose smile still smiled. Whose eyes still pierced. Whose . . . well, *everything* was still doing *everything*.

"May I help you?" he asked.

May *he* help *me?* May *he* help *me?*

No one ever wanted to help *me*. But that was just like him. Just like my Troy. The bell went off. Oh, no! Not the man in coach again. I wish he *would forget me.* Then another bell. And another.

I turned to Troy and exclaimed, *"I HATE PEOPLE!"*

I suspect that Sandra Dee had departed from reality now and then because Troy knew exactly what to do. He touched my hand and softly assured me, "We don't have to love them, you know. Not en masse."

I got the message. He wanted to be alone. With me.

Three bells from the cockpit. I rushed back to my jumpseat. We took off. I don't know who fed the people in coach but I was sure glad to see them eating when I floated back down the aisle to first class. He was still there. As real as before. As I stood beside him; it started again. The music. He was lying on a picnic blanket waiting for Sandra Dee. He asked me again if he could help me. I gave him the agenda.

"Troy, this will be in three stages. First I'll stare. Then I'll jump on your lap. Then I'll kiss your face."

"Well, you've stared long enough," he laughed. "Get on with the second stage."

Obviously he was asking me to join him. So, in spite of the darts I was receiving from the two Barbies working first class, I sat beside him. And we talked and talked. We talked about *Summer Place.* Whatever happened to Dorothy McGuire, Richard Egan, Arthur Kennedy? He shared a bit of his personal life with me. I invented one and shared it with him.

Just about the time we had really, really begun to bond, I heard the approach announcement from the cockpit. We were landing in Baltimore in ten minutes. Troy and I had played out our last scene. Almost.

He was nervous about making his connection.

"You're fine," I assured him. "You're gonna make it."

"No, *we're* fine. *We're* gonna make it," he smiled. He produced a pen and wrote down what I assumed was his autograph. It was his phone number in L.A.

The Barbie was watching.

"You gave it to *her*? You gave *HER* your phone number?" she marveled.

He turned and gave me a look Sandra Dee would kill for. "Yes, I gave it to *HER*," he grinned.

He wrapped his six-foot something frame in a full-length leather coat and gathered up his briefcase and computer as I watched him prepare to leave.

The Barbie wouldn't give up.

"Well, when are *we* gonna get the number? *Huh? When?*"

I looked at him one last time as he walked down the jetway. With one hand, I clutched the phone number. With the other, I freed this young woman's hand from my sleeve.

"*When?*" I smiled. "I'll tell you *when*."

"When *LEE'S* stops making press-on fingernails and *TEENAGE HELL* freezes over.

That's when."

40.
Don't touch that bag. She works for the company.

"Come on, stewardess, don't tell that closet is full! I *KNOW* you've got some hanging areas you aren't showing me!"

For the first time in airline history, a passenger was right. I had some hanging areas alright, and it took a very brave man to point out what any fool could see. My life was exactly as he had said. It was all about hanging. Hanging and aging. Aging and hanging. I was just another flying airbag—living for her layover—waiting to chase down catered, saturated fat with mini-bottles from first class.

The morning following this four-day trip I woke up resigned to my fate. As I faced the big 5-0 in my mirror, I told myself I could *be* who I wanted and therefore *say* what I wanted; my thoughts were, in fact, just down right profound. It was when I took a second look at the new, wiser me that my world came screeching to a halt like a wheelchair with bad brakes.

Seemingly overnight, Judy Garland had been replaced by that old tree in *The Wizard of Oz's* famous forest—a sagging, bent-over piece of brittle wood, with lines circling its trunk and dead limbs flopping in the breeze, marking time until a young sprout took its place. An inanimate piece of dispensable scenery without so much as a speaking part was what I'd become.

"Yes! What I think *is* important!" I had thought, but that was before I discovered the terrible Truth. The mouth that had earned exclamation points had been awarded parentheses instead—two lines running from the base of both sides of my nose to the corners of my upper lip. *Semi-circles!* My shrunken lips—too tiny and upside down to accommodate anything larger than a capful of Geratol sucked through a hospital straw—were now surrounded by semi-circles!

No way around it, the mouth that should have been set free had been framed. The lips that once smiled back at me in the mirror had now turned into an upside down U that reminded me daily: "U, bitch, should never leave the house.'"

Above my upper lip, vertical creases traveled up to my nose like tributaries and grabbed everything that crossed their path. Even the raspberry gloss intended to bring the plumpness of youth to my disappearing lips now shot up my nose like bright red cocaine.

This was the same mouth that once said, "If I were Arkansas Junior Miss, I would give the money to each and every one of the judges," and should have said, "No, I really don't think I belong in a mental hospital," and for years had said, "Ladies and gentlemen, if you'll observe the fasten seat belt sign . . ." and, most recently had said, "If you'll take me to dinner, I'll cook it."

The mouth that was prepared to shout, *"What I think IS important!"* could now deliver no more than a parenthetical phrase in a faint whisper:

("Not as important as the rest of the sentence.")

It was a sentence I would be serving for the rest of my life.

Obviously, psychiatric therapy was in order. But if you think I went that route, you'd better hold on to your seat cushions because let me assure you that for once, this flying airbag put that psychobabble pile of rubbish aside in favor of a solution that would jump out and pull the eyeballs from the sockets of any man—first class, coach class, cockpit, whatever. It was a solution that wouldn't have to be bandied about, analyzed, and mauled beyond recognition. It was one that would, finally, S H O W!

41.
Cosmetically correct

Quite possibly, the smallest piece of plastic on a flight attendant's body is her credit card, which is where the real surgery should probably take place. Nevertheless, it was my need to be like the Barbies—but more, Truth be known, my need to *not* be like myself—that propelled me forward with that card and had me agreeing to what the plastic surgeon called a min-lift. ("Mini," in plastic surgery talk, refers to the limit on one's credit card. Just so you know.)

It was one day post-surgery. I waited in his reception area to see this plastic surgeon, a man who, throughout this grueling process, had been the best straight man and comedic partner I'd ever had. Our partnership began just after my fiftieth birthday when I walked into his Upper East Side office and tossed my Arkansas Junior Miss banner onto his desk and then challenged him to recreate the 8x10 photograph I had placed beside it. Yes, it was a picture of my coronation. No, I wasn't kidding.

I had spent the night before in the room adjacent to his office, one of several cost-cutting perks included in my facelift package. But now I wondered if that generous discount hadn't placed me on the bottom of the appointment list. For what seemed to last longer than the aging process itself, I waited, eyes swollen, eyelashes stuck to the bandages below them, bruises on top of everything, and more bruises on top of those. I felt the glares of the Park Avenue Hollywood wanna-be's who filled the chairs surrounding mine. They came and they went, seemingly with very little waiting time. Just the same, as though waiting for a second martini or late limo, they fretted and fidgeted.

And they pouted. *Jesus! Did they!* At least I think they did. With lips the size of bananas, it was hard to be sure. Before today I, too, had wanted lips—even had it written into my package deal. Okay, The Truth is that I wanted to look like my sisters who, of course, wouldn't go anywhere without lips any more than they'd go within ten feet of a "package deal" to get them, or anything else. Naturally, neither of them *needed* lips. Their own God-given ones were perfectly shaped already, as perfectly shaped as their perfectly shaped lives. Full, pouty, pink lips. Perfectly perfect. Naturally.

Damn! I was sick of waiting. My sisters would never have had to wait. I handed a note to the nurse and asked her to deliver it to the surgeon.

> *Doc:*
>
> *As I begin my second hour in your waiting room, I am aware that your outdated magazines have become more outdated and your other patients—bigger snobs. It would also appear that their lips and breasts are taking up the small bit of space their enormous egos have not filled up in this teensy space you call a reception area. In fact, during my stay in this room, I have come to understand that the only thing worse than a New York chip on your shoulder is your very own butt on your lips.*
>
> *That being said, if I ever get back to see you—"package deal" or no "package deal"—don't touch my lips.*
>
> *Rosemary*

"I'll get you back. I'll swear I will." The surgeon stepped inside the door of the reception area, then waved the note in my direction and mouthed words that were unmistakable, especially to the mother of a lip reader. Suddenly I was overcome by an irresistible urge to empty the room and get my appointment underway.

I leapt from my chair, raced to the doorway, grabbed his sleeve and shrieked, "You quack! Just look at my face! I told you liposuction!" Which I thought was absolutely hilarious. On the other hand, it was most likely from an event like this that the expression emerged, "Don't dish it out if you can't take it."

The group of flawless New Yorkers appeared to be rethinking those initial consults and/or scheduled surgeries while attempting to frown through their Botox—unfortunately, at me. As I observed their obvious lack of anything, mostly humor, I understood how important it was for them to keep their appointments.

The doctor chose the center of the reception room for his announcement: "Ladies, may I have your attention," he said, as he turned toward me. "This woman is crazy. However, if she checks her butt, she'll find that I did, indeed, do liposuction. I put part of it on her face and part of it on her chest, and, still, there was enough remaining for this entire waiting room, the Upper and Lower East and West Sides, and Chinatown as well. Unfortunately, my plans to plug up her enormous mouth have just been aborted as she has instructed me to stay away from that particular portion of her face."

Only in New York.

Post-operative note: Facelifts are intended to help a woman go forward. Mine took me backward. Two weeks post surgery I saw in my mirror the face of a younger woman I once knew. She hadn't needed to leave her children in search of a better mother then any more than she needed a better face now.

A couple of weeks later, I looked into that same mirror and saw a young father standing beside his daughter. "You can be anyone or anything you want to be," he was saying.

Even someone old.

42.
The longest runway

"Hello, Mama. This is Travis. I'm in love, and her name is Susan. Well . . . here's Susan."

That phone call from Travis six months before his wedding day was reminiscent of many others. As always, he stated whatever was on his mind, then turned the phone over to some poor soul who got blasted with my reaction. That poor soul then turned to Travis—who could read lips from across a football field—and relayed my every word. This time, the poor soul was my future daughter-in-law—the young woman who had swept away this special man in my life. Before I could respond to his first shocker, Travis took the phone from her hand and finished me off.

"Listen, Mama, we're going to get married. So, I guess you'll be a mother-in-law, and, someday, a grandmother. Now, what do you think about that, Mama? Here's Susan."

This was the first summer following college graduation and he'd been hired as Director of Sports for the employees at a popular theme park. With more than a thousand employees to oversee, I thought that all of his time would be occupied; that's what I thought. *That's what I hoped.* Truth be known, I needed more time to get to know the boy I once tucked into bed with only a night light shining up from the baseboard—the little boy who had responded to, "I love you," with:
"Turn on light. Can't hear you."
Now that boy was handing the phone to his bride-to-be while I visualized her face as she waited—and waited—to hear me sound happy. But I couldn't, so I faked it. Then I hopped on a flight to meet her. Face-to-face.

And what a face. I wasn't prepared. Susan. Beautiful, gentle, nurturing, free. With traits that don't usually mesh, she was artistic and uninhibited, yet practical and meticulous. Everything within her reach seemed to fall into perfect order effortlessly, yet nothing took precedence over the present moment. I think it was her laugh that really got my attention. Like Travis, she seemed to be on to something I couldn't see but found myself looking for just the same. But unlike Travis, she could hear.

On the last night of our visit, we sat up late and talked. With only a nightlight shining up from the baseboard in the living room, Susan leaned closer to me and whispered,

"Sometimes it's nice to talk in the dark."

I always knew I would survive the federal government, aging and menopause, a mental hospital, divorce, panic attacks and a commercial airline. But since the day my sons were born, I was afraid I wouldn't survive their weddings. Today I understood why.

I had so hoped by now I would know who I was. As always, The Mayor knew exactly who he was and had a title to prove it. He was now asking to be called "The District Attorney," so I, like most everyone else, just assumed he was one. I wasn't sure what a District Attorney did, but had heard it had something to do with locking people up.

It would be our first up-close encounter since the day he said goodbye to me at The Rose Garden all those years ago. I had made it through two years with lunatics and twenty more without this one, yet I was pretty sure I wouldn't sarvive this day. The problem was not my son, his wife, or her family. Emily Post and Miss Manners would have been hard pressed to find a more acceptable group. But, of course, the new First Lady, The District Attorney, and a myriad of former friends and relatives showed up, too.

I know of nothing to prepare a woman for such an event. But if you take a look at my mistakes, perhaps you won't make the same ones. These are the secrets of survival I figured out from the second pew:

- Don't flirt with the preacher. It makes you look lonely. No matter how hard you try, you can't talk him into holding your funeral early, like the day before the wedding.
- Don't try to reconcile with your ex-husband at the reception. Remember, this is the first time you've seen him wear a suit or drink his liquor from a glass.

- The rehearsal dinner is not the place to discuss back alimony. And don't try to settle up by taking the current wife's mink coat. Chances are she killed the thing herself with one of those *LOOKS!*
- The groom's parents are financially responsible for the rehearsal dinner. True. But don't get roped into paying for more than your share. *Do Not* pay for the current wife's outfit—no matter how cheap it appears to be. Feathers and pop beads are more costly than you might think.
- Don't pitch a screaming fit if you get cake on your dress. People will suspect you were planning to take it back to the store after the wedding.
- If your escort was hired through an agency, make payment arrangements before the wedding. You're gonna want to *die* when he asks for his money at the reception.
- Don't break your neck trying to catch the wedding bouquet. It makes you look even lonelier than flirting with the preacher.
- Airline training helps. Know the location of your medical kits, oxygen masks, fire extinguishers. And when the heat gets too intense, crawl on your stomach to the nearest emergency exit.

Travis and I had rehearsed for many important performances when he was a child. I was right on cue as I sat in the front row at his kindergarten graduation and mouthed the words to the songs, just as we had rehearsed at home. For a TV fund-raiser with Minnie Pearl, we had practiced the words I would feed him from behind the camera. "Y'all come," he said, even better than Minnie. But this was different. There had been no rehearsal for tonight—no rehearsal for the rehearsal dinner.

I almost missed the whole thing. My seat of honor was just a stone's throw from the heating and cooling system and at least a mile from the head table.

The Mayor was from Mars—and Mars was getting farther away every day.

Immediately after sitting down I felt the need to escape by assembling the kind of obsessive facts and figures always left to Mr. Jones. It was suddenly important to me that the age of the new First Lady was the approximate number of hours I had gone through labor and that we were wearing identical fur coats, and I desperately needed to count the individual strands of fur on both. But even from that distance, when I got to the fiftieth hair on mine, I realized that our coats were much like our jewelry and the color of our hair. Hers: Real. Mine: Not so much.

A perfect time to usher my mind to a better place. I took a deep breath and switched to earlier memories of Travis. He was just out of high school and had umpired a farm league baseball team. There was a phone call, one in a very long line.

"Hello, Mama. This is Travis. Now get this. Remember my coach when I was seven—the one with the temper? Well, today I umpired his game. When his team got behind he went berserk. I waited to see the first cuss word leave his mouth. Then I said, 'Coach! You're out,' and he walked off the field. You would've loved it, Mama."

As a deaf person, Travis had been an enigma. Even the United Givers' Fund folks thought so when he was five and they fired him as their poster child. A few days before appearing in a television spot which was to feature him, followed by a taped message from President Nixon, I got word that they'd chosen another child—a deaf four-year-old who was just beginning to use sign language. "Your child is profoundly deaf but he's talking all the time," one of their representatives explained. I apologized. "It's just not going to be believable to the public," he said. Briefly, Mr. Nixon's credibility came to mind, but I accepted defeat with dignity, concurring that my child was, indeed, too normal to be marketable.

I apologized again when he got to high school. This time, to the football team. At an age when his friends would not admit the existence of their parents, he invited me to eat with his teammates after the game—and I accepted. I'll swear, if there was a macho bone in this kid's body, it was well hidden. Surely his peers tried to tell him he wasn't being cool. I guess he just didn't hear them.

Like everyone else, I was impressed with the way he either maneuvered around or faced head-on the hurdles set up by his deafness. I was especially pleased when he asked for my advice. Sometimes it was about girls. Others, his deafness. Often, both. Occasionally, sports. But almost always, it was long distance. When he got to college the distance got longer, and the calls—more and more about sports.

"Hello, Mama. This is Travis. Listen, I'm in the hospital and I can't feel anything on my entire left side. I had a concussion. Don't worry, Mama. My roommate's here—you know, to feed me and all. Well, here's Mark."

Poor Mark. He was ill-equipped to handle a hysterical mother. But in his own way, he offered support.

"Mrs. Hamilton, he's 'Kamikaze.' That's what they call old Travis. He really gets 'em head on. But, uh, Travis didn't really get hurt in the game. He got in a fight . . . on the bench . . . with one of our guys. You know, on his own team."

Travis never was one to pick on strangers.

The little boy who had wanted only one baby Jesus for Christmas was now distributing boxes of them to underprivileged children. As a member of the Association of Christian Athletes and Vice-President of the Student Education Association, Travis became a speaker. His favorite topic was sports. The favorite topic of sportswriters was his deafness.

Tonight, the young man who stood in front of his friends and relatives needed no notes. But I remembered when he did.

"Hello, Mama. This is Travis. Listen, I've got a problem. When I look up to see the teacher's lips I can't take notes. When I look down, I can't see the teacher's lips!"

Abruptly, my zone-out was interrupted by the still familiar voice of The Mayor who was introducing the groom-to-be. It would be my first time to hear Travis speak to an audience, but it was immediately apparent that it wasn't his first speech. He was relaxed and confident and he was looking at me.

"If it wasn't for that woman in the back of the room—*Mama, can you hear me?* —I wouldn't be talking tonight. In fact, I probably wouldn't be talking at all," he smiled.

The years I spent without him and tonight, without a seat of honor at his table, suddenly took a lower number on my list of life's cruel jokes. I was back in that kitchen at the hearing and speech center, standing on the tabletop, hearing his first words strung together perfectly. I was on top of the world.

I remembered his freshman year in college and the day we stood on the steps to the girls' dormitory, his favorite hangout. It was then that I observed him for the first time as a young man. As always, his intense blue eyes studied my lips, and at the same time, pleaded with me to keep them quiet. His thick black hair attempted to cover his ear-level hearing aids, but stopped short to curl up and away from his tanned skin. He wore white tennis shorts with a matching shirt, and carried a sweatshirt wrapped around his tennis racket—a picture that could have been the cover for any sports magazine. That's what you thought of when you saw Travis. Sports. Achievement.

That day I had taken the opportunity to stumble over an old explanation for my two-year hospitalization and the following years apart. As before, I hoped at least one of us would understand. I reminded him of our special relationship during those years when he was learning to talk. The other self-serving references to our past that I have conveniently forgotten were, no doubt, also laced with guilt.

"Listen, Mama. Just listen," Travis stopped me, as his piercing blue eyes followed the trail of mascara that ran down my cheek and stopped just short of my mouth. His expression was familiar, just like his words. Again, his eyes studied my lips while simultaneously begging me to keep them quiet. This time I did. "A boy never forgets," he said. "He just never forgets those early years. Don't you think I know what you did for me when we were together?" He took my hand. "Can you read my lips, Mama?" he asked. "Can you read my lips?" He leaned forward. His eyes shifted from my mouth to my blurred stare, forbidding me to look away. "I understand, Mama. I understand that you love me."

Once again Travis had saved me. This time with only five words: "Mama, a boy never forgets."

Well, son, read my lips. Neither does his mama.

The time I spent on his college campus became one of my favorite memories. The day I arrived, first thing, he took charge and drove us to lunch. I suddenly realized I'd never seen him drive a car. I felt like a total stranger.

We pulled up to McDonald's and I immediately began campaigning to go inside, hoping to spare him the frustration of the drive-through and that dreadful speaker contraption. Even for the normal hearing, it was difficult to understand the person on the other end. He disregarded my suggestion and reminded me he was grown now, old enough to know what he could and could not do. After a few *"Oh! Mama's!"* followed by a couple of hard looks, I didn't feel like a stranger anymore.

"Mama, it's no big deal. I do this all the time," he said, as he pulled up to the speaker. After he gave the order twice, I tapped him on the shoulder.

"She heard you, Travis. She repeated the order. She understood," I let him know.

He turned toward me and unleashed an expression that eliminated the need for spoken words. Then he leaned out the window and spoke loudly into the speaker. "Listen. I'm deaf and Mama's afraid you won't understand me. But I told her nobody can understand you people, either. Just kidding."

When we reached the drive-thru window, it was clear the girl inside had mistaken Travis' humor for a proposal of marriage. Giggling like a hyena, she turned away from her microphone and as best she could, twisted her large frame toward him. "Can I throw in a couple of whoppers for free?" she chuckled, as she dangled hers out the window.

"Don't you want *me* with those fries?" I fully expected her to ask, as she winked with one eye and took in the campus hunk behind the wheel with the other.

Without sufficient warning, her voice dropped to something resembling a dying cow in a Texas hailstorm. "You're Travis, aren'cha?" she asked in a painfully slower, throatier, and more irritating voice than the one that had squawked into the speaker box. "You're some athlete," she said. "If you'da honked, I would'a came outside to git your order myownself, Travis," she tried to purr.

I was pretty sure that if the hunk had'a honked, she'd'a came out and tooken a far sight more 'n 'at.

I was about ten steps from my car when I made a u-turn and headed back toward Travis' dormitory to say good-bye one last time. As I approached, someone turned on the light in his room on the first floor; then I heard Travis' roommate's voice blasting through the open window. "Turn down the radio," he was saying. "I'm not deaf, you know! Nobody around here's deaf but you! Wish you'd get those hearing aids fixed," he yelled.

"No," Travis retaliated, "You're not deaf. But you're crazy. And you can't put hearing aids on 'crazy.'"

I had spent three days and two nights on campus the night I left. As I listened to my son's exchange with his housemates, I remembered our conversation that same afternoon. "Do those boys treat you well?" I wanted to know. "Do they speak in a normal tone, not too slow, but not too fast? Do they face you so you can read their lips?"

"Mama," he had said, exasperated, "I'm not a baby anymore. Besides, college is different. These guys don't really care about that stuff. They're too busy looking out for themselves."

"I know," I sighed. "But, you know how it is—a mother never forgets . . . ."

As he talked to his fellow jocks, I was reminded of the day his father and I observed him as the self-appointed coach of his T-ball team. Verbal commands to his hearing teammates were prefaced with, "Can't you hear? *I'm* the coach! Now, y'all *listen* to me . . . *LISTEN!*"

His father gave me a look that normally preceded a dissertation about how smart his child was, what a good job we'd done—the usual. Instead I heard, "Someone needs to tell the little son-of-a-bitch he's deaf!"

Like that would've convinced him.

Travis' roommate was still going strong as I headed toward my car. Someone turned off the light in their room. I knew it was Travis. It was a weapon he'd used before, believing it assured him the last word. The momentary silence was broken as his roommate's voice cut through the darkness, "Hey, guys, tomorrow we're gonna get Travis real good. Okay? We'll roll down his car windows and just before he stops to let us out, we'll turn up his radio full blast—you know, like we did before."

"Then he'll get stopped by the police—*again*," one of the other boys chimed in.

His roommate was jubilant. "Cool!" he sang. "Tomorrow we'll get him good. "Tomorrow . . . you hear?"

Tonight not even the good memories were getting me through my son's rehearsal dinner. Trapped by vaguely familiar faces from my distant past, and the aroma of a salmon-surprise entree from my unfortunate present, I was surrounded by well-wishers who offered even more surprises than the fish. They seemed to approach my chair exactly as they spoke. Slowly, cautiously. Yet, like my hearing had taken off with my highly publicized missing mind, they also spoke loudly. Luckily, all I could hear was my own voice, reminding me that I could survive anything because I had, definitely, *been there. . . .*

I was facing a room filled with cheap furniture, psychiatric aides, a dubious odor, windows with bars, and deranged foreigners. . . .

Wasn't I the one who told that woman on the bus, *"Don't ever take a back seat unless it's in the back of a limousine!"* Wasn't I the woman who gave life to this extraordinary soul, the groom-to-be? How did that woman wind up next to the boiler room instead of at the head table next to him? How could she have landed in the back of this room, or worse, in The Rose Garden? Was the answer in this room? Had the person in charge of seating arrangements tonight been in charge of my living arrangements all those years ago?

And why was this happening to me at my own son's wedding, for gosh sake? Had the humbling experience of wearing a fake fur done no more toward releasing me from the unyielding grip of Southern Belle Disorder than sky-waitressing, entertaining the troops, or doing time with the federal government? Hadn't I groveled enough? Lord have mercy, had I not earned a little respect? Why was my life spinning around like those old records from the seventies? Why did I feel like yesterday's greatest flop stuck on perpetual replay?

The words of that Yankee shrink had no business at this particular gathering, but they jumped right in just the same because that is what Yankees do.

"Your Southern Belle Disorder escorted you right up to the locked doors and barred windows of this nut house and, naturally, you're being treated accordingly."

As always, I had overdone it with the groveling. I'd chosen my own seat in the back of the bus.

I was in a room filled with strangers, but thank goodness I didn't have to sit next to one. Sam found my table and took the seat beside me. A very big man on campus, my son was the president of his fraternity; at the other end of the table were many of the guys he was president of. But tonight his attention was on the young man who was addressing his guests in perfectly constructed sentences—words that had likely originated from him.

Sam operated differently from his brother, with an ever-present caution, like he was waiting for the next obstacle—the next question from his brother or hurt he might need to tuck away. I assumed he had not escaped our separation without that somewhat genetic, but well-earned fear of abandonment. I hoped that like Travis, he had held on to the good memories and would someday say, "A boy never forgets." I wondered if he had.

A fan of many things academic and athletic, and all things social, he still found time for his brother, making sure he hadn't missed a word coming from the TV, the football coach, or someone in the next room—fearing, as always, he'd get beat half to death if he didn't. However, much of his attention had now turned toward his admirers, which seemed to include a pretty big chunk of the college's female population.

After graduation I would see where his need to help man (and woman) kind would take him. But what probably led him to the halls of justice and his eventual profession was his analytical little mind. He was only five when it surfaced.

"Think about it, Mama. The cows are just like us. Sure they cry, sure they have feelings. They just don't show them. Cows don't just eat grass, you know."

Why, years later, was I not surprised that his feelings were so often for others but that much like the cows, when it came to himself, he chose to keep them inside. Why am I not surprised today that despite his allegiance to The Bar Association, he is a lawyer who actually cares.

Sam had often taken a back seat to a disability that wouldn't go away and had attempted to replace a mother who had. As his brother's teacher, he had helped build the confidence we saw in the man now addressing his friends and family at his rehearsal dinner. Tomorrow he would join me in watching his father give his student away to a marriage that had not been part of the lesson plan.

I had so wanted to believe that I could enjoy this day—that The Mayor and I would have a let bygones-be-bygones moment, fall to our knees, kiss and make up.

. . . and it got me exactly what that sort of thinking has gotten every woman in the universe since the reign of Adam and Eve. The SOB got worse.

For twenty years I had lived with my homicidal urges toward the man which, after years of therapy, I learned were not only valid but should be acted upon at the first opportunity. On this day I came close, literally. Unlike the rehearsal dinner where the approximate distance of a football field had separated us, in the reception line I stood right beside him and his second—or third—First Lady; I was loosing track. I wanted to turn off my mind, I'll swear I did, but it was stuck in the past, spinning out of control.

We decided to send me away for help . . . well, I helped all right! I helped the new First Lady move right into my little white house and take over my title!

I tried to recapture the good memories, but the bad ones were getting in my way. If only mentally, it was time to leave. Before, I had dodged the administrator's all-knowing crystal ball by visiting my own private, self-supported institution, a safe haven in that small corner of my half-a-brain where I often took refuge. Today I had found just enough remaining space for one more getaway. I trusted that the technique used to break away from that other frightening world would once again take me to a better one.

> *This book was not intended to be a workbook, but write this down: just get your head the heck away from the whole mess. That's right. Forget that nonsense about living in the moment. The idea here is to get OUT of the present moment—and fast! In psychiatric circles the labels attached to this behavior are many. "Disassociating" is one; "psychosis," another. "Spacing out," and just out-and-out "escape" also work.*

You just pick a diversion and go with it. Like, say, plan your wardrobe for the next ten years. Count the feathers on you-know-who's boa. Or my personal favorite—"Making Impossible Resolutions." If you don't have any of your own, try mine.

By this time next year . . .

1. I will be teaching an aerobics class to women the same age as my ex-husband's wife. They will be makeup-less and outfitted in large denim overalls and floral muumuus. I, of course, will be stunningly shapely in hot purple spandex with matching sweatband, walkman, and eye shadow.
2. I will figure out why each Christmas, when my sister puts a wreath on her new Mercedes, it's festive. And when I put one on my aging van, it dies twenty-five or thirty times between Georgetown and downtown D.C.
3. I will no longer make dates with men I meet on the airplane, especially if they're handcuffed to law enforcement officers.
4. I will have the wisdom to accept life's painful realities which I know I cannot change: my arthritis, my son's wedding, The Rose Garden, and me.
5. I will acknowledge that the night I sat in the far corner of a room—enjoying the company of one son while observing the other—I realized that this occasion had little to do with *The War of the Roses* that took place years ago. That no matter how far away my place card; how fake my fur; how old my car; how grey my roots; or how empty my dance card, tonight I faced the greatest two accomplishments of my—and, okay, The Mayor's—life. And that the main attraction did not nor does it now nor has it ever had everything to do with us.

I will acknowledge this, if it kills me, and I will also acknowledge that acknowledging this was a giant step toward the dismantling and ultimate reconstruction of this Southern Belle.

When your son gets married, it can be just one more reminder that you are not and that normal people usually date before they do. At first I turned to self-help books for answers, but quickly discovered that while finding oneself is next to impossible, finding a man is worse.

Obviously, I needed more therapy—but for once I chucked it all in favor of those individuals who put

m-o-s-t o-f u-s
t-h-e-r-e
i-n t-h-e f-i-r-s-t
p-l-a-c-e.

VII. Men . . . (and other delays and cancellations)

43.
I was picking up trash when I met him

"So I'm walking through my neighborhood, coming off a four-day trip, when a homeless man approaches me and holds out his cup. He's hungry. I'm tired. I extend my hand and whisper, 'I'm sorry, sir, I'll have to take that now.'"

Me, New York Comedy Club

At first it seemed simple enough. The rules for finding a man were darn-near identical to the ones for finding myself. Therefore, I decided at the onset to be happy with whichever one showed up first. The general consensus was that I should (1) join a group, (2) eat right, (3) give the appearance of having good mental health, and (4) get physically fit, which would, (5) get me a man, with—*oops!*—(6) no guarantee whatsoever he would be doing (1), (2), (3), or (4) himself.

Screw that.

I had just about exhausted all options when it occurred to me; I hadn't been looking for Mr. Right at work. Since I worked on an airplane, the process of elimination was fairly obvious: bypass the pilots (b-o-r-i-n-g); eliminate the coach section (they're letting *anyone* in these days); and reduce the hunting ground to first class.

The problem is that affairs with passengers are about as rare as on-time arrivals. Regardless of what you've seen on the news, when a flight attendant says, "I'm sorry sir, I'll have to take that now," she is not referring to a man's home and family—and certainly not his congressional seat. Politically speaking, she could care less whether he is on the right or left wing. What she does care about is *character*.

Sadly, it took the following relationship to teach me that "first class" on a man's boarding pass has nothing to do with it.

Girlfriend, with this one I would've faired much better had I bypassed first class and scrounged around beneath the caged animals and human body parts in the bowels of the rear-cargo bin. Just so you know.

It was flight 1505, Charlotte to L.A. I was the flight attendant. He was the passenger. Right away I knew he was different, you know, in the important ways.

"Gimme the chicken," echoed from the jetway minutes before he stepped onto the plane and put in the rest of his order. "Fix me a scotch and soda," he mumbled, as he handed me his coat while making additional requests of the person on the other end of his cell phone. He continued to multi-task as we climbed out of 10,000 feet. "Heymiss, Heymiss," he shrieked before mastering the flight attendant call bell, which he had down to a science by the time we landed. Ignoring the safety demo, he explained to everyone three rows forward and back, "I've seen it a million times. I'm a frequent flier."

He had only two carry-ons (which fit perfectly beneath the seats in front of the men on both sides of him), and he wasn't wearing designer anything, carrying his own booze, or reading a decorating magazine. So there he was—the man of my dreams. Aside from his obvious charms, he was, you know, worldly. My fantasies went berserk. At last I'd get to see how the other half live: villas, estates, The Admiral's Club at the Raleigh-Durham Airport.

I had scarcely released the brake of my beverage cart when he bombarded me with aspects of his life which were, I am sure, painful revelations. He was a Yankee, a Jew, and a Republican. A graduate of the Harvard Business School, class of God-knows-when, he was now a professed tycoon—a corporate mogul of world renown. From what I could surmise, his travels took him mostly from his summer home to his winter home to his summer home. The rest of the time he rescued fallen corporations and worked on his biography, which he proceeded to share with me (as something inside pleaded, *"Oh, please, make me wait for the movie!"*).

He suggested we meet for a drink in some exotic place, so for many, many months we headquartered out of South Hampton and worked the globe, meeting in many places for many drinks. As the months flew by, I learned many new and exciting things about this man. Though mostly about himself, he spoke openly. And often. His vocabulary was astounding, but I ignored the words that seemed to rush together when he was under pressure. A favorite was tossed at me often, and always, with feeling. . . .

"Idonwannacommitment, I really donwannacommitment," he'd plead.

But it doesn't take a Harvard man to throw out big words. I had one of my own. And I'd called on it enough to feel comfortable as I threw it back at him.

"GimmesometimeandIcanchangethatbaby. . . ."

But he didn't and neither did I.

> *And another thing about me and men.*
>
> *It seems important, before I go further with this story or this man, to explain that therapy does not necessarily guarantee wisdom and insight in every area of a person's life. I also assume you know by now that I normally spend less time in my selection of men than I do in the produce section at Food Lion. That being said, I did not take a huge detour from my usual course when, immediately after seeing this man's penthouse on the Upper East Side of Manhattan, I moved in.*
>
> *Moving out? Now that was different. This time my departure had little to do with running out of insurance and losing a marriage, but everything to do with running out of patience and hocking an engagement ring.*

44.
I was taking out trash when I left him.

"Mama, for goodness sake, first tell Travis what trash IS and then tell him to take it OUT."
Sam

I had lived with him only a week when I began questioning the circumstances under which we met, specifically, how the man ever got on the other side of that curtain. Truth be known, his upgrade to first class was likely due to the airline's rumored alliance with a well-known bus company. But this and all other revelations didn't really matter as I chose to ignore them anyway. This was, after all, a man in the process of some big changes. He was agreeing to finance and attend couples therapy (contingent on the therapist lowering her fee. God forbid he should pay retail). It was a step farther than others had been willing to take. So together, we took it.

A minimum of ten years with no possibility of parole was what I had assumed my sentence would be. Since my fiancé had unresolved asshole tendencies, I expected couples therapy to last at least that long—long enough to figure out what I was doing to make him throw anything not attached to the floor into the hallway of his building, usually something directly related to my faith, like Christmas. Or directly related to Christmas, like the tree. And once, directly related to me. Like me.

Although I never looked for witnesses, they were generally close by, as these outbursts could be heard from the twenty-third floor of the man's condo on East Seventy-Second Street to the corner deli on East Seventy-Third. Of course, he was usually as lit as the Hanukkah candles on his mantle when he went berserk which, in his defense, may very well have been part of that whole bizarre custom.

In the New York therapist's office, he was charming. Go figure.

I was somewhat apprehensive about a female therapist. The idea of being in the same room with another woman and not competing for *something* was just plain weird. With this one, I either had nothing she wanted or so much she didn't know where to start. I couldn't be sure. But five minutes into the session, it was clear there was definitely one thing I had that she didn't want, and that was the man I'd brought with me to therapy.

When I recovered from the experience of facing an ex-Broadway actress/therapist with Grace Kelly good looks; no desire to be me; zero designs on my fiancé; and, rumor had it, a brilliant mind to boot, I relaxed. (I later realized it was the brilliant mind that kept those last two things from being a problem.)

We were scheduled for an hour session, but this woman had a way of wrapping it up quickly, bottom line, to the point. After ten, maybe fifteen minutes, she stood and asked my fiancé to leave the room. The door had scarcely shut behind him before she turned to me and said, "Get rid of him. He sucks."

Get rid of him he sucks?! Oh! My Dear Lord and Precious Savior! Where did this shrink go to school? Where was the analyzing, the compromising, the philosophizing, the going off to find the answers even if it took the rest of your life, your children, and all your insurance?

Nope, no time for that. Just time to get rid of him because he sucks.

Well, I had never disobeyed a therapist in my life—so I got rid of him. Because he did, indeed, suck.

VIII. There was a Rose in Spanish Harlem

45.
Sometimes you win. . . .

"Perhaps I always knew I could have simply packed my bags and walked out the door. Perhaps I always knew I should never have been in that Rose Garden."

It was this woman who convinced me I hadn't needed The Rose Garden—that a divorce, a couple of Broadway plays, and a few hours in Barneys most likely would have sufficed. She persuaded me to stay in New York.

I had become quite proficient at initial meetings with shrinks. During my first solo visit with this one, I presented my file, just so she'd know I'd done the work. I dredged up as many inner children, fears of abandonment, conflicts with my mother, and variations of excruciating pain and failure as I could, then proceeded to unload them. As I wrapped it up with the old familiar lowering of my head and uncontrollable sobbing, she observed me and continued to take notes. I was waiting to be assigned a new label when she handed me a tissue, then leaned forward to deliver what I assumed would be a whopper of a diagnosis. Instead, she whispered, "You know, you *can* watch too much television."

"You know, you can watch too much television?"

How simple was that!? Finally . . . I was free to be happy! Freud was dead!

*For one glorious moment I forgot that I was still in therapy and must now begin the painful process of figuring out what was **really** causing the happiness. Which, of course, required—*

MORE THERAPY

My past affiliation with therapy had acquainted me with an initial phase which must be endured before patients can explore their own problems. It involves the projection of the therapist's unfinished issues onto the patient and the patient's role in assisting the therapist in finishing them up. In this woman's case it was men.

I don't know what they had done to her; I don't want to know. But in the beginning of our sessions I discovered that I was a woman who ran with the wolves, whatever that meant, and was identical to the women in a book by that name. Although I knew who *REALLY* had the problem (*hello!*) I promised to read this and all other books relative to men and wolves and running with either of them.*

"You're a comedian; that's clear," she told me. "You've been to hell and back with your sense of humor. And just look at your determination to hold on to your dysfunctional past, or, as they call it in the business—your 'material.'"

She finally hit on something I could understand, and because she catered to the world of the entertainer, I listened. At one of our sessions she came up with a list. It was just analytical, complex, and disturbing enough to get my attention. It was all there, my twisted past, neatly arranged:

- A father who encouraged happiness and free expression and a mother who thought that was alright. As long as everyone else was doing it too.
- A minister who talked about hell and all of us burning in it when women wore shorts, but would drive through fire and brimstone to photograph me in swimsuits for beauty pageants.
- A culture that told me to feed the hungry but not at my table.
- A mother who wanted me to enter beauty pageants as long as I acted like a lady and didn't look too sexy, give anyone "the wrong idea," or win.
- An aunt who could give a rip how I acted or looked or what anyone thought—as long as I won.
- A husband/Mayor/District Attorney with gubernatorial aspirations.
- The psychiatric hospital where he dropped me off when I was well so I could stay until I got sick or my insurance ran out or he married his girlfriend, whichever one came first.
- An airline that calls me a safety professional but plants a team of beauticians and plastic surgeons in the crew room—beneath memos from the FAA.

*I would eventually admit it was I, not her, who had hung out with the wolves. But I had hung out with enough therapists to know that so far, this woman led the pack!

There it was. I was as confused and dysfunctional as any stand-up comic on any stage. I had soared so far above 30,000 feet the control tower was history, completely out of range. I was a comedian, with a past.

And now I could put it to work: the twitches, jerks, and insecurities; the ritualistic behavior that began after my father's death and revisited me throughout my life; the magical thinking that helped me through The Rose Garden, my divorce, and the airlines; the compulsions I'd been punished for by my stepfather; the comedy routine I performed as I represented the typical American teenager; the nights I entertained the Marines; and the days I survived the federal government.

Those years of guilt and sexual confusion I had picked up from other women could at last be blamed on men and assigned the popular label, "man bashing." I could finally throw every disorder and socially and politically incorrect part of myself onto my resume and then write every bit of it off on my taxes. I had arrived.

Actually, it was the same old routine with a different diagnosis and a shiny new label. It was now called stand-up comedy. It was also called just one more step toward this Southern Belle's reconstruction. And this time it worked. I forgot about the audience, competition and judges. It was just me. I was on no one else's runway; I'd found my own. I could now take on the character of anyone because I knew who I was and who I was not. I was the granddaughter of no one, the alumni of no hospital, and the peach of no one's crop. I was not Judy Garland and I was no one's First Lady. I was not that troubled child on the kitchen counter and, above all, I could finally listen to—and love—my own laugh.

You can be anyone you want for make believe as long as you come home to Rosemary.

Daddy's words finally made sense.

I could go wherever I wanted on that stage because when I stepped down, I knew *who* I'd be returning to and *what* I'd be returning as. I was the master of my own ceremony, and I knew—r e a l l y knew—the MC!

275

Onstage I portrayed a wacky Southern Belle in distress while my insides made an abrupt u-turn when I remembered how unfunny it was to be one. The character was someone I knew; the routine was real; performing it was as natural as breathing. I already had the outfit, the job, and the attitude. I was a Southern Belle. And that Southern Belle was a flight attendant. I could forget lines, repeat others, stutter, stammer, shake, and screw up 'til the cows came home because I was not *just* a flight attendant; I was a flight attendant consumed by her own Southern Belleness, trapped beneath her tiara, and afflicted with terminal cases of ADD and OCD.

Brilliant.

46.
There goes the neighborhood!

"His penthouse was incredible, the view fantastic. From the living room, dining room and both bedrooms, I could see Manhattan. From the living room, dining room, and both bedrooms, I could also see his mother. Well, girlfriend, I showed him. I moved to Harlem."

Me
Stand Up New York

I left my fiancé in his Upper East Side condo—an impressive address, status, the perfect life. But now, being in control of that life seemed more important than where I lived it.

Our relationship had made it through one Christmas and two Hanukkahs. In retrospect, the break-up had less to do with his abuse than the beating I was taking from New York's Upper East Side. I tried to fit in, Lord knows I did; I always do. Lord knows that, too. But although I am a longstanding member of numerous oppressed *minorities*—southerner-gone AWOL, divorcee, ex-mental patient, etc., etc., I refused to join the privileged *majority* from Midtown Manhattan—those poop-scooping, fast-talking, draped-in-black mannequins with perfect resumes. No known past affiliations with southern beauty pageants or insane asylums; no matching pieces from "Rooms to Go" on their hardwood floors; and not one impulse purchase from the Home Shopping Network on their skinny wrists and fingers. Odds are, an embarrassing delivery or relative had never once shown up in their lobbies or on the front porch of their brownstones.

Although my previous life was now out of my price range, it took only one day to find one that was. But in my haste, I once again went too far—this time, about fifty blocks.

I'm pretty sure it was that old sitcom theme, *I'm Movin' on up to the East Side,* that got me thinking higher was better and Park Avenue was best. Well, I wound up on a street that was way up in the numbers, alright. I also landed on Park Avenue. *The corner of Park Avenue and Harlem!*

If I thought I'd been looking in from the outside before . . .

"I was the only white thing left. . . ."

Beneath a New York blizzard I found my apartment, blanketed by a mantel of perfectly arranged snow. My introduction to graffiti corresponded with the melting of that snow from my building and preceded the realization that "New York walk-up" does not refer to property on a hill-top in the better part of town. It simply means that you wheeze your way up six flights of stairs past rattling radiators, strange kitchen smells and blaring bongos to a ten-by-ten square with shower and commode. A shower and commode if you're lucky, that is. And because there's no way you can make it back down those steps in the same day, the words, "I'll take it" slip from your lips and head straight for the pages of a one-year lease.

The neighborhood aroused visions of Currier and Ives, Christmas and Crosby, Aspen and Vail. At first. But when the snow melted I looked around, and I was the only white thing left. That's when I added yet another label to the ones I already carried. It was "white girl," and there wasn't another one in sight.

> *Dear Rosemary,*
> *We hear you've moved to New York! How exciting! Sure would like to drop in on you.*
> *The Pageant Committee*

> *Dear Pageant Committee,*
> *Sorry, there are no pageant committees in Spanish Harlem. No first class. No coach.*
> *Rosemary*

I was pretty sure I'd made the right move, although the family of rats frolicking on my front door steps almost changed my mind. But it was too late to go crawling back to the bellman on East Seventy-Second Street. So I made a clumsy attempt at humor instead.

"I thought I left the rat race behind," I said to the statuesque black woman walking beside me. Pretty funny, I thought. But when I asked her how to get past the rodents, she answered with something even funnier. "Pretend you don't see them," she said, never once looking down. "Pretend you don't see the rats."

Pretend you don't see them? Pretend you don't see ten, maybe fifteen rats? I wonder how many other rats in my path I could have avoided with that philosophy?

As she made her way up those steps, the critters parted like they'd been waiting for her royal highness' arrival to assume their stations on both sides of her feet. But as I became friends with this woman named Rosa, I could see that she would never have assumed that role. When confronted with anything she categorized as pretentious, just plain ridiculous, or simply blocking her path, Rosa maintained her philosophy: "Pretend you don't see them. Pretend you don't see the rats."

So Rosa missed a lot, it seemed. She was nothing but a prisoner, poor Rosa, of her own wisdom, soul, and dignity—everything but those rats.

I wondered if Rosa also ignored the plastic wreath of dusty roses that hung on her door. I thought often of how quickly the ones on my mother's grave were taken away because they "didn't belong beside the real ones." But I also remembered the night I stood in judgment on a stage flocked with plastic red roses at a Marine base in Arlington, VA., and did exactly the same thing.

In the years to come I would learn that when Rosa arrived at my door with flowers, it didn't really matter that they were real and the ones on her door were artificial, because this was Rosa, and poor Rosa would never have even noticed the difference in bus children and town children, blacks and whites, first-runners-up and last-runners-up, first-class people and coach-class people—not even Republicans and Democrats.

Much less a bunch of stupid flowers.

47.

There are no pageant committees in Spanish Harlem (no first class, no coach).

"It was at my daddy's liquor store that I learned about life and how sometimes you have to stay put for awhile until you get happy."

It was day two for me in the neighborhood and I was still in the moving process. I had just made my second trip to the dry cleaners, this time to pick up my flight attendant uniform—one of the many signs of procrastination I would exhibit that day. My mission: to avoid the apartment building across the street and the task of shoving my entire life into what would formerly have served as my broom closet.

The urgency of getting off the street and safely inside that apartment was brought to my attention when I faced a human version of the party of rats I had encountered the day before. I'd been told to step over those, but the ones waiting outside the dry cleaning establishment today were hard to ignore.

As I walked out the door, cleaning bag in hand, I was surrounded by a group of young men, at least ten of them, and they weren't asking for directions. If they weren't cast members from *West Side Story,* they were doing a right decent impersonation of a neighborhood gang. As they moved in on me I, who appeared to be just minutes away from a horrible death, could only think of what they were thinking about me. Were they thinking I was white, or old—or too white to even matter whether I was old or not.

Weren't these the guys who had snickered the day before as I unloaded the box marked, "Arkansas stuff—crowns and trophies?" The only thing more out of place than me, I was thinking, would've been, maybe, a southern politician. (Like that would ever happen in Harlem.) As they approached, I realized what they thought really didn't matter. It was time for my talent routine and I'd left my baton at home. I was dead meat—dead white meat.

Damn that first grade teacher! When she took away my sheriff's badge and Trigger, she stole my identity! Understandably, I wanted to get back at her. But why had I picked 125th Street in Harlem to do it? Why was I still determined to rewind that tape and tack on a different ending?

As Harlem's Welcome Wagon closed in on me, one of the greeters got in my face, then reached for the cleaning bag. I was frozen in that moment, yet I chipped off just enough of it to bludgeon myself because of what had just left my mouth. "Now, y'all just quit it. Right now!" is what I'm afraid I said. I had never felt this helpless, this vulnerable, this un-black, this alone.

It appeared the cowboys had left with my daddy. . . .

"Here she comes, Miss Arkansas," one of the men sang, or rapped, I wasn't sure. "Oh, Miss 'Thang, wha'cha got in that bag? Is it your Miss Arkansas dress? We've seen your trophy. Now, come on, show us that dress!" Well, I didn't have a dress but I did have a flight attendant uniform, and Miss Arkansas was about to perform.

"N Y P D!" I threatened as I, for the first and probably last time in my life, was about to get my money's worth from a dry cleaners. I snatched the plastic from the hanger covering my navy blue flight attendant uniform, pointed to it and shouted, "Now do you want me to put on this son-of-a-bitch or do you want to get your fucking butts off the street?" They stopped cold.

Have these soldiers never been exposed to CLASS? And what the fuck have I said to make them think I don't have any?

As they turned and walked away, my elation that I had actually worked son-of-a-bitch and fucking butts into the same sentence was short lived as I realized that theirs were, most likely, the fucking butts that would be my neighbors.

48.
With both feet on the ground, I was high.

After a few months I saw my neighborhood as that perfect playground where everybody had ridden the same bus to get there and would ride the same one when they left. There were no back seats, not that I could see.

In the vacant lot separating my apartment building from the housing projects next door, I enlisted the help of my neighbors in planting a vegetable/flower garden, painfully aware that the unleashed creativity of some might summon the Drug Enforcement folks back into the neighborhood. I remembered another garden, but that one was on a windowsill, and I wasn't looking out for the DEA. In those days, I shielded a neighbor's imaginary marijuana crop from armored gladiators and man-eating dinosaurs so he could go to therapy. It was a time when the marijuana plants were phony, the gardeners were crazy, and the therapists, in some cases, were both. Then, a visit from the DEA would have meant the plants were real and the gardeners were sane enough to grow them. But that was a Rose Garden—a different garden altogether.

Just one more step in this honkey's reconstruction, Harlem became a vehicle for healing my past and moving forward. I was eating Thanksgiving dinner at the table of the people who had served it to me—the "help" Mama drove to the wrong side of town to pick up—women I'd loved and allowed to love me back when I was a child. The same ones I had shut out of my life when I got old enough to know better.

The day I saw Mama Woman walk up those steps and head toward that balcony, she turned into Colored Woman and she remained Colored Woman from that day on.

I had my own Secret Service now, the local surveillance team, so living on a tough block was normally no big deal. But that almost changed the night I was stalked from a comedy club into my neighborhood. I was only three blocks from my apartment building when my power walk turned into a marathon as I felt the stalker catching up. But suddenly the gang members took flight from their perch on the street corner, invited the villain to face the mud, and then made me an offer. It was hard to refuse.

"Hey, Rose, ya' want us to kill the son-of-a-bitch?"

Reluctantly, I allowed the stranger to live and opted for a group escort to my apartment door instead.

There were no Junior Leagues in Harlem, not a country club or symphony ball. But there were fundraisers on the sidewalks, celebrations in the streets, foot traffic everywhere—sometimes swift, sometimes slow—and, always, music pulling at your feet.

There were neighbors like I'd never known before, the kind who'd give you the air conditioners off their windows or pick up new ones, if need be. Whatever a person required usually showed up pretty fast. And talent. It was all over the place. My building was fairly evenly divided between those who struggled to be actors, and those who struggled with everything—everything but sex. It was in the music, the clothes, the sounds from the apartment next door.

Nothing was disguised; it was what it was. Dirty dancing was, unmistakably, dirty dancing. Drinking was done on the street. Sex too, or something pretty close to it. Music was loud, tempers hot. There were bars on apartment windows that opened onto fire escapes leading to the streets. But the crazy people weren't behind those bars. They took up residence on blankets on the streets below.

I had ignored *The Book of Rules* only to discover I should have done it long ago. It seemed that everywhere I looked I saw myself and every time I saw myself, I saw my neighbors. I was in a place where I should have been an outsider, yet I was looking at a neighborhood that felt like home. I had no desire to jump from the top step of my porch and land flatfooted on the sidewalk below. I was safe and I was happy.

With both feet on the ground, I was high.

49.
There goes the neighborhood—again!

My transition from *white girl* to *white girlfriend* took place about the time I learned that my people have not one clue about dirty dancing, the best recipes are not found in *Southern Living,* and *Architectural Digest* is a doorstop. And I learned another thing. Brothers live by a code. You don't unload precious antiques, valuable memorabilia, most of the West Wing and all of the Oval Office without being viewed as either unscrupulous or uppity.

(You know who you are.)

And there's more:

In Harlem:

- Your word is your bond. You lie you die.
- The Puerto Rican Day parade—wild and rowdy, a drunken brawl—may be as close as it gets to a Republican Congress.*
- The closest thing to a golf course would be the pot-holes, grass, hard liquor and men whose pants don't fit on the corner of 125th Street and Lexington. And, for the rest of us:
- Guys whose jackets say DEA are not from the neighborhood. Run!
- Curry powder works on grits.
- Food stamps are staples and Jamaican Rum—a religion.
- Life's greatest tragedy is not when the dog-sitter doesn't show.
- Drug stores don't have a monopoly on drugs.
- The people who sell them are always quite pleasant.

With the renovation of Harlem came one Starbucks, two Kentucky Fried Chickens and one ex-President of the United States. As for my own personal renovation, each day I was laying more bricks toward the reconstruction of this Mid-town Manhattan recovering Shiksa Belle.

After six years in this neighborhood, I'd gotten comfortable with my new life. Now the old one was moving in next door. For the first time in Harlem, USA, I was petrified. What next? Would I start

---

*And weekends in Arkansas (with your brother).

making promises I couldn't keep to people I didn't know about stuff I knew even less about than the promises and the people? Would I become one of *them . . . again*?

There was little doubt those old memories were about to be revived in my neighborhood right along with Granddaddy—the man who first introduced me to the brouhaha of politics and brought to my attention our Tree's propensity for leaning toward the left.

It was the day he announced, "I wouldn't vote for that son-of-a-bitch if he was the last person on earth," that I learned, in one fell swoop, about sons-of-bitches, how they could be spotted by animal-type (elephants), and that they should never be allowed to win—*anything!* I concluded that there were no elephant sons-of-bitches on Granddaddy's side of The Tree because there were no losers, not even one.

But when Granddaddy's candidate for governor lost and the "elephant man" won, suddenly elephants weren't sons-of-bitches anymore. In fact, Granddaddy grew so fond of the man with the long trunk, he affectionately referred to him as Boss Man. Overnight, all his efforts to "run the sorry son-of-a-bitch out of town on a rail and to hell in a handbag" were history. And my history? Well, Granddaddy's way of thinking became a big part of mine.

"It doesn't matter *what you do*, it's all in *who you know*," was the lesson I learned as I observed Granddaddy exchanging hugs and favors with Boss Man. But I also lived five miles from a little girl who, many cotton crops and governors down the road, would grow up and rearrange that expression.

"It doesn't matter *what you know*, it's all in *who you do*," she would say, as she made some new laws—and The Governor as well. The expression really caught on after a second woman came forward and swore she'd been kidnapped by the Arkansas State Police and delivered to that same governor's hotel room with a double order of cheeseburgers and fries. We all knew the story was true because each time the woman told it, her nose got shorter and shorter.

"It doesn't matter *what you know*, it's all in *who you do*" had now replaced the state's famous "calling of the hogs," and, in our nation's capitol, would round up even more.

FYI: It is truly important to recognize the profound effect of each and every vote on the affairs of our government—but perhaps more important to understand the effect of each and every affair on the votes for our government.

Just so you know.

The old neighborhood was barely recognizable, with prices skyrocketing, rents doubling, boom boxes disappearing, and disoriented white people from Little Rock all over the place, looking for—according to Rosa—a restaurant featuring authentic Negro cuisine in a predominately white neighborhood with Emeril Lagasse in the kitchen and valet parking. And did I mention safety? Out the window! I mean, really, has anyone ever been safe among the politically confused?

Hell had sure enough frozen over. So, with the demise of life as I'd known it and the take-over of my neighborhood by this undesirable element, I packed my bags. In fact, if you saw two U-hauls passing in the night, that would be *him* moving in and *me* moving out.

It was time to go home. My sons were still in Tennessee, and both had begun filling their own Family Trees with wives and children. It was my opinion that every last one of them needed me desperately. No doubt about it, I had turned into my Aunt Allie B.

My going away party lasted a week and would have been memorable had a good portion of it not drowned in Puerto Rican Rum. I do, however, recall the day it got underway when our resident poet/graffiti artist taped the invitation to my front door:

> **Plumbin' don't work,**
> **Landlord's a jerk.**
> **People can't talk,**
> **Stairs she won't walk.**
> **Argentina don't cry,**
> **Puerto Rico good-bye.**
> **Fed up to her nose,**
> **With the pimps and the Ho's.**
> **Good-bye forever,**
> **Good-bye Harlem's Rose.**

Leaving this place and the remaining gang was hard. Abandoning our garden, worse. But leaving it in the hands of a politician, now that was excruciating! In the words of one planter, it would now be fertilized with surplus political bullshit.

I couldn't think about that now. I didn't need the memories. Okay, it wasn't the memories. I didn't need the competition. Of course, folks here certainly knew I wasn't leaving the place as I'd found it, and, no question, I had accomplished more during my term here than this intruder ever would! But I enlisted the help of my neighbors just the same, and together we made sure that no one forgot. We simply replaced the graffiti that had been washed away from our building by a recent snow.

Just like my mama, the message was honest. Just like my daddy, I had been drinking wine when I helped write it. Also like my daddy, it fit my purposes. But even *more* like my granddaddy, it was political:

**Since history has a selective memory,
Let's not forget how it goes:
Long before there was a President in
Spanish Harlem, there was—
—inside this building—
A Rose**

I also said goodbye to my favorite comedy club where I was, finally, getting some respect. But on my last night, no more than five minutes into my act, I realized this was not going to be one of those nights. In the audience my Harlem supporters were laughing at all the right times. But there was also a heckler, probably the worst I'd had so far. The man wasn't black and he wasn't about to laugh with people who were. He let me know that about five minutes into my routine.

It had changed. I no longer bashed myself and men. I was on a crusade. Single-handedly, I had taken on stigma and discrimination—and it came from a character I knew very well. "I was prejudiced before I moved to New York," I drawled, as I faced my neighbors I had smuggled into the club. "Oh, yes, I was a racist. Back home I was a big time bigot. Backward as they come. Eat up with backward. But since

I moved to Harlem I have learned," I said, as I fixed my eyes on Rosa. "Oh! Lord, girlfriend, you *know* this honkey has learned . . . I mean . . . just ask my people right there at that table, surrounded by all the whites. I live with 'em, plant roses with 'em and grow marijuana, too. No more ignorance spewing from this girl's mouth. And you know why? Well, let me tell you why," I said, as I paced back and forth across the small stage. "Because she's finally learned, you know what I'm sayin,' this white girl has learned—thank you Jesus—to hide it."

Their responses were just as I had hoped, but their laughter took a backseat to the heckler as he sabotaged each line. In my head were Rosa's words, my mantra. Over and over I recited it to myself,

> *Pretend you don't see him.*
> *Pretend you don't see the rat.*
> *Pretend you don't see him.*
> *Pretend you don't see the rat.*

It wasn't the best sendoff I'd ever had—but a far sight from the worst.

As I left the building and approached the taxicab, their cries—begging me to turn around, to unlock the door behind me—were muffled by the silent ones of my mother. I stepped up my pace.

The heckler was out of control—back in my face, winning the game. Then I got my first glimpse at the men in sleeveless t-shirts sitting at the table next to Rosa's. It was my second glance that caught them pouring rum from the bottles so blatantly displayed on their table, reminding me I had arranged admission but forgot about the drinks.

Homeys. My guardian angels had arrived—the only men I knew with enough *chutzpah* (an expression meaning one thing in certain Manhattan neighborhoods and another *[weapons]* in mine) to bust the dress code and bring their own liquor into the club. I was looking at an interesting blend of store owners and the welcoming committee from my first day in Harlem. It was the 125th Street Chamber of Commerce and the neighborhood gang!

"Hey yo' . . . Snow White! We're gonna miss your honkey self, girlfriend," one of them shouted.

That did it! The heckler stood.

I didn't flinch. I was a woman who'd been heckled by an evil white man before.

First you'll be locked up in one of our seclusion rooms and when you run out of insurance, there's the state hospital down the road. . . .

My glance in their direction was apparently taken as a signal. One of my neighbors jumped to his feet, sending his chair in the direction of the heckler behind him. Then he swung around, waved his fist, and turned to me as he shook the walls with his familiar concern:

"Hey, Rose, ya' want us to kill the son-of-a-bitch?"

Neighbors. No matter what street they're on or which institution they're in—you gotta love 'em.

IX. Only when I'm high

*". . . and one day the magic lines on my sidewalk will
have all turned to dust and happiness will fly through the
sky. But never again must I jump high into the air to
catch it or travel to the end of a runway to find it. It will
be mine not 'only when I'm high'—but only because it
always was."*

50.
The gospel truth about getting high

I was five years old the first time I got high. I discovered that if I climbed to the top step of my front porch and jumped as high as I could—while making a wish, mid-air, and then landing with both feet aligned perfectly just over the line on the sidewalk below—I could turn my whole life around instantly. It was, of course, magic. Later I learned that when I performed this ritual in private, I was safe. But if someone was watching, I was crazy.

In psychiatric circles my behavior was labeled many things. Magical thinking was one, obsessive-compulsive disorder, another. If I'd gotten really high and then fallen on my face, bipolar disorder would have been another. I don't know which of these things other children got called, but I'm sure it wasn't crazy-as-a-damn-bat which is what I recall answering to most of the time. Just the same, I secretly performed these mental and physical gymnastics for my happiness, believing it was a privilege that must be earned in some private, punishing way.

Unbeknownst to me, this method of blocking pain and creating instant pleasure would govern the rest of my days. Books would be written about it; seminars would be taught on it; a President of the United States would be punished for it; folks would walk over hot coals to get to it; Buddhists would stare into it; The Rose Garden would line its pockets with it; and the whole process would be labeled "living in the present moment."

Today my favorite label for this compulsion is "changing one's state," which can easily be confused with "sending your wife to another state." (There is at least one documented case of this mix-up.)

Thankfully, I have found enough variations of this phenomena that I haven't been limited to porch steps. My compulsions have opened up a frightening world of magical diets, quick-fix weekend retreats, magical romances, and "liar, liar, pants on fire"—thin thighs in thirty days.

I took my porch-jumping magic to new heights when I became a flight attendant. Safety kicks in now much as it did on those sidewalks when I was five. I leave my problems on the ground and the higher we climb, the smaller they look. Neurotic, perhaps, but it seems like a good plan to me, with clouds being much closer to God than steps on the front porch.

On September 11 the magic was gone.

As the world changed overnight, I found I was never safe, not above or below ten thousand feet, not at home or at work or on a comedy stage. Not even on a sidewalk somewhere.

A few days following the World Trade Center massacre, I had set my alarm for 4:00 a.m. to begin a three-day trip. My emotions had been unraveling slowly, except for the anger which was fast turning into rage. I marveled that with so many feelings, this was the only one I'd been able to express.

I was experiencing more difficulty than usual attaching my airline wings onto the pocket of my uniform. But I struggled even more with the TV morning show co-host whose words were about to be challenged by my own. "Flight attendants should have anti-terrorism combat training," she announced, and I was thinking,

"Lady, *you're* the terrorist!"

Her face was as familiar as her voice, and no wonder. From a first-class seat this woman had recently demanded every service we provided and some we didn't. The flight attendant mantra, "Ma'am, I am here primarily for your safety" had meant no more to her than the two-bag carry-on rule. Visualizing the overhead compartment as her mouth, I had attempted to cram her bags into it as she swore the space had shrunk since her last flight.

"*How, lady? How?*" I said to the TV. "How can we turn our flight crews into police when we're wearing so many other hats? In case your incessant ringing of the call bell rendered you unconscious, let me fill you in: *I'm* the one who hung your coat, settled your double seat assignment, served you three drinks, removed the drunk sitting next to you from the aircraft, completely unaware that he was your husband, threw the rest of your excess baggage onto the jetway and performed numerous other duties before strapping myself into my jumpseat and preparing to go to work. *Remember me?*"

Given my current state of mind, I wasn't sure *I* remembered me, certainly not the stranger who was about to maneuver herself and her luggage into the car. But I would find that while I was headed for the last place I wanted to be—it was also the only place I should have been.

I tackled the moments ahead one step at a time, one foot in front of the other. It occurred to me that these robotic movements must have gotten me to my car when I saw the menu at a McDonald's drive-thru just off the interstate. I was hoping against hope the second McMuffin would make me miss my flight, but as I pulled into the employee parking lot at the airport, I realized things had gone better than I thought. I had accomplished Step I of my Master Plan.

Step I: Leave the House.

Enroute to my gate, I was welcomed by the heightened state of security I'd heard about. An airport security person was rummaging through my suitcase—confiscating a McDonald's plastic fork—when suddenly a belligerent ramp agent ahead of me got smart with the FBI, choosing to saunter off rather than produce his company I.D. A perfect opportunity to shed some rage and take control. "Chase him!" I shouted, as I began my own security check of those who had somehow slipped through, ever mindful, of course, to conduct my investigation fairly, with no discrimination against a particular group.

I could now mark off Step II.

Step II: Do not discriminate against a particular group.

No problem. I hated *everyone*—men, women, and children of all faiths and races. I hated carry-on-dogs and cats, cell phones with dumb rings and each and every crew member. I hated everyone equally, regardless of first class, business class, coach class, or no class. The guy with the tattooed arm—I hated him, too, even after I was yanked aside by a crew member. "Get a grip," she said. "It's a tattoo of the American flag, for gosh sake!"

This is the way I began this three-day trip on a peaceful September day, a day of unlimited ceiling and visibility, a day of unlimited rage.

My head was exploding. Everywhere I looked I saw the flag being displayed in ways and places that were, though disturbing, not safety violations. Shiny red, white, and blue sequins made their way through the security checkpoint as they pledged their allegiance to polyester pants, tube tops, handbags, earrings and necklaces—most anything that could be trapped long enough to be flagged. I reminded myself that displaying patriotism with bad taste had nothing to do with our national security, only with the security, perhaps, of those who display it. In my presence, these well-meaning patriots were no more secure than if they'd been carrying weapons of mass destruction in see-through backpacks.

I thought it couldn't get worse—until I saw the senior citizen, Las Vegas-bound tour group from Myrtle Beach. One woman had attached an orange and green homemade yarn flag, with fringe, to a walker.

"Everybody had already got to the red and blue. Wasn't one string of it left at the K-Mart when I got there," she explained.

"Looks like a *dyed-in-the-wool* American like yourself could've come up with something," I snapped, like the terrorist bitch I had become.

Since 911 she had been "working daylight to dawn" on that flag, she proudly proclaimed. I was thinking it had been less than a week since that day—not much time for creating such a masterpiece although, Truth be known, I knew very little about the art of crochet and absolutely nothing about fringe.

FYI: In the years ahead, I would learn that this woman had devoted more time and thought to the process of making that flag than our president would devote to the process of defending it.

Just so you know.

Onboard the plane I introduced myself to the crew. The captain's pre-flight briefing included the standard stuff, with no mention of the threat of terrorism. As I tried to put it out of my mind and concentrate on his briefing, the cockpit door kept diverting my attention. Finally, my angry inner voice gave one last encore. "Well, idiot, enough with the small talk, already. Just nail the damn door shut, get yourself a gun, and blow the people who don't look like us off the face of the earth," is what I recall saying to myself.

In the long, slow process of grieving, I understood anger to be one of the necessary steps, but I sincerely hoped the next one was on its way, and it was.

Step III: Find God—a baby Jesus—*something!*
It should've been Step I.

The second morning of the trip, as I boarded passengers onto the same type aircraft that had been used as a weapon in two of the bombings, a passenger held up the boarding process to ask, "Stewardess, do you feel safe?"

I froze, but only for a moment, because then it returned—the magic.

"Only when I'm high," I answered.

And high is exactly where I like to be. It was from the "magic" of those childhood rituals that I learned to change my state instantly by jumping into the present moment. But it was in the close familiar space of an airplane that I found another kind of magic. And I had to look no further than the other end of the serving cart to find it.

We had just flown over the site of the World Trade Center where smoke was rising from the soot and ashes of the flattened buildings. I had suddenly been re-introduced to a childhood nightmare, with fathers dying, little girls searching in dark rooms, and monsters looming around the corner or hiding in the next pile of rubble. I remembered standing with my boys on the observation deck of one of the towers the day I introduced them to the skyline of Manhattan. We had ridden the elevator to the top, anticipating stepping onto that deck, oblivious to the people working in offices on the way up. Today I wished they hadn't been. From one-hundred-ten stories up, we had looked down at the city; today I looked down again, only this time from the cabin of an airplane.

A passenger stood and offered his take on the whole thing. "The terrorists are part of 'a large, extended family,'" he volunteered. But before he could finish his speech, the flight attendant on the opposite end of the serving cart grabbed my hand and raised both of ours into the air. I was expecting the theme from *Rocky* to fill the cabin as she turned to the passengers and triumphantly exclaimed, "Well, God Bless America, so are we!"

Standing right there next to the beverage cart I have always despised, I knew that the human spirit on the other end—with its connection to mine, and ours to something greater than any of us—might be as close to safety as I would ever get.

The remainder of the day I chose to seek refuge in the familiar, safe space of the cabin of this 757-200 airplane. Unable to comprehend the war zone below, I had only been able to make sense of those things within reach—the kindness of the passengers, airport workers and my crew; the buffalo wings we anticipated upon landing in Buffalo; the captain's last french fry he turned over to me; and the challenges of our day-to-day lives which, remarkably, still held some significance.

Earlier, when we boarded passengers for Buffalo, a passenger's credentials had identified him as a Secret Service agent; his business card indicated he was headquartered in the White House. He said he'd had no sleep in a week and had even forgotten to eat. (I believed him when he displayed abnormal enthusiasm for the airline food I placed on his tray.) Moments before I served his meal, I made the decision to ignore procedure and retrieve the person formerly known as me. On his napkin I wrote, "Sir, are you aware that the most unsafe thing about air travel is the food? Enjoy your meal." He deplaned and handed me his card and a stack of cocktail napkins displaying The White House symbol. On the top one he had written, "Thanks. I can't wait to share your note with the guys at The White House. They haven't laughed in a while, either."

In that moment I knew Dr. Phil was right when he said we must continue being ourselves but Rudolph Giuliani was wrong. We could never get back to life as we'd known it. But then I remembered yesterday when I believed those baby steps would never get me this far, and I wondered if just a few more might lead me to the small treasures that once got me through each day. Little things, silly things. At the end of the day, I knew nothing about the enemy, but a lot more about those silly little things I could count on:

- Once in a while a Secret Service agent would have a sense of humor.
- My answering machine would say, "Mama, don't get on that airplane! Wal-Mart's hiring!"
- A crew member would give me his last french fry.
- Buffalo still had buffalo wings.

And I knew that when life's tragedies are incomprehensible, sometimes the most we can handle at one time are its simple choices, just as I was given that night in September when an airline pilot turned in an order 30,000 feet below to some guy in Buffalo, New York. He put him on hold, called me on the interphone, then offered me a choice:

"Mild, medium, or hot?"

It was also in an airplane cabin that I encountered others jumping high to avoid the cracks with no idea where, or if, they would land. It then became my mission to step in and select the routine that would magically remove their demons.

Annoying to some, entertaining to others, but it was stage time for me. Taking this "no fear zone" onto the stages of comedy clubs made perfect sense, as it had brought success to so many of my runways before. It was this "magical thinking" that had sustained me in The Rose Garden, and was, ironically, also labeled a serious disorder.

We are observing the way her moods shift. It seems to happen, this sudden state of contentment, when she steps over the line she drew with that magic marker she stole from the nurses' station. On a really bad day, as we have noted in her chart—she jumps.

Of course, it was this same belief in magic that kept me locked up two years waiting for it.

Out of the tragedy of 911 came my decision to stop postponing a career as a full-time writer and speaker. And since audiences and magic are pretty much the same at any altitude, taking my act on the road has been a fairly easy transition. Besides, I have finally learned that happiness has not so much to do with how high we climb or how far we fall as what we decide before we take off.

I no longer have the power to transform coach-class into first-class people by the mere switching of seat assignments. But I can still transform myself— instantly. In fact—make no mistake about it—I have now reached the age where I can openly and proudly create my magic in any way I choose, and yes, I do believe that would include jumping onto the sidewalk, flatfooted, from my front porch.

Or yours.

51.
The gospel truth about the Land of Oz

If ever I go looking for my heart's desire, I'll look no further than my own back yard.

> *Judy Garland*
> *The Wizard of Oz*

And if I ever go looking for a pile of crap, that's exactly where I'll go looking, too.

> *Rosemary Hamilton*

Oh, Judy, Judy, Judy! You'll look no further than your own back yard, *my arthritic butt!!* Stare at that same back yard and all you'll see is that same back yard. A couple of lawn chairs and you—in your own back yard. Same clothesline, same dirty laundry and you—with not one clue that there are clothes dryers and spot removers all over the world. You know you enjoyed your journey, girl! You can't say that Kansas didn't look a whole lot different when you got back. You know you ran right out and got yourself a clothes dryer.

Gospel Truth? My own journey through The Land of Oz didn't work out for me exactly as I had fantasized. There were a few too many scarecrows and yellow brick roads leading to absolutely nowhere.

Look, I'm no Dorothy, and that's okay. I don't want to be her anymore. I don't want to be Judy Garland. Arkansas' Junior Miss? Forever. First Lady? Forever and ever more. But Judy Garland?

NEVERMORE!

Maybe I'm tired, maybe I'm simply growing up, I prefer tired. But I can no longer hang on to Judy. Of course, I'll never forget her; how could I? The woman took me from a childhood that didn't make sense to The Land of Oz where anything was possible.

Okay . . . I never *really* believed I was Judy Garland. With every verse of *If I Only had a Brain*, I knew I was the tin man. But, hear me roar, I was brave. Oh, Lord yes, I was brave. And the wicked witch? I'm not really sure where she wound up. But you'd better check out your own rainbow because she's definitely *not* screwing with mine anymore. That I'm smart enough to know.

This old beauty queen—this sagging piece of brittle wood straight from *The Wizard of Oz's* famous forest—has learned the lessons. She learned them in Harlem and New York comedy clubs. She learned them from Troy Donahue on a long West Coast flight and at open mic nights in the East Village. She picked up some pointers under the bright lights of beauty pageants and the dim lights of a penthouse. She learned from family and friends, hospitals, and psychiatrists. She learned about crazy people and people who just think they are. And she understands what can happen to those people when their lives take just one small wrong turn.

She knows all about Rose Gardens now. She's learned to stay away from those that cultivate the old and then plant it again—using and reusing the same old crap. She knows about runways and why hers always had the same stage, the same beauty pageants, and the same crazy folks behind the same curtain. She knows that Southern Belle Disorder is not confined to the South (or to women!). She knows it all. She finally got it. Indeed she did.

She knows that getting high has less to do with the dealer on the corner than the cards you've been dealt. She knows that getting high can force a deaf child to speak and that getting "all high and mighty" can move a woman from the back of the bus to the back of a limousine. She's learned about titles and labels and that what you believe you are just might be what you become. And she knows that an obsessive-compulsive disorder is more than a psychiatric label—or a talent routine performed on a kitchen counter. It is a means of survival.

She's at that place in a woman's life where she has had enough light bulb moments to last for the rest of it—a place where she's discovered, many times over, her own creative, sane, resilient mind, and that her daddy was right. She'd had one all along. She's in a good place. She is, indeed.

Now, I want you to take a good long look at that place she's in because it would appear that her big fat ass is stuck in it. Big as life. It is, indeed.

But life is good, indeed it is, as she is also at that place in a woman's life where she knows how to find her answers. And, if she can't find them on *Oprah*, she's not too proud to change the channel or surf the Internet. Girlfriend's grown, alright. She's sure enough found some answers and, by God, she intends to find the rest, no matter how much she has to pay or how high she has to go.

> *Dear God,*
>
> *You may not remember me, but here goes. Bottom line, God, is that I'm struggling. I know you've given me more answers than any one person deserves—and, honest to God—this book is jam packed with revelations, insights, and the like. Still, I search for answers. The past is hard to shake; you know what I'm saying? (Sorry. Sure you do. You planned the whole thing.)*
>
> *Here's the deal. My book needs a happy ending. Of course, I realize that if the ending is perfect, so, too, must be my life, which might also mean getting on with it, something I had never even considered. Anyway, God, you need to step in here. I mean, it's not like I haven't promoted you in one way or another throughout this entire book.*
>
> *As I obsess over this, the final chapter of my memoir, I know that you of all people will understand how conflicted I am. If you've read the manuscript, you know a good portion of my life was wasted trying to please everyone else. So if we tack on a happy ending now—just to please everyone else—what would that say about me (and you)? But if we don't, it would appear I haven't learned Jack, and, just between us, some days I don't feel that I have. See what I mean?*
>
> *Anyway, it has become apparent to me that if I continue turning to therapists for answers, this book—which began as a very short magazine article—will never have a last page.*
>
> *As a first-time caller, am I asking too much? Amen.*

A couple of nights after my prayer I got my answer, and, once again, my grandmother's words, "Be careful what you ask for," were—in the words of my Aunt Allie B—"a day late and a dollar short." On this occasion God, as He has been known to do, copped out and sent a messenger to do His work. I'd be lying if I said I wasn't somewhat put out with Him when my all-too-familiar inner voice showed up—this time, in a dream. "It's all about this dream you're having," the little man said. If you had even half a friggin' brain, you'd understand what this one is trying to tell you," he said, as he left the judges' stand and stepped to the edge of my dream. "Okay, he continued, "this is *your* dream and I shouldn't have to explain it. But then, we mustn't forget, it is *you*. So let me lay it out in a way that, hopefully, even *you* can understand, "You've just lost a beauty pageant. Got it?"

A nightmare. I was afraid of that.

"I was the judge and you lost." "No, the dream didn't end perfectly. And, no, your life isn't going to end perfectly either, and if your book is about your life then—*hello!*—why should it end perfectly? That's life. And life isn't about enchanted forests! You can't see those for the Trees—those damn *Family Trees!*—yours and everyone else's! Look . . . life isn't about winning and it's not about losing. It's not about which runway we choose, or what we decide before we take off. It's not about how high we climb or how far we fall, but maybe it really is about what we discover on our way back up. Oh, hell, I don't even know what it's about!" He threw up his arms. "You've been to the seminars, read the books, and had the therapy. So at least you've learned one thing." He sighed. "*Nobody* does! But if you think it's about figuring out how to wind it all up—perfectly—you'll never have a book *or* a life! Surely, by now, you've seen where that kind of crazy thinking has gotten you. Of course, Lord knows, you don't listen to me. I've been calling you an idiot your entire life and it took two years in mental hospitals to convince you I was right!"

It was that familiar inner voice, alright.

"So come on, get on with it." He was unstoppable. "Leave the magical thinking to Harry Potter. Finish your book. It'll be gutsy, analytical, fun!" He stopped momentarily, obviously surprised by the sudden onset of a positive voice, then regrouped and continued, this time with animation. "It'll be gutsy," he exclaimed, "because the life you've dissected is your own. Analytical because, Lord have mercy, you're still trying to figure it out! And fun . . . well, that's obvious. Throughout this process, in spite of me and your ex-husbands, the mental hospitals and an airline, you have actually had a pretty good time. And, *God knows*, you *have* learned. Unfortunately," he sighed, "*God* appears to be the *only* one who knows that! As for me, girlfriend, I've heard about as much 'woe is me' from one person as I can stand. And, too, the therapy is killing me. I'm history."

Oh, that's just great. My negative but reliable inner voice had turned positive and skipped out on his faithful, co-dependent partner!

Now who's gonna jerk me up and get me back on track and into therapy? Who'll give me issues to ponder so I can preserve the lifestyle to which I have become accustomed? Who's gonna keep these shrinks and insurance companies in the lifestyle to which they have become accustomed? You think I want to single-handedly bankrupt those people? Are you crazy?

Clearly, this was just one more issue that could be answered only with—just when you thought the coverage had lapsed and God had, finally, intervened—

Sorry . . . more therapy.

52.
The gospel truth about the gospel truth!

In psychiatric therapy years it could've taken a decade to resolve this dilemma, but—and I'm guessing here—since God got involved, my next therapist was not from that world. He was from Tennessee. After a couple of months, he and/or God came up with answers. This time, however, I was about to get the shock of my life.

"Girl, no wonder the little guy with the big voice skipped out on you. Everyone needs to feel needed. He simply did not. As I see it, there's nothing wrong with you that's not wrong with me and the rest of us. Probably never was . . ."

> **Patient File: Rosemary Hamilton**
> **Insurance: Yes.**
> **Diagnosis: Nothing wrong with her that's not wrong with the rest of us.**

He lifted a thick, bound manuscript from his desk. "It's all right here!" he said, as he rose from his tattered old chair, walked toward me, and plopped the papers in my lap. "This book is who you are, and other than the Bible, you won't find another one to answer your questions any better." He paused. "Sorry. I know I've made several references to the Bible. Does that bother you?"

"Don't be silly. Of course it doesn't bother me," I assured him, as I cringed. "I grew up hearing about it every day."

"Do you pray?" he asked.

"As we speak," I answered.

Dear God, put your arm around his shoulders and your hand over his mouth.

A faux-leather sofa flanked by walnut wood-grained contact-papered end tables with matching coffee table and filing cabinet doubling as a countertop for a jar of generic instant coffee next to an *I can't believe it's not butter* plastic container filled with artificial sweetener. Right down to the plant on this shrink's desk, everything—*faux, faux, faux!*

(Through the walls of the adjoining room, a Formica dinette with red-leatherette cushioned chairs was heard begging to join the group.)

A Danish Modern reminder of the Rose Garden's outdated décor accented with Jesus memorabilia is, basically, what I saw. Filled with treasures from the *Graceland Museum of Jesus*—if there wasn't one, there should've been—it was a setting so deified not even Freud would've interceded. As I scanned the walls I was struck by the absence of diplomas, but the pictures of Jesus sent out a pretty clear signal that this guy knew very little but hoped to hell Jesus did.

The man was a Christian. A person would have to be crazy not to see that; it was all over the place. Other than that, he'd put little effort into making himself out to be someone or something else—at least nothing or no one I recognized. I'm not convinced he was even trying to be himself. No name plate on his door. No books, no particular theme, not a certificate on the walls for anything—from anywhere.

He wasn't necessarily weird or un-weird, nerdy or un-nerdy, handsome or ugly. Unlike the others, he just sat there acting and looking all normal and boring. Tall, thin, about sixty-years old with the wife, children and grandchildren's pictures on his desk; that was about it.

I had made it through many agonizing sessions with the others only by focusing on their bizarreness, analyzing their weirdness, pushing through their facades, and patiently allowing them to work out their own issues on my time. Naturally, being in the presence of a man so non-descript had me twiddling my thumbs. Confusing and, frankly, unnerving is what it was.

Just the same, for a man who wasn't big on making a statement about himself, he made a lot of them about me.

"Trust me, girl," he said, "you are responsible for your own diagnosis, prognosis and treatment plan, and in your book, you finally figured that out. Woman, you've had more *Aha!* moments than Oprah! You have de-constructed and re-constructed the Southern Belle many times, on your own terms, and you didn't have to give up being one, nor did you spend one night in a seclusion room to do it. To the contrary, you traveled the globe! Your recovery has required the complete and total rejection of stigma and some pretty old beliefs. . . ." he said, as he frowned, then quickly added, ". . . well, except for a few stragglers, like those deeply engrained misconceptions about God. You're still dragging around some pretty tired baggage where He's concerned. Just the same, you are a woman in recovery from many labels, including 'Southern Belle,' which, ironically, is what allows you to be the person who has created her own definition of Southern Belleness, on turf that you fully own. It's all right here," he said, pointing to the manuscript he had just tossed on my lap. "Read it! And, if you run upon parts you don't understand, call me."

Very funny. It was my memoir—the manuscript I'd given him two weeks before. I had handed over my life on paper, expecting to get it back with red pencil marks on every page. Could this be—as they say—a pattern? Had the author found her answers in these pages while the patient-within chose to seek hers elsewhere—anywhere but in her very own book? One could only conclude that a part of this Southern Belle was still reluctant to be dismantled.

> **Patient file: Rosemary Hamilton**
> **Diagnosis: It's in her book.**
> **Prognosis: That, too.**

My hour wasn't up.

"Well, to tell you the Truth—*everything* is *not* in your book," he said, as he took back the manuscript and put it on his desk. "But I'm about to fill in those blank chapters. Now . . . for starters, what if you *do* have that ADD, OCD stuff? It's no big deal. The rituals at least made you *believe* you had control. As for Southern Belle Disorder . . . well, it may have been abnormal in New York and those other Yankee states, but girl, look around you. You're in Tennessee. No one's immune. Surely you've noticed, I've got it too! And, about your mama . . ."

Been there, got the t-shirt.

" . . . I don't pretend to completely understand your relationship with her . . ." *Ever notice how being clueless about a subject never stops these shrinks from being authorities on it?* ". . . but it's fairly apparent that your mama wanted you to win those beauty pageants, but *she* wanted to win even more. Either way, there was guilt!"

God is guilt. God is good. Let us thank him . . .

"And another thing," he said, "someone should've told her that Jesus and his bunch were *not* afraid of success! Matter of fact," he wrinkled his forehead, "there was not one preacher or prophet in the Bible who was *not* prosperous. But your victories meant more than success. For your mama, they also brought about the dismal prospect of sitting through the next pageant, and the next, and the next! It's enough to depress anybody!"

And you honestly think you're going to get paid for this crap, you son-of-a-bitch? I'm calling the insurance company and the American Psychiatric Association and every shrink from here to The Rose Garden! What's next? My daddy wasn't perfect?

With the sudden enthusiasm of yet another shrink about to remove a thorn from his own painful past, he continued, "Oh, yes, that woman was depressed. She could have been on her own stage as a concert pianist, for heaven's sake—if she hadn't had children—and she knew it. Sometimes she wanted to go back, to be free, but that wasn't possible in her eyes, so she lived through her children and their victories. Nothing so strange about that. We *all* do it."

Finally! Confirmation that the man hadn't planned to be a shrink surrounded by plastic Jesus memorabilia or to have a decorator with offices on the boardwalk in Myrtle Beach. He'd wanted more. At one time this man had higher aspirations, I could see that.

"Perhaps the hardest thing in your mama's world was the albatross she carried on her back, the ever-present guilt about her daughter."

She could've done more. . . .

"And that guilt was understandable," he said softly, in a manner one might associate with the prelude to a harmless little afterthought. But one couldn't have been more wrong.

"You simply weren't the child she had in mind," he said.

EXCUSE ME?

Like he hadn't just set off a bomb in my head that would keep me in therapy the rest of my life, damn if he didn't ignite a second one. "Oh, yes! Not caring about your own child can bring on guilt like you wouldn't believe."

SHIT!

"Depression and guilt," he sighed.

"I get the picture," I said, sharply.

"Regrets, too," he mumbled.

What? Even MORE children she regretted having? The woman should've thrown our sorry asses into the burning bulrushes with those lions, or however that one goes. . . .

About now I'd have given anything for one of those "mixed messages" I had always abhorred. This one was clear—about as clear as a southern shrink has probably ever gotten.

"Just as she was not the stage mother you envisioned, perhaps you were not the onstage or offstage daughter of her dreams. It works both ways. You couldn't have pleased her—no matter how many trophies you placed on her mantel—any more than you pleased the administrator of that hospital. And *did you ever* try to please him! You stayed until you produced an almost exact replica of a mental patient. Fortunately you failed; you weren't the real thing. You didn't fit into his plans any more than you fit into your mama's."

"I seem to gravitate toward places where I don't fit in and then try to wait it out until I do," I confessed.

"You don't say!" he teased, then switched gears. "As for your mother's sporadic enthusiasm about those beauty pageants, maybe she was faking it! 'Southern Belles' are born knowing that technique!" he said, as he laughed the laugh southern men are also born knowing. You know the one. "Well," he hesitated, continuing a series of pauses, each longer and more excruciating to sit through than the last, "there's something you need to know about your mama and Mr. Jones, and I believe you already do."

"Do what? Know what?"

"Oh come on, now. You know that they were just not . . ." He started again. "They were just, you know, just not . . ."

I dreaded hearing anything so horrendous it would force this man to finally hold back. He started again and again. "Your mama and Mr. Jones were just . . ."

Jesus, man! Fish or cut bait! Take your foot off the damn brakes!

"Actually, they were just . . .

n o t   t h a t   i n t o   y o u !!"

What the hell has he been reading?

"Tell me . . . did you think you'd find a world unlike the one where you grew up? Would you never again feel trapped in the split of that Family Tree with its trunk full of diverse messages? Oh, yes, Dorothy, the forest is full of Trees. There are *many* places like home!"

Now, wait a minute here. Let me see if this half-a-mind has got the gist of this: I left the cotton fields of Arkansas all those years ago. Now I'm being told I never, really, had to pack up my Bible in my cotton sack and leave. Oh, yes-sir-ee, Toto. We have sure enough landed in hell!

"Maybe Kansas hasn't changed—but Dorothy has," he said. Suddenly his big smile turned upside down. "She just hasn't realized it yet."

He looked first at the clock, then the door. When he moved to the edge of his chair, I assumed I was free to go. He had, surely, sung his last hymn. "Oh, and just one more thing," he said slowly, thoughtfully, as he leaned back in his chair.

Oops! Would the congregation please be seated?

"Most of your life you've squeezed into a very small space, but always gravitated back to that infinite stage your father created. It represented your core, and gave you permission to return to it—probably the only thing that kept you sane!"

"Barely."

"Your world on one side of that Family Tree may have been small, but your stage on the other side was big as life! When you take away those preconceived ideas about how *everything* and *everyone* should be, you're left with a lot of usable space!"

"A never-ending runway, huh?"

"Lit up like a Christmas tree," he smiled.

"Or a Menorah," I added. Like he would know what that was.

"I believe your granny was right. Your mother's half of that Tree *was* occupied by politicians, and no one from your father's side could have ever pleased anyone from hers. Know why?"

"They were Republicans?"

"Worse. They weren't anything. Those politicians are awfully stubborn about who they let in, downright territorial is what they are." He laughed. "They're big on image, you know—titles, protocol, rank . . . that sort of thing. Your daddy's side appeared not to care!"

"They didn't even vote," I whispered.

"Yet when he died," he continued, "you began searching for the thing that would get you to the other side of that Tree, closer to your mama."

"But *everyone* wants to belong. . . ."

He interrupted. "Sure, it's right here in the manuscript: '*They all stood behind the big curtain, waiting for their names to be called . . .*'"

"'. . . *and some of them never were,*'" I said, finishing the quote.

"So it's just as I always suspected," I moaned. "I was one of *those* people, always on the wrong side of everything—wrong neighborhood, wrong clothes, wrong politics, even the wrong idea about what was *wrong*—always struggling to get to the right side of that 'curtain.'"

"Waiting for your name to be called?"

"Yes. That was me, wasn't it?"

"Were you waiting for the magic that would change your life—the next pageant, title, label, or man—the next self-help book or therapist— the next delivery from QVC? It sure it looks that way," he sighed. "And you could've waited behind that curtain for your number to be called; stood in line for a first-class seat; jumped over every crack in every sidewalk in the universe; waited on that empty playground for your mama to pick you up; stayed in that mental hospital until someone named you 'well'; and waited for that UPS man 'til doomsday. You could have hung out 'til the proverbial cows came home, but you were never going to hear your name called until you knew *what your name was!*"

"Until I reconstructed that *Southern Belle within*?"

"Until you found *your* Southern Belle within," he said, "which had nothing to do with your political, social, psychiatric, or comedic labels—not the crown on your head or your seat on a bus or an airplane, not even the title before your name or your husband's name!"

Again, he flipped through the manuscript and read from one of its pages. "*Rich, poor, bus, town, black, white, first and last runner ups, Jews, protestants, Democrats and Republicans . . .*" he said, putting the papers back on the desk, "they'll *all* be standing behind that curtain until they start listening for their *own names*—*not* the ones they've been assigned!"

"Listening for their *own names?*"

"Yes," he smiled, "the ones they finally assign to themselves."

He headed toward the couch but paused directly in front of me, waiting, I assumed, for his own grand finale. Then, like he'd just found a cure for cancer, he triumphantly concluded,

"And that, Miss Junior Miss, *really is*—The Gospel Truth!"

Twenty-five years of therapy had just been squeezed into one piercing bolt of lightning. Son of a gun.

As he ambled back to his chair I positioned myself on the edge of the couch and reached for a Kleenex, unsure of what was coming next but knowing I needed to be prepared. With this one, you never knew. The man I originally believed to be boring was still boring—yet unpredictable at the same time, certainly not like the others. Not your everyday run-of-the-grist-for-the-mill shrink.

"But if you still want a *LABEL*," he continued, "try this one on for size."

Well, maybe he was. . . .

"Agoraphobia. You, woman, are agoraphobic, and understandably so. A person labeled with so many disorders would be crazy to ever leave the house!" He laughed. "You, alone, have designed your own seclusion room. In your mind, you've never left The Rose Garden!"

They longed for freedom. They prayed for freedom. Yet everyone was scared half to death that they would get it.

"Could be," I said.
"So come on out, girl—step down off that stage and join the audience. There's nothing wrong with you!"

That's it, huh? That's why I've peeled my butt off every faux-leather couch from here to Kingdom Come? These are the answers I've been searching for?

"What's left to fear? You don't need a therapist and you didn't need The Rose Garden. You know who you are! You know who you aren't! You know what to do. Most of all," he said, pointing to the manuscript on my lap, "you know what you need. It's all right there," he smiled, "everything you need to know."

Patient File: Rosemary Hamilton
Treatment Plan: She knows what she needs.

Where was this man from—Harlem? Who did he think he was—Rosa? What was he trying to say? Was he saying, "Pretend you don't see them, pretend you don't see the rats?" Or was he saying that there were no rats to see? Was he abandoning me before we even got started? Was this a conspiracy where he and the inner-voice guy would run off together? Maybe it was my insurance that had run out. That damn airline!

Had I finally lost my mind but no longer had the coverage to even be told? Was this God's idea of that "perfect ending" I asked for? Or was my mind—Oh! My Dear Lord and Precious Savior—was it . . .

T H E R E A L L A L O N G?

Nothing wrong with me?
Nothing wrong with me.
I know what to do?
I know what to do.

Treatment Plan: She knows what to do.
Patient File: Retired.
Date of Birth: Today!

It was a diagnosis so simple, there wasn't even a decent label; so ordinary, there would be no way to analyze it; so perfect, it must have been sent from God; so boring, I'm pretty sure it was.

Simple and ordinary.
Perfect and God-sent.
No way to even analyze it.

Not exactly the ending I had in mind.

Dear Rosemary:
  Please send us your new address for our newsletter.

                    The Pageant Committee

Dear Pageant Committee,
  Sorry, address unknown.

                    The Post Office

Rosemary Hamilton's continuing search for a safe place to land is documented in her second book, *Chicken Poop on my Soles*.

<u>Order books at:</u>
www.rosemaryhamilton.com
www.authorhouse.com

To book speaking engagements for book clubs, professional organizations, conventions, seminars, etc., visit Rosemary at: rosemaryhamilton.com

Printed in the United States
131607LV00003B/5/P